"*Wrong Highway* spins a bored cliche—the disenchanted housewife—into a thrilling exploration of how to grasp meaning in the minutiae of family life. Struggling within the confines of suburbia and her family's expectations, Wall Street wife and mother of four Erica Richards finds solace in a drug habit that makes the world seem bright and infinite. Set on Long Island in the technicolor 1980s, *Wrong Highway* is a gripping novel about family, self-hood, and what it takes to escape prisons of our own making."

—**Rhianna Walton**, new book buyer, Powell's Books

"*Wrong Highway* is a captivating debut novel about life in Long Island in the late '80s. Beginning with early memories of Erica and her sister Debbie at the 1964 World's Fair, the path weaves through their dysfunctional jaunt as adults and parents. At times comedic and others tragic, Erica's trip is always entertaining."

—**Kim Bissell**, co-owner, Broadway Books

"*Wrong Highway* is by turns funny, sad, quirky, and surprising, but always engaging. It's Erica's story and she tells it at dazzling speed, with vibrant language, and with high (pun intended) energy and insight. It's a story that captures a full spectrum of family dynamics many of us have experienced, yet viewed through a unique lens that questions the meaning of it all, even if it looks from the outside that you have it all. Babies, children, sisters, parents, in-laws, nephews, a loving but largely absent husband, Erica shares it all with brutal and amusing honesty. Her coping mechanism may be a little unorthodox, but her struggles reflect. . . an important and transformative American decade. A riveting and entertaining read."

—**Nancy Johnson**, arts and nonprofits consultant

WRONG HIGHWAY

SHEPHERDESS BOOKS PORTLAND

WENDY GORDON

WRONG HIGHWAY

shepherdess books

shepherdessbooks@gmail.com

Printed in the United States of America
First Printing, 2016

ISBN 978-0-9970780-0-8

Library of Congress Control Number: 2015919710

Frontispiece photograph © Superstock

Credits are found on page 377.

Copyediting by Kristin Thiel
Book design by K. M. Weber, www.ilibribookdesign.com

To my husband Zak and my children
Gabrielle, Jessica, Alex, and Lukas
You are the center of my life.

PROLOGUE

MAY 1964

In the future, moving sidewalks will propel you forward without effort, but in the present, you only twirl in circles. Your mother is searching frantically for her wallet, which turns up in her coat pocket. Your father is scrutinizing the fair map so carefully you'd think it contains directions to buried treasure. Your sister is sucking her finger and pouting.

"Oh my." Your mother sighs. "I hope this wasn't a mistake."

"I have to go to the bathroom, Mom," your sister whines, pointing to a line so long it curls around the side of a neighboring pavilion.

"I don't," you protest. "Do you, Mommy?"

"No, but it doesn't do any harm to try," your mother says. You get in line.

Even though the New York World's Fair is less than twenty miles from your home in West Meadow, it took a month of nagging your parents to even get in the gate. Your mother dislikes crowds, and weekends are always busy, with your father's chamber music group, his model train group, the never-ending housework and yard work, and your sister's ballet lessons. Finally, they offered you this day as an early birthday present: next week you turn nine years old.

Given your family's inevitable slow start plus horrible traffic, you didn't arrive until nearly noon. Now you are standing in an endless line for the ladies' room. When you finally get in there, your mother insists you try and pee even though you've already told her you don't have to go. A little trickle comes out. You wash your hands and dry them under the blow dryer. Your mother reapplies her lipstick. Your sister smooths her hair.

When you emerge, your father waves you over to an even longer line, this one for hamburgers.

"Best to fuel up before sightseeing," he says.

"I'm not hungry," you protest.

You eat the burger anyway, along with a bag of fries and a strawberry shake, sitting at a plastic table under an umbrella. After everyone dumps the paper garbage in the trash, your father announces you are going to the Canadian pavilion.

"Can't we go someplace else?" you ask.

"The pamphlet says they have an excellent selection of Eskimo artwork," he says.

You trod through a display of masks, harpoons, ivory carvings, and a reasonably interesting igloo you can climb into. Dad tells you more than you ever wanted to know about Inuits and the Bering Strait.

When you emerge into the April air, bugs whiz about, despite your mother's best attempts to bat them away.

"I have twenty-two mosquito bites, Rikki," your sister says, lifting up her skirt to display a particularly gross one on her upper thigh.

"Don't call me Rikki," you say. "My name is Erica."

Your sister ignores you, moving your hand to the bite's pustular white center. "Scratch it—it itches," she commands.

The pimple actually intrigues you, in a perverse sort of way, so you press down, and blood and goo shoot out.

"Ooh, yuck!" your sister squeals, turning and dashing blindly ahead. You chase after her, head down like a bull, colliding with a group of middle-aged men speaking a foreign language.

"Watch where you're going, Rikki!" your father shouts. "Slow down!"

You lift up your head, slightly dizzy. The paths ahead of you twirl, bend, and stretch to the horizon. With all the glass and domes it looks like the kind of world you'd encounter when you stepped out of a time machine into the future.

Your family regathers, leaning against the glass rail of the prototype moving sidewalk.

"Are you feeling all right, Debbie?" your mother asks.

"I think I'm getting a stomachache," your sister says, clutching her belly.

"She ate too many french fries," you say. "Debbie is a pig."

"Be nicer to your sister," your father says. "You know she has a sensitive stomach."

"Maybe we should leave soon," your mother suggests, scratching her neck. She always scratches her neck when she gets nervous, which is often. You roll your eyes in exasperation, which only fuels her nervousness.

"There's school tomorrow, and homework, and if Debbie's not feeling well. . ." Your mother casts her head around, as if searching for other excuses to leave.

"Maybe we should vote on one more pavilion to see and then go," Dad says, readjusting his glasses.

"My vote is for the African pavilion," he continues. "They have some fascinating wooden sculptures. Religious icons and so forth. I read about it in *National Geographic*."

"I want to go to the Seven-Up pavilion," you say.

"What do they have there?" your father asks.

"I don't know." Your guess is unlimited soda, but you know that to voice that hope is to doom your chances. You let go of the rail and cruise along the moving sidewalk. Rubber slides under your feet. You are skating into the future.

"Can we get off this moving sidewalk?" your Mom asks. "I feel like I'm going to fall down."

You step off the end and stand in a patch of grass near a building people enter through the mouth of a gargantuan mahogany head. Your long anticipated day, your alleged birthday present, feels like it is ending before it has barely begun.

"Can I look around by myself?" you plead.

"Are you crazy?" your mom blurts, scratching her neck. "You're not even nine years old. You'll get lost. Remember Tanglewood? Remember Jones Beach? We nearly killed ourselves looking for you!"

Indeed, you remember both Tanglewood and Jones Beach, where, after a dizzying run marred by only a slight knot of fear, you'd been apprehended by security personnel, brought to the Lost Children's booth, offered candy, and returned to the sweaty, anxious arms of your parents. Both times, you'd been driven away by an attack of claustrophobia. The bodily smells and gestures of your family closed in on you, suffocating you with a heavy closeness, like garlic breath. You felt like throwing up. The blanket-dotted sand, the oily waves, the stands of trees, the grown-up strangers drinking wine—anywhere and everywhere seemed fresher, cleaner, and freer.

"I want to go to the Seven-Up pavilion too," says your sister, her stomachache evidently forgotten.

Inspiration strikes.

"We could go together. Me and Debbie." You look to your sister for support, and surprisingly, she flashes you a conspiratorial grin. "She's twelve. She's almost a teenager. We could go to the Seven-Up pavilion together."

"Well, all right," your father says, despite the fact your mother is vigorously shaking her head and scratching her neck again. "That way your mother and I can explore the African pavilion and maybe Latin American too. Meet us at the Scandinavian pavilion, the one by the exit, at eight. That's three hours from now. Debbie, I'm trusting you to be in charge." He lends your sister his special watch, the one with the fourteen-karat gold band.

"Shouldn't you give them the map?" Your mother sighs.

"Oh yes," your father says and hands over his precious pamphlet.

Your sister carefully folds it into her purse.

You and your sister check the map to find your way to the

Seven-Up pavilion, where you both hold cups underneath a series of wall spigots, sampling the flavors of soda, some familiar, some not, that gush forth. "Are you sure it's okay to drink all this?" your sister asks, as she guzzles down cup after cup. On a table in the center of the pavilion, chocolate chip cookies are piled high on platters, free for the taking. Giggling, on a sugar high, you run into the Bell telephone pavilion where you make faces at each other over videophones.

"Hey, Debbie," you say, forming antennae with your fingers: "I'm an alien from Jupiter. We love girls with blue eye shadow and white lipstick. Want to go on a date?"

"Why, sure, Jupiter boy," she answers. "You're just my type."

You ride in little boats along a man-made stream while mechanical puppets in costumes from many countries sing to you about what a small world it is. The boat ride is reasonably entertaining, but otherwise you skip any pavilions featuring fascinating ethnic customs or handicrafts, sticking with glass and metal, with the new machines that promise to make your future so effortless and wonderful. You run from exhibit to exhibit, breathlessly discovering new uses for electricity and coal and nuclear power.

In the Sperry Univac pavilion, a computer occupies half a large room, humming loudly and emitting heat. You enter a series of numbers, and it spits out a recipe for oatmeal cookies, which your sister folds and puts in her purse. One side of the computer flashes a shimmery blue-and-white tic-tac-toe board; visitors are encouraged to play, and the computer wins every time.

Your sister stamps her feet in frustration. She has a mind for games and inevitably beats everyone at anything from Go Fish to Monopoly. But she cannot defeat this computer. The best she can do is take it to a draw. She keeps playing, hissing at the expressionless screen, oblivious to the impatient line forming behind her, until she finally remembers the other thing she's been oblivious to: your father's watch ticking inexorably toward the hour your freedom ends. She frowns.

"Rikki, we should head back now," she says. "It's ten minutes to eight."

It can't be! "A few more minutes," you plead.

Your sister extracts the map from her purse, consults it. "It'll take at least ten minutes to walk back," she says, finally giving up her post at the computer. A fat kid with a crew cut, his striped shirt straining at the buttons, takes her place. Your sister reaches for your hand, but you twist away from her grasp.

You leap out of the Sperry Univac pavilion into the late spring air. The sky is slowly darkening, and lights are blinking on like stars. You are tall for your age, with long legs and knobby knees. You can outrun your petite sister, with her soft dimpled thighs. The path swirls ahead of you. You like being free of the map, having no idea of your direction. You turn right and left at random. Around a bend you glimpse a fountain, water streaming down gray rock, shooting glitter into the air. It reminds you of Jones Beach, the way the waves curl and crash. That day at Jones Beach when you ran away, your mother and sister had sat rooted to the blanket, reapplying sunscreen and complaining about the heat. You jumped up and ran into the waves, letting the water lift you up and carry you, becoming one with a mob of ecstatic bobbing heads.

Your sister huffs at your heels, pleading. "Rikki, c'mon, I'll get in trouble. Mommy and Daddy will worry. They'll never trust us again. It's getting dark."

You balance on the concrete ridge bordering the fountain. A series of flat stones leads to the center, where water tumbles down in a silvery rush.

"Rikki, if you don't stop, I won't let you listen to my albums."

You hesitate. When your sister is in the right mood, she admits you into the pink sanctuary of her room where she plays the albums she buys with her babysitting money: the Beatles, Herman's Hermits, Paul Revere and the Raiders. These records bear no relationship to the dull sonatas Daddy plays in his chamber music group or the show tunes Mommy listens to on the radio. When you listen to your sister's records, the dancing starts deep inside your bones and vibrates out your skin.

But even her music is recorded and abstract. The rhythms of this night, with its warm breeze and promises of summer to come, are immediate. You are carried along by the spanking-new pavilions, the barely trod paths, the endless parade of people, the underlying buzz of footsteps and conversation, the humid stink of sweat and hot dogs, the lavish orange sunset.

A nearby pavilion lights up in blue and red. In the fountain, the water reflects the light like colored cellophane. Hopping from the first stone to the second, you spy a sparkle of copper and silver, reach down into the water, and grab a handful of coins. The dirty water splashes up, making a wet stain on your shorts.

"Rikki, that's not your money. And you look like you wet your pants. We have to go. Now." Your sister pants at the edge of the fountain, her freckled face wrinkling in exasperation.

You stuff the coins in your pocket and reach into the water for more coins, flashing a dripping handful at your sister.

"There's tons of money in here!" you shout.

Another pavilion blinks on in bright yellow, turning the stones golden. You follow the golden path to the heart of the waterfall. The water soaks your hair, your clothes, pours into your sneakers. The coins lie heavy in your pocket. You shiver deliciously.

"We don't have to go home!" you cry through mouthfuls of water. "We can live at the fair! We can buy our own food! All the soda you want! Cookies! Hamburgers too, and pizza, and french fries!"

"Rikki, we're going to be so in trouble." Your sister totters on those heeled sandals she insists on wearing everywhere.

"We won't have to go to school!" You wave your arms in the air.

Your sister places her toe on the ridge of the fountain, draws back. "Rikki! I mean it."

To your ears, your sister's pleas sound faint, disembodied.

Drops pelt your eyes, and through the prism of the water, the sky glistens like shards of glass. In the cold spray of the fountain, you are all sparkles and energy. For a few blinding moments, you see nothing but liquid light.

Your sister is your height but softer and broader, tottering on the edge of adult terrain you are years away from beginning to comprehend. Her rounded breasts and hips fill out her skirt and matching flowered shirt. Her pageboy hair is painstakingly sprayed and styled, frosted with blond streaks. Her eyelashes are curled and lined with mascara; there is a blot of blue shadow below both brows and glossy white lipstick on her mouth. She is wearing a silver locket, a leather pocketbook, and Daddy's special watch with the fourteen-karat gold band. She fidgets, unable to take that first step into the fountain. All those expensive possessions she would damage. All those rules she would break. Her pale freckled face scrunches up, deepens into a frown. Tears trickle out. She wants so badly to please, to do the right thing.

You see all this through the glaze of water. At almost nine years old, you still can't disregard the belief that your sister, at thirteen, is privy to vital knowledge not yet revealed to you. You step out of the flow of water, and when you look up at the sky, it has turned a furry brownish-black, the moon slivery and ominous. You walk back across the stones, bidding good-bye to the flashes of color that streak across them. You step over the concrete ridge and take your sister's grudging but relieved hand. Checking the map under a series of overhead lights, she navigates you along the strange darkened paths, then through the teak doors of the Scandinavian pavilion.

You are met by your mother's scratchy and fervid embrace and your father's worried brown eyes and follow them to the sticky-stale comfort of your family's Rambler Ambassador. You suffer through your mother's inevitable sighing about your ruined clothes, but back home awaits your yellow chenille bedspread, your row of Barbies lined up on your dresser, and a whole box of Debbie's old dolls you have yet to arrange. The next day at school you will get an A on a pop spelling quiz and be the only one in your class to do thirty pull-ups on the Presidential fitness tests. The following Saturday, a boy named Jim will call and ask to speak to your sister. You will answer, telling your mother (at Debbie's request) that it is your sister's friend Barbara instead. As a reward, your sister will let you listen to her new Kinks album on her plastic S and H Green Stamps record player, the two of you bouncing in the filtered magenta light of her canopy bed.

Which makes it all the more unsettling when you hear on the six o'clock news that two ten-year-old boys—only one year older than you—lived off the coins in the fountains of the New York World's Fair for three glorious days.

CHAPTER ONE

MARCH 1986

Erica needed to buy milk and cheese sticks at the supermarket, though she couldn't recall whether she'd remembered the coupon for the cheese sticks. She fumbled through her purse at a red light, finding the coupon safely wedged behind a wad of Kleenex. The red light was a long one, and Vince Volvo started shaking. A vibration came out of the gearshift. Erica held her breath until the light turned green. She accelerated, and Vince slid forward like he was supposed to.

After picking up Jesse and Jake's friend Michael in West Meadow Estates, she plunged into the surge of early-afternoon rush hour traffic. She'd been running all day in this disgusting pelting rain, starting with her hour at aerobics working off the fat from her pregnancy with Sophia, then dropping off some forms at West Meadow Elementary, buying diapers, returning books to the library, and driving all the way to Manhasset to the toy store, choosing a wooden beading set for Stacey. She'd left it, wrapped and with a card, on the hallway table when she'd finally gotten home, just in time for the twins' return from preschool, but then the phone started ringing and didn't stop. Nassau Auto Glass phoned, asking if she had any broken windows needing repair, as if you'd drive around with a shattered windshield waiting for someone to call. Her husband, Ethan, who spoke a numerical language that was as incomprehensible to her as ancient Phoenician, called and gave some excuse why he'd be working late. Something about linear output or n's or m's or x's or p's. Then, when she'd finally strapped all four kids into Vince Volvo, her mother called and she had to run into the kitchen, leaving the kids in the car. Her mother burbled excitedly about some crisis besetting her friend Arlene before announcing that she couldn't talk long because she was late for a real estate meeting.

Erica was certain she'd been holding Stacey's gift while talking to her mother, but she reached over to the passenger seat to reassure herself she hadn't left it on the hallway table. She ran her hand along the shiny wrapping paper, the curlicues of ribbon.

Vince's engine made a weird swishy sound. Maybe the Pakistani guy who worked at the gas station by aerobics had misunderstood her and put in regular instead of premium. The rain drummed down harder. She was always so tired, an exhaustion that coffee only glossed over. Whenever she lay down at the end of aerobics for a minute of yoga-inspired full relaxation, her head sunk into the mat. Her eyes closed, and she almost drifted off to sleep before her instructor, sexy Ari, rang the bell. She rolled to her side, wiggled her fingers and toes, and reentered the world where she always had to stay awake.

In the shimmering halo of the oncoming headlights, she short-circuited. She forgot where she was. Too many details leaped about her brain like uncontrolled electrical signals. She didn't recall whether she was driving on the Northern State or the LIE or the Meadowbrook, or whether she was driving Dylan to soccer, or Jake to T-ball, or Sophia to the doctor for her shots. She didn't remember whether it was 1976 or 1986. Everything was darkness and light, black and white, random dots. She could make out the difference between the white lines and the black road and recognize the circles of light that represented cars in front of her, and she navigated her heavy metal vehicle laden with children by instinct.

"Mommy, can you play the Talking Heads?" Jesse piped up from the backseat. With the sound of her son's voice, a fuse reset in Erica's brain, and all the dots coalesced. She remembered, yes, it was March 26, 1986 and she was driving Jesse and Jake and their friend Michael to Stacey Lincer's ice skating party in Mineola. She slipped the Talking Heads into her tape deck. David Byrne spoke to her personally.

"You may find yourself behind the wheel of a large automobile. . ."

Yes, she thought. Her Volvo station wagon, with its two extra seats in the back, qualified.

"And you may ask yourself. . . how did I get here?"

"I took Glenvere Road to Hillside Avenue," she answered David. "Beyond that, I can't say."

Jake sang along in the backseat, in his clear, perfect-pitch voice. Talking Heads were his favorite band, but as usual, he made up his own words.

"Wrong highway, Mommy. Wrong highway. Wrong highway."

"Is this the wrong highway?' Erica asked David. "Give me direction."

"And you may ask yourself. My God, what have I done?" David said in response.

"Wrong highway. Wrong highway," sang Jake.

"Jake, will you shut up, you stupid dork," Jesse said.

At the ice skating rink, the parking lot was full, and Erica could only squeeze in illegally in front of a BMW. There must have been ten birthday parties taking place simultaneously, but eventually she located Stacey's and bid good-bye to the boys at the skate rental line.

When she turned Vince's ignition on again it hesitated—aruh, aruh, aruh—and all the warning lights lit up. The BMW she was blocking honked impatiently. On the next try, the car started up, but at each red light, which was many in the heavy traffic, the engine knocked, and she gritted her teeth until she could start moving again. If she could just finish her errands and get home, she could call the dealer in the morning. The sun briefly reappeared before disappearing again, setting blearily behind a bank of clouds. There were spots of melted and refrozen snow left over from the surprise storm the prior week, and Erica slid and bumped over them, concentrating on the cars in front of her, terrified the whole time that she was going to lose it again and see nothing but dots and lines.

At the supermarket, Sophia nestled against Erica in her front pack, making whimpering hungry noises. Erica bought the cheese sticks, milk, diapers, and wipes, plus ten boxes of fish sticks that were on sale, and loaded them into the trunk. Now all she needed to do was retrieve Dylan from tennis and shepherd ailing Vince safely home for the night. She could stick the breaded pork chops she'd defrosted for dinner into the oven and sink into her couch, nestled within its brown corduroy cushions which coordinated with the sunny peach tones of her recently repainted family room. She'd nurse Sophia, smelling the sweetness of the baby on her breast and the aroma of the pork chops browning in the oven.

She turned his ignition key. Nothing. Not even aruh, aruh, aruh. Not even any warning lights. Nothing. The car was completely dead. She was already five minutes overdue to pick up Dylan at the club. He would be waiting for her in the parking lot, alone and anxious in the drizzly night. Zipping Sophia into the front pack again, she walked to the pay phone at the edge of the shopping center. She called her mother and got no answer. Of course, she'd forgotten: the sales meeting. Erica dropped another quarter in the phone and called Debbie. Debbie got home from work at four and could, in her better moments, be counted upon to be grudgingly helpful. After delivering a raft of guilt-inducing complaints—too busy, too tired, too stressed—she'd probably grant Erica this minor favor. Erica was hardly in the mood to endure Debbie's inevitable kvetching, but she seemed the most logical choice, living as she did a block away from the West Meadow Pool and Tennis Club.

But Debbie sounded vague rather than irritated. "Rikki?" she answered, like she couldn't recognize her own sister's voice after thirty years.

"Yeah, listen, Debbie, can you pick up Dylan at the club?" Erica asked, her free hand wrapped around the denim of Sophia's pack. "I'm at Pathmark, and the car won't start, and Dylan was supposed to get picked up after tennis five minutes ago."

"I can't," Debbie said, all muffled and wavery.

"Why not?" Erica asked, her breath coming in tight, short bursts. Debbie's strange, weak tone made her nervous. "He's all alone, out in the rain."

"Jared has a terrible stomachache," Debbie said. Damn hypochondriac Debbie. This stomach business was a new one. Usually Debbie fretted about Jared's asthma, or his food allergies, or his weight.

"You can't leave him alone for five minutes?" Erica pleaded. "He's fifteen years old."

Once again, the familiar shapes of the world melted away, leaving Erica with only dots and lines, blots of color. To steady herself, she traced her fingers down the outline of Sophia's small body tucked inside the cloth carrier, her knitted cap peeking out, her hungry lips nuzzling the padded area against Erica's sternum. The rain beat down harder. She knew she should give up and think of somebody else to call, but Debbie was making her so disconcerted she couldn't let go of the phone.

"Please. The club is around the corner from your house."

"You don't understand, Rikki," Debbie said. "Jared is on medication."

"What kind of medication? Pepto-Bismol? Dylan is only nine years old, you know. He's all alone in the parking lot."

"I'm not feeling so well myself," Debbie continued. "I'm exhausted. And Ron doesn't think I should leave Jared alone these days."

"Ron's not home?"

"It's his bowling night."

"Well, thanks for nothing," Erica said, slamming down the phone. She should have known Ron lay at the root of this. She bent her nose down inside the baby carrier, catching a whiff of Sophia's yeasty breath, and called her best friend Lisa Schrabner, sweet, reliable Lisa, who of course agreed to pick up Dylan even though she'd just gotten a new puppy and had pick up her daughter Lyndsey from dance team in the opposite direction. She called Michael's mother, hopefully referring to her by the correct name (she settled on Dorrie), catching her right as she was leaving for the ice skating rink, asking her to drop off the twins at Lisa's. Then Erica called AAA, where a bored operator instructed her to wait by Vince Volvo for a minimum of forty-five minutes.

She settled down in the driver's seat to wait. Her hands felt stiff and cold. Sophia's nuzzling noises transformed into a sustained wail. Erica removed her from the denim carrier, lifted up her shirt, and undid the top flap of her nursing bra. Her breasts were hard, leaking milk. Sophia latched on, sucking sharply and anxiously at first, then settling into a steady rhythm. Her intense and innocent need was settling: Erica found her own breath calming as well. She pondered with some satisfaction how much Debbie would disapprove of Erica exposing her breasts, albeit behind a rain-spattered windshield, in a busy parking lot.

Ron wouldn't mind, she was sure. He was one of those guys who always undressed you with his eyes. He was a DJ at WBEZ, an easy listening station based in Mineola, presiding over the morning show, dishing out news, traffic reports, and the kind of music Erica despised above all others. His greasy voice floated out over countless insurance agencies and dental offices. When Debbie met Ron, he was just home from Vietnam, and she was only nineteen, working her first job out of beauty school. She mowed his hair into his preferred sidewall style, week after week, until one day he asked Debbie to marry him, a proposal perhaps inspired by the fact that Jared arrived eight months later. Premature, their mother insisted, despite Jared's hefty nine-pound birth weight.

Erica never liked the scurried, tense-browed manner Debbie displayed around Ron, always catering to his whims, always looking to him for direction. "Should I serve chicken today, Ron?" "Do you think Jared should play tennis with his asthma, Ron?" "What brand of toilet paper should I buy, Ron?"

But now, apparently, she'd sunk to a new level. "Should I leave the house, Ron? Should I help my sister and my nephew out even if it means leaving my fifteen-year-old son alone for a few minutes?" Despite the calming presence of Sophia, Erica's blood pressure rose.

Flashing red lights signaled the arrival of the tow truck.

CHAPTER TWO

When Erica walked into the kitchen, the pork chops were leaking blood all over the counter. A sullen tow truck driver had hauled Vince off to the Volvo dealers, to await diagnosis. She'd picked up the boys at Lisa's. Sophia was fast asleep in her car seat. Ethan wasn't home yet. Erica glanced at the oven's digital clock. 7:30 p.m.

"You guys hungry?" she asked.

"Lisa gave us pizza," Dylan answered. Pizza seemed to be the default meal at the Schrabner house. "I need help with my math homework." Dylan extracted a crumpled sheet from his backpack.

"In a few minutes," Erica promised as she wiped down the thin trail of blood that led from the counter, down over the white Formica cabinets, onto the white floor. Jesse and Jake were battling with Lego weapons in the family room. As soon as she wiped the blood up, more flowed down the cabinet door, like it was streaming from a cut. The sight made Erica feel inexplicably nauseous; maybe she was just hungry. The last thing she'd eaten, she realized, was a bagel right after aerobics. She swept the meat into a Tupperware, stuck it in the refrigerator for the next day, and scrubbed the whole white area—counter, cabinet fronts, and floor—with Windex and paper towels. She heated up some leftover pasta in the microwave, poured herself a glass of Chianti, and sat down to eat.

The wine settled Erica's stomach. She grabbed a chocolate chip cookie and, gently disengaging Sophia from her car seat, managed to change her outfit and diaper without waking her up. She settled her in her crib and then noticed Dylan standing quietly behind her, still waiting. "The math?" he prompted.

Dylan, who was in the advanced math track, showed her a sheet of what, if Erica trusted her memory correctly, looked to be quadratic equations. "I'm not sure what to do here," she said.

"Well if X is sixteen and Y is eight," Dylan said, "then I think n is two."

"Sounds like you got it," Erica said. She had no idea.

"Jesse threw a Transformer at my head!" squealed Jake, crashing into her hip.

"Why don't you finish the assignment, Dyl, and then I'll look at it when you're done?"

Erica dragged the twins into the bath and then read them a story and lay with them until they fell asleep. She kissed them, all sprawly and sweet in their beds with their curly dark hair and long-lashed eyes, and picked up the stray toys lying around their room.

"Do you need me to check your homework, Dyl ?"

Dylan was already brushing his teeth, his notebook stuffed in his backpack.

"Nah, I called Jason and compared answers with him."

Downstairs, she heard the garage door open and then the squeak of the door. "Hi, hon!" Ethan called out.

He met her at the base of the stairs and kissed her. His face felt cold and wet. "What took you so long?" she asked.

"I had to take a client out for drinks, and then the traffic was terrible. Some truck spilled mayonnaise on the LIE," he said, opening the refrigerator door and prying open the Tupperware of bloody meat. "What's for dinner?" he asked.

"Not that," Erica said. "I can heat you up some pasta. No. That's all gone. I'll make you a turkey sandwich."

"Throw in some lettuce and tomato and sunflower seeds, and that would be great." Ethan pulled off his suit, leaving it crumpled on the family room carpet atop the Legos and Transformers. He settled onto the couch in his jockey shorts. By the time Erica brought in his sandwich, he'd flicked on one of his assortment of cop shows. They all seemed interchangeable to Erica. The only one she liked was *Miami Vice*, and only because of the gorgeous Don Johnson, whom she was actually going to meet, next week, at one of Ethan's business functions. The rat a tat of machine guns filled the air, differing little in sound from Jesse and Jake's play battles. Ethan bit sloppily into the sandwich and, wiping mustard from his mouth, asked Erica how her day was.

"Kind of aggravating," Erica replied. "The Volvo broke down."
"You're kidding," Ethan said. "It only has—what—ten thousand miles on it? What a lemon." Ethan turned his head to watch a policeman knock down a door and slam a bunch of drug dealers up against a wall. From the baby monitor on the coffee table came a rustle of shifting limbs and then a steadily intensifying cry. Erica ran upstairs and settled down in the armchair with Sophia sucking at her breast; then Erica fell asleep. When she woke up, Sophia was lying tightly held in her arms on her lap, and the house was dark. Erica put Sophia back in her crib and walked downstairs where she put away the Legos and Transformers in their appropriate plastic bins, put Ethan's clothes in the hamper, and set up the coffee for the next morning. She changed into an oversize T-shirt, washed her face, climbed into bed, and buried her nose into Ethan's hair. He was already snoring, tucked against his oversize pillow. He still smelled like Herbal Essence, which was what they had washed each other's hair with the night they met, at Ethan's frat party at MIT. He grunted, turned over, and withdrew deeper into the blanket.

Erica stared up at the skylight. Sophia's cries would wake her before long. In the distant past, when she had had time to sleep, she'd never taken advantage. As a child she was tucked into bed at eight o'clock, come hell or high water, where she traced pictures on the wall with her fingers, listened very quietly to the radio or read books by the flashlight she had tucked under her pillow. She listened to Debbie chat on the phone outside in the hallway, heard her shower, cream off her makeup, set her hair. She listened to her father practice his flute and her mother bustle around cleaning and straightening things. Then she would listen as the house quieted down: her parents' door shutting, their TV going on, and later off; Debbie toweling off her hair in the bathroom and then the gentle slam of her door as well. Erica would peek out of her room, into the shadowy hall with its nightlight, watching the lines of darkness leaking out of her parents' and Debbie's closed bedroom doors.

Now she lay in the bedroom of her own home, staring at those same lines of darkness.

CHAPTER THREE

Debbie called the following morning during her coffee break. Erica had already arranged rides for the twins to preschool; reluctantly skipped aerobics; engaged in a long, unpleasant, and inconclusive conversation with the Volvo service manager; rented the car guaranteed by her insurance (a Dodge Aries with vinyl upholstery and a creaky windshield wiper); and sat down at the kitchen table ready to tackle a toppling pile of mail. Sophia lay next to her on a quilt, rocking back and forth on her belly like an airplane about to take off.

"How's Jared's stomach?" Erica asked.

"Oh, better, I hope." Debbie's voice no longer wavered. It sounded rather brisk, actually. "He wanted to go to school, so I packed him a lunch with rice cakes and peanut butter. His pediatrician thinks he might have a wheat allergy. And I told him, in no uncertain terms, to call me at the salon if he wasn't feeling well. But I haven't heard from him."

"That's good. My brand-new car is completely dead, and no one knows why."

"You shouldn't have gotten that foreign car, you know. Ron always says American-made are still the best, even if they're not trendy these days."

"The Volvo 760 got excellent ratings in *Consumer Reports*." One of Debbie's many annoying habits was to quote Ron's platitudes. Erica ripped open a manila envelope and pulled out a lengthy registration form for Camp Whispering Wind, Dylan's summer camp in the Poconos.

"Well, anyway," Debbie continued, "You wouldn't believe how busy it is here today. Wedding parties up the wazoo. You'd think the whole North Shore is getting married this weekend. I even had to do an eyebrow wax when the aesthetician didn't show up. I don't really have time to talk on the phone."

"What did you call me about?" Erica reminded her.

"I called to invite you to Shabbat dinner. Are you free this Friday?"

"Sure, I guess so."

Sophia propelled herself over on her back, off the blanket, and onto the shag carpet. The abrupt change in perspective frightened her, and she started to scream. Cradling the phone against her ear, Erica knelt to pick her up.

"Are you there, Rikki?" Debbie asked. "Well, see you Friday, then. Gotta go."

Maybe this invitation was Debbie's roundabout way of apologizing. She hoped Jared would be there. Maybe Debbie would even allow them to have a conversation.

She'd been fifteen and a sophomore in high school when Jared was born, shocked by the rush of wonder and envy she'd felt holding this miraculous creature her sister had produced. A placid, happy baby, Jared grew into a cautious, pudgy child, prone to ear infections and asthma, suffering through a life-threatening bout of pneumonia at age two and a lazy eye that required thick glasses as a toddler and an operation at age four. This did not dissuade Erica from playing with him in a way his mother did not: pushing him so high on the swing he squealed with a combination of fright and joy, chasing him around the furniture in games of tag, allowing him to eat forbidden cookies and stay up way past his bedtime.

As Jared neared adolescence, though, he could no longer spend the night without Erica getting a dressing down from Debbie the next day. She fed Jared fish and wheat when obviously she should have known it aggravated his ear infections. Ethan said a four-letter word in his presence. One weekend they let him watch an R-rated movie with full-frontal nudity, and after that he became a polite stranger Erica only saw at Sunday family dinners and other public occasions. She missed Jared. He was the first newborn she'd cradled in her arms.

The auto shop couldn't figure out what ailed Vince Volvo, tossing around ideas from the solenoid to the central computer. It needed more tests, and then, who knew what kind of parts had to be ordered and how long they would take to arrive. The Dodge Aries stunk of cigarette smoke, Erica couldn't adjust the seat comfortably, and worst of all, the Aries didn't come with a tape player. She missed her music desperately.

She didn't feel like getting in the stupid vehicle if she didn't have to, so even though Friday afternoon rolled around chill and drizzly, she decided to walk over with the kids to Debbie's for dinner. Ethan could drive them all home later in his Mercedes. She envied Ethan's snazzy sports car, which sat all day in an outdoor parking lot, getting corroded by acid rain.

The boys dragged their feet. They meandered past West Meadow Elementary, past the wood play structure that had replaced the old metal jungle gym, past what used to be a decrepit chain-link fence with an equally decrepit frame house behind it. The old lady who used to live there would watch Erica and her schoolmates' games intently from the window and the second a ball flew over the fence, dart out to steal it. She was long gone now, the chain-link fence replaced with a cedar one, the frame house replaced with a faux Georgian colonial. They took a turn to the right and then a soft left onto Debbie and Ron's street.

As always, Erica stalled at the high ranch on the corner, the one that used to be Jeff Russell's. Through the window of the daylight basement, halfway hidden by a hedge, she could see the family room where she first slept with Jeff. Even though they found lots of other cool places later, like the mossy concrete foundations of the Mackay mansion or his sister Eve's playhouse, her favorite remained that floral-printed plastic-covered family room couch. Sometimes his mother would walk around upstairs, making dinner or whatever, and Erica got a kick out of listening to her footsteps approaching and then receding.

Jeff did the odd thing and attended some little college all the way in Oregon, where, rumor had it, the students ran around naked and committed suicide at alarming rates. His parents did the odd thing too and followed him out West, to Arizona. Since then their house had changed hands three times, twice brokered by Erica's mother, Suzanne. The newest owner was a dentist. He'd opened a little office in what used to be the garage. The orange-and-avocado-flowered curtains in the daylight basement, sewn by Jeff's mother, had been replaced with generic beige Venetian blinds.

"Let's go, Mommy, I'm cold," complained Dylan, kicking at the wet plastic casing of an advertising mailer lying forlornly on the driveway.

Two more split-levels and a high ranch and they arrived at Debbie and Ron's, a Dutch colonial identical to Erica and Ethan's prior to their renovation. It was testimony to their mother's real estate prowess that she had managed to sell them both the same house, three blocks apart.

Now Erica's kitchen was twice the size, with a center island and a shiny outsize refrigerator with a cold-water dispenser. Her family room opened out from where Ron and Debbie's living room ended, extending to sliding glass doors and a wooden deck. While Ron and Debbie's bedroom was a cramped affair barely containing their Ethan Allen queen bed, night tables, and dresser set, Erica and Ethan's boasted a king-size waterbed, a skylight, and closets replete with Formica cubbies. Erica knocked on Debbie's front door, which was the same as hers, a dull brown wooden rectangle. Peering through a gap in the curtains in the dining room, a bay window just like their own, she saw Ron get up from his easy chair and shuffle toward them.

"Shabbat shalom," he said. "Come in and rest a while." He returned to his La-Z-Boy and the NCAA Final Four. The boys made a mad dash for Jared's room; Jared still recognized their existence, treating them like the little brothers he never had. Debbie and Ron's house looked like Laura Ashley threw up in it: new floral wallpaper in the entry hallway, a crocheted bunny doorstop, and a needlework picture stating, "Bless our home." As children, according to the neat definitions preferred by their parents, Debbie had always been "the artistic one." She did not possess the unsettling kind of talent that might lead to a bohemian lifestyle and a loft in Greenwich Village but rather a contained artistry that produced drawings of houses with two neat curtained windows, a chimney puffing smoke, and a pathway leading up to it in proper perspective, lined with abundant cheery flowers. She knotted lanyard necklaces, made macramé plant hangers, and rolled her hair into a flawless French twist. When she graduated high school and announced she wanted to go to beauty school instead of college, her parents were not thrilled but accepting.

Erica walked past the dining room table, carefully set with blue-and-white china, a shiny challah, and candles, finding Debbie at the kitchen counter basting chicken legs with a tomato-and-soy marinade. She was wearing a blue pantsuit with a blue-and-white-striped apron over it. Her hair was newly streaked blond and cut into a perky bob. Erica felt oversize and sloppy staring down at her sister's rounded but neatly proportioned body. Errant flesh bulged out between Erica's leggings and the sweatshirt she'd pulled on early that morning, no makeup, hair back in a banana clip. A few oily strands escaped, and she pushed them back before they drooped too near the chicken.

Debbie stroked Sophia's head. "Hello, cutie," she said. There it was again, that disturbing wavery voice. As she drew her hand away from Sophia, her hand holding the basting brush shook softly, like it was buffeted by some private wind. On her sister's wrist, sneaking out from under her sleeve, Erica could swear she saw the purple rim of a bruise.

As Debbie slid the pan of fluorescent poultry into the oven, a tremor ran up her arm, starting at her fingers, rippling past the faint white scar at her elbow. Her grip on the pan loosened, and for a split second the handle hung precariously off the edge. Just before the pan tipped past a point of no return, Debbie grasped it with her other hand, gave it a nudge, and closed the oven door. Then she opened the refrigerator and removed a head of iceberg lettuce like nothing had happened.

"Are you all right, Debbie?" With one hand, Erica poured herself a glass of water.

"I'm exhausted, that's all. Work is insane," Debbie said. "What's new with you?"

"We're meeting Don Johnson tomorrow," Erica said.

"No kidding," Debbie said. "From *Miami Vice*? How did you swing that?"

"He's starring in a new movie," Erica said, sitting down at Debbie's kitchen table, "and Ethan's company, you know, Grant Fishel, is throwing a movie premiere party. I'm hoping I can shake his hand, and maybe get his autograph, although I guess that's kind of dorky, don't you think?"

"I can't blame you. I'd do the same if I had the chance." Debbie poured the same orange pseudo French dressing their mother had served them as children in a thick gooey stream all over the iceberg lettuce. "Ethan works in the movie business now?"

"No!" Erica and Debbie had engaged in this conversation, in many variations, as long as she'd been married to Ethan. "Ethan is a quantitative analyst," Erica explained for the thousandth time. "He devises computer programs that predict the movement of world money markets."

"What does that have to do with Don Johnson's new movie?" Debbie asked, mixing up a box of Betty Crocker scalloped potatoes, pouring them into a pan, and putting them in the oven next to the chicken. Her movements were deft. Erica began to think she'd only imagined the shaking hand, the hesitation at the oven door.

"Grant Fishel financed the movie," Erica said. "So we get to go to the party."

"Where are your boys?" Debbie stiffened in sudden concern.

"Playing with Jared, I assume." Sophia twisted her way out of Erica's arms, dangling her chubby fingers dangerously near the bottle of orange dressing. "They ran off to his room the minute we came in the house."

Debbie twisted the ends of her hair. "Well, I hope they don't make too much noise. He still isn't feeling well."

"I'll go check," Erica said.

Jared and Dylan lay on Jared's bed, contentedly playing Atari. Jesse and Jake were gleefully running pint size Mercedes and Porsches from Jared's old matchbox car collection between the legs of his desk.

"Hi, Jared," Erica said.

Jared lifted his head up, and as he did so, she noticed he'd changed his hairstyle. It was short, almost shaved, but self-consciously so, as if to parody his father, and dyed a peroxide blond. He'd grown into his weight too, his limbs stretching out long and sinewy like Ron's. "Oh, hi, Aunt Rikki," he said, without averting his eyes from his video controls. She felt so awkward around him now. Perhaps Debbie had only accelerated the speed at which adolescence would draw him, like any child, away from her. She knew that one day in the unimaginable future there would be a time when her own kids would no longer cling to her leg, or chatter so incessantly she thought her brain would burst out of her head, or turn to her out of the blue to tell her, "I yove you." At nine, Dylan already ran upstairs after school and closed his door, and he no longer asked her to towel him off after his bath.

Sophia wriggled, heavy and restless, rooting at her shoulder. Erica felt like a hulking, unnecessary presence among the boys. She returned to the living room and, tired, settled onto the creamy-white cotton sofa across from Ron. The glint of yellow streetlights through the drawn blinds cast tinted dashes on his closed eyelids.

"Wake up, Ron," Erica said.

"Sorry, some of us have to work for a living. Speaking of which, where's your hubby?" Ron asked, blinking. Behind him hung Jared's bar mitzvah pictures and a series of needlepoint tulips, all in gold frames.

"He should be here any minute," Erica said. "He can't get out of work until the market closes, and then there's usually a meeting, and there's Friday traffic."

"That's the price you pay for working in the city." Ron flicked from the basketball to a golf tournament to the basketball, then back again, clutching the remote like a weapon. Ron had learned radio engineering in the service and referred to his tour in Vietnam as if he'd spent two years rewiring faulty connections. She couldn't imagine how he'd survived two years there without killing a man, or at least having his synapses permanently skewed from the sight of dead babies and brain tissue leaking out of shattered skulls.

Debbie joined them in the living room and leaned her head against Ron's. Her eyebrows knotted tensely. "All these crazy weddings are making me hate spring," she said. "Thank God it's Friday." Her thighs looked thinner than Erica remembered and her skin rubbery. Erica could see the veins pulsing underneath. Ron set the remote down at his side and put his arm around Debbie, massaging her shoulders.

"What's keeping Ethan?" Debbie asked. The wooden salad bowl sat on the table, as did the challah, the candles, the casserole of chicken on a heating tray, everything awaiting Ethan's late arrival.

"Traffic, I guess." Erica looked down disparagingly at her own chubby thighs, encased like sausages in their black leggings.

"Can I interest you in a whiskey sour, Rikki?"

When Ron married Debbie in a catering hall with crystal chandeliers, Erica wore a hideous pink bridesmaid dress, drank too many whiskey sours, and got sick. At least it gave her an excuse to throw away the dress, but the whiskey sour incident provided Ron with conversational fodder forevermore.

"No, thanks," Erica said. "I'm nursing. I'm not drinking hard alcohol." Sophia lay next to her in the grooves of the couch, dribbling a thin line of spittle between the cushions.

"A 7-Up?" Ron asked.

"Sure, thank you." Erica leafed through the record albums in Debbie and Ron's wall unit. What a pathetic bunch of crap it was: Paul Anka, Tony Orlando and Dawn, a Roger Whittaker collection advertised on late-night television. They were probably all throwaways from Ron's easy listening show.

"Debbie?" Erica asked. "What happened to your old albums? You know, *Sgt. Pepper* and stuff?"

Debbie shrugged, her face a blank. "I don't know. I haven't listened to them in so long. They're probably in the basement somewhere."

"Do you think Jared has them?" Erica asked, her arm gripping Sophia, who'd edged dangerously close to the perimeter of the couch.

Debbie snorted. "Jared? I can't stand the music he listens to. Nothing but noise."

"What bands does he like?"

"Who knows? They're awful."

"When are you getting a CD player?" Erica asked.

"We're still paying off Jared's stupid Atari thing," Ron said.

The doorbell rang. Erica sprang up and admitted Ethan. He looked tired, his suit pants wrinkled, his damp curls sticking to his forehead, slightly stunned to find himself in the shelter of Debbie's orderly living room.

"Boy, it's nice to be here," he said, smiling benignly. "The week was a bitch. The traffic was terrible."

———

The chicken was surprisingly tasty, but as it was red in color, Jake threw it on the floor.

"Can I make him a peanut butter sandwich?" Erica asked.

"It's in the refrigerator," Debbie said, eyes rolling.

Erica spread Skippy and grape jelly onto white bread. Figuring Debbie's floor was spotless enough to eat from, she laid the two rejected chicken legs on Ethan's plate. Ethan ate with gusto, and so, Erica noticed with interest, did Jared, who was shoveling in chicken, potatoes, salad, challah, and Jell-O with shaved carrots in it.

"Great stuff!" Jared exclaimed between bites. He sported new straggly moustache hairs on his upper lip. He took a third helping of Jell-O and jiggled it around his plate, to Dylan's wild laughter. Erica met Jared's wide-eyed gaze, all pupil. All of a sudden, it came to her: Jared was stoned. How could she have missed it up to now? The stomachache: her family's traditional, foolproof excuse for escape and privacy. She'd used it to handy advantage all through high school when she was too chemically altered to face her parents. And it came to her, in a sharp and unexpected pang, how much she missed that sensation of being so intensely engaged with her surroundings yet somehow floating above them. She couldn't recall when she had last gotten high. Not in this decade.

"Want the rest of my chicken, Jared?" she asked. "I'm kinda full."

"Sure," he said, grinning. "Thanks."

After a dessert of lemon bundt cake, Debbie's favorite recipe made with pudding mix, everyone rose from the table. The boys ran back to Jared's room.

"Think you could give me a hand with the computer again, Ethan?" Ron asked.

"Do I have to?" Ethan blurted out but then caught himself. "Just joking," he reassured Ron. They'd given Ron the Apple IIGS for Hanukah and now he requested technical assistance every time Ethan came over.

"We can't all be brainiacs like you," Ron said.

Debbie started clearing the table, and Erica would have helped her, except that Sophia was nuzzling and whimpering and clearly needed a feeding. She sat down on the living room couch and unbuttoned her blouse, listening to the click and splash of Debbie loading items into the dishwasher, wondering what Ethan and Ron were up to. Probably installing an updated version of *Leisure Suit Larry*.

Driven by the mysterious impulses of little boys, Jesse burst into the room and heaved a Matchbox Volkswagen at the coffee table, knocking over a globe in Debbie's prized snow globe collection. The snow globe fell to the ground, rolled against the sharp corner of the bookcase, and shattered, sending shards of broken glass and water across the carpet. Both Ron and Debbie rushed in from opposite directions.

"What's going on here?" Ron's tone was calm, but his pale skin reddened, his lips contorting as if they were holding in something unpleasant. Thin bristles of white-blond hair vibrated at the base of his receding chin. Jesse, frozen and wide-eyed, stared wonderingly at the miniature wood-frame colonial and snow-covered trees sinking into the white slush of the soaked carpet. "Car accident," Erica explained, detaching Sophia from her breast and wrangling the buttons of her blouse quickly into their respective slots. "Sorry." She picked shards of glass out of the carpet with her one free hand as Debbie rushed for rags and rug cleaner and then vigorously scrubbed at the spot.

"Hey, what's all the noise about?" Ethan asked, appearing belatedly at the entrance to the room. "Hey, Ron, come back here," he urged, steering Ron back down the hallway. "I added a new memory card and defragged your hard drive."

"Sorry about this," Erica repeated while swabbing at the perimeters of the spot with her one free hand.

"Ron bought me that paperweight the year Jared was born. It's his favorite." Debbie poked around the legs of the coffee table with her Dustbuster. "You buttoned your blouse up wrong," she noted. "It's hanging funny."

"I could buy you another one." Erica rebuttoned her blouse, but it still pulled at the bustline.

"Ron found that one at an antiques store in Albany. I doubt it's replaceable." Debbie wiped down the coffee table with Windex. "This house looks like a hurricane hit it," she complained.

"Then why invite the hurricane to visit," Erica thought. Her four children were like her body: overflowing, excessive, unruly. "I think that table is as clean as it's going to get," she said as Debbie dug her paper towel into the interstices between the glass and the brass knobs at the corners.

"Oh, I suppose," Debbie said, giving it one more swipe. "I just wanted to make sure any slivers of glass are gone. If one of those gets ingrained in your skin, you can get a nasty infection."

Debbie looked at her expectantly, as if expecting Erica to say something to restore the social equilibrium. Erica couldn't remember a time when Debbie hadn't made her feel guilty of crimes sometimes obvious but more frequently undisclosed. She'd never been "nice" enough to satisfy Debbie, if one accepted Debbie's definition of "nice." She'd never been appreciative enough of Debbie's obligatory kindnesses, never considerate enough of her troubles, never respectful of her immaculate housekeeping, on the whole an aggravating embarrassment.

She wanted to get the hell out of Debbie's house. While Erica feeling inadequate around her sister was a standard condition of her life, Debbie's aspect this past week differed in an uncomfortable way. There was something wrong going on with her, something as erratic and unpredictable as Vince Volvo's stalling engine. That wavery voice that came and went, that ephemeral tremulousness, those bruises that showed themselves only to vanish under a neatly cuffed sleeve. They all called out to her to pay more attention than she had the bandwidth for. Debbie was hiding something, but Erica wasn't sure she wanted to find out what it was. Not tonight, anyway.

"We'd better go," she said. "It's past the twins' bedtime." She stuck her head into the den, where Ron sat hunched over the computer, playing a defragged version of, no surprise, *Leisure Suit Larry*. "Where's Ethan?" she asked.

"I bored him, I guess," he said. "I think he's outside."

She retrieved the kids from Jared's bedroom, wondering where he hid his stash, safe from Debbie's relentless housekeeping and Ron's evil eye.

"Bye, Jared," she said.

"Yeah, it was good seeing you, Aunt Rikki. Thanks for coming."

Debbie pressed several chocolate bars into Erica's hand, already overcrowded with Sophia's car seat handle, the twins' sticky fingers, and the diaper bag. "Here, take these. I want to get them out of the house. Ron and I could skip the calories, and Jared is allergic to chocolate."

"I'll call you Monday." Erica backed rapidly down the stairs, tearing open a chocolate wrapper as she did so. "We need to go shopping for Lauren's bat mitzvah." Ethan was standing on the sidewalk smoking one of his disgusting clove cigarettes. The door shut, and the edgy fear rising in her settled into a faint pulsing at the back of her skull, eclipsed by an overwhelming sense of relief.

CHAPTER FOUR

Erica decided, just for that night, to break her rule about no hard alcohol while nursing. She always looked forward to attending large parties in theory but inevitably changed her mind as soon as she arrived, then threaded her way through the crowd toward the alcohol source. The alcohol made her feel dizzy but settled. One night's deviation could hardly turn her bright-eyed infant into a blithering idiot.

On a Saturday night the spring of Erica's junior year of college, she'd been on her third glass of Purple Passion, watching the smoke rise up from the Everclear, when she spied Ethan through the haze. Outside in the Boston April, timid new leaves huddled against the gray wind, but inside his MIT dormitory Ethan carried a halo of sun about him. Ringlets of reddish-brown hair brushed his shoulders and framed the honeyed complexion of his face. He wore jeans and a collarless Indian cotton shirt and a vest that looked like it had come from a vintage store. The combination of shock and Purple Passion glued her in place.

Ethan remained capable of movement, though, and responded to her dumbfounded stare by sidling over. "Hi," he said.

"What's your major?" she asked, because her conversational gambits were as pathetic as the pimply, polyester clad physics students surrounding her.

"Economics," he replied, and after a couple hours she followed him upstairs into his dorm room and into the rest of his life.

—

The door to the banquet room of this Grant Fishel extravaganza consisted of two thick panels of etched-glass flamingoes edged with cherrywood. Erica fixed its location in her head, like she would the exit door of an airplane. A couple of conversation clusters away, Ethan's head bobbed up and down enthusiastically. The drink of choice at this gathering was a frothy combo of peach puree, champagne, and liqueur, called a Bellini; Erica was sipping her third, but she still felt in danger of either floating away or crashing. The oversize room—converted industrial space—felt insubstantial and fragile. There were tin squares on the ceiling, green glass tiles on the walls. The conversations of hundreds of people echoed metallically.

She wore a black washed-silk dress with a low-cut V-neck, all slinky and slidey, procured by her mother at a 75 percent discount. She'd assured Erica it was a designer dress with timeless style. Erica's thighs pressed against the smoothness of her skirt, which skimmed the tops of her knees. She wasn't sure it was the most flattering length or fabric. Parts of her anatomy jutted out at every opportunity. At least, unlike most of the other women in the room, she wasn't wearing a poufy floral dress with a giant bow at the back, looking as if she'd been stranded in time at her senior prom. She was wearing her mother's jewelry: sunburst earrings of twenty-four karat gold and cubic zirconia, a gold bracelet with another chunk of zirconia at its center, and a genuine diamond pendant Dad had given her for their twenty-fifth wedding anniversary. Erica fingered the pendant to reassure herself that the diamonds were still there. A waiter walked by offering beluga caviar on toast points, and she tossed a couple in her mouth.

She maneuvered her way to Ethan and placed her hand lightly on his arm. He squeezed her arm back in recognition but continued his stultifying conversation about designations or assignations or acquisitions. Erica drifted off again. She worried about the foundation she was wearing, another suggestion of her mother's. When she'd glanced in her rearview mirror after dropping the kids off at Lisa's, her complexion had looked sallow and fake.

Driving here, she'd cruised sleekly over the Fifty-Ninth Street Bridge and parked in a garage only two blocks away from this renovated factory. Ethan was happy to let her drive the Mercedes. At home in California, he navigated freeways with equanimity, shifting lazily between lanes, adjusting the radio, resting his hands ever so lightly on the wheel. But he'd never truly adjusted to driving in New York City, intimidated by the maze of roadways, the squeegee men, the taxis darting out of nowhere. Erica planted her gaze on the etched-glass birds marking the exit. If only she could walk through those swinging wooden doors, retrieve the Mercedes, and dart through tangles of lights like one of the bouncing balls in her boys' Nintendo games.

"Erica! You look wonderful as usual! Where did you get that dress? Is it vintage?"

She turned in the direction of the voice to see Ethan's boss's wife, whose name she had forgotten, wobble towards her in five inch heels. The wife was about ten years older than Erica, sporting a lavender-and-turquoise concoction that bunched like runaway cotton candy just below her tush.

"Thanks," Erica said. "But it's not vintage. My mother gave it to me."

"Well, I love it," said Mrs. No-Name. "So different! How's your new baby girl?" She jiggled her alligator skin purse, which matched her alligator skin heels and clashed totally with the prom dress. Mrs. No-Name seemed as uncomfortable as Erica was, shifting back and forth in her tight shoes, her designer tag jutting out from her neckline.

"She's doing great," Erica said. "This is our first night out in the city since she was born."

"Oh, you must be so exhausted. I remember those times. My littlest one is fourteen now, you know." Mrs. No-Name smiled expectantly while Erica's mind raced, searching for her name. Maybe if she wasn't so exhausted, her mind would function more efficiently. From a cooperative neuronal cluster, she retrieved a comment this woman had made at the last Grant Fishel event—a moonlight cruise—about her upcoming kitchen renovation, accompanied, thank goodness, by her conveniently alliterative name, Shelley Stanley. "How's your kitchen coming along, Shelley?" she asked, accenting the Shelley part. A waiter—cute, with curly brown hair—proffered Bellini number four, and Erica accepted.

"Oh, the kitchen's taking forever," Shelley said. "Our first contractor quit in the middle of the job, would you believe it? Left our new center island sitting in the middle of the family room and disappeared. I finally found another contractor—we're suing the first one—and then it turned out that the Sub-Zero refrigerator I ordered was too high for the alcove, so we had to break open the ceiling, and you wouldn't believe the dust! Of course, Stewart didn't notice anything out of the ordinary, he's so oblivious. . ."

Erica let the stream of words pulse over her like a soothing shower, obviating her need to respond in any way but a pleasant smile. But Shelley eventually paused, awaiting a response.

"Shelley, I know what you mean," Erica said. "Our kitchen renovation took forever too. They sent the wrong tiles, six-inch instead of four-inch, so for two weeks we had no floor tiles at all, only subfloor, and now I hate the tiles I ordered. My sister convinced me to get them. They're white. Do you know how constantly you have to clean white tiles with four kids?" Erica wobbled slightly, spilling her Bellini down the V-shaped bustline of her dress. The drink dribbled down her cleavage, leaving a sticky trail and finally clotting at her belly button.

"Let me clean you up," Shelley said, blotting up the exposed part of the mess with her cocktail napkin. "Nice talking to you," Shelley said after she was done and sashayed off into the crowd.

"Ah, the lovely Bellini," said a short guy with thinning hair and horn-rim glasses.

"Pardon me?" Erica looked down at the trace of stain at her belly.

"Alcohol is always better than soft drinks. Soft drinks go straight to your hips while providing no pleasure."

"So true." Her dress, wet from where Shelley had dabbed it, clung to her rounded belly.

"Stephan Langston," said Mr. Horn Rim, extending his hand. "Hey, look over there," he said.

Don Johnson, brighter than TV, brighter than life, was striding toward them, unintentionally perhaps, but nonetheless drawing closer and closer.

"Oh my God," Erica whispered.

"I'll leave you two be," said Stephan.

Don and Erica's shoulders brushed. They were the same height. She could see directly into his warm brown eyes, rich and languid. "Excuse me," Don said, presumably in relation to their accidentally bumping into each other. But now that he'd stopped, he smiled, all white teeth, extending his hand.

Somehow Erica managed to return the gesture, saying, "Nice to meet you, Don," looking down at their clasped hands, fixing the moment in her consciousness.

Don was wearing a *Miami Vice* suit: white jacket, black T-shirt, a hint of tanned chest. A golden glow radiated from his every pore, reminding Erica of her first sight of Ethan, only more so. Her silky dress untethered from her belly and slithered over her skin.

"I love *Miami Vice*," she heard herself say. "I watch it every week." Their hands remained clasped.

"Thanks," Don replied offhandedly. "It's fun."

"I'd love to see Miami sometime," Erica said, even though she'd never before connected televised Florida, the one encapsulating her ineffable desires, with the Florida she knew personally, the one containing elderly relatives and all-you-can-eat Chinese buffets. "I want to stand on Miami Beach," she continued, "you know, my toes in the water, the sunset turning the ocean all pink, and there'd be a slight breeze up, and I'd be standing there in a cotton dress, with a margarita in my hand."

Don's hand dropped away, but his maple-syrup eyes still latched onto her like she was the only person in the world, his expression soft and serious. He did not pass judgment on the Bellini clutched in Erica's half-open palm. "Yes," he said. "I know."

Erica sank into his rapt, intense gaze. She loved a gaze like that more than anything. In her mind, guitar chords built to a crescendo. She allowed herself to believe that he did know, that he grasped the enormity of her desires, that pulsing hunger. She imagined the two of them standing under a palm tree, having narrowly escaped with their lives. In her fantasy world, Don tipped her chin up with his hand, as if to kiss her. She could see the blond stubble on his chin. Back in the real world of the Grant Fishel party, that stubble hovered so close she could touch it.

"So, what's your movie about?" she asked. "I assume it takes place in Miami. Do you play a police officer?"

"Actually, no," replied Don. "It's set in Maine. It's a saga of three generations of a shipbuilding family. I play the heir to the fortune. I'm trying to engage in more serious work."

Erica was trying to wrap her mind around Don trapped in a winter coat, buffeted by frigid North Atlantic winds, engaging in whatever he believed to be serious, when one of his handlers whisked him away. She floated through the rest of the reception, drifting in and out of conversations and finally reconnecting with Ethan to sit down to a dinner that meandered dreamily from tuna tartare to chocolate mousse pie, each course accompanied by continually refilled glasses of red wine.

The movie was disappointing. The plot revolved around three generations of family secrets and dysfunctions, with Don looking more tight-lipped and constipated than serious. She'd anticipated him loping among palm trees evading gunfire, and instead he strode stiffly along cold and rocky cliffs colored in navy and purple and gray. Erica's cocoon of soft sand and fragrant tropical air evaporated, and she became aware of a dank odor in the theater and her heavy head. She rested against Ethan's shoulder and fell asleep, waking to see the credits drift across the screen.

Outside she revived slightly. In the city, the night was young. People were still eating in outdoor cafes and walking down the sidewalk arm in arm. She crooked her arm through Ethan's.. A light rain pelted her shoulders; the air reeked faintly of garbage. They waited on the first floor of the parking garage for the attendant to fetch the car, inhaling the wet exhaust.

Ethan offered to drive. Erica started to complain, but feeling six Bellinis, uncounted glasses of wine, and years of inadequate sleep, held her tongue. He pushed the driver's seat back to accommodate his knees while Erica leaned against the leather passenger seat, and then they were moving, and she was staring numbly at the taxis whizzing by, too exhausted to even give direction. Ethan headed for the Manhattan Bridge, a route Erica always avoided because the stone arch at the beginning gave her the creeps. To her, it resembled an archaeological find, like the head of the Statue of Liberty at the end of the *Planet of the Apes* movie. When New York City inevitably imploded, nothing would remain of this vibrating and glittering metropolis but rubble and floating plastic bags, save this one ornate granite arch.

As they crossed over the Manhattan Bridge, the Mercedes heating system kicked in overly hard. "It feels like the Sahara in here," she said.

"Adjust the vent," Ethan suggested. He jerked his head right and left, trying to remember which way to turn after exiting the bridge.

"Turn left," Erica told him, playing around with the little black knob. All it did was increase the flow of hot dry air. A layer of sweat pooled under the neckline of Erica's dress, trickling down between her swollen breasts. "Nothing helps. It's still hot."

Ethan didn't respond. He was concentrating intensely on his driving, navigating past an overflowing garbage truck and some fallen construction debris, casting his eyes about for a street sign that would tell him what to do.

"Turn right here," Erica said, slipping off her mother's cape with the golden embroidered collar. "Take the BQE."

She unzipped her dress down to the center of her back and placed her hand on Ethan's thigh. "I met Don Johnson at the reception, did I tell you? He's actually better looking in real life than he is on *Miami Vice*."

"You already told me," Ethan said, gripping the wheel tightly and leaning forward to read an upcoming sign. He'd taken his contacts out and put on his glasses, like he often did when he was tired. The glasses gave him a vulnerable, nerdy look. "I exit here for the Grand Central, right?" he asked. The exit ramp to the Grand Central popped up with little warning, a black hole in the sulfurous haze. Ethan slid over into the right lane, cutting off yet another garbage truck. The truck honked loudly.

"Asshole," Ethan muttered softly to himself.

Erica opened the window a crack and let the cool, stinky air ripple through the car.

Many years ago, on another night when Ethan was driving, a night shortly after they were married and living in a rental on Beacon Hill in Boston, a thick heavy summer night when it was 4:00 a.m. and they were still wide awake, Erica slipped her entire dress off in the car. Then she pulled her panties off. She wasn't wearing a bra. She unbuttoned Ethan's shirt while he was driving, unzipped his pants, nuzzled his neck as he narrowly missed the fender of a double-parked taxi. He pulled into an illegal parking space by a water hydrant, where they made love in the front seat. Stark-naked, Ethan then drove them home and parked the car in a legitimate spot. They walked half a block down to their brownstone, opened the deadbolt, walked through the lobby with its dirty marble floor and rows of mailboxes, walked up two flights of stairs, and then negotiated the three locks on their apartment door. Nobody noticed, or nobody cared. All their neighbors were gay or asleep or both. Dylan was born exactly 270 days later. Ethan accepted the job at Grant Fishel, and Mom sold them their Dutch colonial in West Meadow Knolls.

The neon Hebrew National Salami sign shone through the fog, signaling their arrival in Queens. Ethan relaxed now that they had passed the most insane tangles of traffic and were cruising relatively unimpeded past row houses, pizzerias, and bagel bakeries, sailing toward home with James Taylor on the tape deck.

"I'm looking forward to a good night's sleep," he said. "I think I'm going to start running again. I feel like a slug."

"Don't forget, we have to stop at Lisa's and pick up the kids," Erica reminded him. Her head hurt. Her skin itched. The tag on her new dress poked stiffly into her neck. She slid uncomfortably around the leather seat.

Lisa helped Erica and Ethan carry heavy lumps of sleeping child into the Mercedes.

"I'm still waiting up for Lyndsey," Lisa said. "She's at a party with your nephew, Jared. They've got an English class together. She told me she'd call. Stupid me, I didn't get the number of the house the party is at. I'm not even sure of the kid's name."

Erica thought of Jared's new haircut, his wide stoned eyes. "I'm sure she'll be home soon," she said. She didn't want to worry Lisa.

"Oh my God, the phone is ringing," Lisa said, running toward the house.

When Ethan and Erica walked into their kitchen, Erica noticed that her own answering machine blinked an angry neglected red. It bothered her, but she left it alone. Four sleeping kids needed settling in their rooms, and she could barely stagger up the stairs.

CHAPTER FIVE

Despite her exhaustion, Erica lay awake for a long time, prostrate on her new 100 percent Egyptian cotton pinstriped sheets, listening to Ethan's snores and watching clouds drift by the skylight like celestial TV. When she finally fell into a spotty sleep, images—not quite dreams—startled her awake. Red blinking lights. Red blinking sun. White sky, white-hot sand, burning feet, sun-bleached camel skulls. Whimpering, bleating emaciated goats. No, red blinking lights on the baby monitor and the whimpering bleating of baby Sophia. She staggered to her feet, stumbled into the bathroom and gulped water still warm from the tap until it pooled heavily at the base of her belly.

The sight and scent of her mother threw Sophia into even stronger paroxysms of screaming. She arched her back against the sheets, her mouth opening into a perfect circle. Erica picked her up, her nightgown down at her shoulder, inhaling Sophia's intoxicating brew of urgency and milk. The baby attached to Erica's nipple with a satisfied snap as they stood by the crib. Together, the two of them clumped down into the big chenille rocking chair.

It was unusually warm for March, and humid. A fetid odor of defrosting mud and diesel exhaust blew in from the window, cracked open a notch. Malodorous as it was, the breeze still carried with it a note of spring. As Sophia sucked hard on her breast, Erica turned her head, observing the rectangle of nighttime observable through the window: the oak tree to the right, limbs shuddering in the wind; the line of black road behind it; the Krauscheks' brick house across the street, its windows blank and dark.

She burped Sophia. Milk dribbled down Erica's back. Sophia's mouth dropped open, indicating deep sleep. There was a milk blister on her lower lip. Erica lowered her gently into her crib and then climbed back into bed with Ethan, pressing her body against his back, slipping her hands around his sides and resting them against the softness of his belly. He grunted gently, rolling onto his stomach, and as he did so, the baby monitor once again emitted an insistent cry.

Erica and Sophia resumed their position in the chenille chair. "I'm sorry, Sophia," Erica whispered to her daughter, sorry for leaving her with Lisa all evening, sorry for attempting to drug her with Bellini-laced milk, sorry for any other ways she might have failed her. Her mind drifted toward sand again, but this time gentle, enveloping sand, lapped by turquoise water, warmed by a benevolent sun. Don Johnson lay next to her wearing white swim trunks. His head rested on his raised right elbow; a shock of dirty blond hair fell into his eyes. He smelled of coconut oil and salt.

In the rectangle of the open window, a touch of light infiltrated the sky. A lone car, an ancient wood-sided station wagon, drove by, its headlights shimmering in the navy-gray light. The car skidded to a stop in front of their house. A gnome-like man stepped out, tossing the Sunday paper with his gnarled hand. The paper missed the front stoop, falling with a clunk into the arborvitae. As it did so, from a distance came a high-pitched shriek, like a radio disaster test. When the shriek sounded again, Erica realized it was the phone.

Cradling Sophia to her like a football, Erica raced down the stairs, managing to pick up just as the answering machine went on.

"Rikki! Where have you been? I was just about to hang up!" Erica's mother shouted, competing with the message machine recording of Jesse singing "Baby Beluga."

"I was feeding the baby. It's 6:00 a.m. I almost dropped her running down here. You could have left a message on the machine."

"I already left a message on the machine. Didn't you check your messages when you got home from that party?"

Erica leaned against the counter for balance. Her answering machine was blinking, scarlet as a blood clot.

Debbie. It had to be Debbie. Debbie's bruises, the ones that unnerved her so on Friday. The bruises were leukemia, blood gone fiendishly wrong, blood pooling against her skin. Debbie was lying flat in a hospital bed, IV lines threading in and out, monitors registering her heartbeat in cold white lines. No, more likely it was another one of Debbie's accidents. She had fallen down the stairs. She'd slipped off the ladder she climbed so often, dusting figurines on a top shelf or vacuuming her drapes.

"What's wrong with Debbie?" Erica squeaked.

"Debbie?" Suzanne sounded startled. "There's nothing wrong with Debbie. It's Jared!"

Jared. His stomach. So his stomachaches weren't an excuse to avoid the family, to lie on his back on his own bed, in his own world, staring up at the glow-in-the-dark stars on his ceiling, letting whatever Debbie termed his "horrible music" wash over him. No, there really was something seriously amiss with his digestive system, some undiagnosed disease rotting his insides, and now he was bleeding, hemorrhaging, lying in a hospital bed with IV tubes threading in and out and his heartbeat registered in cold white lines.

"What's wrong with Jared's stomach?" Erica pulled a footstool over with her big toe and leaned against it, Sophia heavy on her chest.

"His stomach?" Mom sounded more befuddled than ever. "They pumped his stomach, but. . ."

"Why did they pump his stomach?" Balancing Sophia precariously against her shoulder she filled the coffee carafe with one hand, pressing the phone between her shoulder and her stiff neck.

"He was unconscious. Ron found him lying on the front lawn and rushed him to the emergency room. He drank too much at some crazy party. His alcohol level was twenty-three!"

"Nobody's blood alcohol could be twenty-three, Mom," Erica said. "They'd be dead. Are you sure you don't mean point twenty-three?"

"Well, what does it matter—he almost died!" Mom's disembodied voice crackled loudly through the receiver, so high-pitched it set Erica's eardrum to vibrating. Her bladder swelled to bursting.

"I have to pee," Erica said.

"What are you going to do?" Mom bleated. "Jared is in the hospital. Your sister is besides herself."

"Pee," Erica said, walking toward the bathroom. As she sat on the toilet, still juggling the baby and the phone, she assured her mother she would call Debbie immediately.

She did call Debbie, but no one answered. She drank a quart of orange juice directly from the carton, a bad habit she'd picked up from Ethan. The baby was finally sleeping. Not wanting to risk waking her on the trip upstairs, she placed her in the playpen in the family room. A better sister would have, she supposed, checked her answering machine last night and been there for Debbie during this time of trouble. A better sister, she supposed, would not be so exhausted by the demands of her own inconsequential life. She lay down on the couch, her limbs splayed out among Matchbox cars and stray Cheerios, and fell soundly asleep.

When she woke up, the sky was fully light, a uniform gray. Sophia was still sleeping, resting against a stuffed bear in her playpen as Jesse and Jake circled around her, eating Fruit Roll-Ups and chasing each other with plastic swords. "I'm going to throw you into the dungeon!" cried Jesse, stabbing Jake in the abdomen. On the TV, a green furry creature sang a song about world peace. In the background, she heard the hum of the Apple IIGS, Dylan playing *Rosella*. To the accompaniment of ominous music, cyber zombies swarmed a cyber graveyard.

"Daddy said to tell you he went running," Jesse said.

The coffee carafe was filled with Ethan's allegedly superior hand-ground artisan coffee, a Christmas gift from his parents. Honestly, she couldn't detect a major difference from Chock Full O' Nuts, but she poured herself a large mug.

This time she called North Shore Hospital, asking for Jared Lassler's room.

Jared answered the phone, sounding healthy enough.

"I wanted to make sure you were okay," Erica said.

"Yeah, I'm just great," he answered in a sardonic tone new to Erica. "Grandma and Grandpa are here making disappointed faces at me."

"Where are your parents?" Erica asked.

"Downstairs. Signing me out of here. Probably signing me into a psycho hospital."

"I doubt they'd do that," Erica said. She hung on the phone, listening to the interplay between Jared's breathing and her household's ambient noise: the zombies, still making their creepy music; dancing giraffes on the TV; the clash of plastic swords. "Say, Jared," Erica said. "All hell is breaking loose here. I'll come see you at home this afternoon."

"Sure," Jared said. "If you want. If they haven't sent me to a psycho hospital."

Erica told Ethan about Jared when he returned from running.

"Wow," he said, guzzling the remainder of the juice from its container and panting. "That run was more than I bargained for. I gotta quit smoking. I tell myself they're only herbal cigarettes, but it's smoking nonetheless. Is Jared okay?"

"I guess," Erica said. "I told him I'd visit this afternoon. Can you watch the kids?"

"Sure," Ethan said. "As long as you're home by four. I've got a tennis game. God, I could use a nap."

In Ethan's family, the phone did not ring at six in the morning. He really didn't talk to his family very much at all. Birthday presents and newsy Christmas letters arrived from his parents on schedule. Every other year, the Richards family gathered for a reunion at some tasteful and interesting spot like Yosemite or Mendocino. His family boogie-boarded and cross-country skied. Every summer his sister, Pauline, who lived in Santa Rosa, sent them a spice rub made from herbs growing in her organic garden.

———

Debbie was in the process of loading the dishwasher when Erica stopped by. From the backyard Erica heard the whirring of Ron's hedge clipper.

"Want some tea or something?" Debbie asked. "What a day."

Erica caught a whiff of lemon air freshener. "No, thanks," she said. "I promised Jared I'd come see him."

Debbie's face tightened, revealing thin vertical lines Erica had not noticed before, on either side of her bare lips. "He's taking a nap," she said, sweeping crumbs down the sink drain.

"Can't I say hello?" Erica leaned against the spotless refrigerator, dislodging the magnetic parrot clip Debbie used to hold messages.

Debbie frowned. "I guess so," she said. "But don't wake him if he's sleeping."

Jared was perched on his elbows, lying on his bed watching Nickelodeon and eating chips. REM's album *Fables of the Reconstruction*, which she'd wanted to buy but hadn't gotten around to even though it had been out almost a year, played on his stereo. His walls were still papered with the same soccer ball motif Ron had put up ten years before, but Jared had covered the paper over almost totally with posters of rock stars in leather and studded bracelets, plus one incongruous photograph of Darryl Strawberry straddling home plate.

Jared's skin was a mite sallow and still pimpled; short strands of peroxided hair were plastered to his scalp. But basically it was the same baby face, the same full lips and wide eyes he'd had when she'd pushed him for hours in the rubber swings at West Meadow Elementary School.

"Hi, Aunt Rikki," he said.

"That's *Fables of the Reconstruction*, right?" she asked.

"Yeah." His voice betrayed the slightest hint of enthusiasm.

"REM is so much better than most of the junk you hear on the radio," Erica said, sitting down at the edge of his bed. Jared assumed, she was certain, that all adults were alike: that once you hit a certain age, all your spirit disappeared. She wanted to break through the wall of indifference that separated them and prove him wrong. She wasn't anything like his parents. "Most music now is so cold and commercial," she added.

"True," Jared said. Cartoon cats leaped across the television screen. He pointed at her mother's zirconium-studded evening bag, which Erica was still using, having forgotten to transfer her keys and wallet back to her everyday leather one. "Nice bag," he said, in his newly acquired sardonic tone. In the light of day, it looked like some spangly thing a six-year-old girl might wear.

"I met Don Johnson last night," Erica said.

"Really?" Jared seemed genuinely impressed. "That's cool! How did you manage that?"

"Ethan's company financed a movie that Don Johnson is in."

Debbie peeked in the door, holding a vacuum cleaner. "Would you like some fruit juice, Jared, honey?" she asked.

"No, thanks, Mother dear," he said. Debbie hesitated at the door a minute and then pushed the vacuum down the hall.

"My Dad is a DJ, but he wouldn't recognize anybody worth listening to if he bumped into them on the way to the bathroom," Jared said.

Erica nodded in silent assent.

"Did you know that Bloody Tampax is from the Island?" he asked.

"No way," Erica said. She had never heard of Bloody Tampax.

"Yes way," Jared said. "They went to high school in Hicksville."

His fingers were long and pale; suited for the violin, Debbie had decided, when he was in fourth grade. Erica recalled dutifully attending several elementary school recitals. She didn't think he took lessons anymore.

"Say, Jared," Erica said, mindful of the need to finesse the topic at hand. "How did you wind up in the hospital getting your stomach pumped?"

Jared sucked on his bottom lip and scratched his chin. Erica could see the imprint of his raggedy fingernails, faint red scratches, on the dimple directly below his lip. "We were at a party at this guy Matthew's house. We were drinking vodka from a bottle. Then I walked home. Or so I believed."

"Dumb, dumb, dumb," Erica thought. "You could have killed yourself." But unsure how to phrase this sentiment in an acceptable manner and wanting, unlike his parents, to be a good listener, she maintained empathetic eye contact and said nothing.

Fables of the Reconstruction came to an end and Jared changed the record to some intensely jarring music, all screeching guitars and synthesizers and barely comprehensible lyrics reeking with self-conscious angst. He flashed the record cover at her: a metal trashcan overflowing with used feminine hygiene products.

They listened silently for a few minutes.

"I thought Dad was going to kill me," Jared finally said. "They didn't say anything about psycho hospitals to you, did they? The parental unit?" There was a frightened pitch to Jared's voice that Erica typically associated with bogeymen in the closet and monsters underneath the bed.

"No," Erica said. "To tell you the truth, I haven't really spoken to them." She supposed she should. She checked her watch. "Listen, I'm sorry to leave so fast, but I have to get back home to your little cousins. Take care of yourself, okay?"

"Don't worry about me, Aunt Rikki." Jared turned his face back to the television set.

Erica padded down the thickly covered hallway, ridged with vacuum cleaner marks. In the living room, Debbie was pulling knickknacks out of the bookcase and vacuuming behind them.

"Jared seems all right," said Erica. "We had a nice conversation."

"I don't like this teenage thing." Debbie pulled a glass bowl of marbles off a lower shelf, sucking up the faint dust circle under the bowl. "Little kids, little problems. Big kids, big problems. That's what Ron always says. Are you sure I can't interest you in a cup of tea?"

Erica looked toward the bay window. The slatted blinds, down as usual, blocked the light like jail bars. "I promised Ethan I'd get home in time for his tennis game," Erica said, but Debbie was smiling tightly and expectantly at her, already pouring hot water over orange pekoe tea bags and setting out a tray of pastries.

Erica noticed another bruise on her shoulder, a soft blue quarter moon edging out from under her bra strap.

"Debbie, what are those bruises all about?" she asked.

"Bruises?" Debbie blinked, all innocence.

"Yeah, bruises," Erica said. "You know, the purple blotches on your leg and your arm and your shoulder. They're pretty obvious."

"Oh, I was hoping you wouldn't notice them and worry about

me," Debbie said. "You know, with Jared and all. They're nothing really. My internist is doing tests. Apparently I bruise easily. Especially when I'm under stress." She sighed.

"You don't have leukemia or anything, do you?" Erica asked.

"Of course not," Debbie said, wiping her arm wearily against her face. "I never should have let Jared go out with Lyndsey Schrabner. It wasn't really a date. The kids all hang out in groups these days, instead of pairing off like we did, but she's the one who invited him, and not to criticize Lisa or anything, but there's no structure in that household. Those kids eat whatever and whenever they want, and did you know that Lisa and Les gave Lyndsey and Jason their own personal TVs? With cable?"

"Yeah. I caught Dylan and Jason watching the Playboy Channel once."

Lisa Schrabner was Debbie's age. They'd met in sixth grade, at baton-twirling lessons, and back then Erica had leaned against Debbie's closed door, straining to decipher their giggly secrets. But it was Erica who had ended up as Lisa's friend.

Debbie pushed the tray of Entenmann's in Erica's direction. While Debbie never failed to serve fattening treats, she rarely partook herself. "What did you do? Weren't you shocked?"

"No. I thought it was funny. It's not like they understood anything that was going on." Erica ate the white half of a black-and-white cookie and then nibbled at the black parts. Somehow pastry fragments that were merely nibbled at, never forthrightly chewed, contained no calories.

Debbie sighed. "Well, I sure don't understand what's going on with Jared now."

Erica checked her watch—five to four. "I absolutely gotta go," she said, standing up. "I'll see you Tuesday to go shopping for Lauren, okay? Tuesday is your day off, right?"

"Yes. But one more thing," Debbie said, lifting up the placements and sweeping crumbs off the table. "On your way out, can you stop and say hello to Ron? He doesn't think you and Ethan like him very much. He's out the back."

Ron was applying grub control to the newly replanted lawn around Jared's old play gym, the one where he used to swing round and round on the metal bars, the bristles of his hair flashing in the sunlight. Ron's shoulders hunched from years of ducking his six-foot-five frame through doorways. His body was tight and twitchy, like a tensed wire. He was wearing a face mask, aiming a plastic spray tube with his skinny red-knuckled fingers at a square of sod. A white film oozed across the mud, and Erica smelled something metallic and acrid. Everything Ron held looked like a weapon. "Way to go, Ron," Erica thought. Defoliate those weeds. Agent Orange for the home. Destroy your lawn in order to save it.

She didn't feel like calling out to him over the din of the sprayer. The club would cancel Ethan's tennis reservation if she didn't get home pronto, and Ethan would have a cow. Plus, it was true—, she'd always disliked Ron. Ethan was just more public about it. Give Ron credit—he perceived their mutual distaste. He didn't look up as she scurried around the side of their house and down the street.

CHAPTER SIX

Erica slouched on the front stoop with Sophia, waiting for Debbie to pick her up. The Volvo dealer had finally determined that Vince's central computer was to blame for his malfunctions, but the replacement was still en route, apparently on a slow boat from Sweden. Everyone's lawns were slimy from the winter, and only the most tentative of green buds mounded up from the tree branches. A garbage truck huffed by, leaving a stink and a scatter of Styrofoam plates.

Debbie pulled into the driveway in her new gray Oldsmobile sedan and honked. The vehicle reminded Erica of a hippopotamus. "And that was Englebert Humperdinck," announced a familiar voice as Erica hooked in Sophia's car seat. Ron's tone was melodious and resonant, intimating a totally different personality over the air than in person.

Debbie wore an aqua pantsuit with padded shoulders and matching pumps. Her nails were perfectly rounded, a pale pink. "We're going to Macy's," she said, merging onto the Meadowbrook. "It's got a broad selection, and it's close by. I need to squeeze so much into my day off, and I have to take Jared to the gastroenterologist at two."

"How's Jared doing?" Erica asked.

"Don't ask," Debbie sighed.

———

At Macy's Erica suggested an underwater watch, complete with timer, in crystal blue. Debbie shook her head. "It's a scuba diving watch," she said. "Lauren doesn't dive, as far as I know."

"I thought she did," Erica said. "Plus there's a barracuda

engraved on it. Isn't the theme of her bat mitzvah the underwater kingdom?"

Debbie decided a watch wasn't a smart idea, period, so they drifted over to jewelry, where they surveyed practically their entire inventory of necklaces and bracelets, asking the saleslady to remove them one by one from the locked glass case. Debbie dangled each one from her pearly fingers, held them up to the light, wrinkled her nose, and dismissed them. They were all too expensive, too cheap, too showy, too dull, just not right somehow. Finally, Debbie cradled a bright-blue semiprecious stone dolphin on a gold chain in her palm and granted her grudging approval.

Then she suggested lunch. If there was anything Debbie loved it was a frilly ladies' lunch in a department store. They settled into wicker chairs and looked at each other over the lace tablecloth.

"What do you want to eat?" Erica asked.

"Oh, I don't know," Debbie said. "I'm not very hungry."

"You were the one who suggested lunch," Erica reminded her. She couldn't relate. She was always hungry. The waitress appeared, pouring them lemon-scented water. They both chose the special: chicken walnut salad and cream of broccoli soup.

By the time the soup arrived, Sophia was whimpering and nuzzling at Erica's blouse. She unbuttoned it partway, and Sophia snuggled into her contentedly as Erica alternated soothing spoonfuls of soup with gulps of black coffee.

"How are the boys?" asked Debbie, averting her eyes from Erica's chest.

"Oh, crazy as usual," Erica said. "Dylan is entering a Lego robotics contest. He scored in the ninety-ninth percentile on his math aptitude tests."

"How nice," Debbie replied absently, blowing her nose in her napkin. "Sophia looks like Mom, don't you think? Those wide-set blue eyes."

"Yeah, I guess so," Erica said. "Now that you mention it."

The waitress removed the soup bowls, replacing them with plates of chicken salad attractively arrayed on watercress.

"I can't believe you went for another baby, after the twins." Debbie blew her nose again.

"I wanted a girl," Erica said, switching breasts.

"Yes, well you're lucky. When all you have is one. . ." Debbie listlessly lifted a forkful of chicken to her lips, letting it dangle there for a moment, and a greasy walnut fell onto her leg. She dipped her snotty napkin into her lemon water, dabbling furiously at her pantsuit.

"One what?" Erica asked.

"One boy. One precious only boy. I tried to have more, you know, but then I had that ectopic pregnancy and nearly died, and the doctor said no way could we have another child." Debbie's face collapsed, tears streaking down her cheeks, bunching up her face powder into little mounds like mauve sand. Her eye shadow clotted into little polka dot pimples beneath her painstakingly plucked brows.

Erica proffered a baby wipe from her bag.

Debbie placed the wipe over her shut lids like a compress. "I'm sorry to make such a scene, Rikki," she said. "I can't eat. I haven't slept. You have no idea of the stress I'm under with Jared."

"Did he get drunk again?" Erica grabbed a burp cloth out of her diaper bag and slung it over her shoulder.

"He wouldn't have the chance!" Compact case in hand, Debbie redid her makeup. "He's grounded! It's not just the drinking—it's everything! He's getting Cs and Ds, and he used to be on the honor roll. He quit violin, and he showed such promise. He quit the tennis team, and you know how important sports are to Ron. We got a progress report from school, and he's been cutting French class. French is his last class of the day, at 2:10, and he never gets home until at least 4:30, so tell me, what's he been doing all that time?" Debbie gasped and sniffled, and her newly applied makeup started running again. "I think he's"—she hesitated, nearly swallowing her next words—"using drugs. He's going to drop out of school at this rate. He'll never go to college. He'll wind up on the streets!"

Sophia burped loudly, spitting up a few curds of milk. "Don't you think you're overreacting?" Erica asked. "I mean, like the tennis team. Jared never liked sports, as far as I can recall."

Debbie sighed. "Don't you remember? He made the semifinals last year at the club! Now look what's happened. You have no idea how serious this is, Rikki."

The waitress reappeared, presenting the check and removing Erica's empty plate. Erica put down her credit card. "Let me treat you to lunch," she said.

Debbie sipped listlessly at her cup of Earl Grey tea. "Thank you. I haven't said anything, but this has been going on, you know, for a while. We've been to so many doctors. His allergist said he might be allergic to wheat, and that could be causing his stomachaches and maybe the fatigue and his lack of concentration in school. That's why I'm taking him to the gastroenterologist today, for more tests. And his ear, nose, and throat specialist said that maybe his middle ear membrane was damaged from all those ear infections he had when he was little, and he hears words differently than most people do. I mean, he hears them as loud as normal but at a different pitch so he can't interpret them correctly. It's called dystympania."

"There's no such thing as a middle ear membrane," said Erica, signing the check. "And wheat allergies aren't nearly as common as they're made out to be."

"Oh, Rikki, stop pretending you're a medical expert just because you went to nursing school ten years ago. These are some of the best doctors on the Island. And that's not the worst of it."

"Tell me the worst of it," Erica said.

Debbie sucked in several deep heavy breaths. "At the Nassau Family Clinic, Dr. Rafferty diagnosed Jared with DDD."

Erica stared at Debbie in perplexed astonishment. "What on earth is DDD?"

"Defiant disobedient disorder."

"It sounds like something Ron might spray on the lawn."

"Rikki! Why must you make light of everything! It's a real physical syndrome! Mental illnesses aren't always in the head, like people used to think!"

"How do you treat DDD?" Erica signed the credit card slip and fastened Sophia back into her stroller.

"Well, he needs more tests," Debbie said. "He needs therapy—we've already started that. And medication."

They descended five floors in the elevator and exited at the parking lot. Debbie fumbled in her purse. "Where's my car, do you remember, Rikki? Why can I never find my car when I'm running late?"

"Over there, by Bloomingdale's."

Debbie pulled out of the parking lot and onto the busy parkway. Ron's closing selection, a Tom Jones ballad, droned through its final chorus.

"I still don't get it," Erica said. "Aren't all teenagers defiant and disobedient?"

"Maybe you. I wasn't. Ron wasn't," Debbie said.

"Oh, please. What about Randy Wasserman and those open cans of beer in his car?"

"He was the only one drinking it. Beer always made me sick."

"And what about Ron? Didn't he beat up some kid on his college basketball team? Isn't that why he lost his scholarship and got drafted?"

"You weren't supposed to know about that, "Debbie said, exiting onto Glenvere Road.

"You told me once. When Jared was in the hospital with pneumonia."

"It was different with Ron."

"How?"

"It just was. His buddy started that fight, and you know how frat boys can be. Listen, Rikki, I want to ask you a favor. I was wondering if maybe you could talk to Jared, spend a little time with him. I thought you might have more insight into his mindset, given the kind of teen you were."

"The kind of teen I was? That sounds more like an insult than a compliment."

"Well, you know. Everything." Debbie slid to a stop at the four-way intersection by the entrance into West Meadow Knolls.

"The way you were always stealing Mom and Dad's liquor, for instance. I saw you sneak a bottle of Connemara whiskey—the one the Lipmans gave him at his fiftieth birthday party—and it upset me so much I told Mom."

"You snitched to Mom? You weren't even living at home anymore."

"I felt she should know. It was Dad's! And it was expensive!" Debbie inched forward as the Audi opposite her did the very same thing.

"I can't believe you snitched to Mom. They grounded me for a month for that."

"Get over it. This was fifteen years ago. You put Mom and Dad through their paces, believe me."

"Do you always have to be such a goddamn sanctimonious saint?"

"Rikki! Stop harassing me!" Debbie accelerated, turning toward the stone gates of West Meadow Knolls. Brakes squealed. A horn barked shrilly.

Erica jerked her head around. The Audi's grille hovered directly out the rear passenger side window, inches away from Sophia's car seat.

"Debbie!" Erica screamed.

"God, Rikki, you totally distracted me!" Debbie slammed on the brakes. The Audi driver gave them the finger. Erica looked back at Sophia, her sleeping breathing unaltered, her pulse beating regularly under her thin new skin.

A chilled sensation rose up in Erica—an icy draft from a rip in the earth.

"What was that all about?" she squealed. "You almost killed us."

"Let's just forget about it, okay?" There was a finality to Debbie's tone, a warning to go no further. Erica steadied herself by turning to look at the bland face of the Bergmans' high ranch. Steve Bergman, accompanied by his Jamaican nanny, pedaled down the sidewalk on his tricycle.

Debbie pushed up her sleeve to check the time on her watch,

and another bruise revealed itself, deep purple and unmistakable. "I have to stop at the high school first," she said. "I'm late."

They arrived at the school. Jared stood glumly at the end of the parking lot.

"You can have my seat," Erica said, opening the front door.

"I can drive you and the baby home," Debbie said. "I still have time."

"No, thanks," Erica said. "I could use the walk."

CHAPTER SEVEN

One wedding, one fiftieth birthday party, and two bar mitzvahs were taking place simultaneously in the catering hall, but there was no mistaking Lauren's party. That would be the room illuminated with blue lightbulbs, framed by banners announcing, "Under the Sea." Erica and Ethan stopped at a large table with a model of a harbor, constructed from paperboard and tongue depressors. Ethan plucked a sailboat with their name on it from the Styrofoam sea. Table six.

"Are we sitting with Ron and Debbie?" Erica asked.

"How would I know?" Ethan asked. "Should I care?" Ron and Debbie's sailboat still sat untouched in the harbor. They were sitting elsewhere, at table seven, which was just as well. Debbie had called Erica Wednesday evening, informing her that she'd had second thoughts on the way home from Jared's gastroenterologist appointment and exchanged the dolphin pendant for a jade bracelet. Debbie, the queen of returns. Erica did not have the time to return things. Once she bought something, she owned it. Nor, precisely because of Debbie's insulting manner of asking, had she found the time to call Jared to chat and relate. He'd most likely classify her as a clueless adult and not give her the time of day anyway. Though, now that she thought about it, maybe she should do so of her own volition, not as a favor to Debbie. Perhaps it was just a function of exhaustion, or medication, but by the time they'd finished talking that afternoon he got out of the hospital, it seemed liked Jared had actually opened up a bit.

The room filled up. Scaly turquoise helium balloons with silvery eyes floated by. The DJ started playing outdated disco hits and handing out shark-head masks; all three boys ran off to dance.

Dave Luskin, Dylan's orthodontist, snagged Ethan for investment advice, leaving Erica alone in her red spaghetti-strap dress. She'd bought it herself, at a new boutique across from aerobics. If she needed to wear a size 12, it wasn't going to be another dress selected by her mother. She gulped down two glasses of mediocre chardonnay, then grabbed a third and meandered through an obstacle course of conversations. Her mother commented on the scarlet hue of her dress, although, thankfully, not the skintight fit. Sherry Luskin requested the name of her kitchen contractor. Some woman she recognized from aerobics inquired after Dylan's summer camp plans.

The DJ transitioned into a Cars song—at least he acknowledged the advent of the '80s—and Erica watched the crowd of kids jumping up and down in their shark masks, waving fins above their heads. She felt disconcertingly light, as if she could float up and join the helium fish. She let the murmurs of the crowd flow through her like the ancient Hebrew prayers did at services and searched for safe anchor. She considered sitting down at table six, but no one was sitting at any of the tables yet, save some ancient relatives and her uncle Barry, who suffered from a rare muscle-wasting disease. She pressed herself against the wall, underneath a blowup of Lauren vacationing in Bonaire, sporting scuba gear. So she was right; Lauren did dive after all.

Looking toward her escape hatch, a swinging door at the end of the long blue hall, she watched Debbie, Ron, and Jared enter. Jared was wearing a clearly homemade pair of pants, black in the front, white in the back, held together by safety pins, topped by a sloppy black T-shirt. He'd spiked his green hair around the crown of his head. Ron was wearing a blue-gray polyester suit. Sinuous in his diamond twill, he reminded Erica of a rattlesnake. He stalked along the edges of the room, heading directly for the bar. Both he and Jared looked sullen as hell.

Debbie, on the other hand, shimmered like one of the decorative fish. Curvy and resplendent in a clingy full-length silver garment, topped off by long silver gloves, she dove into the crowd as if off a high board. She swam straight for Erica, grabbed her by the arm, slipped a shark mask over her head, and dragged her to the dance platform. "Let's let bygones be bygones, Rikki. Let's dance! Let's have some fun!"

"You look pretty," Erica said. Through the stiff plastic eyes of her mask, she watched Jared stride back out the swinging doors, out of sight.

"I bought a new dress." Debbie giggled, gyrating with abandon. "Isn't this cool?" she squealed, shaking her hips. "Isn't this fabulous?" She was a good dancer, smoother and more rhythmic than Erica, who nodded in agreement and flung herself about. Someone shoved glow sticks in their hands. The group formed a conga line. Debbie swayed along, her arms on Erica's shoulders.

"I've decided to have some fun in my life," Debbie announced. "I mean, why not?"

"Why not?" Erica agreed, trying to lose herself in the moment, all silvery and blue and laughing and empty. The last time she'd seen Debbie this manic was shortly after her ectopic pregnancy when Jared, two years old, developed a nasty cold that turned into pneumonia. He ended up in the North Shore ICU. Mom and Dad were attending a wedding in Chicago, Ron was out of town at some music industry conference, and Erica was a week away from leaving for Boston University. "He's on a breathing tube, Rikki," Debbie told Erica when she called from the hospital, in a high-pitched airy voice. "His lungs are full of water." And then in a higher pitched voice: "They don't know if he's going to live." When Erica talked her way into the ICU, she found Debbie grinning, which struck her as odd. She'd paced around their little cubicle, circling Jared's crib, babbling about anything and everything. How she'd wanted to go to beauty school ever since she put French braids in her Tressy doll; how she wanted to open her own salon someday; how Ron beat up that kid on his basketball team, breaking his collarbone (by mistake, of course); how she wore a thong bathing suit on their honeymoon in Barbados.

Antibiotics and luck worked magic. Jared came off the respirator, and Ron rushed back from his conference. Jared returned home with asthma meds and a special humidifier. Erica left for college, and by the time she returned for Thanksgiving, Debbie was back to her zipped-up, holier-than-thou self.

"Let's get something to eat," Debbie said. "I've decided to eat whatever I want at parties like this. You only live once, right?"

The appetizer stations resembled a mall food court: a pasta bar, a cold seafood bar, burgers and fries, Italian antipasto, a lineup of uniformed waiters serving Chinese food out of warming trays. Erica removed her shark mask. Underneath, her skin was sweaty and her lipstick smeared. By the Italian station, Jesse and Jake slurped pasta under the solicitous arms of two thirteen-year-old girls. Nearby, Ethan peeled the skin off a giant prawn while presumably giving Erica's uncle Nathan an update on the stock market. Back on the dance floor, Dylan sank to the ground and twirled around on his butt.

Debbie plowed into her orange beef while they were still in line for the seafood. Erica piled her plate with boiled shrimp, balancing her empty wine glass on the edge of her plate.

"Let's get a cocktail," Debbie suggested. Sipping Cosmopolitans, they passed Uncle Barry, who was sitting alone with his cane, picking at ravioli with a toothpick. Debbie leaned close to Erica. "I feel so bad for Uncle Barry," she whispered. "Did you know that on top of everything his wife left him? For another woman! Can you believe that? She's a lesbian!"

Ron stood by the burger station, engaged in a back-slapping exchange with Dave Luskin. As she passed him, he slapped her on the back as well, spilling her drink into her shrimp. "Whoa, baby!" he said. "That's quite the dress!"

"Oh, get lost," Erica muttered.

"Leave Ron alone," Debbie said nervously, steering her away until they were out of sight, on the other side of the dance platform. "We had a fight," Debbie whispered. "Ron's real mad about Jared's outfit," she whispered. "And that awful hair! Ron wasn't going to let him out of the house looking like that, but we can't leave him alone these days." Debbie lowered her voice even further, so low that Erica could barely make out her words over the disco music. "So I pleaded with Ron to please let us go, even with Jared dressed like that. I told him I absolutely needed this party for my mental and physical health."

"Well, I'm glad you came," Erica said. "Where is Jared any-way?" she asked, scanning the room for green spikes.

"Oh, I don't know," Debbie said, breaking into an odd little leap. Her heels skidded against the floor. "And I don't care! Don't you get sick of men, sometimes? Maybe Barry's wife had the right idea. Don't you wish we could get away for a week or so? Just us girls. Go to a spa or something. Something wild!"

"I guess so," Erica said without conviction. Debbie's hot dry palm rubbed against Erica's; her diamond band dug into Erica's finger. A bell clanged, calling them to dinner. The lights darkened. Lauren's baby picture flashed on a giant movie screen, and Caesar salads appeared in front of Erica and Ethan. Table six proved to be a cousin's table: first, second, and third cousins from Westchester and Jersey. A fishbowl sat in the middle of the table, with a single hardy goldfish swimming round and round. Erica downed her glass of cheap sweet champagne and started in on Ethan's.

"So, I've figured out this program," Ethan was saying to her cousin Mike from South Orange, "similar to the programs that I've developed to predict movements in the bond market that predicts standing in the NBA for the upcoming year. I tested it this past winter, and it proved 95 percent accurate."

Mike's wife (Kerri? Gerri?) turned to Erica, smiling brightly. She was approximately Erica's age. Erica remembered their mutual mothers forcing them to go together to USY dances in high school. Kerri/Gerri had been voluptuous and vivacious then, dancing with stringy bespectacled boys whose garlic breath made Erica want to gag. But marriage and childbearing had transformed her into a stout, short-waisted woman, middle-aged before her time, with a heavy bosom hanging close to her waist. She was wearing a purple suit of an unnatural-looking matte material and a white blouse with an oversize bow.

Erica's nipples tingled, leaking milk onto the silk of her red dress. She missed the pull of Sophia's urgent little *O* of a mouth closing down upon her, the damp pressure of her small body against her chest.

"You've got spots on your dress, Erica," Kerri/Gerri said.

"Milk," Erica dabbed ineffectively at the two dark circles.

"Oh, dear," said Kerri/Gerri. "What did you order for your main course?"

"The salmon, I think. It's lower calorie."

"You know, you should always order the prime rib at affairs," Kerri/Gerri said. "Never the chicken—it's inevitably rubbery. And absolutely not the fish. The salmon could be crawling with salmonella!" She tugged her white bow for emphasis.

On the movie screen, Lauren's thirteen-year-old life flashed before Erica's eyes: Halloween costumes, birthday parties, swim meets, Caribbean vacations. Across the way, at table seven, a screech of metal chair against the linoleum announced Jared's return from wherever he had been. He forked large bites of salad into his mouth.

The video entertainment ended, the salad plates were cleared, and the lights came back on, far too glittery and bright. The airy, dizzy, almost nauseous sensation Erica had felt before returned, intensified. Ethan was still chatting with Mike about stocks and basketball while tearing pieces off his roll and spreading them with butter. Kerri/Gerri, having exhausted her line of conversation with Erica, was chatting with her second cousin Pamela about the cost of orthodontia. Dylan, Jesse, and Jake were bending themselves under a limbo rod on the dance floor. At table seven, Ron appeared to be telling a story from his endless cache of jokes. He cackled, waving his long arms toward the goldfish bowl. Debbie reapplied her lipstick. Ron cackled again, this time pointing at Jared, who slid his chair back and once again walked out the swinging doors.

"I'm going to the women's room," Erica announced to no one in particular.

She followed Jared's retreating green spikes around a corner and then down a flight of steps into the basement. Right past an open utility closet jammed with mops and green buckets, he pushed open a door labeled "Men's Lounge."

Erica followed. The door clanged shut, and Jared looked up in surprise. The room stank of Lysol but still looked dingy, with trough-like urinals and a roll of toilet paper snaking out the stall door. Jared sat on a torn vinyl couch tamping dope into a pipe.

"What are you doing here?" Erica asked.

"Shouldn't I be the one asking you that?" Jared said. "This is the men's room."

"Your mother wanted me to talk to you."

Jared chuckled grimly. "That sounds like a thrill and a half." He lit the pipe.

"Can I have some?" Erica asked.

He looked at her, incredulous. "But what about the baby?"

"She's home with a sitter," Erica said, as if that answered the question. She held out her hand.

He handed her the pipe. A silly flood of excitement rustled through her body, like she was fourteen years old again, sitting on the mossy stones of Mackay Estates in the gathering fall darkness with her friend Allison and her cute big brother home from college. She hesitated for a second, afraid she would do something embarrassing like she'd done back then: cough her lungs out. It had been a long time. But no, the smoke in her throat felt good. Grounding.

"So, what's going on?" she asked.

Jared handed her the pipe again. "You know Mom. She's convinced herself I'm sick. She hauls me to one doctor after another. As well as the psycho doctor at the family clinic. And the drug and alcohol counselor at school."

Erica took another drag on the pipe. She felt steadier than in high school or college, as if her neuronal pathways had cleared up along with her skin. "Do you actually get stomachaches?" she asked.

"Not really," Jared said. "And this is rich. We're starting family therapy next week, on Fridays. You should have seen Dad when Mom informed him about the family therapy. He exploded! He never had any of that touchy-feely stuff when he was growing up. When Grandpa Joey spoke, it was the law. Blah, blah, blah."

They kept passing the pipe back and forth. She felt exposed, sitting there in a public restroom for the opposite sex, using illegal substances on a grungy couch. Jared's voice seemed to be coming from far away.

"Did you know my Dad's jokes always have a priest, a minister, and a rabbi in them?" he said. "Or else an Italian, an Irishman, and a Scotsman? And Mom laughs every time, even when she's gotta know they're not funny."

"What was the joke he was telling just before you walked out?"

Jared looked down at his pants, running his hands along the line of safety pins. "He called these things diaper pins." The mucoid-colored tiles lining the bathroom walls shimmered to the distant thrum of the disco beat. "I've never seen a diaper pin," said Jared. "Have you?"

"I used them on my Tinkly Winkly doll," said Erica.

"What'd you say? Your Tinkly Winkly doll?"

"I got her for my seventh birthday," Erica said. "I was jealous of your Mom's Tressy doll, so Grandma and Grandpa gave me Tinkly Winkly. She peed out of a little hole. I changed her diaper a hundred times a day. Practice for my current life."

"Tressy! Tinkly Winkly!" Jared clutched his belly and bent over, laughing hysterically. He proffered Erica the pipe again.

She reached for it but could not assess its location in space. She shook her head no, inhaling deeply of the overheated, pseudo-antiseptic air instead, aware of its slow drift down her bronchi and into her lungs. "I'd better get back," she said.

Jared regarded her with his luminous, thick-lashed eyes. She grasped one of the green spikes fringing his head and wiggled it. It felt like a papier-mâché horn.

"How do you get the spikes to stay this way?" she asked.

"Elmer's glue," said Jared.

"You look like the Statue of Liberty," Erica said, giggling.

"That's what this is," he replied, deadpan. "A Statue of Liberty hairdo."

"Are you sure you don't want to dance to 'YMCA' with me?" Erica asked. "I have no idea how a song about casual gay sex came to be so popular at bar mitzvahs."

"You've got to be kidding." Jared grimaced. "I think I'll remain in these elegant environs for a while."

<hr />

Erica steadied herself under the crystal chandelier in the marble lobby and then dove back into the sea. The entire blue room teemed with schools of fish: whales, sharks, brightly colored tropical species warbling their bubbly oceanic songs, ancient fish with bald tops and gray tops and even flaming red tops, parentfish and cousinfish and neighborfish. There were tons of teenfish, the females preternaturally mature in their low-cut black dresses and mascara, the males shorter by a foot, hanging back in their ill-fitting suits. Kiddiefish, in miniature tuxes and elaborate pink taffeta dresses with matching hair ribbons darted through the under layer. On the dance platform, Debbie, the silverfish, performed an approximation of her high school cheerleading routine, jumping up and clapping her hands over her head, then crouching and kicking her heels out in a pushup. Ron, the slithery eel, stood flattened against the wall, ready to pounce and gobble his prey whole.

Erica swam over to Debbie and did ten jumping jacks.

"Rah, rah, go, Wolverines!" Debbie cried, grabbing Erica's hands and swinging her around, just as the DJ went silent, and the room darkened again.

Up by where the movie screen had been, Lauren and her parents stood in front of a large candelabra. Lauren read shyly from a folded yellow sheet:

> *They always like to joke and play.*
> *I love them more than I can say.*
> *Grandpa Stan and Grandma Jill, come*
>   *and light my first candle.*

Erica rejoined Ethan at the table as Grandpa Stan and Grandma Jill, wearing a lime-green pantsuit with tufts at the shoulders that resembled giant kelp, walked smilingly over to their granddaughter Lauren and lit their candle and then posed for both the photographer and videographer. Erica clenched her jaw muscles to suppress her rising laughter. Lauren continued to the second verse.

> *Whether we swim or whether we ski,*
> *at their Vermont house I like to be.*
> *Grandpa Dan and Grandma Hetty, come*
>   *and light my second candle."*

Grandma Hetty stood close to six feet and two hundred

pounds, wearing a shocking-pink sheath dress. The laugh rose higher and settled in Erica's mouth.

"Why do they make so much fuss about a thirteen-year-old's birthday party?" Ethan whispered before turning his polite face back to the crowd. Verses droned on, as Erica gripped Ethan's hand tightly, averting her eyes from any more giggle-inducing fashion mistakes by watching the fish float by overhead. Lauren's voice shook her out of her reverie.

Their house is fun and full of toys
with a baby girl and three boys
Ethan and Erica, come and light my tenth candle.

Still gripping Ethan's hand, Erica rose unsteadily to her feet, and they walked toward the candle table. Her cousin Amelia, Lauren's mother, handed her a lighted match. The world was drenched in royal blue, luminescent and ludicrous. Fish swam gently through the air, their glassy eyes fixed on her. At table seven sat Ronfish, the slimy diamondback eel with the greasy-blond-hair fin. Next to him sat the small, round brown-fringed, silver-bodied Debbiefish, her impassive marine eyes betraying nothing. Erica gaped dumbly in the blueness, the beady eyes of the fish upon her, murmurs rippling through the ocean, an impatient white flash of the videographic sun. Ethan guided her hand, as if through mud, toward the candle. The wavering flame infused the room with a certain beauty.

Back at her seat, a plate of salmon, rice, and undercooked zucchini awaited her. She chewed a bite of salmon slowly and carefully. Lukewarm and drowning in an unctuous white sauce, it tasted distinctly off. She imagined bacteria crawling up and down the flakes of fish, a salmonella superhighway. Lauren continued reading:

They've always been my special friends,
with lots of books and games to lend
Ron and Debbie, come up and light my eleventh candle.

Debbie, poised and smooth, lit candle eleven as Ron stood stiffly at her side.

"I met my best friend in second grade—" continued Lauren.

From table seven a voice drowned out Lauren's monotone: a growl, arising from the Ronfish.

"Don't give me that look, young man!"

Jared rotated his green scales in the direction of his father.

"Are you making fun of me?" Ron roared. "Wipe that ridiculous grin off your face!"

Debbie, the pretty silverfish, hung motionless, riveted to her chair.

There was silence as Lauren stopped midpoem. Then a splat, as Jared took the roasted potatoes a waiter had just placed in front of him and tossed them at Ron's chest. Then a louder sploosh as Ron heaved his entire plate—rare prime rib, potatoes, spinach—into Jared's face. Then Debbie's muffled whimper, and Jared rushing to her lap like a little child, and blood, either from the prime rib or Jared's nose, dripping onto her silver dress.

"What in God's name?" said Ethan, clearly wishing he could teleport himself from the scene.

Erica knew she needed to do something, but her body refused to react. A bumpy, clumpy sturgeon of a fish, she stood plastered to the sea floor.

Lauren, newly thirteen and clueless, returned to the verse she'd already started:

I met my best friend in second grade,
when with My Little Pony we played.
Steffie, come up and light my twelfth candle.

CHAPTER EIGHT

Back home, Erica dumped the boys' party favors—goldfish swimming gamely in plastic bags—into a glass salad bowl. Ethan stripped down to his underwear and settled next to her on the couch.

"Want to watch that movie about Amazon women from Venus?" he asked. "It's on again."

"Debbie isn't answering her phone," Erica said. "What do you think is going on?"

"Haven't you had enough family melodrama for one night?" said Ethan, flipping on the movie.

"All Jared did was give Ron a funny look!"

"Yeah, Ron. My delightful brother-in-law. The one who's always asking me to program pornography into his computer. The one who tosses his dinner around."

On television, gargantuan blond women sunned themselves in a tropical Venusian valley.

"Jared is innocent," Erica said.

"I feel sorry for the kid. But, you know, we have four of our own—isn't that enough to worry about? My sister lost her job and my brother drinks too much; you don't notice me dropping everything and hopping on a plane, do you?"

"Our family is different." Erica ate barbequed potato chips out of the bag.

"Jared's going to be all right," Ethan said, grabbing a handful of chips. "His hair color will return to normal. He'll reconcile with his good old dad. Maybe he'll even join the Marines."

"I doubt it," Erica said.

Ethan sighed. "You know, just for once on a Saturday night it might be nice not to go to a bar mitzvah or a wedding or a graduation. We could go to a movie. A restaurant. We could get a good night's sleep."

Erica turned her attention to the movie. A flying reptile attacked. The Amazon women wore seashell bras. She laughed so hard she rolled over and fell into Ethan's leg.

———

Monday, Erica poured the last of the coffee into the oversize mug Dylan made for last Mother's Day. Vince Volvo was finally home and humming, one hassle off her back. Lisa called to remind her to fill out registration forms for Camp Whispering Wind, where Dylan and Jason had spent their summers the past three years. But overwhelmed by their number and complexity—page after page of health, legal, and athletic preferences—Erica dialed Debbie's number at the salon instead. She couldn't let go of the image of the blood dripping down Jared's face, and most of all she couldn't let go of the image of Debbie passively watching events unfold, pretty and stunned and frozen.

The moment Debbie answered the phone, in work mode, all brisk and assertive, Erica regretted her impulse. Why was Debbie assertive only at times when it didn't matter? She could have tossed some undercooked broccoli. She could have dumped a glass of cheap Chianti on Ron's greasy head.

"What's wrong, Rikki? I'm rolling crème developer in a client's hair. She'll turn platinum blond if I don't get off the phone quick."

"I wanted to let you know that I talked to Jared, like you asked me to. At Lauren's bat mitzvah. But the next thing I know your husband is throwing a plate of meat in his face, so I was wondering how he was doing."

Debbie sighed. "You interrupted me at work for that? Everything is under control, Rikki. It's all right."

"No, it's not all right! You don't throw food in your child's face!" Erica crumpled a corner of the *Sunday Times* in her fist, a paper she had not yet even glanced at, even though it was Monday afternoon already.

Debbie sighed again, weak and reedy now. "I can't have private conversations like this at work, Rikki, or I'll lose my job. Jared presses Ron's buttons, that's all. He's got serious problems, and we're dealing with them. I really have to go, Rikki. I've got the most awful headache today."

Well, all righty then. A headache she claimed, an ailment no doubt as dubious as Jared's stomachaches. The blood dripping from Jared's chin, and Debbie's bruises, for that matter, were physical facts, but evidently it wasn't nice to call attention to them.

Erica uncrinkled the *Times*. Maybe, as Ethan always implied, the incessant Lassler family drama resembled those tropical storms weather forecasters so eagerly reported, the ones that never coalesced into the disastrous hurricane they kept predicting. Might as well shift gears and see what was happening in the wider world. Under a boldface headline, an article about Grant Fishel stared her in the face:

"Grant Fishel's quantitative analysis department is changing the stodgy face of investment banking, plunging into areas that prior generations dared not touch."

And then her husband's name: "'We aren't reactors—we're actors,'" stated star analyst Ethan Richards."

And more: "Buoyed by success, analysts, brokers, and traders are pulling down seven-figure salaries. Trader Stephan Langston is reputed to have earned a record three million last year."

Stephan Langston's name sounded vaguely familiar.

Ethan rarely spoke about his work, and when he did, he totally confused her. What he did for a living sounded significant yet tedious, with the tiniest hint of thrill and defiance, if thrill and defiance could coexist with investment banking. Whatever he actually did, it generated money like nothing she'd ever experienced. No matter how much money she managed to spend, their bank balance inevitably floated upward like a constantly rising lake.

She presumed their economic status was another thing Debbie must resent. Debbie never mentioned anything specifically, but Ron never missed an opportunity. "Well, if I worked on Wall Street, I might have ceramic tile on my floors instead of linoleum.

If I worked on Wall Street, I might vacation in Carmel instead of on the Jersey Shore. If I worked on Wall Street, I might buy those snazzy running shoes."

Mom always rambled on about how Ron barely made ends meet at WBEZ, as if the circumstances of Debbie's life rained down on her from above, with no agency on her part. No one had commanded Debbie to marry the creep. Just like no one made her date that idiot Randy Wasserman, the one with the open bottles of beer in the car, who rolled his car into a ditch after homecoming, tearing Debbie's left meniscus. Her parents never so much as lectured Debbie after the accident but actually bought her a Volkswagen Beetle, so she wouldn't have to walk to school.

On the other hand, despite the genetic misfortune of being Ron's son, Jared struck her as someone she could spend time with, not merely out of obligation but out of genuine affinity. She couldn't push him out of her mind. What was he doing now? Taking a history test? Waiting to see the gastroenterologist? Getting high in the boys' room?

The doorbell rang, and as if she'd summoned him up from her imagination, Jared stood in front of her. He looked a little sheepish and a lot less outrageous than at Lauren's bat mitzvah, wearing a loose pair of olive khakis and a Clash T-shirt, greenish hair flattened down messily against his scalp. A petite skinny girl with long blond hair, tight jeans, and a fuzzy sweater stood next to him, her thin arm wrapped around his waist. She had a vague, lost look in her eyes and a strange but oddly attractive air of premature dissipation. She looked to Erica like a cheerleader gone wrong.

"I was telling Ashley how cool you are, and she said she wanted to meet you," Jared said. "She babysits. I thought you might need a babysitter."

"Nice to meet you, Mrs. Richards," Ashley said, sauntering over to Sophia's playpen. Sophia, sporting a new pair of yellow overalls with an embroidered parrot on the chest, was poking the squeaky cow on her baby activity box.

"Oh, Mrs. Richards, I just love your little girl's overalls!" Ashley reached down and tickled Sophia's chin. "This one family

I babysit for, they have a little girl with the same overalls, only they're red. I love dressing her. She's like a little baby doll. I can't wait until I have my own babies."

"Thank you," Erica said. "But you don't need to call me Mrs. Richards."

"My father taught me to call adults by their last name. He was real strict about that." Ashley moved a plastic pig along its grating Busy Box track.

"I appreciate the sentiment," Erica said, "but 'Mrs. Richards' sounds pretty dorky. Almost as dorky as Rikki Richards."

"My name's Ashley Ann. Talk about dorky." Ashley wandered through the family room, playing with Dylan's, Jesse's, and Jake's scattered toys. She pushed their Brio train over the bridge, past the woods, and down to the station while Jared slouched around, his hands in his pockets.

"Aren't you supposed to be in school?" Erica asked.

"Yeah, lunch is over in fifteen minutes." Jared nodded.

"Why don't I walk you back?" Erica said, getting Sophia's stroller.

"What happened after the bat mitzvah?" she asked, relinquishing the stroller to Ashley at her request. Ashley carefully tilted the wheels and, looking both ways, crossed the street.

"Nothing really." Jared shrugged. "Mom said she had a headache and shuffled off to the bedroom; then Dad followed her in there, and I took a shower and watched TV and tried to forget the whole thing. And then the next day, Mom's all over me asking if I feel okay. She even took my temperature."

"And your Dad?"

"Oh, he lumbered around stripping wallpaper or something. Not speaking to anyone. Then he asks me if I want to go with him to the hardware store, like some father-son bonding thing the therapist probably suggested, and I said no, why would I want to go to the stupid hardware store, so he stalked off, and I just went into my room, saying I had to do my homework and just listened to music and stuff until the evening when I snuck out my window and went to the park. You know, I can climb out my window, perch on that box where Mom grows those purple flowers, and jump down into the bushes? Mom wonders why the birds are always trashing her flowers." Jared chuckled.

They walked past the elementary school parking lot and then cut along the paved path that adjoined the playground, continued past the middle school and all the way to the north end of a grassy plain that used to be a potato field and before that, presumably, a meadow. That was one of the selling points of West Meadow Knolls: children of all ages could walk to school. The linear progression of the schools promised orderly growth, predictable, visible steps toward maturity.

The high school was a sprawling U-shaped brick building, constructed in the '50s. To the left lay the football field; to the right lay a parking lot and a thin strand of trees that bordered Mackay Estates. All around them, teenagers spilled out onto the grass and squealed out of the parking lot. They sat on top of cars, stood in small groups in the muddy field, climbed onto the football bleachers.

"We have open campus since last year. Dad hates it," Jared said.

Ashley stopped the stroller, eyeing a bunch of kids by a giant old oak tree, the last remnant of the Mackay estate woods before they were cut down to build a development of outsized Georgian colonials. Erica remembered the spot.

"When I was at West Meadow we called that the dope-smoking tree."

"That's kinda what it still is." Ashley looked embarrassed.

Erica watched the kids around the tree: slouching, sitting cross-legged, posturing to each other, a few of them smoking something. A girl whispered something in a boy's ear. Their body language had a sweet intensity to it. Erica knew she was trespassing in a world no longer hers. She couldn't understand where all those years had vanished—thirteen years, such a long span of time, over so quickly. When she'd attended this high school, she'd wanted nothing more than to grow up and leave all this behind, to enter the magic circle of adulthood. But now the tangible reality of that passage of time made her feel sad and full of longing.

"Hey, Jared," she said softly. "Do you think you could get me some dope sometime?"

His mouth hung open. "Did you just say what I think you said?" he asked.

"Yes," Erica assured him.

"I can get you some right now, if you want. You wanna wait here, with the baby?"

Fast-moving clouds covered up the sun, a hint of chill drifted in. The afternoon bore a potential for excitement. Anything could happen. She watched Jared strike up a conversation with two other boys, one tall and ruddy, wearing only gym shorts and a West Meadows High T-shirt, the other one skinny and small with spiky orange hair, looking barely older than Dylan. Thirteen years ago, she had stood in this same place, made similar exchanges, felt the same intimation of deeper dimensions hidden under the thinnest of veils. Thirteen years ago, she was the one standing under that tree, the gangly girlfriend shivering in her cotton skirt and tank top, with Jeff Russell's warm arm around her waist. Or after he broke up with her, one of the Jeff substitutes, Rob or Chris, or that guy with the wavy red hair with a weird last name like Lemonpie.

Thirteen years later, the secrets of the world still danced their elusive ballet. The magic circle did not exist. Jared sidled up to Erica and handed her a baggie. "It's good stuff," he said. "Jamaican."

Erica looked at it quickly and then stuck it in her diaper bag. "How much do I owe you?" she asked.

"Oh, for you, nothing," Jared mumbled.

"That's not fair," Erica said, handing over forty dollars. She had no idea what an ounce of dope cost these days.

"Uh, thanks," Jared said. "See you around."

———

Late that evening, Erica put away laundry while Ethan undressed and shaved. She asked him if he'd read the Grant Fishel article in the *Times*.

"Yep," he said, drying his chin off with a towel. "It was very superficial."

"What do you mean?" Erica asked.

"My work is more global in nature." Ethan wrapped himself in the cushy cotton bathrobe he'd stolen from a Hyatt Hotel on one of his business trips.

"Global?" Erica shoved his underwear into a drawer.

"I'm isolating the essential elements of exchange in capital markets and converting them into universal guidelines. Investment banks have traditionally been reactive. If Grant Fishel uses my systems, they can be proactive—you understand what I mean?"

Erica didn't really, but "proactive" had a positive sound to it.

Ethan placed his hands over hers and gripped them tight. His eyes looked close and far away at the same time. He turned off the lights.

"Tuck me into bed," he said.

Erica extracted her arm from under Ethan's chest and rolled to the far end of her pillow where she could breathe. She got out of bed and breathed even easier. She padded down the hall past the bedrooms where her family slept and walked downstairs to the basement laundry room, where she'd hidden her baggie of dope in a plastic blue case originally intended for crayons.

She liked getting high. She liked the way the ordinary became slightly different, the colors slightly heightened, the sounds a deeper vibration. She lay on the playroom carpet, savoring the sensation of the altered room.

But what she liked best, she realized a few days later, was the illicit thrill of pulling the dope from its hiding place and smoking it late at night, in a stolen secret moment all her own. She liked that first second, when the blood rushed to her head and her limbs got all light and tingly. Illicitness is cheap when you you're fifteen. For Erica it was a rare commodity. She carried that little kernel of a thrill around all day long.

CHAPTER NINE

Ari, the Israeli fitness instructor who thought he was God's gift to women, strutted around aerobics class with his T-shirt riding up his six-pack abs. Erica's heart raced after forty-five minutes of step. She paced back and forth, letting her pounding heart settle down before doing a hundred sit-ups. All this effort and her belly still bulged out of the top of her tights. In the first row, Justine Baum, wearing a Victoria's Secret underwear set instead of a leotard, applied lipstick midstretch.

"I'm going to quit this class," Lisa said as they put away their steps. "I swear, half the girls in it are professional models. I don't have time to deal with the damage to my self-esteem anymore. Speak of the devil—"

Justine, who had worked as a model before marrying a back surgeon and giving birth to two children, and with whom Erica had never exchanged so much as a full sentence in her whole life, inserted herself between them.

"Hey, Erica! Your husband, Ethan, works for Grant Fishel, right? I read the article in the *Times*." She shook her sleek auburn hair out of its ponytail.

"Yep, he's quoted in there," Erica said, fluffing her depressingly limp hair. Maybe she needed one of those extra-volume shampoos.

"Does Ethan know Stephan Langston?" Justine pulled a pair of leather pants over her bikini-cut panties.

"He works on Ethan's floor," Erica said. I met him at a party. I met Don Johnson there too."

"You didn't! Wow! I never would have thought it!" Justine reached in her Louis Vuitton bag for a leather appointment book. "We should set up a playdate for Dylan and my Andrew," she said. "How about next Tuesday?"

"Erica, let's get going." Lisa picked up both gym bags and shifted on her feet.

"I'll call and confirm," Justine said.

———

Justine, true to her word, called and confirmed, and Erica dropped a reluctant Dylan off at her house in West Meadow Estates on Tuesday. Ethan was off in the Florida office on one of his business trips, which were becoming increasingly frequent.

"Again?" Erica had asked him as he threw a bunch of shirts she'd just picked up from the dry cleaners into an open suitcase, plastic and all. "You've been spending so much time there you're going to develop a Southern accent."

"I'm setting up my systems in the Boca Raton office," he said. "But, hey, something for you to look forward to: get a babysitter for Friday night. I'll be home in time for us to go to a party this trader I know, Josh, is having. He lives in Tribeca. You'll like him."

Between dropping the twins off at Kindermusic and Dylan's planned pickup time from Justine's, Erica managed to nail down Mrs. Lutock for Friday night as well as swing by her mom's real estate office to drop off a sweater she'd borrowed.

"I wonder if Debbie's gotten the results of her blood tests," Mom said, scratching the back of her neck. She enjoyed alluding in a serious tone to information she suspected Erica wasn't privy to.

"About those bruises on her arms and legs? She's blaming them on some mysterious blood disease."

Mom erupted in a short, nervous laugh. "Oh, I don't know, honey. Medicine is a foreign language to me. If only she didn't have to stand on her feet all day. I wish she could afford to quit her job and stay home, like you."

"I'm on my feet all day," Erica noted. "Often nighttime too."

"Well, you know what I mean," Mom said, checking her appointment book. "I have to run. An open house over on Clavier. But let me know if you need something special to wear for Friday. We seem to wear the same size these days."

Great, she fit into the same clothes as her sixty-year-old mother. Debbie must wear a size 6. Erica sat in the car thinking of blood and feeling slightly sick, which was odd, because blood never used to bother her in the slightest. In her one year as a nurse in Boston, she'd drawn plenty of blood.

If she still worked as a nurse, would that qualify in her mother's eyes as standing on her feet all day? At the time, her parents were disappointed by her career choice. If Debbie was the artistic one, then Erica, by default, needed to be the academic one, but she'd failed to fulfill her potential. In school she had quivered with a restlessness that made it impossible to concentrate on the causes of the War of 1812, or when a train traveling 120 miles an hour would crash into another train traveling eighty miles an hour in the opposite direction, or for that matter, any knowledge confined to pen and paper. She drummed her hands against the desk or passed notes to her friends, watching the big clock at the front of the room ticking away her life.

So, second-tier college instead of Ivy League; so, nursing instead of premed. And the irony was, at BU she concentrated, because she saw a light at the end of the tunnel. As a nurse she could immerse herself in a real world that demanded competence and split-second action. She drank tons of coffee and stayed up all night to make up for party weekends; sealed herself in her room through the endless snowy winters, struggling through organic chemistry and biophysics and calculus; passed them all with flying colors; and landed a job at Brigham starting the first day after graduation.

She started in the emergency room, drawing blood, mostly. She was good at it: finding the sturdy vein popping up out of the forearm, jabbing the needle in quickly, pulling her wrist back, watching the red blood fill the syringe, withdrawing the needle, applying pressure and a bandage, all the while distracting her patient with a calm hand and conversation. In the emergency room, there was never any slack time. You never knew what the next minute would bring. Even during stretches of quiet, she remained on alert, awaiting the next all-absorbing crisis.

Then, perhaps impressed by her skill, the powers that be transferred her to the cancer ward. That was a different kettle of fish. Time moved excruciatingly slow there for her, but it was running out for most of her patients. She coaxed protein shakes down the throats of emaciated men dying of lung cancer. She attached tubes to orifices, changed unpleasant messes, stood pointlessly by as bad news was delivered. One day a woman in her twenties, her body ravaged by breast cancer that had spread to the brain, asked for a pen and paper. Erica gave it to her, and in a few minutes she handed it back. In shaky script, she'd written one word: "why?"

Why indeed? In this nightmare world, Erica's only purpose was to serve as an efficient and kind voyeur of tragedy. This was not the kind of purposeful action she'd anticipated. She was already pregnant with Dylan then, and she quit her job. They were moving to New York soon anyway. She thought she might apply for a job on Long Island, back in the emergency room, but when Dylan was born, he filled up her whole world in the most solid way she had ever known. For a magical period, she did not watch time tick by; she simply lived within it. Then came, in short order, Jesse and Jake, and Sophia, and a series of promotions for Ethan at Grant Fishel that precluded any ambition of hers to work for pay.

She retrieved Dylan from Justine's. Justine gave her a tour of her five-bedroom colonial, complete with fifty-inch projection television, suites for both her kids, and a West Indian housekeeper busily erasing mess.

Back home, Erica sank into a chair, blurry-headed, and absorbed the wealth of her own kitchen: her cherrywood cabinets, hand-built by Amish craftsmen; her Italian tile backsplash hand-painted with sunflowers; the sturdy wooden Brio set scattered carelessly on the floor. Their shiny surfaces, so deceiving, shattered into component atoms. All this abundance merely camouflaged danger bubbling up from a rent in the earth. There wasn't any point in sharing such perceptions, which came upon her increasingly often, with anyone. Lisa would tell her to buy a new dress. Mom would nag her again about losing weight and hiring a housekeeper. Debbie would advise her to call the doctor. Ethan would tell her to get a grip, and he was never home anyway. Maybe Jared would understand, but he was only a kid.

Ethan liked home-cooked meat, grains, vegetables, and salad to be waiting for him when he came home for dinner; the consequences of growing up with a mother who ground her own wheat berries. But with him in Florida the whole workweek, she didn't need to exert such effort. She splashed water on her face in a partially successful attempt to clear her head, put a tray of fish sticks in the oven, julienned a few carrot sticks, and heated up a can of baked beans.

After dinner and bath time, with Dylan closeted in his room working on his Lego robot, Erica read about Horton the Elephant to the twins while nursing Sophia. They all fell asleep together on the boys' double mattress. Erica woke up an hour or so later in a tangle, Jesse's feet at her shoulders, Jake's head on her foot, Sophia nestled against her chest, Dr. Seuss hard under her right arm. Her foot tingled where Jake lay on it. Slowly, she disengaged herself and edged toward a vertical direction, clutching the baby. She padded down the hallway, placed Sophia in her crib, and then sat on her new bedroom rug staring up at the skylight. The moon was full and sat smack in the middle of the glass, making her new rug shine beautifully, thick and slightly yellowed, like heavy cream. It was woven from the hair of rare North African goats, imported from Morocco by a real estate friend of her mother's whose cousin owned an exclusive carpet store in Long Island City. With Ethan in Florida, she could perform her dope-smoking ritual here on the clean soft carpet rather than in the basement. And that was what it was rapidly becoming, she realized regretfully: a ritual, like Dylan's tennis lessons and her aerobics class.

Later, stoned, she started obsessing about blood again. She saw blood dripping down Jared's shirt and Ron's eyes all bloodshot. She saw Debbie wiping down her glass coffee table, spraying Windex on bloodstains that wouldn't come clean. She saw blood on the floor of the emergency room and blood spurting from a punctured arm and red veins bulging in a dying patient's withered neck. She was scared to stand up, and she couldn't make the blood go away, so she closed her eyes and fell asleep on the carpet, waking up only when Sophia's hungry cries came over the baby monitor. Her body felt numb and heavy. She picked up Sophia, and they settled down in their corduroy chair.

CHAPTER TEN

Erica bought a new outfit at a boutique in Huntington for Josh Hendrie's party, still size 12, two sizes bigger than before Sophia. It was a burgundy washed-silk item with shoulder pads, a dropped waist, and a short skirt, accessorized by retro-patterned nylons and three-inch strappy heels.

Friday afternoon she ran her hands along the silk, sucking in her stomach. She still looked three months pregnant. As she trotted gingerly down the stairs in her new heels, Sophia in her arms, her mother burst in the door.

"That's a pretty dress, Rikki, but isn't it a bit short?"

"No, I don't think so." Erica smoothed the silk over her belly bulge, wishing she could sand it flat.

"I don't know—it seems perhaps you should wear something more matronly, but what business is it of mine?" Her mother smiled brightly. "I'm in a rush, but I had to bring by the most adorable baby outfit from Julia Olsen. You know the Olsens. I sold them that colonial in Manhasset?"

"Thanks, Mom. It's real cute." Erica dangled the tiny velvet pantsuit with her spare finger as she nudged aside a pile of mail on the kitchen counter and mixed up rice cereal and defrosted breast milk for Mrs. Lutock to give Sophia.

"You know what I've been thinking, honey," said her mother, wincing at the clutter. "Isabella once a week isn't enough help. Not with all you have to do. You need a live-in housekeeper who could work here all the time. All the girls have been talking about a wonderful agency, right here in West Meadow. Housemates."

"Whatever." She opened two cans of Spaghetti-Os, poured them into a saucepan, and set it by the stove with a note for Mrs. Lutock to heat it up.

Shaking her head, Mom scraped a few toast crumbs off the kitchen table, set down a business card for Housemates, and dashed out the door.

———

Erica caught the 5:35 out of Mineola. A minor surge of excitement rippled through her regarding the party. Even if it proved disappointing, at least no one would be discussing Jared's wheat-induced diarrhea. She sat on her cracked leather seat, alternating between watching industrial nothingness drift by through grimy windows and leafing through a *Newsday* someone had left behind, catching up on all the news she'd missed. An unsolved murder in Texas. A hurricane in Bangladesh. Genocide in Africa. A weekend section reviewing all the movies she hadn't seen and plays she hadn't heard of. Everywhere, events were spiraling out of control.

When she finally arrived downtown, it was past rush hour and the emptied-out streets of the financial district looked shadowy and canyon-like. The rectangle of buildings at the end of the street framed a strip of orange, the last remnant of the setting sun. The early-evening air felt cool and humid, and a mingled effusion of odors emanated from restaurants and bus tailpipes. It seemed like a movie set: the action was about to begin. She met Ethan in Grant Fishel's lobby.

They walked hand in hand through the cool dark streets. "You look really pretty tonight," Ethan said. "It's so nice to be alone for a change."

"Yeah," Erica agreed. "This was a crazy week. Justine Baum invited Dylan over for a playdate. Would you believe she reads the *New York Times*? She read the article about Grant Fishel."

"Who's Justine Baum?"

"That woman in my aerobics class who wears underwear instead of a leotard. I thought I told you about her."

"Perhaps. I don't remember." Ethan stuck his other hand in his slacks pocket, pulling out one of his noxious clove cigarettes.

"And apparently Debbie took a bunch of blood tests to find

out why she's getting all those bruises. You know, she keeps claiming it's a disease, but I don't buy it. I think maybe Ron's beating her, and she's covering it up. Battered wives do that, you know."

"I think you're overreacting. Just because he's a boring, meat-throwing jerk doesn't make him a wife beater. Listen, no offense, but do we have to talk about your sister and her family every time we have a conversation?" Loose Life Savers and used Kleenex tumbled out of Ethan's linen pocket, joining moldy leaves in the gutter.

"I'm sorry." Erica tightened her grip around his hand. "I don't mean to obsess."

"You know why they don't have any windows in the New York office? For the same reason they don't have windows in a gambling casino. They don't want workers distracted by the weather outside. Or maybe they don't want them jumping out the windows."

"That clove smell is gross," Erica said.

"Sorry." Ethan stubbed out the cigarette and added it to the gutter mess. "I should quit these things. I don't smoke them in Florida, you know. The Florida office has windows."

Erica pictured the Florida office as a gleaming new building overlooking white sand, surf, and palm trees. She imagined Ethan sitting amid reflected sunbeams, perfecting his algorithms while somewhere nearby Don Johnson leaped onto a docked yacht, which would speed off, kicking up exhaust and spray. Such a light-infused image, so opposite from these dusky and mysterious streets. She found it difficult to hold both places in her head at the same time.

"Tell me about this Josh, again," she said.

"He's a trader. One of our sharpest ones. One of the few guys who truly understands my system." He extracted a crumpled Post-it from his pocket with Josh's address on it. "He's a talented musician too. He plays keyboard for a band in his free time."

Josh Hendrie lived in a renovated factory by the Lincoln Tunnel. Around the corner, cars funneled into the dark maw of the tunnel like an army of fireflies. Erica and Ethan rode up eight flights in an old-fashioned freight elevator, which creaked to a halt a full foot below floor level. They stepped through a propped-open door into a loft space with refinished wood plank floors and exposed rafters bleached white. Again Erica experienced that tantalizing ripple of excitement, that lightness in her veins.

"This is Josh," Ethan said, introducing her to a tallish, thirtyish man, fit, with sandy hair and a round baby face, wearing white cotton pants and a tight lime-green scoop-neck shirt. There were about fifteen other people present, all in their twenties or early thirties. Preliminary introductions revealed that they all lived in downtown Manhattan or just over bridges in Hoboken or Brooklyn. Erica sat down next to a woman wearing a knit princess-waist dress over tight leggings. She worked in advertising and told Erica that she and her husband wanted to get pregnant but that the birth of their child needed to coincide with the end of the sailboat-racing season.

"That sounds challenging," noted Erica, hoping the conversation would soon slide toward more exotic realms, perhaps those movies and plays she hadn't seen or music she hadn't heard of. She asked Josh about his band.

"We do light jazz, some jazz fusion," he said.

"Did you ever hear of a band called Bloody Tampax?" Erica sipped the standard-issue chardonnay that was the only drink on order other than diet ginger ale and sparkling water.

"No, I don't believe so. What kind of music do they play?"

"Heavy metal, I guess. Sort of punk heavy metal."

"Sorry, not my thing." Josh's eyes glazed over with faint distaste and significant disinterest. He initiated an intense discussion of the New York Marathon with two skinny ladies in designer running suits. Everybody in the room was discussing physical fitness: optimum heart rate, lower-ab exercises, caloric intake versus energy output, their personal levels of body fat. Even Ethan got in on the game, talking about how he'd dispensed with the golf cart and now walked the entire eighteen holes down in Florida. Erica felt the excitement dissipate from her bloodstream.

"My aerobics instructor has the most amazing body and a sexy Israeli accent," she said. "He's got these groupies who always set up in the front row and apply eyeliner in the middle of class."

"Who said nothing exciting happened on Long Island," said Josh Hendrie, sarcasm evident.

"Did you work before you had children?" asked Knitted Dress.

"Not nearly as hard as I do now," thought Erica, but what came out of her mouth was "I was a nurse at Brigham Young Hospital in Boston."

"Oh?" Knitted Dress smiled brightly. "When was that? I know a cardiologist there."

"Ten years ago."

"Oh." More eye glazing. Knitted Dress turned her attention to her husband, a lanky man with a shock of black hair who was describing a yacht race off of Connecticut.

"I've developed a fear of blood," Erica said to no one in particular. "Kind of weird for a nurse, huh?"

No one gave evidence of hearing her. Erica poured herself some more chardonnay, even though it tasted like wood pulp. She looked around for something to eat. She was hungry, her last meal a yogurt at noon. The only food option she could see was a platter of crudités with onion dip that a couple people were picking at listlessly. The last thing she needed was onion breath.

Josh's apartment was as spare as his food and drink offerings. Milky-white walls, the exact tone no doubt selected by a decorator; a pair of tasteful modern oil paintings; two modular sofas in complementary cream and brown; a Tibetan throw rug; a gleaming black baby grand piano in one corner. Off to the right she saw a kitchenette with doll-size appliances, sandy granite counters, and a microwave. There was none of the clutter that accumulated in Erica's house as naturally as breathing, not even the framed needlepoints, globe paperweights, and lemon air fresheners of Debbie's house.

She tried imagining such a stripped-down life, a life simplified to work and workouts and carefully delineated hobbies, not complicated exponentially by the needs and desires of five other human beings. By bedtime your slate would be wiped as clean as these cream walls. You'd think such freedom would lead to a bigger life, but given these people, and their limited conversations and appetites, it seemed, strangely, to diminish them.

She needed to pee, not desperately, but enough that it seemed like an excuse to leave this boring situation and explore Josh's still mysterious bedroom, separated from the rest of the loft by a bamboo screen.

Hidden behind the screen, Erica took inventory. A double bed with a Hawaiian-print bedspread. A television on a stand at the foot of the bed. A night table, a slightly scummy water glass, and a book entitled *Fitness or Fatness: The Choice Is Yours*. A door to the bathroom, which was closed, and sliding doors leading out to the balcony. After a few minutes, the bathroom door opened, and a short, slight guy with horn-rim glasses stepped out holding something and smiling at her like they shared a secret. She recognized him: Stephan Langston.

"I met you at the Don Johnson party," she said, returning the smile. "You made some strange remark about soft drinks. You work with Ethan, don't you?"

"Tired of those health freaks?" he asked.

"You'd think they could find something else to talk about," Erica agreed.

"You want this?" he whispered, as if needing the toilet was a desire as potent and suppressed as a craving for Oreo cookies, and Erica nodded yes, even though she still didn't need to go that badly. Stephan hovered by the bathroom door, and as she walked in, surreptitiously shoved the something he was holding into her hand.

It was a thimble-size snifter of cocaine, with a miniature silver spoon on a chain.

Erica had never done coke before, never even seen it except on TV and movies. This was the type of thing that was supposed to go on at parties all the time, she knew, but never at any party she'd attended with Ethan, on Long Island or in the city. All people ever did was sit around and talk about home renovations, summer camp, or diet and exercise routines. People talked about boring stuff and went home by midnight because they were tired from the workweek, or tired from their kids, or tired from running around like chickens without heads, or tired on general principle. But now, in her sweaty palms, lay an opportunity to transcend all that.

Leaning on the vanity, she tentatively filled up the little spoon and sniffed it, half expecting it to scatter over the floor and reveal her for a fool. But no, the powder went neatly up her nose like she was an old hand at this. Her nostril grew numb, and she felt slightly light-headed, nothing more. She sat on the toilet, producing a trickle to authenticate her presence there, flushed the toilet, walked out of the bathroom, and not quite meeting Stephan's eyes, passed him the snifter. She stood by Josh's night table, leafing through *Fitness or Fatness,* and in a few minutes Stephan came out and handed her the snifter again. For the next half hour or so, they did a little dance, in and out of the bathroom. A steady hum of conversation issued from behind the bamboo screen. She kept expecting others to feel the urge of nature and poke their heads in, but perhaps people who didn't eat or drink didn't eliminate either. After a while, she ceased to care.

"Sayonara." Stephan grinned, vanishing back into the living room. Erica stepped out on the terrace and into an amazing revelation. The outside world for once in her lifetime was moving at the same pace as her interior one. No background noise, no to-do lists, no blood, no hurricanes or kidnappings, just this glittering perfect alignment. Down at street level, everything was fog and shadows, stretching past the filthy Hudson River to the green expanse of Staten Island; up here on the top of the city, she stood on the cusp of a sea of light.

She'd felt like this when each of her four children were born, but that was earned ecstasy, colored with pain and sweat. This evening was a gift. She feared she didn't deserve it. She reached deep back in her childhood, and like that evening at the World's Fair, New York City blinked on for her, stretching to the horizon, sparkling like jewels.

CHAPTER ELEVEN

Erica felt a hand on her shoulder, a kiss on the back of her neck. The kiss felt really good. She waited for more.

"Where the hell have you been?"

She turned around. Ethan's suit jacket, now past its fifteenth hour of service, hung limp and linty from his shoulders. His pinstripe shirt had worked its way loose from his waistline and bubbled over his leather belt. He picked at his ear in a tired, abstracted way.

"I'm looking at the world transformed." She nuzzled close to him, hoping he would kiss her neck again.

"It's quite the view!" Ethan agreed, but Erica knew he didn't see what she saw out there, the bouncing electrons, the dusty light. She almost spilled her secret, tossed it into the sky and let it sparkle, but a residual caution residing in her brain told her that was not a safe idea.

"Stephan Langston told me you guys got into a long conversation." Light glinted on the tendrils of dirty-blond hair at the base of Ethan's neck and the reddish scab on the curve of his ear.

She'd almost forgotten about Stephan. "Oh yeah! We talked about soft drinks, you know, the health effects." She turned back toward the lights. "Look! Can you believe that galaxy of lights over there is Staten Island? Does that remotely resemble Staten Island?"

"In the morning it'll look like Staten Island," Ethan said. He steered her indoors. "C'mon, hon," he insisted. "I'm all zonked out from the week, and now I'm all revved up for the marathon. That'll give me a goal, to finally quit smoking and get into fantastic shape. I want to go running first thing tomorrow morning." The pressure of his fingers sent sparks through her arm. The floorboards bounced like rubber under her ankles.

Josh sat at the piano, playing a lush rendition of "Uptown Girl." All the guests save Stephan had left, and the room was a quiet mess: sticky glasses scattered here and there, a cucumber wedge stuck in a puddle of fat-free hummus, a forgotten jacket. The whole mundane scene shimmered with a glow that, as Erica noted with dismay, was already breaking off into golden droplets and floating away. "It was nice meeting you," said Josh, his fingers not straying from the piano keys. "Same here," said Erica.

Stephan was traversing the limited length of the kitchenette, practicing tai chi kicks. She waved good-bye to him and bestowed what she believed was a warm and meaningful smile. He gave her an odd little salute in return and kept on kicking.

"What'd you find to talk about so long with that guy?" Ethan said, as the door closed behind them. "He's a major weirdo."

"I told you, soft drinks." Erica said. She and Stephan hadn't exchanged more than a few words. "And yoga. He takes yoga classes. Oh yeah, and he wanted to know about our vacation in Jamaica."

"Would you believe he made three million dollars last year?"

"I read that in the *Times*. Which department does he work in?" Erica asked. The freight elevator creaked too slowly down the eight floors.

"He's a trader. Josh's boss. He's another big fan of my systems."

Erica concentrated on the diamond filigree of the elevator door. The shine was off, but her mind still felt extraordinarily clear, all information and sensation neatly shelved and accessible, like a giant mental library. Stephan must have approached her at the Don Johnson party, and again this evening, because he recognized a commonality between them, something longing and vulnerable.

They stepped out of the lobby onto the sidewalk. "Why wait until morning? Let's run right now!" Erica said. Her legs felt like springs. She leaped through the air, the front of her foot only lightly touching the sidewalk.

"Hey, slow down," Ethan said. "I'm tired."

In the street, a rush of steam shot up from a manhole, dispersing a spray of white vapor. Under the streets, water rushed through pipes. Trains rumbled through tunnels. Who knew what mysteries lay at the heart of the city, while she ran above it all on the illusion of solid ground? She could keep running forever, through the yellow vaporous night, the canyons of towers, the shadowy caves of industrial space, all the way to the lapping waves of the filthy Hudson. If only she could keep running. But, there, obstructing her path, sat Ethan's trusty Mercedes.

"You'll drive, hon?" he asked, climbing expectantly into the passenger's seat.

She averted her eyes from the giant stone archway as she powered over the Manhattan Bridge and through the dodge game of shooting stars that was the BQE, shifting seamlessly to the Grand Central, the Northern State, the LIE, all the way to the West Meadow exit. She couldn't place the precise moment when her sense of extraordinary clarity dissolved all the way down to sludge.

She navigated through the dense molecules one at a time. Thankfully, these dark roads were etched into the crevices of her brain; she could drive them in her sleep. She pressed the electronic garage opener, and the door went up on her own home where her kids were sleeping. Mrs. Lutock blinked herself awake on the family room couch, a late-night horror movie rambling dumbly on. Erica dug into her purse and handed her a couple twenties; Mrs. Lutock hauled herself upright on her arthritic knees and out to her car.

Erica stripped off her washed-silk dress and left it on the bedroom floor. She heard Ethan in the bathroom, brushing his teeth, flushing the toilet. Sophia, no doubt sensing her presence, started to cry. Erica nursed her, feeling a vague guilt that she was polluting her baby's body with drugs, thinking that maybe she should substitute one of those cans of formula they'd given her in the hospital. But that would mean giving up their intimate embrace, that absolute trust that exhilarated her and crushed her at the same time. If only she could get back to that shiny place again, that point of light receding so rapidly, like a bubble drifting into outer space.

Back in her bedroom, Ethan gently snoring, she ran her fingers over the rumpled surface of her dress, searching for remnants of white powder. She thought she found a trace and inhaled, but it was only lint, or maybe some particulate from the Manhattan air. Disgusting. She was disgusting. Lacking an alternative, she fell into bed and slept.

CHAPTER TWELVE

The alarm clock jangled her awake long before she was ready. She detected a familiar cool emptiness on Ethan's side of the bed—he was out running, no doubt—and stumbled downstairs into a world propelled by noise: cartoons, Nintendo, pillows thudding into the family room walls, and Dylan, reminding her of his Saturday morning basketball party.

She felt unusually jerky and unsure on the road. Even Jefferson Starship, which bore the character of a floating dream, failed to calm her down. She slammed on the brakes too hard, took the turns too wide, and parked so close to the neighboring Ford Taurus in the parking lot that she and the kids had to slide out sideways.

In the gym, basketballs pounded against the floors. She engaged in driblets of conversation with the women who darted in and out, moving between watching the party and buying grape juice at the supermarket, going to the bank, and working on the seating arrangements for their sons' bar mitzvahs. Conversation was an effort. All these women, her friends and neighbors, struck her as trivial-minded drips.

When Erica got home, Ethan was pulling on his weekend sweatpants, showered and refreshed from his run.

"I might go for a run myself," Erica said. "Can you watch the kids?"

"Sure," said Ethan. "Maybe you could even train for the marathon with me."

Hey, maybe she could train for the marathon and beat those fitness freaks at their own game. She was a fast runner, probably faster than Ethan, though she hadn't run consistently since high school. She'd trained on these very streets for the West Meadow cross-country team, temporarily released from the confines of the stuffy classroom, her long legs exploding with seemingly infinite energy.

But in the current day her legs had lost their spring. The cold dry winds of the spring afternoon slapped at her but couldn't penetrate her torpor. She was slow. She tripped on the curb. She replayed the events of the previous evening—the dark, mysterious streets; Stephan and his knowing smile; their dance in and out of the bathroom; her illuminating moment on Josh's balcony—but the entire experience felt like something that had happened a long time ago, in a different country. In West Meadow, everyone's lawns looked identical: carpets of grass, rounded hedges, the occasional purple or yellow crocus, an early azalea, damp patches of dirt awaiting the obligatory May visit to the nursery. It all seemed so predictable, so pointless. Her heart beat hard against her chest.

When Dylan was four years old, he'd scraped his leg on a shard of glass in the Bar Beach surf and who knew what toxic slime was in that water. He'd scratched and picked at it until it swelled up into a red, angry boil, which Erica lanced with a sterilized needle. Blood and pus gushed out. No doubt the same river of blood and pus ran underneath Debbie's bruises, despite how their faded colors, rose and gray and lavender, almost blended with her pastel pantsuits. Erica sat down on the street curb with her head in her hands. She didn't understand what had happened to her, how she'd lost her sturdy implacability. She wanted to scrub her brain cells with Ajax.

That evening they went out for dinner and a movie with Lisa and her husband, Les, who worked in the garment business. Lisa was a regular, down to earth sort, but Les wore ill-fitting Cavaricci jeans, actually patronized a tanning parlor, and grossest of all, manicured his nails. Ethan cut his nails flat across the top. His hands were rough, workingman's hands, even though the most physical work he did with them was punching numbers on a computer keyboard, or maybe swinging a tennis racket.

Lisa and Les insisted on eating at their favorite steakhouse— more blood. Erica ate only the stuffed potato and creamed spinach, layering her steak onto Ethan's plate. The husbands chatted about golf and tennis, while Lisa yammered on and on about how she'd hired a girl from Housemates to work Monday through Friday. She felt kind of guilty because she didn't work outside the home and her youngest was in fifth grade, but hey, there still weren't enough hours in the day, and Les had just got a promotion. "It's so great," she enthused. "Dinner appears magically on the table, and then, after dinner, you go relax, and the dishes disappear. Like a hotel!"

"Everybody's talking about Housemates," Erica agreed. "My cousin Amelia's been singing the praises of her housekeeper for months. My mother's after me to call them."

"You should," Lisa said. "My God, you have four kids! What are you waiting for?" She leaned over the table, stroking Erica's arm. "And to tell you the truth, hon, you're looking awfully tired."

The movie, a spy thriller, held everyone's rapt attention except for Erica, who kept dozing off at critical moments and waking up with a start; she pretended to follow the discussion afterward over ice cream cones at Baskin-Robbins. At home, in bed, she could not sleep. Ethan threw his arm around her, sticky and enclosing. She wriggled away so that only his fingertips touched her. The baby monitor predictably filled with the sounds of hungry crying.

She fed Sophia for longer than necessary, breathing in her sweet baby-lotion scent, and then went down to the basement and then pulled her plastic suitcase out from behind her underwear and smoked her dope. She was almost out. She'd told herself a couple of days before that she wasn't going to buy any more from Jared—it didn't seem right. But now, staring at the almost-empty baggie, she changed her mind. She cleaned the boys' paint easel and stacked their wooden puzzles. As she shoved the last puzzle into place, it tipped over a box of Colorforms, scattering plastic shapes all over the floor. She should have realized: chaos always won. She left the mess and stumbled back to bed. This time when Ethan put his arms around her, she did not roll away.

In the morning she woke to Ethan's limbs wrapped around her like a fuzzy towel and a small child tapping her on the back. She opened her eyes, and there stood all three of her boys, serious faced. A tear trickled down Jesse's cheek. "Mommy," he said, "something very sad has happened."

"What is it?" she cried, her mind reeling through its usual litany of bloody and mangled bodies.

"The goldfish died. All three of them. They're floating on top of the bowl."

"We think we should bury them by the tulips," Dylan said.

They lined a shoe box with tissue paper, placed the three bloated fish in it, and dug a hole by the tulips. Dylan read a Shel Silverstein poem about a fish, and the twins sang "Baby Beluga," with appropriate hand motions, substituting the word "goldfish" for "whales." Ethan said a prayer he remembered from Unitarian services as a child. Erica promised the boys new fish.

"Can we get an iguana instead of fish?" Dylan asked. "It would be more interesting."

"If you want," Erica said. Agreement seemed the simplest path. An iguana wouldn't require walking or petting or obedience classes, or membership in a special society like Lisa's beloved cocker spaniel.

She called the local pet store, up the street from her parents', but it was closed on Sundays. After lunch, Ethan packed for another week in Florida, called the limo, and retreated to his Apple IIGS. The afternoon dribbled on disconcertingly slowly.

Erica poked her head into the computer room. "Um, that Stephan guy," she said, hoping to casually get Ethan's attention. Just saying Stephan's name made her feel sticky and hot.

"Who?" said Ethan, barely looking up from the screen.

"Stephan Langston? Who we met at Josh's party? The big-shot trader? The guy with the horn-rim glasses? Who was doing tai chi? Do you have his phone number?"

Ethan frowned. "Jeez, I don't know his number. I don't call him on the phone. Just let me finish this program, okay?"

"Well, do you think you could get me his number?" There was a high panicky undertone to Erica's voice that she didn't like.

Ethan punched a few more numbers and letters into the computer and then looked at her for the first time since she'd entered the room, scanning her face slowly and carefully. "What's the big hurry?" he asked. "Do you need to continue your hour-long conversation about soft drinks and yoga? Do you like him or something? I wouldn't think he was your type."

"No, are you crazy?" Erica scrambled to compose herself, to come up with a credible answer. "Um, we were talking about Jamaica, like I told you, and I said I'd get him some information on that hotel we stayed in last year."

"You mean Coconuts? I have the number on my Rolodex. I'll give it to him at work." Ethan picked at his ear.

"Well, you could do that," Erica said, shifting Sophia to her other hip and making a show of unbuttoning her jacket. "But you know, he asked me, and you always get so busy at work and forget stuff like that. Plus, you're flying to Florida in an hour."

"Yeah, well, I suppose you have a valid point there." Ethan pulled his earlobe and scratched his butt. He didn't seem satisfied, but he did seem eager to return to his calculations. "Check my black leather phone book. In my jacket. Upstairs."

That evening, before she could lose her nerve, she took the cordless phone into the powder room and called Stephan. His answering machine pronounced, "This is Stephan. Sorry I can't come to the phone right now, but your call is very important to me."

"This is. . ." she started and then stopped. Leaving a recorded message about illegal drugs seemed a really stupid idea.

CHAPTER THIRTEEN

She woke up, in the gray light of dawn, to the pulsing shriek of the burglar alarm. Her foot had fallen asleep. Numb and heavy, it slid heavily on the floor as she tried to stand up and shuffle to the closet control pad and turn off the alarm. The pulsing changed to a louder, faster, more urgent beep and then a shrieking wail. She made it to the closet just in time to avoid triggering a police visit.

Then the thought hit her like a sick punch: maybe she needed the police. She crept down the stairs. The front door was closed. The downstairs hallway, kitchen, and family room appeared tranquil and undisturbed. From the backyard came a faint rustle, a slap of something against the wood.

She spied a gray rounded shape on the damp redwood of her patio. Sticking out of the lump was a hand, pale and seemingly too small for the body attached, with two silver rings on the index finger. And rising from behind the lump, another, larger hand clutching a red rubber volleyball, followed by an arm and a spiky green head. Jared! The ball slipped from his hands and rolled toward the door, where it bounced off with a mild thump. Jared leaped for it, losing his balance and hitting his chin on the gas barbeque.

"What the hell?" Erica squeaked, shivering outside in her cotton leggings and a U2 concert shirt.

"Oh, Aunt Rikki, that's not going to set the alarm off again, is it?'

"The alarm's turned off," said Erica. "You scared me half to death." The pale ringed hand, now clearly attached to Ashley, rose, still clutching the gray woolen blanket that Erica last recalled seeing neatly folded at the base of Jared's bed.

"I tossed the ball at the door, and the alarm went off," Jared said. "I'm so sorry."

"We added extra wiring to the windows last winter," Erica said. "It's real sensitive. Come on in. It's freezing out here."

They straggled in, Jared wearing jeans, a T-shirt, and a dirty pair of running shoes, Ashley still cocooned in the blanket.

"I'm sorry for the inconvenience, Mrs. Richards," Ashley said.

Jared launched into a soliloquy. "I get home at 2:00 a.m., and Dad's waiting up, all red-faced like he gets, and he's having a cow because my weekday curfew is 10:00 p.m. He's ranting and raving, about how could I do this to Mom, how I'm making her sick. I didn't even used to have a specific curfew, but that's one of the stupid rules we worked out in family therapy. So Dad's ranting on about how even when we negotiate rules, I break them, and why was my trashy girlfriend out at that time of night, didn't her parents care, and if I didn't like the rules of the house, why didn't I leave. So I left."

"Want some coffee?" Erica asked.

"Yeah, sure, absolutely!" he said. "Mom never lets me have coffee. She claims it aggravates my DDD."

Erica ground some glossy Costa Rican beans Ethan had special-ordered. This morning, Ashley was as quiet as Jared was voluble. She entwined her hand somewhere between Jared's waistband and the small of his back. She looked congested and red-eyed. Erica fought back the urge to wipe her nose, to feel her forehead for fever.

She poured the strong coffee into three mugs. "Do your parents know where you are, Ashley?" she asked.

"My mother is in St. Thomas," Ashley said. "Only the housekeeper is home, and she doesn't care. Her name is Georgia. The last housekeeper we had was also named Georgia. Don't you think that's kinda weird? And she cooks jerk chicken every single night. It's so fattening. She must dump a stick of butter on it."

"You want to take a shower or something?" Erica gulped a long, satisfying draft of coffee. "You can borrow my clothes if you want, not that they'd fit."

"No, thanks—we gotta get to school by 7:30," Jared said. "I have to carry around a green attendance sheet that gets signed by all my teachers. It's another negotiated psychologist rule."

"I have to carry around one of those stupid sheets too," Ashley said. "Not that anyone ever reads them."

"We met in family therapy." Jared stirred a heaping tablespoon of sugar into his coffee. "That's the only good thing to come out of all this bizarreness."

Erica popped a waffle in the toaster. "That sounds really dumb," she agreed. "Green sheets."

"I knew you'd understand," said Jared.

"Do the sheets go on your permanent record?" Erica asked.

Ashley looked confused. "What's a permanent record?"

"Maybe they don't have them anymore," Erica said. "When I was in school, teachers always used to threaten you about putting things in your permanent record. And you know what? When I was in high school, there was a court decision, and students got the right to examine their records. So I looked, and it was really boring. Just grades and test scores and a psychological evaluation from the school psychologist saying I was hyperactive and some other evaluation from a graduate student who observed my sixth-grade class and said I was a spirited child with advanced fine motor skills."

"I got diagnosed as hyperactive too." Ashley nodded sagely.

"Do you want to be my approved friend?" Jared asked. "We negotiated a list of approved friends in therapy. We could party."

Were it not for her four children sleeping upstairs, soon to awaken, Erica thought they could have all been high school kids, chatting in the kitchen after a sleepover. "Yeah, sure," she said. "But I think it would be best if I knew when you were coming over. Why don't you tell your parents you're lending me a CD? That can be our secret code."

"Cool," Jared said. "Thanks."

From upstairs Erica heard coos from the crib and Dylan's clock radio. She needed to try Stephan again but he would be on his way to work already. She could call him in the evening, but with Ethan gone, she probably couldn't find any private phone time until all the kids were in bed, and suppose Stephan also went to bed early like Ethan, or went out to dinner, or movies, or late-night yoga? She still couldn't see leaving messages on that phone machine.

When Ashley disappeared into the powder room to brush her hair, Erica asked Jared something she hadn't planned on until it popped out of her mouth. "Jared, I do have a favor to ask you. Can you get me something?"

"You want more pot?"

"Well, yes, but also something else."

"You want lots of CDs for real? My friend Rich works at Tower Records in Roosevelt Field, and he rips them off all the time." Jared bounced a stray rubber ball against the refrigerator.

"Well, that would be nice too, but could you get me a gram of coke?" Erica said.

Jared dropped the rubber ball. "You do coke?" he asked. "This guy Colin in my therapy group went to rehab for that."

"I thought I'd try it," Erica said.

Jared rubbed a strand of greenish hair. "I don't know. Let me ask around." He rubbed his hair some more, bit his lip. "Wait a minute—I do know someone, this guy Nick Stromboli. I know him from the family clinic. It might be kind of expensive, though."

"That's no problem," Erica said. "Thank you."

"Where's the toothpaste, Mom?" Dylan called from upstairs.

"Try the second shelf of the vanity," Erica called up.

Ashley emerged from the powder room hairsprayed and mascaraed, but still shivering in her T-shirt.

"Here, borrow this," Erica said, offering her a sweater from the front closet.

"Thanks so much, Mrs. Richards," said Ashley, pulling on Erica's pink Liz Claiborne, which hung on her narrow chest like a tent.

CHAPTER FOURTEEN

Erica wore a sparkly lavender leotard with a matching thong to aerobics class. A friend of Lisa's sold these at house parties, where Lisa had pressured her into buying several. She fought her inclination to remove the thong. Five months after Sophia's birth, her stomach still felt round and soft, and when she slapped her inner thighs, a shaky arc of flab rippled all the way through to her ample butt. Perhaps her inner discomfort would increase her motivation to exercise.

In class, sexy Ari lingered extra long correcting her leg lifts. As she did jumping jacks and hamstring curls, she tried to blank out her mind like Ethan's mother, Clara, claimed to do when she meditated. Despite her valiant efforts, clutter surfaced: Dylan's camp labels for Whispering Wind; the suspicious way Ethan had looked at her Sunday; the Audi grille inches away from Sophia's car seat; the way Ashley's pale hand traced across Jared's back; whether Jared thought less of her since she'd asked him for the coke; the way Debbie was sure to call her about Jared's vanishing act; the blood—she could never blank out the blood. Her beating heart stuttered, light and slippery, like Sophia's newborn breathing. When, at last, Ari told the class to sit down on their mats for abs and stretches, her heart rate took its time cooling down, and she lay against the foam rubber of the mat, light-headed and panting.

"Nice leotard," said Justine, buckling her spiked heels.

Debbie called Erica the minute she walked into the kitchen and didn't let her get a word in edgewise.

"I took the morning off from work, Rikki. I hardly slept a wink all night. Jared got into a fight with Ron and ran out the house! For the life of us, we didn't know where he went. We called all his friends, and he wasn't there. I suspect he was with that trashy Ashley, because they're always together these days, but I don't know for sure because her mother is in the Caribbean. Her parents are divorced. They left her with some housekeeper who didn't have a clue where she was and didn't care—you can't believe how some people raise their kids. Anyway, we were about to call the police when Ron says, 'Why don't we call the school first,' and guess what. La-de-da, they showed up at school like nothing was wrong. We still don't know where they spent the night. I never thought I'd say this, but I wish he was still dating Lyndsey Schrabner."

"Well, at least they're safe. Isn't that the most important thing?" Erica took the cordless into the garage where Sophia was still sleeping in the car. Debbie evidently didn't suspect her in the least. She leaned against the cold concrete.

"Yes, of course! And I'm trying to be understanding. I know Jared doesn't have good impulse control because of his DDD. But Ron is furious."

"Can't you tell him to chill out?" Erica bristled at the very thought of Ron's bulging eyes, his quivering chin.

Debbie sighed. "You know how hard it is to tell Ron anything. And on top of everything, he's under so much stress at work. They're switching from easy listening to adult contemporary and he has to familiarize himself with performers he's never even heard of. But, say, Rikki, on a cheerier note, did Mom tell you she's hosting Passover this year?"

"You're kidding! You usually do Passover."

"Well, this year she got it into her head that she's going to do it. She said she's worried about me because of all the stress with Jared and, you know, my blood condition."

"Yeah. I'm surprised she didn't palm it off on me." Erica sunk into an unstable sitting position on top of a net bag of soccer balls, attempting unsuccessfully to keep blood from cascading into her vision.

"She's having it catered. But she asked me to ask you if you could pick up the matzoh?"

"No problem," Erica said, her sweaty hands scrambling for purchase on the nylon bag strings. She slid off the bag onto the greasy floor of the garage.

Her butt still hurt when she took the boys over to pick out their new iguana after Dylan's tennis lesson. The pet store, up the street from her parents' house, was a neighborhood relic, left over from prewar days when West Meadow was a farming village and Meadow Heights was the commercial town center. Owned by a garrulous elderly couple, the Petersens, who remembered Erica from childhood, the shop sprawled sloppily over a two-storied clapboard house. Parrot cages hung on the front porch.

"We only have one iguana now, two months old," said Mr. Petersen. "He's used to the name Sammy, if you don't mind." Sammy was larger than Erica anticipated, exotic and beautiful Day-Glo green, with a dinosaur face and strangely compelling eyes.

Mr. Petersen led them around the store as they purchased what seemed to be an endless list of supplies: a fifty-gallon tank (only temporary; when the iguana grew to full size it would re-quire a custom-built cage); a heat lamp; branches for climbing; even silk orchids to replicate the jungle. The total cost surpassed eight hundred dollars. No matter, thought Erica as they loaded Sammy and his luggage into Vince's hatchback, where he took up the entire child bench, forcing Jesse to squeeze illegally against Erica in the front seat.

"They eat collard greens and raspberries," Dylan pronounced, leafing through a booklet entitled "Iguana Care and Feeding."

While Sophia batted at fabric birds in her playpen, they set up Sammy's cage on a card table in the family room, in a corner with plenty of the essential natural light. They arranged climbing branches and orchids, filled his feeding bowl with greens and ber-ries, and hooked up the heat lamp.

"The lamp should be turned on a minimum of ten hours a day," Dylan read.

"Hi, Sammy," said Jesse. "Do you want to eat your greens? Let me show you where the bowl is, Sammy."

The doorbell rang.

Jared and Ashley stood in the entrance. Jared wore an antsy, sheep-ish grin and his safety-pin pants. Ashley clung to him, wearing a pair of denim bellbottoms with flowers embroidered on the cuffs and a cotton Mexican blouse with a lace neck, her hair parted into two odd, perky little braids and tied with plaid bows. She looked like she'd wandered out of a couple of different decades and wasn't sure where she'd ended up.

"I've got a CD for you," Jared said, handing her *Fables of the Reconstruction*. "Thanks! I love this!" Erica said, scanning the song list. "But what's up?" she whispered. "It's kind of crazy around here. We're introducing a new iguana to the household, and we haven't even had dinner yet."

"I guess I should have called and said I was bringing a CD, huh? Sorry." Jared licked a drop of blood off his chapped lips. A nervous energy radiating from him belied his carefully cultivated air of nonchalance. He reached into his backpack and pulled out a paper lunch bag.

"I brought you a goodie bag too," he said. "From my good friend Nick Stromboli."

Ashley giggled. Erica peered inside the bag, where a smaller glassine bag nested inside. Displaying her own brand of fake in-difference, she dangled the bag at her side, swinging it casually back and forth.

"Mommy, Mommy, Sammy ate a piece of lettuce!" Jesse cried, dragging Jared by the hand into the family room to meet Sammy.

Jared inspected Sammy with clearly feigned interest. "Cool," he said, staring past Erica into the backyard.

Erica shoved the paper bag behind some cans of soup in the pantry. "Well, thanks for the goodie bag, guys," she said, setting water to boil for pasta. "We're getting ready for dinner here."

"I can't go home," Jared said. "The parental unit doesn't ap-prove of me. They're going to send me to the psycho boot camp if I don't shape up. I heard them talking to Dr. Rafferty about it. She's the head therapist at the family clinic."

"A friend of mine got sent to a place like that," Ashley said. "She was, like, really traumatized. She got bit by a poisonous spider, and they didn't treat it, and it swelled up and left a permanent scar on her arm."

"A poisonous spider?" Erica shuddered. "Was this camp in Montana or something?"

"They don't tell you where they're taking you," said Ashley. "They haul you off like you're a prisoner of war."

Erica pictured an evil cousin of Camp Whispering Wind. "So, how are you supposed to shape up?" she asked.

"That's the other problem," Jared said. His voice sounded weak and reedy, like Debbie on a bad day. "I don't know what they want me to do anymore. I go to stupid school, I get my green sheet signed, I go to stupid family therapy, I take my meds and eat my wheat-free diet." He shrugged, his shoulders fell, and he looked very thin under his baggy Mets sweatshirt. "They don't like my friends. They hate Ashley. My grades aren't up to potential. I quit tennis. I smoke dope. So what? So do you."

Dylan ran out onto the patio, waving the cordless. "Mommy, Aunt Debbie is on the phone for you."

"Hi, Deb," Erica said. "What's up?"

"What's up is I can't find Jared again. School ends at 3:15. We live three blocks away. He quit all his extracurriculars. So, tell me, where is he? Do you have any idea, by any chance? You seem good buddies as of late."

"Isn't that what you wanted?"

"I guess. I did ask you to reach out."

"Well, actually, Jared's here. He wanted to see our new iguana."

"Your new what?"

"Our new iguana. A lizard. I told you we were getting one last night at Mom and Dad's, remember? To replace the goldfish."

"No, I can't remember anything these days." Debbie sighed. "Send him home, will you? He needs to start on his homework."

"Okay. Will do."

But Jared resumed his monologue like the phone hadn't rung, as Jesse and Jake raced around him throwing Legos, Sammy's novelty apparently already faded.

"They don't like my att-i-tude," he said, drawing out the word.

"How do you change your attitude? They say DDD is chronic. They say you'll suffer from it your whole life if they don't attack it at the source. And who is the source? The source is me. They're attacking me."

"Jared, please go home," Erica said. The faster he went home meant the faster she could initiate the dinner/bath/bedtime routine, and the faster she could sample from her new glassine baggie. "Your mother is very upset."

"I don't want to ever go home. I want to run away." Jared picked at his chin. There was a raw red scab at approximately the spot where the edge of Ron's plate had landed. The cut was deep and probably should have been stitched; she wondered how Debbie explained its existence to Jared's numerous doctors. He kept picking at it as if he didn't want the wound to heal, as if it reminded him of something he needed to remember.

Erica pulled his fingers away. "Leave that alone. It'll get infected." Her arm edged around his thin, tensed shoulders, meeting Ashley's fingers somewhere on the back of his bony neck.

"I ran away to Times Square once," Ashley said. "It was gross."

"Jared." Erica flipped *Fraggle Rock* on on the television set, inducing instant, albeit temporary, calm in her chaotic family room. "I need you to go home now. I'll try and put some sense into your mom, okay?" She dumped a pound of fettuccine into the boiling water.

His eyes probed hers, moist and long lashed, beautiful as a baby's. "Good luck," he said.

—

When everyone was soundly asleep Erica extracted the baggie of coke from behind the cans of Progresso minestrone and appraised it, as if she were trying to figure out the buckle on a new make of car seat. This time she lacked the advantage of Stephan's jewelry thingie, so she improvised: the plastic mat from Sophia's diaper bag (sanitized) and a straw from an unused box drink. If it wasn't transformation this time, at least it was elevation, the ordinary ratcheted up a notch, the knot of fear diminishing. The white tile of the kitchen shone glittery clean; the nectarines ripening on the counter bore a mellow, fruity scent. She listened to her heart thump against her chest.

She played *Fables of the Reconstruction* on the CD player, softly, but still loud enough to wake Sophia. She rocked her back to sleep, caressing her tendrils of dark-brown hair, kissing her fragile neck, swaying around the family room. The music was moody and slow, depressing even, but it was a dreamy, indulgent depression she enjoyed sinking into. All these hours of the night, previously lost in sleep or hoping for sleep, opened up to her with limitless possibility, as if she were rambling through the rooms of a mansion she'd always known was there but that only now had become visible.

REM's music felt replete with hidden meaning. The lyrics all sounded like convoluted messages from Jared.

Maybe's he caught in the legend
Maybe's he's caught in the mood
Maybe these maps and signals
Have been misunderstood, been misunderstood
Is he to be reached? He's not to be reached.
Is he to be reached? He's not to be reached.
Is he to be reached? He's not to be reached anymore.

CHAPTER FIFTEEN

Debbie's instincts were kind, Erica reminded herself. She'd realized this as a young child. Debbie always waited by Erica's classroom to walk her home from kindergarten, her dry warm hand in Erica's, looking carefully both ways as they crossed the street. She cooked nachos piled with cheese and olives when their parents went out. More recently, she'd crocheted blankets for all four of her children's births. Erica reminded herself of all these things, but all it did was trigger guilt at finding her so exasperating. But then there was the fact of Jared's round baby eyes. The following afternoon, in between Jake's speech therapy appointment and Jesse's playdate, she called Debbie.

"Did Jared come home last night?" Erica asked, simultaneously rummaging through the pantry, extracting a couple cans of clam chowder for dinner.

"Yes. He told me you asked him to, so thank you." Debbie sighed. "I get so panicked these days. He still won't tell me where he stayed the night before. I assume someplace with that Ashley. He's not ready for a steady girlfriend at his age. Especially a troubled creature like that one."

"He's fifteen years old! You dated that guy Lewis from auto shop when you were thirteen, and he was already in high school. Remember, you made me tell Mom you were studying at Annie Lachulsky's house?" Erica needed a crunchy item to balance out the soup. Maybe some carrot sticks. She peeled the carrots, tossing the scraps down the disposal.

"I don't remember."

"You must. He had red hair and always wore chambray shirts and lived next to the pizza place that used to be by the railroad tracks? He taught me how to change the oil in Dad's car."

"Are you sure this isn't some story you're making up, Rikki?"

"Of course not. My point is, teenagers have hormones, and they go out with the opposite sex."

Debbie snorted, yet another one of her annoying habits. "Jared is a young fifteen. And it's a different world these days. Scarier. Look, Rikki, I appreciate your concern, but you don't seem to understand. He's got severe allergies, and I keep telling you, he's been diagnosed with DDD! It's a serious biochemical disorder."

"He's very afraid you're going to send him away to some boot camp." Erica placed the chopped vegetables in a bowl of water and then in the refrigerator.

"Well, we're keeping it as a last resort. It's not a boot camp, by the way—it's a boarding school, and I've heard very good things about it. It took the Marines to screw Ron's head on straight, and he wants to nip this thing with Jared in the bud right now."

"You could make up your own mind. You don't have to listen to Ron," Erica said.

"But I want to listen to Ron," said Debbie. "He's my husband."

"Uh," Erica began. This conversation gave her nothing reassuring to report back to Jared, but it was clearly over.

"I gotta go, Rikki," Debbie was saying. "Listen, don't forget that matzoh. Go to Rothman's. Get their egg matzoh—it's Ron's favorite."

———

The week sped by, and Erica forgot about the matzoh. She developed a new habit of discreetly disappearing into the bathroom a few times a day, for a little longer than it normally took her to pee. Her day grew brighter, sunnier, and most of all more manageable, as if the zillion disparate points of energy that comprised it coalesced into a single wave. All the extraneous blather fell away. The world glinted like metal in the sun. Rays of light shattered into rainbows on the walls, and every tone of every sound rang sharp and discrete.

The notes of the ringing doorbell lingered in the air like a bell she'd once rung with Ethan on a balcony overlooking Big Sur at one of the Richards family reunions. This time the bell, in the more mundane location of West Meadow, only admitted her four-year-old sons, home from preschool. Still, she remembered how the deep thrum reverberated over the waves.

She tossed a beach ball back and forth with the boys and, when they tired of that, pushed them on the tire swing. The thwack of the ball and the whoosh of the swing took on a rhythm of their own. Erica looked up at the sky, as intensely blue as the Pacific ocean was that day in Big Sur. Her boys clutched the chain of the swing, their curls glittering golden in the sun, so precious and beautiful the day could barely contain them.

She pushed the swing toward that azure sky, a little too high, a little too rough. Jake lost his grip, slipping through the center of the tire, hitting a rock and scraping his knee. Blood oozed out. Erica's glimmering private space dissipated, blather swirling back, and with it, an inchoate sense of apprehension. Her children broke and bled so easily. And there was no denying it: she was scraping the bottom of her magic baggie.

After cleaning and bandaging Jake's knee, gritting her teeth and squinting her eyes all the while, she treated both boys to lemon popsicles. Once they were suitably entranced in a video about talking poodles, Erica called the number scribbled on the back of Jared's algebra homework.

"Are you Nick?" Erica asked.

"Yes."

"Um, Jared gave me your number. He thought you might have something for me that I want."

"Jared?"

"Jared Lassler. Um. I believe he knows you from the family clinic?"

"Oh yes, Jared. Great kid." Nick had a calm, steady voice, not a whole lot of change in inflection.

"Um, he said you have something I might want. Some new CDs."

"Oh. Well, yes. If you're interested in my music, why don't you come over now?"

Now—with the twins in the family room watching TV, Dylan

arriving home any second requiring transport to tennis, and Sophia needing a diaper change and milk—was obviously not the right time. In fact, she'd forgotten, she needed to take Jesse to his speech therapy appointment right after tennis. "How about tomorrow morning, Friday?" she asked. "Around 11."

"I can make that work," said Nick. "I live at 845 Locust. Right across from the pet store."

CHAPTER SIXTEEN

At aerobics Friday, hunky Ari strutted between everyone's step platforms, shaking his hips to Wang Chung. Maybe Erica was imagining things, but it seemed like her belly felt tauter underneath the spangled lavender leotard, and she could swear her clothing fit more loosely, the thong no longer digging into her butt crack. She lifted five-pound weights in bicep curls while simultaneously performing a V-step. She even found herself singing along to "Dance Hall Days" as Ari circled by and tapped her on the rear. "Looking good," he said in a move that unfortunately reminded her of Ron.

"He thinks you're cute," Justine said afterward, reapplying her mascara. She was wearing a pink lace underwear and camisole set.

"Don't you think he looks like Michael Bolton?" Erica fiddled with her gym bag, looking for the new patterned leggings she'd bought, but Justine was already pulling on her six-inch heels, paying not a mote of attention to anything Erica was saying.

"You'll have to excuse me—I'm running like crazy today. I have to go to the dry cleaners, pick up cat food, and then go to the doctor. I may have an infection at the site of my tubal ligation. I've been having cramping and bleeding. If I have time, I really should talk to you. Someone told me you were a nurse."

"I used to be." Erica patted her thighs, which still rubbed together uncomfortably when she walked, fashionable patterned leggings or no.

"You've got bags under your eyes." Justine brushed her scalpel-like nails across Erica's cheek. "You should call Housemates and get yourself some help."

"My mother gave me the number."

"Well, call them for God's sake." Justine clattered out of the locker room, and as she did so, Lisa sidled up from the other side of the locker room.

"Sorry, but I can't stand that woman," Lisa said. "Do you think her boobs are fake?"

"Probably. Do you think Ari looks like Michael Bolton?"

"There's a resemblance, now that you mention it. Do you have time this afternoon to go order the boys' camp labels?"

Camp labels. She'd forgotten about ordering them, as well as buying something Debbie kept requesting. Her mind felt razor sharp yet pocked with inexplicable holes.

"I can't make it this afternoon. I have an appointment."

"Doctor?" Lisa's eyes clouded over with concern.

"No, no. A friend. Um. Nicole."

"Who's Nicole? I thought I knew all your friends. Even the lovely Justine."

"No, she's not really a friend. A cousin. My mother's cousin."

Lisa shrugged. "Let's make it next Monday, then, okay? We need to get the labels before we reserve the trunks."

"Sure," Erica said.

She was operating on two planes: one here sitting on this locker room bench pulling on her jeans, one existing entirely beyond this constricted world. She could carry on friendly conversations, pick up Sophia from the gym's childcare, and buy matzoh at Rothman's—because she remembered that was the thing Debbie kept reminding her about—all the while flashing on Stephan and his little silver locket, and the lights of Staten Island, and the lush way Josh Horton's fingers raced over the piano keys, like they were unleashing a force far beyond the capability of his hands.

But she didn't have time to drive all the way over to Rothman's. Egg matzoh was disgusting anyway. Ron's taste in matzoh was as bad as his taste in music. She'd pick up regular matzoh at the regular supermarket later. She took Sophia to the pediatricians for her checkup and then fed her milk and cereal before picking up the preschool carpool and depositing the twins at their friend Andy Spicer's house, before driving across the railroad tracks to Nick's, across the street from the pet store, two blocks up the street from her parents'. Blood skated through her veins like helium.

Nick lived in a rundown Victorian. A few straggly irises

bloomed in the front yard. The screen door had rusty hinges and torn wire, but the wooden door behind it was thick and hand carved, with a stained-glass porthole.

He opened the door, a stocky man heading into premature middle age. His skin had the yellowish tint of an olive-skinned person who didn't get outside often enough. He smiled at her through thin lips, with the same aura of detached bemusement that characterized his phone manner.

"Oh, well, hello, Rikki," he said. "Come on in."

The small entryway opened onto a parlor room, which, despite the ornate fireplace mantel and built-in bookshelves, bore a neglected bachelor air about it: dingy shag carpet, an overly elaborate stereo system with shoulder-high speakers, a television, and a round tiled coffee table with a Styrofoam container on it filled with dried-out chow mein. A stack of magazines rested unsteadily against the arm of the overstuffed couch.

"How did you know my stupid nickname?" Erica hovered uncertainly over the couch. "Nobody but my family calls me Rikki."

Nick fluffed the sofa pillows in an impotent attempt to straighten up. "Last time I spoke to you, I believe you answered to Rikki? Debbie Shapiro's your big sister, right? Debbie Lassler these days. Mother of Jared?" He winked.

With that wink, it came back to her. She knew Nick from school. He'd entered Mrs. Twombley's third-grade class late, having moved from Illinois, and she'd been assigned against her will to show him around. He was one of those kids who sat in the back and didn't call much attention to themselves. He'd won a multiplication prize on upper elementary math night, she recalled. In high school he'd starred on the wrestling team. He'd even signed her senior yearbook, she was sure.

"I don't believe I've seen you since high school," she said, though as she uttered that sentence, she realized she had, just the other day at the pet store, buying dog food. His dog, an Irish setter, lounged on the couch, shedding hair.

"You haven't changed a bit," said Nick. "You still look like you could beat me up."

"Right," Erica said.

"No, I'm not kidding. You've got those naturally sexy shoulders, those muscular arms, those long legs. You were on the track team, right? You still do any sports?" His eyes washed over her body.

"Just aerobics class and jogging once in a while," she said.

"What beautiful eyes on that baby!" Nick exclaimed. "Your first?" He fluffed Sophia's tufts of black hair.

"No," Erica said. "My first girl. My fourth child."

"Wow. You don't look like a mother of four." Nick motioned for her to sit down. He didn't remotely resemble Erica's notion of a drug dealer.

"Jared and Ashley and some of their buddies come and hang out here after school. I like to set up a friendly space for them, when they don't feel like going home." Nick waved his hand around, indicating the couch, the stereo, and the TV.

"Do you know my sister Debbie?" The couch bounced under her rear end.

"Oh, sure," Nick grinned. "She's a nice enough lady, on the anxious side. Her husband's an asshole, though. Sorry."

"That's okay. I don't like him either." Sophia wriggled madly in Erica's arms but she hesitated to put her down on the grotty couch. She didn't want to sit around and make small talk. "So," she said. "About those CDs."

"I've got them right here," Nick said. "Same music you've listened to before. Want to listen right now, with me?"

The idea appealed to Erica, quite a lot, in fact, despite the smarmy Nick and the smell of decaying Chinese food. But the necessity of putting Sophia down on a carpet where she saw dried cheese fragments and a broken paper clip made her decline. "I'll just buy them," she said.

"That'll be $150," he said, reaching into the drawer of an antique roll-top desk, sending a pile of pamphlets tumbling to the floor. Erica picked them up, shuffling the pile back into shape. Housemates.

"Don't tell me this is your business too?" she asked. "Everybody I know is recommending you."

"Yeah, I'm a multifaceted guy." Nick stuffed the stack of pamphlets into a cubicle at the back of the desk. "Need a housekeeper?"

"No. Everyone else just thinks I do." An Elvis Presley clock chimed the noon hour by bellowing out "You Ain't Nothin' but a Hound Dawg." Erica dug in her purse for the cash, balancing Sophia precariously on her hip.

"Thanks for the stuff," she said.

For good measure she stopped by the pet store and picked up some decorative orchids and a better heat lamp for Sammy before getting back in her car.

CHAPTER SEVENTEEN

Ethan stepped out of his town car late afternoon, tired, distracted, and smelling of airplane air. He dumped his suitcase in the hallway and dropped his suit jacket on the stairs. Erica reminded him they were due at her parents in a half hour for the seder.

The small brick three-bedroom house where Erica grew up sat literally across the railroad tracks, in West Meadow Heights. Everything within remained essentially the same as she remembered from childhood; furniture accumulated on sale, with care and taste, maintained diligently with a dust rag and lemon oil. Before her mother got her real estate license, she'd sublimated her significant nervous energy making things: curtains, slipcovers, crocheted doilies for her potted plants. Her father, an engineer, now retired for two years, still built things: an entertainment center, a backyard deck, cabinets to hold the toys that still filled the basement. Dad received a decent pension, but despite the money flowing in from her mother's real estate business, they still couldn't bring themselves to buy new. So all their carefully accumulated and crafted possessions stayed in place, verging on the edge of shabbiness, in time-warped hues of avocado and orange.

Erica's boys didn't care. They loved their grandparents' house, especially the miniature railroad in the basement, which they ran down to as soon as they arrived. Her father was setting the table with Mom's good china, Haggadahs, wineglasses, plastic cups for the kids, and a full seder plate. Debbie was centering a sponge cake from Leonard's on a silver tray. Ron was watching the Mets game. Jared sat on the floor, leafing through a copy of *Guitar* magazine. Erica smelled aluminum-foil pans of roast chicken reheating.

Ron pumped Ethan's hand. "So how about those Mets!" he

asked in his smooth, melodious DJ voice that was completely at variance with his stringy body and annoying mannerisms.

"What about them?" He smiled politely, as if Ron were a pesky client he needed to accommodate.

"They're on a roll." Ron waved his arms enthusiastically. "And how about those Yankees?" he continued gleefully. "Fading fast!"

"I'm more of a basketball fan," shrugged Ethan, following the boys downstairs to the model railroad.

Ron turned his jovial beady eyes toward Erica. "Well, at least you like baseball," he said. "Even though you root for the wrong team. Watch out for Mookie Wilson. He's the best first baseman the Mets have ever had."

"He doesn't hold a candle to Don Mattingly," Erica said.

Debbie emerged from the kitchen, holding a blue platter. "Why don't you put the matzoh on here, Rikki?" she asked.

"Oh my God, I completely forgot!"

"I told you to go to Rothman's. I told you several times. I remember distinctly."

"The stuff's kind of tasteless, to tell you the truth," said Erica.

"Matzoh is the major symbol of Passover!" Mom, hovering over Debbie, scrunched up her forehead and scratched the back of her neck.

"I'll go to Rothman's right now, before they close at sundown," Erica said. A car ride appealed more by the second.

"I'll come with you," Jared announced, slamming the door behind them before his parents could register any objection.

Erica pulled out of the driveway, plugging in her Jefferson Starship tape. "I tried talking to your mother about the boot camp," she told Jared. "I didn't get anywhere."

"So, what else is new?' He slumped down in his seat, fiddling with something in his pants pockets.

Erica hummed along to the Starship's song "Sara." Like most of her favorite songs, it had a dreamy, floaty quality. "Don't you love this song?" she asked.

"It's all right," Jared said.

They drove along, listening to the music, not really conversing, arriving at Rothman's just as the grumpy proprietor was locking the door. They convinced him to reopen the cash register and sell them his last two boxes of matzoh.

"Wanna get high?" Jared asked, pulling a joint from his pocket as they passed West Meadow Park on their return.

"Sure," Erica said. "By the duck pond?"

They sat down on a bench across from Porky Pig the Litter Eater, a larger-than-life pink pig face that opened its mouth every ninety seconds, repeating, "I'm porky pig the litter eater. Give your litter to me."

"This stupid pig has been here ever since I was in high school," Erica said. She took a hit off the joint, then another, then a third.

"So, did you like my little present?" Jared asked.

"Yeah," said Erica, embarrassed, wanting to change the subject. "So, what are you reading in *Guitar* magazine?" she asked.

"About Van Halen. About how he's the best guitarist in history."

"No way. He doesn't compare to Eric Clapton. Did you ever listen to 'Layla'?"

"Clapton was on heroin then."

Erica looked at her nephew, cross-legged, leaning forward, his expression earnest and frowning, his black T-shirt loose at his shoulders. Debbie didn't understand that teenage indifference was a fraudulent front, slender protection against a raw pit of emotion deep enough to drown in. Waves of purple and orange swirled along the horizon, backlit by the setting sun, as Porky made regular pronouncements from his open maw.

"Feed the starving pig!" Erica cried.

Gathering up paper cups, scrunched napkins, and discarded notices, they stuffed them down Porky's mouth, laughing hysterically, their faces pink from the evening chill.

"We'd better get back, "Erica said, when they'd exhausted their supply. The purple and orange stripes had faded from the sky. It was nearly dark.

Jared zipped his nylon jacket up around his neck. They walked toward the car in damp grass, dodging duck poop.

"Dad hits me," he said softly. "He used to spank me when I was little, any time I did anything remotely bad. Now he hits me for real, for nothing. Once he hit me because I wouldn't eat my meatloaf!"

A chilly breeze whipped through. They both shivered.

"Nobody believes me," Jared said. "Nobody but Ashley. I'm the dropout from the gifted program, and I'm the bad boy."

"Has your Mom seen him hit you?" Erica asked.

"Yeah. She doesn't like it, but it doesn't matter. Whatever he says goes."

"That's inexcusable." Erica grabbed both his hands, looking deeply into his eyes. It was an odd sensation, like mother to child, but not quite. Both their sets of eyes, so similarly round and long lashed, their swollen black pupils surrounded by hazel, flecked with gray, took up all the available space. "Does he hit your Mom too?"

"Oh no," Jared said, averting his eyes ever so slightly, twisting out from under her grip. "He treats her like a princess."

As she was parking in front of her parents' house, Jared said, "I saw him hit her once."

"What did he do? Where did he hit her?" Erica drummed her fingers on the dashboard in time to the music.

"I didn't actually see it. I heard it. They were in their bedroom, and Mom screamed. She was screaming, 'Don't do that to me, Ron!'"

"And then what? What did you do?"

"Oh, I dunno. I didn't know what to do. I think Ashley called, and then when I got off the phone, Dad was working in the yard, and Mom was boiling some potatoes or something."

"Jesus," Erica muttered. "I can't believe this."

Debbie banged on the car window.

Erica turned off the engine, opened the door and stepped out.

"What took you so long?" Debbie asked.

"Fighting litter," Jared muttered.

"You're holding up the seder."

"I got your matzoh," Erica said, handing Debbie the bag. She peered in. "You didn't get the egg kind," she said.

———

Dad raised the first glass of wine—Ethan's merlot—for the blessing.

"I can't drink because of the medication I'm on," said Debbie, taking delicate sips of seltzer water. Jared took a sip of wine before Ron grabbed the glass and exchanged it for grape juice.

"Oh, let the boy drink the wine," Dad said. "It's Passover."

"I think this young man caused quite enough excitement this spring with alcohol, don't you think?" said Ron.

"Babe, will you read the blessing for the bitter herbs?" Dad asked Mom.

Debbie refused the bitter herbs. She said the horseradish hurt her stomach and that Jared shouldn't eat it either due to his DDD medication. She didn't think he should eat the matzoh either, because of his wheat allergy, and produced some rice crackers from her purse. They sat untouched on Jared's plate.

Dylan read the Four Questions, a task he'd been practicing daily. "Halilah hazeh, halilah hazeh," he sang softly and quickly, his curly head bent down over the book, his right hand pulling nervously at his ear.

"Fantastic," Erica said, reaching across the table and squeezing his hand. She drank her second glass of wine.

Mom, Debbie, and Erica served the dinner—gefilte fish, matzoh ball soup, brisket, chicken, potato kugel, green beans. "This is delicious," Mom proclaimed. "Can you believe it's all takeout?"

"It's great, babe," Dad said.

"Great matzoh ball soup," Ethan concurred, flashing his engaging smile. Mom often told Erica she liked Ethan's smile, though she'd also told her on numerous occasions that she found him too slick, too workaholic, too reserved, too Californian, in so many ways not the husband she'd imagined for Erica. Somehow even her marriage to a wealthy investment banker had managed to be a disappointment.

"This brisket is too salty," muttered Ron.

"Would you like something else, Ron?" Mom fluttered and hovered. "A chicken leg? Some tuna fish? I think we've got leftover lentil soup."

"No, don't bother," Ron said, picking at the roast potatoes. "I'm not very hungry."

After dinner, dessert, and the afikomen hunt, Jared suggested a singing contest. "I can sing 'Chad Gadyah' all in one breath," he said, rocketing through all twelve verses in a squeaky fast voice. "Two zuzim," he finished breathlessly, red-faced and coughing.

"Jared, are you all right? Do you need your inhaler?" Debbie reached inside her purse.

Jared shook his head.

"Jared hyperventilates," Debbie announced to the table. "His asthma comes on when he gets overexcited. "It's part of his DDD. Jared, honey, are you sure you don't need your inhaler? You look awfully tired."

Shaking his head again, Jared got up from the table and disappeared.

"I hope his stomach is okay," said Debbie. "There was wheat in that chicken breading."

The boys ran back down to the model trains in the basement. Ron and Dad retreated to the living room. Ethan stepped outside, presumably to smoke one of his clove cigarettes. Erica didn't think he'd cut down at all. In fact, she even suspected he was substituting some regular tobacco ones for the clove. She was not about to call him out on his bad habits, though.

Mom and Debbie commenced cleanup. Erica sat down in the living room to nurse Sophia. Ron was complaining to Dad about the new adult contemporary format on his morning show.

"I can't relate to the songs on the playlist. They all sound alike. Three-chord wonders, all of them. No depth. No romance. You know what I mean, David?"

"I'm not the best judge. I've never been one for popular music. Well, I think I'll see what the boys are up to downstairs." Dad made a quick exit, averting his eyes from Erica's semiexposed breasts.

"Well, nice of you to join me," Ron said, exhibiting no such discomfort. "Your husband's done one of his vanishing acts."

"He likes to be outside. He's indoors all day at work."

"Poor baby. You know, I wanted to continue my college education, become an electrical engineer. I was going to when I got out of the service. But then I met Deb, and little Jared came along, put the kibosh on that fantasy. Now I'm stuck playing Loggins and Messina."

Erica burped Sophia. Curdled milk dribbled onto Mom's rust-colored tweed couch. She mopped it up with the fringe of her shirt.

"Is her little tummy upset?" asked Ron.

"No, it's normal," Erica said.

"Little children, little problems, big children, big problems. You give everything to these kids, and then they grow up and treat you like crap."

"I gotta change her diaper," Erica said.

———

By the time she made it back to the kitchen, Mom and Debbie were bundling the last of the leftovers into Tupperware, loading silverware into the dishwasher, and cleaning crumbs out of the crevices of the aluminum containers. Somehow they'd managed to create as much work out of this takeout dinner as if they'd cooked it from scratch.

"Can I help?" Erica asked.

"No," said Mom. "We're nearly done." They looked robust and purposeful, a matched pair.

"I wonder if Jared's in the bathroom," said Debbie, as she stashed the last pan away. She followed Erica into the rear hallway. "His wheat allergy gives him terrible diarrhea."

"He's not in here," Erica noted superfluously, while Debbie looked down the toilet as if Jared might have fallen in. The rear window was open to the backyard, letting in a breath of fragrant evening air.

"I wonder where he went. It smells like oranges in here," Debbie said, sniffing.

In the dimmer light of the powder room, Debbie looked paler. Her upper arms flapped like chicken wings. On the inside of her right elbow, a square flesh-colored bandage stood out, loose at one edge, vaguely menacing.

Erica pictured blood, scarlet and viscous, pulsing beneath the thin surface of Debbie's skin. She took a deep breath. "Did you get the results of those tests?" she asked.

Debbie whispered tentatively, "It's a blood disorder." She opened the medicine cabinet as if Jared could shrink and disappear there among the aspirin.

"You told me it wasn't leukemia, right? Erica asked, getting that pressure sensation at the back of her head. She followed Debbie aimlessly into Mom's sewing room, on what used to be the back porch.

"No, no," Debbie said. "Nothing like that. It's some kind of rare disorder. Nobody knows what caused it." Debbie turned her right hand palm up, revealing one pale, veiny wrist. "My capillaries? Is that the right word? They bleed easier than normal."

Erica averted her eyes from Debbie's mottled skin. She searched her rusty nurse's brain for names of obscure blood disorders but couldn't come up with any that didn't manifest themselves shortly after birth. "That's really weird," she said. "Debbie, tell me the truth. Has Ron ever hit you?"

Debbie recoiled. "How could you ever say such a thing?"

"Well, I never heard of a blood disease like that, and Ron's always had a bad temper. And Jared's said some stuff to me."

"Stuff? What kind of stuff?"

"Oh, nothing. I mean, he thinks Ron is very hard on him. He says Ron has hit him for all kinds of minor offenses."

Debbie bristled, her spine erect, her dimpled chin, identical to Jared's, jutting out of her round face. "Rikki! That's the most ridiculous thing I've ever heard! I'll try and forget you ever said it."

"You know, Ron's a Vietnam vet and all. Sometimes they get violent."

Debbie's almond eyes clouded over, impassive and impenetrable. "Rikki, you've seen too many movies. Ron is strict. He believes in discipline. But he's never laid a hand on Jared."

"He threw food in his face."

"Would you stop bringing that up? I don't want to talk about this anymore."

Mom's fancy Singer with the quilting attachment sat on a specially designed table, protected by a tea-green cozy, crocheted by Debbie. Spriggy flowered cottons, folded and arranged by color, lined the shelves, awaiting incorporation into quilts that Mom no longer found the time to sew. Even in the shadowy dark of the sewing room everything looked sprightly and innocent on the surface, but surfaces betrayed nothing of what lurked underneath. Sparks sputtered in Erica's belly. If only she could retreat into the shelter of her body and burst into flames. She was starving for air.

"Do you feel all right, Rikki? You look very tired." Debbie said.

"I am tired," she admitted. "I have a headache."

Debbie's face softened. "I have Advil if you'd like." She dug into her purse and handed Erica a plastic canister. "Maybe Jared is in the basement with your boys. He always loved those trains." She scurried into the hall and down the stairs.

Erica walked out onto the patio where at least she could breathe. Jared sat quietly by the barbeque in the moonlight. Above him, her mother's hanging pots, overflowing with pansies, swayed in the breeze.

"Well, hello there," she said.

"Hello," said Jared, smashing an ant with his foot. "Sorry you couldn't join me in the bathroom for a mood refresher."

"That would have been difficult to facilitate."

"I meant to ask you, what do you think of Nick? He told me you stopped by for a visit."

"Oh, he's okay, I guess. I went to high school with him."

Jared scraped his foot across the concrete, massacring more helpless ants. "He's a Safe House leader at the family clinic. He leads therapy groups and retreats and stuff. Mom loves him. Isn't that a kick? I mean, they're all so clueless."

"Did your mom tell you about her weird capillary disease?" Erica asked.

"Yeah. Have you seen those bruises on her arms and legs? She tries to hide them, and she keeps telling me and Dad that its nothing, but I think she's lying. I think they're more serious than she's letting on."

"I don't believe she really has a blood disorder." Erica ineffectually scraped off chunks of charred detritus from the barbeque grill.

"Do you think maybe that when she said, 'Don't, Ron,' to Dad, they were just arguing about something? Like maybe that he sprays Roundup on the cherry tree? She doesn't like it when he does that. It makes me break out in hives." He twisted the ends of his black T-shirt, which had a skull on it and flowers for eye sockets.

"Could be," Erica said. "But I doubt it."

"It's me he hates," Jared said.

Ron's resonant voice boomed from within the house. "Get your tuchas out from wherever you are, Jared! We're leaving right now!"

"I have a CD for you. Tomorrow morning," Jared whispered urgently.

"Okay," Erica said, half listening. A robin nibbled at the bird feeder. The pansies gleamed in the creamy light of the full moon. She wanted to bathe in that light, to swallow it whole.

CHAPTER **EIGHTEEN**

Erica rushed home from aerobics, begging out on further discussion of Dylan's and Jason Schrabner's Whispering Wind camp trunks. She didn't have the patience for mundane conversation. The sun was rising steeply in a vivid blue sky. The haze from the expressway and the parkway had drifted elsewhere, and the mild breeze smelled pure as the Catskills. The impatiens in front of Jeff Russell's old house glistened purple and pink. The whole world seemed supersaturated. When she arrived home, only mildly surprised to find Jared and Ashley at her doorstep, it only accelerated the sensation.

Jared looked lankier and paler than ever, his hair devoid of green glue, bleached at the ends and hanging limply over the tops of his ears. He wore tight black jeans and that same black skull T-shirt. She noticed a new stud in his right ear. Ashley wore tight jeans too and a clingy flowered Betsey Johnson top. They both wore heavy backpacks.

Jared handed her the new Robert Palmer CD. "It's kind of pop, but I figured you'd like it," he said.

"Thanks," she said, standing there with Sophia on her hip, awaiting what might come next. If Jared had warned her last night, she didn't remember.

"Well, this is it," he said. "This is the day. I can't stand it anymore. I'm leaving home."

"But where will you go?" Erica asked, hitching Sophia up onto her shoulder. This was more than she had bargained for.

"To my friends Roger and Griffin in Philadelphia," said Ashley. "They were teachers at my old Waldorf School. They're like, at least forty, but they're cool, like you." Ashley tickled Sophia under the chin.

"He's got this house where we can stay, and Ashley says he can even get us jobs," Jared added. "I'd love to earn my own money. Dad never pays me for all those hours I spend slaving away on his stupid lawn."

"How will you get there?" Erica asked, unbuttoning her jacket. Underneath her zipped-up cotton jacket, beads of sweat trickled down her stomach.

"We're taking the train," Ashley said. "Don't worry—we're not hitchhiking or anything."

In high school, on hot days like this when summer seemed close enough to touch, Erica would cut class and take the LIRR into Penn Station and then the subway to the Village or the Upper West Side or even Times Square. Just to walk around through the streets and shops permeated with light and color and noise, breathing in the air filmy with dirt, feeling part of whatever might be going on. Just to open herself to the possibility that something earth-shattering was about to happen. Not that anything ever did. She always caught the train home in time for dinner, telling her parents she'd been studying at the library or that cross-country practice ran late.

On her square of green front lawn, the earth crinkled and shook. She could dither and second-guess or plunge ahead on blind instinct. Her instinct, in the bright immediacy of the day, repeated the same message as Jared's: get out while you can. She dug into her wallet and handed over three hundred dollars. "For whatever," she said. "Call me. Let me know you're all right."

"Of course I will, Aunt Rikki. Thanks so much for everything." Jared put the money in the zippered pocket of his backpack.

Ashley poked him in the side. "We gotta catch the train."

"Call me. Please." Erica watched them run down the street, toward the train station, backpacks jiggling, and the way their images were caught in the filtered sunlight made Erica think of a photograph, as if the event occurring right before her eyes had already happened some time ago.

The street filled with a thick silence. From a distance came the hum of the expressway, the whine of a leaf blower. A bright-yellow bird with red striped wings, so luminescent in color that it looked to have escaped from a cage rather than existing freely in nature, landed on their one tree, a big old maple. Overnight the maple's leaves had transformed from tentative pastel to full-blown summer green. The bird cawed.

"Da!" exclaimed Sophia, swiveling to track the bird as it soared up from the branch in an arc across the sky. "Da. Da. Doo. Doo. Da!"

"'A da da da. A doo doo da. That's all I want to say to you,'" Erica sang, cradling her daughter.

She walked inside, put Sophia down on her play mat, and chopped up a batch of collard greens for Sammy, who had grown a foot since his purchase. He stared at her with his dinosaur face. She was being paranoid, she knew, but those amber eyes seemed to be observing her, rendering judgment.

CHAPTER NINETEEN

Erica could not sit still. She folded laundry, paid bills, scrubbed fingerprints off of all the doorknobs of the house, ordered some art materials from a children's catalog called Strawberry Alarm Clock and swim trunks from another one called Watery Wonderland, and then shopped for groceries and picked up the camp trunks with Lisa.

Debbie's inevitable call came after school, as she was leaving to pick up electrical wiring for Dylan's Lego robot.

"Oh my God, Rikki!" Debbie screeched. "I went by school to pick Jared up for his allergist appointment, and he wasn't there! Apparently he never showed up for school this morning! They were supposed to call me if he skipped class! They promised!"

The photographic image returned to Erica: Jared and Ashley rounding the corner and walking off into the clear perfect morning, their backpacks bobbing behind them. With that action, they'd mutated into bouncing dots, location unknown.

"Though guess who else is missing," Debbie's shrieks dissolved into tremulous, tearful snorts. "Ashley. I'm trying to get in touch with her mother, but she's such a flake—she could be in Aruba for all I know."

Erica pictured tears running down Debbie's cheeks, streaked with blue eye shadow. A lump rose in her throat, thick and sad; she punched it down.

Dylan fidgeted by the refrigerator, nibbling on an apricot Roll-Up. "Mom, hurry up," he whined. "I need you."

"I'll be right with you, honey," she whispered.

"Do you have any possible idea where he might have gone?" Debbie pleaded. "Did he say anything to you? You know, he likes you. He told me Sunday that you were the only person in the family who wasn't a total idiot. Those were his exact words."

Even Debbie admitted that Jared knew who was on his side. Erica was protecting the child, and when it came down to the wire, wasn't that her obligation as a mother? Debbie lied to Erica about her marriage, her bruises, her whole life. Surely she could lie to Debbie about Jared.

"No, I'm sorry, I have no idea at all." Erica felt dizzy, her cheeks flushed and hot. "I have to go now."

"Are you all right, Mommy?" Dylan asked. "You look all red."

"I'm fine," she said. "Let's get that robot together."

That evening Ethan called to tell Erica that he could not fly home that weekend. He'd given a presentation on his nonlinear asymmetric frameworks, allowing for comparisons of non-nested models, and the CEO of West Coast operations, James Ranken, happened to be in the Boca Raton office. He'd told Ethan he was really impressed with his work and invited him and Erica's buddy Stephan, remember him, out to LA for a meeting Monday. So, as long as he had to fly out West anyway, he thought he'd spend the weekend surfing with his sister Pauline in Mendocino. Erica didn't mind, did she?

No, of course not, Erica assured him. "Jared ran away from home," she added.

"Jesus," Ethan said. Erica swore she could hear him picking his ear over the phone. "It's a dangerous world out there for a naïve kid like him."

Jared was naïve, Erica admitted to herself. At his age, she'd routinely hitchhiked with her friends across the Island to Nassau Beach. She doubted that Jared had ever before so much as ventured on a public bus. "Yeah, but—" she started to say.

"Not to change the subject," Ethan interrupted, "but something else I forgot to mention. I'm going to be working in the Boca office the first ten days of June."

"So," Erica said. She paced about the kitchen with the cordless, wiping up spills: raspberry jam, cereal crumbles, dirt from Dylan's baseball cleats.

"So, but this time they've offered to put everybody up, the kids too, in a really nice hotel for ten days. It's right on the beach. There's a pool. Everything paid for. They'll even get you a rental car. You can take the kids to Disney World."

"They're still in school in June," she said, wiping down the handle to the refrigerator. "Dylan has his robotics fair."

"Can't he stay with a friend or something?"

Erica thought of Don Johnson and coconut oil. She thought of breezy quiet: no phones, no lies, though, probably, no coke, which already seemed difficult to imagine, shimmering as it did, consistently, at the edge of her consciousness.

"Whaddya think?" asked Ethan expectantly.

"I'll make it happen," Erica said.

—

Sunday night brought the standard family dinner at her parents', featuring takeout from Taste of Tuscany. Everyone sat quietly, picking at their chicken parmigiana; only Erica's father, David, ate with any gusto.

"Mom sold a travel agent a six bedroom house in Westbury Manor, new construction," he announced proudly. "And not only did she earn a tidy commission," he said, his arm around her mother, "but she booked us—at considerable savings—on a tour of European capitals for our fortieth anniversary this August."

"That's nice," muttered Debbie weakly.

"I'd be so happy now," Mom sniffled, "if it wasn't for Jared."

Erica arranged her stuffed shells in a spiral as her father detailed the Athens leg of the trip.

"Oh, David, how can you talk about vacationing at a time like this!" Mom scratched the back of her neck.

"Life has to go on. As best as it can, babe. Let me show the kids the whole itinerary." He left the table to rummage around on his desk.

"That's a sweet tank top, Rikki," Ron said.

Erica ignored him, though she did like her new tank top, a size 8–10, ribbed, with a T-back.

"Didja see the game last night?" Ron tapped the dining room table for emphasis. "Mookie Wilson got five hits against the Padres."

"You know I never watch the stupid Mets." Erica drizzled tomato sauce in lines across the pasta, like it was one of the twins' preschool art projects. She didn't mind Ron's baseball banter. It perpetuated the illusion he was actually the jovial, all-American fellow he made himself out to be.

"At least you're a baseball fan," Ron said, as if reading her mind. "Your husband is too good for sports. What does he do in his spare time, watch algebra competitions?"

"He plays tennis," Erica said. "He runs. He plays basketball. He's surfing this weekend. He just doesn't sit around in an armchair watching sports on TV."

"Well, well," said Ron, pushing a piece of bread around his plate. "Aren't we special."

Dylan and the twins vanished down to the basement to play with the toy trains, followed in short order by their grandfather, who had evidently forgotten about showing them the tour itinerary. Her mother stood up, repackaging the barely touched food and beginning the nightly kitchen purification. For once, Debbie did not leap up to join her, instead picking at a hangnail on her index finger. Ron disappeared to regrout a leak in the powder room tile.

Mom reappeared with two cups of tea. "Why don't you two girls relax a bit? Given everything."

Erica felt exposed, alone with Debbie. She missed the buffer of the phone. Nor did she relish sitting on her butt and drinking tea. She tapped her fingers against the table.

"Ooh, can you stop that?" Debbie asked. "I have a headache."

"Sorry," Erica said, but her fingers drummed of their own accord. Headache or no, Debbie rehashed Jared's fifteen years, attempting to pinpoint the specific moment when things started going wrong. She blamed Ashley for most of Jared's mistakes. "I should have known," Debbie confessed. "Jared was always such a sweet, vulnerable little boy. She put all kinds of crazy ideas into his head. The little bitch." Debbie sighed, leaned back in her chair, and put another spoonful of real sugar, with its full sixteen calories, into her coffee. "Do you think he's having sex?"

Erica pictured the way Ashley traced her hands around Jared's hipbones. "It wouldn't surprise me."

"He's not ready. He's just a little boy." Debbie sat straight up in her chair. "Oh my God," she cried. "Do you think he could get AIDS?"

"From who? From Ashley? Don't only gay people get that?"

"Oh, Rikki." Debbie collapsed her head onto her arms, narrowly missing her coffee cup. "You have no idea what it's like to try and sleep at night not knowing where your baby is."

"Did it ever occur to you," Erica ventured, "that Ron's temper might have driven Jared away?"

"Oh, my goodness, no," Debbie said. "I mean, Jared's been testing Ron's authority for months—it's a sign of his DDD—but we've been working on that in family therapy. I can't believe tensions were at the point that on his own he would have run away without the urging of that awful girl. He's got poor impulse control—that's another sign of DDD. He's overinfluenced by his peers. And you've got to have some understanding for Ron. He's under terrible pressure." Debbie sighed. "They're changing the format of his show from easy listening to adult contemporary."

"You told me."

"He can't choose his playlist anymore. And they don't like his voice, his beautiful voice. They want more youthful patter, whatever that is. Probably jokes about penises. There's even talk the station might get bought out! And then all this trouble with Jared—it's the last straw. I don't understand this world."

"I'm planning a family party for the twins' fifth birthdays," Erica said. "Their friends party is going be at Music Makers in the morning and the family party at our house in the afternoon."

"How can you talk about parties right now?" Debbie groaned.

"The twins are turning five. They deserve a birthday party. Like Dad said, life must go on."

"That's easy for you to say," Debbie said. "Did you see those whole cloves of garlic in the tomato sauce? They gave me heart-burn."

Mom reappeared with a pitcher of hot water. "It's so sweet of Ron to fix our bathroom tile, Debbie. He told me he found a leak under the sink too. David says we should redo the whole room, but I can't bear to spend the money." She refilled their cups.

"I can't drink any more liquid, Mom." Debbie sighed.

"It's only tea," Mom said.

"Didn't you read—tea has almost as much caffeine as coffee." Debbie burped loudly. "Oh, jeez, can you smell that garlic breath! My stomach is absolutely in spasms!"

"Do you need to lie down dear?" Mom asked. "I have Tums."

"I have to pee," Erica said.

Her head was buzzing. She needed some clarity, some strength, some distance. She was already fumbling for her coke, now sharing space with excess pennies in her change purse, when she noticed Ron's flat ass sticking out of the bathroom vanity. He was tightening a screw on the sink drain. She pictured those arms pummeling into Jared's face.

"Mom can call a plumber, you know." She wasn't scared of his arms at all. She wasn't a kid like Jared. Ron had been out of the Marines for a long time now, sitting on that flat ugly butt at the radio station. He didn't work out with weights like she did. She bet she could beat him up if she really tried.

Ron kept turning the screwdriver, his face reddening with the effort. "Not everyone can waste money like that," he said. "Plumbers charge seventy-five dollars an hour for a home visit."

A stray tissue from Erica's purse landed on his buzz cut. He rotated his head slowly upward in that wiry, snaky way of his. She could feel his pale-blue eyes burning through the cotton rib of her tank top. "Looking good, Rikki," he said. "You working out more or something?"

"It's those naturally sexy shoulders," she was tempted to say, but she didn't say anything, just took a couple steps backward, banging into the doorknob. If Jared had been there, they would have winked at each other and shared a secret laugh. They would have snuck off to the park and gotten high together.

"There, I fixed it. No plumber required." Ron slammed his screwdriver on the counter as if it were responsible for the leak. "The police are useless," he groused. "And so are all those 'I'm okay, you're okay' psych airheads. That Nick Stromboli, the Safe House counselor—did my wife praise him to the skies? He's a wimpy pervert, if you ask me. I'm hiring a private detective to find my son."

CHAPTER TWENTY

On the advice of both Ron and her boss at the salon, Debbie took a leave from work. On her first free morning, she showed up with a new and unlikely friend, Ashley's mother, Patti.

Running away was nothing new for Ashley, Patti assured them, though she admitted that this, Ashley's most recent misadventure, was putting her over the edge. Patti's husband, a garment district executive, had filed for divorce. He was refusing to pay any child support, and she had no idea how she was going to cover the $3,000 monthly mortgage on their house, much less pay the housekeeper, Georgia, not that she was any great shakes.

"Did you get her from Housemates?" Erica asked, pouring coffee and passing around a tray of cookies.

"Yeah, doesn't everybody?" Patti nibbled on a pistachio biscotti.

"Weren't you going to call Housemates?" Debbie asked. "Mom told me she gave you the number."

"I thought I might, but then I changed my mind," said Erica.

"You know, I can't get it out of my mind how you and Jared were spending so much time together before he ran away, Rikki. Every time the family got together, you two would mysteriously disappear. What were you doing, gossiping about what terrible parents Ron and I are?"

Erica looked into her sister's condescending face. She was only five years older, but it could have been an entirely different generation. "Just talking. About music and school and stuff. Being friendly. Isn't that what you asked me to do?" Erica sipped her coffee, one of Ethan's highly caffeinated Brazilian blends. He'd complained that it tasted too "winy," whatever that meant, but as far as Erica was concerned, it could have been her mother's three-year-old can of Chock Full O' Nuts—she needed all she could get.

"Well, I did suggest you reach out to him," Debbie said, "but that obviously was a mistake on my part. You don't seem to understand that we are the adults here. Jared is a child. When you interact with him like a friend, you undermine our authority. We just discussed that issue with Dr. Rafferty at the family clinic."

"You had a discussion regarding me?"

"Well, yes," said Debbie, pouring herself another cup of coffee, apparently unconcerned about the caffeine. "We discuss all relevant family members."

"Do you discuss how your husband throws plates of food at your son? Or that he hit him for not finishing his meatloaf?"

Debbie hand trembled, spilling coffee on the cuff of her sweater. "Who told you that?"

"Everybody at Lauren's bat mitzvah saw the plate of food."

"That thing about the meatloaf."

"Jared did."

Debbie furiously blotted at the cuff of her sweater and then dumped water on it, wringing it out on a stack of paper towels. "And you believed him? That is exactly my point. You may have four children, but you act like a teenager yourself, Rikki. Why, before this even started, as you recall, I limited Jared's access to you because of the language he heard at your house and your inappropriate movies and your utter disrespect for Ron's and my values." She tugged at her sweater cuff, now a uniform tan. "I think I've ruined this sweater, and it's one of my favorites."

"Now, now," said Patti. "Everyone is upset. We're all suffering."

"Dr. Rafferty said I should not be afraid to defend my values," said Debbie.

"Can we cut the drama? Isn't our priority to find out where the hell our children are?" Patti grabbed another biscotti. "Are you going to eat any of those or just feed them to us, Rikki?" she asked. "You've got the flattest tummy. I can't believe you just had a baby a few months ago."

"Yeah, you have lost weight, Rikki," Debbie said. "What's your secret?"

"Probably low carbohydrates," Patti said. "Everyone's swearing by low carbohydrates. Whatever works, that's what I say."

———

Debbie did not return for more coffee klatsches. Buoyed by Dr. Rafferty and her tentative friendship with Patti, her mysterious illness faded into the background. She tossed her hair into a casual ponytail and laid off the makeup. Her nervous exhaustion translated into a curious vibrancy. She spoke to all Jared's teachers at West Meadow High, all the kids in his multiple therapy groups, and even the kids who hung out by the smoking tree, questioning them about Jared's possible whereabouts. Almost daily, she picked up Patti and drove all around Soho and the Lower East Side, speaking to bums on the street, searching for any sign of Jared and Ashley.

Avoiding one-on-ones with Debbie, those loaded moments when something untoward might pop out of her mouth, proved a relief. One minute bled into the next as the days melted away. She sent out last-minute invitations to the twins' birthday parties, to both friends and family. She introduced Sophia to rice cereal and made it to aerobics every morning just in time to set up her step in the front center of the room, next to Justine. She lifted her legs, executed T-steps and L-steps, moved up to eight-pound weights. She sang along with Ari: "'We were so in phase in our dance hall days. We were cool on craze. Dance hall days.'"

One day after class she and Sophia went to the swimwear store next to Rothman's and bought a bathing suit for Florida. Nothing fit quite as well as she had anticipated. Taut as she'd believed she'd become, pouches of runaway flesh still popped out above her bikini bottom and around her side straps, and lumps of cellulite rippled down her legs. She bought a blue bikini anyway, size 8, with ties at the hips.

Weeks went by without Jared calling. Erica couldn't shake the image of her head of him and Ashley disappearing around the corner, backpacks bobbing, melding into the vibrant colors of the spring morning. It was an unsettling image, yet strangely compelling. She couldn't deny the suspended excitement that filled her days. She was opening herself up to the sensation of muted danger. It was starting to feel good. She supposed a war might feel like this, or at least a minor catastrophe like a tropical storm, the way all your senses were heightened and your blood flowed electric and the trees looked greener than green before the lightning hit.

She'd portioned her coke out in precise, small quantities, like Weight Watchers. Nonetheless, she'd been reduced to dredging up suspicious specks on the sides of her glassine bag. Even fortified by multiple cups of the industrial-strength winy Brazilian coffee, she dragged her feet. If only she could snort the grounds. She called Nick Stromboli again and asked him if she could buy more of his CDs. No big deal, she told herself. A household necessity like milk or diapers. Sure, he said, no problem, ten the next morning would be fine.

At 9:30 a.m. she parked in the pet store parking lot, justifying her presence by stopping in the store first and buying more decorative rocks and replacement bulbs for Sammy's heating lamp.

After putting her bags in the trunk, she surreptitiously crossed the street to Nick's house. She glanced up and down the sidewalk, seeing no one except a grandmotherly woman following a little blond girl on a scooter.

Nick did not answer the doorbell. She knocked hard and rang again, panic shooting through her like darts. This time she heard footsteps and a turn of the lock, and then Nick swung the door open. "Sorry," he said. "I was reading on the toilet. Come on in."

His living room was as airless and grotty as two weeks previous. Out of the corner of her eye, Erica could see a yellow Formica kitchen, vintage 1965, and off that, the open door to the bathroom. Deep Purple played on the stereo. On top of the speakers, a goldfish, healthier than her recently departed ones, navigated cloudy waters. Nick wore gray sweatpants and a T-shirt featuring two humping pigs and the slogan "Makin Bacon." The difference between this time and last time was that, oddly, the whole scenario comforted her. She sank onto the overstuffed couch, moving aside a pile of magazines as she did so.

"Did you like the CDs I gave you last time?" Nick asked.

Erica nodded.

"Wanna listen to the CDs with me this time?" "Under the Gun" blared out of the stereo, and the TV played some recycled situation comedy.

"Okay," she said.

"You can take your kid out of that carrier if you want," Nick said.

"No, thanks," Erica said. She might not be a housekeeper like Debbie, but between her and Isabella, the cleaning lady, they managed to suck up the obvious dust balls. Here at Nick's they took on a life of their own. God knew what Sophia might discover here, in the interstices of the brown shag carpet.

"Please yourself," Nick said. He laid out the lines of coke with the precision of a Benihana chef, all social and civilized, out in the open on a regular table. It felt kind of strange, with Sophia sleeping against her chest, but after a couple snorts, she felt clear and clean. The *Deep Purple* record clanged to an end.

"Can you put some better music on?" Erica asked.

"'Rikki, don't lose that number. I don't want nobody else,'" Nick sang.

"I hate Steely Dan! Don't make me sick. You have no idea how I got teased about that one in college." Erica leaned back against the scratchy couch.

"Journey?"

"Don't make me sicker." Erica groaned. "Do you have any Bloody Tampax?"

"Can't say as I do," said Nick. "My body doesn't work that way."

"It's the name of a band. They're a favorite of Jared's. I thought you might have heard of them."

"Oh, I suppose I might have." Nick wrinkled his nose. "I tend to tune that crap out. How about Fleetwood Mac?"

"That would be tolerable." She looked over at his turntable. "Don't you have a CD player?"

"Nope," said Nick, as "Tusk" tootled through the speakers. "I'm a dinosaur."

"You've got that in common with Debbie and Ron," Erica said.

"Even though Ron is a DJ. He was just switched over from easy listening to adult contemporary. Can you define adult contemporary?"

"Beats me. I haven't heard a good new song since 1975." Nick laid out a couple more lines, and Erica almost asked him to stop—that was enough—but she reconsidered. Once she was alone, she'd be economizing, parceling it out.

"Do you know anything about that boot camp for teenagers?" she asked.

"You mean the Pritima Center?" Nick chuckled. "Of course I do. I'm a community counselor for the family clinic, remember? The Pritima Center is Arlene Rafferty's pet project. She must get a commission from them."

"It sounds like some creepy military school. Is it?" Erica tentatively unzipped Sophia from her carrier, where she was awfully warm, and laid her on her lap.

"Not military, exactly." Nick said. "But the kids who go there come out podded. You know what I mean? You ever see *The Invasion of the Body Snatchers*?"

Erica nodded. "It's one of my husband Ethan's favorite films."

"I gotta thing for '50s sci-fi too. Maybe we should all go to the movies." Nick chuckled. "You know, given what you were like in high school, I couldn't picture you as you are today. Or then again, maybe I could." He leaned back against the couch cushions, only a few inches away from her. When he stuck his elbows behind his head, she could feel them gently grazing her hair. "You dated that guy Jeff, right? The one who always played guitar under the stairs?"

"Yeah, for a while." She was feeling so good, totally without reference to the outside world. Just good inside her body. Nothing could touch her. "Did you ever see *Lobsterman from Mars*?" she asked. That was another favorite of Ethan's. She'd watched it several times with him in college. She hungered for those aimless weekends, that luscious purposelessness. To lie around watching dumb TV until they all ventured out for burritos or peanut noodles, the afternoon already shot, the pale sun slipping below the winter horizon.

"Oh yeah, man, that movie was hilarious." Nick chuckled. "You remember how they finally killed him? They boiled him in water!"

Midday sun flitted in lacy patterns on the rug, illuminating a knot of dried pasta here, an indeterminate yellowish stain there. It was comforting to be in a place where nobody cared about such superficialities as vacuuming. Maybe that was what brought back such intense memories of Ethan's dorm room, with its discarded beer bottles and piles of tangled wires. She could see why kids gravitated here after school, for drugs, yeah, no doubt, but also Nick had a gentle, patient way about him. In this room, time slowed down, and she too started giggling like a stupid kid. Perhaps feeling the reverberations of her mother's laughter, Sophia stirred against her legs, and Erica, with a start, returned to a land where Jared was missing and time mattered.

"I gotta pick up Jesse and Jake at preschool," she said. She reached in her purse for ten twenties, just garnered from New Westminster Bank.

CHAPTER TWENTY-ONE

Ethan constructed a play castle from a kit by the glow of a flashlight. Erica, unable to sleep, lay on a futon on the upstairs balcony, listening to the rustles of the bags of parts, the bang of his hammer.

In the morning, he left for Florida again, apologizing profusely for missing the twins' birthday party, citing unavoidable meetings, bond market liquidity, governmental overreach, issues with Stephan Langston. He'd see her and the kids in Florida.

The boys were jumping off the turret, playing Masters of the Universe, when Erica opened the front door, admitting her parents, Ron, Debbie, Amelia, Jason, and their kids, Lauren and Jonathan.

"So, where are the birthday boys?" gushed Amelia, brandishing a large, brightly wrapped package.

"I didn't bring a gift," Debbie said. She was dressed crisply in a lavender pantsuit and hoop earrings. "I hope you understand. It's not like I've had time to shop."

"Don't worry, Deb. Dad and I brought enough for all of us," said Mom, displaying an overflowing bag from Roger Rabbit, the local high-end toy store. "I've been spending too much time on the Miracle Mile these days. Shopping as therapy." She sighed.

"What's to eat? I'm starving." Debbie lifted up the plastic on the cold-cuts tray and stuffed a slice of pastrami in her mouth. "Ron's really hungry too," she added. Debbie snapped open a can of Diet Coke. "He didn't have any lunch."

"I couldn't reach the damn electrician," he said. "Tried to rewire it myself, three trips to the hardware store, no luck."

"Debbie and Ron's kitchen lighting went bad," Mom explained to Erica. "Just what the poor things needed, with everything else on their plate."

Debbie and Ron nibbled cold cuts from the trays, dipping them in mustard. Erica gazed longingly at the lively tableau outdoors, wishing she could play the evil Skeletor chasing a crowd of helpless Earthlings, instead of Rikki, dutiful sister.

Amelia ran breathlessly inside. "How do you ever keep up with those kids?" she panted.

"Amelia," Mom said. "I've been trying to convince Rikki to give Housemates a call. You got your girl from Housemates, didn't you? Don't you love her?"

"Oh, Dahlia? I couldn't live without her!" Amelia downed a cup of Diet Coke in one gulp.

"Nick Stromboli must be doing very well with that Housemates business," Mom said. "I sold him his house last year, you know, and he paid cash! It isn't much to look at, but he told me he has all kinds of plans to fix it up. You know, Rikki, I could swear I saw you going in there the other day."

"Nope, never met the man," Erica said. She laid three slices of turkey in overlapping circles on top of a slice of rye bread, topping each slice with a bread-and-butter pickle at the precise center and a pimento stuffed olive at the center of that.

"Don't you remember—he starred on the West Meadow wrestling team? I believe you went to a couple of his meets. He owns that house across the street from the pet store. He's part of the Safe House program at the family clinic. Jared likes him a lot."

Debbie gulped at the mention of Jared and inhaled a dill pickle rolled up in a slice of salami.

"You must have seen me going into the pet store. Sometimes their parking lot is full and I have to park across the street." Erica sucked on a cherry tomato, letting the seeds spatter against the inside of her cheeks. "Have you met our new addition to the family? You can hold him if you like."

"That gross salmonella-carrying lizard?" said Debbie, coughing salami fragments into a napkin. "No, thanks."

"Debbie, do you think I should test Jonathan for DDD?" asked Amelia. "He's only in first grade, but he's spending half the day in the principal's office."

"Perhaps." Debbie guzzled the rest of her Coke. "Symptoms

can show up very early, and they're easier to treat then. I wish Jared had been diagnosed sooner."

The doorbell rang again; Erica admitted a slew of guests, including Lisa and Justine.

"You know Penny, my cocker spaniel?" Lisa poured herself a Diet Sprite.

"How could I not know about Penny, your cocker spaniel?" Lisa updated Erica on Penny's doings daily.

"Well, you know how crazy I am about her. I've been thinking of showing Penny, maybe breeding her, so I joined the American Spaniel Association, and would you believe they're having a formal ball?'

"A ball?" Erica couldn't bring herself to eat the turkey sandwich she'd so artistically constructed. She was rarely hungry anymore. Food looked pleasant enough displayed in its colorful variety in the supermarket, or in the refrigerator, or on the plate in front of her. But actually consuming it seemed irrelevant. She'd lost eight pounds in the past two weeks.

"Yeah, a ball, a whole big shebang, like a wedding or a bar mitzvah or something. Only you bring your dogs with you! They're having a whole cocker spaniel table! Say, Erica, I've been meaning to tell you, by the way, you look great! You've lost all your baby weight."

"Yeah, I wish you'd tell me your secret," Justine added.

Erica massaged the area around her belly button that until recently had been all bulges and wrinkles and folds. It still wasn't anywhere near flat, but it felt smoother and younger and tighter.

"Low carbohydrates," she said. "Like everyone."

The guests scattered: some outside by the castle, some downstairs with the Brio trains, Debbie and her mother clattering about in the kitchen. Erica sniffed Sophia's diaper: odorous. On her way back from changing it, she ran into Ron, fiddling with the stairway light switch.

"I think your connection is loose," he said. "Can't fix my house, I can fix yours."

"I'll ask my electrician to look at it," said Erica.

"You could have me look at it, you know. I might not have the official license, but I know what I'm doing."

"Not right now, okay? Can I get by? They're waiting for me in the dining room."

Ron waved his hands expansively, as he was prone to, blocking her progress. "I thought you might want to know that the private eye I hired spoke to Stromboli. He didn't have much to say. He's a loser, if you ask me. Most of those folks at that family clinic are losers, with their diagnoses and their therapies. Fat lot of good they did with Jared."

"I have to agree with you," Erica admitted. "But can I get through?"

Ron stayed resolutely put, standing with a stretched-out askew posture that gave him the aspect of a Gumby toy. "So, by any chance, do you have any idea where Jared ran off to?" he asked.

"No, why would I?" she replied. She couldn't stash Ron in a safe mental slot. He was so quick with the jokes, the facile compliments, the sports patter; he wasn't a DJ for nothing. She suspected he saw through her more readily than her earnest and sanctimonious sister.

"You and he being such good buddies of late and all," Ron continued.

"I told you, I don't know," Erica said. "I have to get back to the party."

Ron leaned close to her. His skin was pale and dotted with moles, including one irregular purple one that looked like it could be a melanoma. Not that she would point it out to him. Her body stiffened, but his manner seemed more confidential than hostile. "Don't tell anyone I told you this," he said. "I'm not even telling Deb—I don't want to get her hopes up. Ralph thinks Jared might be in the Philadelphia area. Apparently his little girlfriend has some associates there."

He was on to her, maybe in his own limited way, but on nonetheless. Her skin flushed, hot and itchy. She feared her body would betray her if her mouth did not. Jesse and Jake ran in at just the opportune moment, pulling at her legs, begging her to light the candles on their birthday cake.

Ron left right after cake and ice cream, allegedly to prepare for a WBEZ staff meeting the following morning. The rest of the guests scattered soon thereafter. Dylan settled himself in front of Apple IIGS, while the twins bounced about the family room, rolling wrapping-paper fragments into balls and throwing them at each other.

Debbie lingered, seeming less guarded than usual, slipping cold cuts into Ziploc bags and coleslaw into Tupperware. "I don't feel like going home," she said. "It feels so empty without Jared."

"So, Debbie"—Erica shoved paper plates into the garbage—"are you having any luck with your search missions?"

"No, nobody knows anything." Debbie furiously swept cake crumbs off the counter into a paper towel. "It's like Jared's vanished into thin air. And it's such a dangerous world out there. Male prostitutes. Heroin. And crack! Have you heard about the crack epidemic?"

"Ron hasn't come up with any clues, either?" Erica stacked the leftovers neatly in the refrigerator, the pastrami, corned beef, and turkey nestling next to Tupperware containers of coleslaw and potato salad.

Debbie dumped the crumbs into the trash and, pantsuit or no pantsuit, knelt down on the floor to wipe up a soda spill. "He trusts that private detective of his, Ralph Rossiter." She sighed. "But I find him cold and unfriendly. He leaves me out of the loop. Let me be honest with you, Rikki. Ron and I have been fighting. I don't blame him for Jared's running away, goodness knows, but he simply never understood about the DDD. About Jared's lack of impulse control and the need to watch his diet. And the need to keep him away from that awful girl. He actually encouraged his dating Ashley! As if it made him manly or something! He doesn't realize that Jared is still a vulnerable adolescent!"

"Were you fighting even before Jared ran away?"

"Yeah, yeah." Debbie clutched the small of her back. "God, my soaz hurts," she groaned.

"You don't need to sanitize my floor," Erica said, covering up the remaining cake with plastic wrap.

Debbie stood up, grimacing and rubbing her back. "I understand now how Mom must have felt when you disappeared as a kid.

Like at Jones Beach? Even if it was only for a few minutes. You could have drowned."

"I was only swimming," Erica said.

"But how could she know that? And I despair, Rikki. I try not to show it, but I despair. Sometimes, and I can't tell Ron this, sometimes I worry that Jared's dead. Except I'm sure I could sense it—if that was the case—but if he's alive, why hasn't he called me. Can you give me a good answer, Rikki?"

Erica's mind refused to go there. Jared hadn't called her either. "Debbie, I'm sure he's alive. I guarantee you."

Debbie wrapped Erica in an unfamiliar hug. "One mom to another," she said. "We may be different, but we're both moms."

Erica twisted gently free.

"I better go home and have a hot bath," Debbie said. "You're coming to that special meeting I'm running about DDD next Wednesday, right? At the high school? I left you a phone message."

"I'm leaving for Florida the next morning."

"Rikki, please. Mom told me she offered to babysit."

Erica nodded yes.

CHAPTER TWENTY-TWO

West Meadow High School's parking lot was completely filled, with additional cars lining the adjoining streets. The gymnasium smelled of chewing gum and sweaty socks. Erica, running late, squeezed into the back, wedged between a water fountain and a muscular man with graying hair and a gold chain around his neck. Debbie stood at the podium, hair twisted into an unfamiliar bun, wearing bifocals Erica didn't recognize, looking like she was wound up so tight that any second she would burst, sending springs and fasteners bounding throughout the room. Patti stood next to her, tight-lipped in a Bettina Riedel pantsuit.

"As many of you know," Debbie was saying, "my fifteen-year-old son, Jared, has run away from home. My husband, Ron, and I are still searching for his whereabouts." She choked up, hesitated a moment. "What many of you do not know is that Jared is handicapped by an invisible disability—defiant disobedient disorder, or DDD.

"Jared did not run away alone," Debbie continued. "He was accompanied by his"—Debbie glanced sideways at Patti—"his friend Ashley, whose mother is standing right next to me. Ashley has not been diagnosed with DDD, but she is under treatment for ADD, a related disorder." Debbie scratched her neck in a gesture reminiscent of their mother, and directed her eyes toward a gray head in the front row. "I want to introduce you to a woman who has been of special help to my husband and me and to our precious son, Jared, in his struggles. I proudly introduce you to Dr. Arlene Rafferty of the Nassau Family Clinic."

Dr. Arlene Rafferty took the podium, and Erica took an instant dislike to her. Short and stocky, with a helmet of steel-colored hair, Rafferty reminded her of every substitute teacher she'd ever thrown paper airplanes at.

"DDD is a destroyer of young people's lives," she pronounced.

In a series of slides, she outlined the cardinal signs of DDD: a lack of respect for authority, poor grades, refusal to attend school, lack of interest in formerly enjoyed family activities, substance abuse, and "new and unsavory" friends. She reviewed the possible physical causes of DDD: vulnerable genes, emotional stress, wheat or dairy allergy, even exposure to common childhood vaccines. As Rafferty droned on, she reminded Erica more and more of Mrs. Law, her eighth-grade gym instructor, the one with a neck like a turkey who gave lectures on the rules of field hockey. Erica had heard all this DDD claptrap from Debbie before and found herself worrying about whether she'd packed the twins' rain jackets for Florida.

She hadn't eaten all day. Her blood sugar dipped, her head swam, her stomach gurgled acidly. Dr. Rafferty turned the overhead projector off and flipped the lights back on. The fluorescence drilled into Erica's skull. She sighed and paced in place.

Rafferty extended herself to her full gnomish height, fixed her audience with a steady eye, and pronounced, "But the main problem, my friends, is not physical." She paused for dramatic effect. "The problem, my friends, is a lack of old-fashioned discipline. I know, 'discipline' is not a popular word these days. Since the 1960s, 'discipline' has been a dirty word. But discipline is exactly what we need to rescue our children from the messy world they've been born into. DDD children may look different from one another, they might have superficial differences in their interests or talents, but inside they're all alike. What they need more than anything, fellow parents, is behavior modification."

A rustling arose from the crowd, some tentative applause, a few hands raised for questions. West Meadow traditionally was not a land of discipline, more a territory of gentle parenting, of negotiations, of family conferences. A woman with an auburn bob called out, "But what exactly do you suggest?"

Rafferty calmed the crowd with a wave of her hands. "We offer many excellent behavior modification groups at the Nassau Family Clinic, groups that have benefited the Carrera and Lassler families as well as several other families I recognize in this audience." She smiled, a thin, tight stretch of teeth that made her appear even more unpleasant. Upon reflection, Erica decided she looked considerably more venal than Mrs. Law, who, despite her stupidity, was never vicious, actually praised Erica's field hockey performance, and brought heart-shaped cookies to class on Valentine's Day.

"Sometimes, despite our best efforts, family therapy is not enough," Rafferty continued. "Sometimes residential treatment is necessary."

Murmurings arose again from the crowd, not uniformly positive.

"Sometimes a vacation, shall we say, away from the pressures of everyday life is exactly what these young people need. A chance to be out in the country and reflect. To experience physical challenges. A chance to escape peer pressure, societal pressure, and yes, even parental pressure—to discover who they truly are. An opportunity for a disciplined life."

The lights dimmed again; the overhead projector lit up, this time displaying shots of pine-covered hills and wholesome youth feeding horses, playing soccer, and harvesting fresh vegetables. Brittle rage coursed through Erica—her pulse racing, that sharp pain at the back of her skull. All the verdant countryside and mooing cows in the world couldn't conceal the fact that this must be Jared's feared boot camp. Dr. Rafferty yammered on, selling the boot camp like a time share in Hawaii.

"At the Pritima Center, young men and women complete their high school curriculum while learning discipline and self-respect. They do chores on the busy farm and learn athletic, outdoor, and practical life skills. And as they do so, they learn how to make appropriate decisions."

Blah, blah, blah. Her words all ran together. Erica scratched her scabby wrist, blew her nose, picked a pimple on her chin.

"Through hard work and periods of reflection, the children regain a spiritual center, Rafferty intoned.

"Whoa! What was that all about? Were they a bunch of Jesus freaks?" Erica's stomach felt like an empty pit.

The fluorescent lights blared, the crowd shifted in their seats, a few people left.

But most of the crowd lingered, shouting out questions.

Was the Pritima Center only for boys? No, but they segregated the sexes to minimize distractions.

Where was the center located? Sorry, but to protect the families involved, they couldn't release that information.

Erica waggled her arm in the air, eventually catching Rafferty's attention. She struggled to make herself audible from her perch at the back of the large room. Her voice emerged squeaky and tentative, nothing like the firm, strong voice she heard in her head.

"What are your criteria for sending teenagers to this program?" she asked.

"It depends on the individual situation," said Dr. Rafferty. "But we find it works remarkably well for a wide variety of young people. Now, if you'll excuse me," she said, looking at her watch, "I think it's getting late, so I'll turn this program back to Debbie Lassler."

Debbie announced that cookies and coffee were available at the side of the gymnasium, informational pamphlets at the front. Erica forged her way over to the side and stuffed a couple of cookies in her mouth. Their butterscotch sweetness settled her nerves as well as her stomach; she'd never realized how delicious cookies could be, even these, straight from their Sam's Club box. She grabbed three more, plus a full cup of black coffee, as she navigated through the crowd to the front. Parents recognizing her as Debbie's sister nodded sympathetically.

Debbie manned the informational table, straightening a pile of pamphlets. She was wearing white slacks, a nubby teal sweater, and mauve lip gloss. "Thanks for coming, Rikki," she said.

"That was nervy of you to get up and speak like that," Erica said.

"I'm getting used to it. I even wrote this pamphlet for Dr. Rafferty on ten warning signs of DDD. It's funny; I'm so desperately unhappy and worried, but when I do work for Dr. Rafferty, it settles me down somehow."

Erica guzzled the acrid, steaming coffee. "I gotta tell you,

Debbie. That woman puts a pretty gloss on that Pritima Center, makes it sound like summer camp, but it sounds pretty abusive, if you ask me. You don't know anything about this place except what she's showing you on those slides! How do you know if the kids get enough to eat, or where they sleep?"

"I respect Dr. Rafferty implicitly." Debbie's lips tightened as she corralled all the pens and pencils into a plastic case. "She's done wonders for Jared."

"Wonders for Jared! Last time I looked, Jared ran away from home. Some wonders!" Erica crushed her Styrofoam cup with her fist. Remnants of hot coffee dripped through her fingers. She wasn't quite sure how she'd accomplished that. Styrofoam seemed difficult to crush. She licked her singed thumb.

"Rikki, control yourself. People are listening." She composed herself in a deliberate way that she'd clearly learned in therapy. "Rikki, I know deep down we both want the same thing. We both want Jared home and safe, don't we?"

"Of course," Erica answered, truthfully. A presumption of ultimate safety underlay the ripples of risk in which she and Jared swam. It allowed her to look back at the image of Jared and Ashley disappearing around the corner, and all the lies and evasions that necessarily followed, with a degree of equanimity. But that equanimity was wavering, that high-pitched luster of controlled danger fading. Two months had passed since he ran away. He'd never called, despite his promise. If only she could see his face, and reassure herself, as she'd reassured Debbie, that he was not dead.

"He'll come back," Erica said.

"How do you know?" Debbie sobbed.

"I just do." Jared was no doubt terrified, out there in the world. Debbie looked at her sharply.

"I mean, he has to." Erica sucked her thumb, bright red and developing a blister. "I mean, probably Ron's detective's going to find him, right?'

"Ron thinks so. That thumb looks scary, Rikki. I think I have a Band-Aid in my bag."

"I don't need one." Sharp bursts of pain were shooting down

through her thumb to the base of her palm. The sensation seemed separate from her, an interesting phenomenon. "Promise me, whatever happens, you won't send him to that Pritima Center?"

"Yeah, yeah, Rikki, I promise," Debbie said. "Do me a favor. Take this Band-Aid."

Patti materialized at their side, and when she saw Debbie's red eyes and Erica's burnt finger, plus the runny nose that she was dabbing at with a Kleenex, she enveloped them both in a fierce embrace. Her body was a reservoir of competing fragrances: mint, tobacco, an unctuous floral perfume. Erica wangled her way out of the press of skin and jogged back in the cool rain to her home and her children waiting in their footed pajamas.

Ethan called from Florida, telling her he was eagerly anticipating their arrival. He'd rented her a car. They'd love their big suite at the Ritz Carlton. He'd even arranged for her to meet a real estate agent.

Until late in the night she threw summer clothes and bathing suits into suitcases. She pulled the Band-Aid off her thumb, where a large blister had formed. She picked at the thick skin of the blister until it burst, sending a spurt of fluid onto one of Sophia's cotton stretchies. The pain vanished. Her thumb was already healing, though if Debbie were there, she would no doubt instruct Erica to rub Neosporin on it. Erica looked at the pile of unpacked items in front of her, plus a tilting pile of papers that included their plane tickets and a mass of coloring and dot-to-dot books. Ten hours before departure, the mess on her family room floor represented one thing: escape.

CHAPTER TWENTY-THREE

JUNE 1986

The nice thing about being on a plane is that you are floating above the earth, totally enclosed. No one can call you. You can't go anywhere. So even if you are tending to the never-ending needs of three restless preschoolers, you are free.

When you're driving a car that is not your own, where your tush has yet to carve an imprint into the seat, where your tapes aren't stacked in the center console and the floor is not littered with wrinkled to-do lists, you remain free.

There are no right or wrong highways in a state you do not know. There are only new highways. You rarely check direction.

No one knows exactly where you are, save your children in the car with you. Your husband spends 90 percent of his waking hours in a dreary over-air-conditioned cubicle. He thinks it's better than his one in Manhattan, but you can't tell the difference. You will not run into your neighbors at the supermarket or your mother at the dry cleaner's. A few elderly relatives do live in your vicinity, but you did not notify them of your presence. Besides, the Florida you are currently experiencing bears no resemblance to the Florida you've previously known: acres of look-alike bungalows surrounding a golf course; mosquitoes buzzing around overwatered grass, thick and spiky as cactus; the horrible all-you-can-eat Chinese buffets stinking of overcooked cabbage.

This Florida saturates every cell of your body with light and heat.

Your children are very young. Your twin boys have just celebrated their fifth birthdays, and your daughter is all of seven months. If they had their druthers, they would spend their days in your luxurious hotel room, watching cartoons on the king-size bed or, in the case of your daughter, propelling herself on her tummy like a caterpillar over to the electrical outlet by the lamp. The twins are fascinated with the hotel bar and wash down bags of potato chips and M & Ms with cans of soda. Every day the goodies are replaced like magic, and you don't care, you just sign your name and room number, and your husband's company pays the bill.

The twins like swimming in the big pool with the slide, and for a time you enjoy this too, plunging down the slide with one or the other in your lap, inhaling sharply right before the cold blueness envelops you. You raise the white flag by your pool chair and a well-built waiter with spiky blond hair, maybe ten years younger than you, brings you BLTs and frothy piña coladas on a tray. He smiles at you, and you can tell he admires your body.

But soon you grow restless, and the backs of your thighs chafe against the plastic strips of the chair as if your muscles were about to burst through your skin and propel you through the air. So you drive.

Your kids are young, so you can pile them in the car and cart them wherever you want to. As long as they are with you, they will be happy. You know this will not last. Already your nine-year-old son asks questions. He seeks privacy. He is developing a life you know nothing about. But he is not with you now. He is back home in New York, staying at his friend's house and attending his last weeks of elementary school. Meanwhile, these little ones open themselves up to you with absolute trust.

You comfort yourself that you live up to that trust, and most of the time you do. You feed them and clothe them, laugh and play games with them, wipe their noses, press their sweaty, needy faces against your breast. You balance that against the part of you that keeps driving, and the Ziploc bag of cocaine that enables you to transport these children until the sun sinks down in an orange splash, a hazy moon rises up, and the highway empties out until it seems like only you in your private space-ship are sailing through the night sky.

Your kids, or more precisely your baby daughter, have made the presence of that Ziploc bag feasible, if unwise. It's sitting right in your diaper bag, between a nearly identical bag of rice cereal and a tube of Desitin. The airport personnel gave no more than a cursory look to your diaper bag as you carried it through security and stuffed it beneath your seat on the plane. You were wearing leggings and an oversize flowered sweatshirt, hair in a ponytail, the baby in her stroller, holding your twins by each hand—how innocuous can you get? Nevertheless, you told yourself you weren't going to take the chance. But in the end, you couldn't bring yourself not to.

Besides, you tell yourself, the coke is not changing you. You've always been restless, a seeker of thrills. Even as a little girl, your mother always told you to settle down, to play with dolls or read a book like your older sister. Your energy has always amazed people. You've always been a night owl. All the drugs are doing is potentiating your true self.

This bad habit of yours does not hold a candle to how so many people you know are screwing up their lives, compromising themselves beyond endurance. Your sister lives in fear, your brother-in-law in anger, your parents in a tangle of lies and ignorance. Your friends live lives stultifying in their monotony. Your husband, whose intensity and penetrating brilliance you have always loved, seems to have lost his rudder. Even your nephew, only fifteen, who should be young enough to see more clearly, for the fires to burn stronger, even he seems destined to return to his prison.

They are all in danger. They are in more danger than you. And they aren't having fun. You are having fun.

At first, when you drive, you don't stray too far from the hotel. You drive past spanking-new developments, large houses with burnt-orange stucco roofs and oval, jewel-like pools, vast shopping malls, dentist offices, and health clubs. You drive past miles of this until little breaks the flat landscape but produce stands, roadhouse bars, and the occasional sagging frame house. Then even those outposts of construction end. Reedy swamps, housing nothing but alligators and swooping herons, stretch on to the horizon. Only then do you turn around, and drive all the way back to A1A, the coastal road, where you drive through archways of waving palms and fuchsia flowers, catching glimpses of the mansions behind their wrought-iron gates.

Next you venture farther, south to Miami, where you buy a clingy black dress. The kids are restless in the dressing room, but they are very young, and you ply them with lollipops and toys. You stand for a long time in front of the mirror, smoothing the dress down your hips, feeling its rough-hemmed edge, right where the curve of your butt intersects with the top of your tanned thigh. You are tanning despite your lack of pool time from the sun streaming in through the windows of your car. That sickly yellow tone, so obvious under fluorescent lights in West Meadow, has vanished. Your skin is a caramel brown.

Not bad. That thick brown hair with just a touch of a wave to it, cascading past your shoulders, red highlights gleaming in the sun. Despite the heat, you've freed it from its ponytail so you can feel the fullness of its weight on your back. Those dark-brown eyes, that nose that's a mite too long, those high cheekbones—an angular face, but one that ages well. Those full breasts, a little saggy after four kids but still respectable, milk-white against your tan. Those long legs with muscles well honed from a lifetime of track team and aerobics. Your knees are bony and scuffed like a child's. Your right forearm has a cut on it that you've had for a while but don't remember getting. The scab on it is picked raw. Your nails, too, are ragged: the sparkly red nail polish you painted on your first day at the hotel has worn off in uneven ridges, and your left thumbnail is chipped. You don't mind these small imperfections. They mean you're active and alive. Debbie's fingernails have been perfectly manicured pale peach half-moons for as long as you can remember.

Fifteen years ago you admired yourself like this, in your pink room full of stuffed animals, while your mother unpacked groceries in the kitchen. At any moment she could have barged in on you, as she had the propensity to do, with a pile of clean laundry or a reminder to walk the dog. The night before, you lost your virginity to a guy you didn't particularly like, whose shallowness was part of his perverse appeal, who had gorgeous sleek hair that hung down past his shoulders and jeans that wrinkled perfectly at the backs of the knees. His name was Max. He wasn't the guy you truly had a crush on, the one who always strummed his guitar with his eyes closed on the stairs beneath the school auditorium. You were always tongue-tied with stupidity around any guy you really liked. This thing with Max of the sleek chestnut hair was just something that happened at a party, one of those overnight ones at the Mackay estate, but it was time, and you were glad.

You smoothed your hands over your body then like you had never seen it before, and in a way you hadn't—so much was new over the past year in your lanky, late-to-mature frame. You felt like you'd burst through the tunnel you'd been living in for so long and out into the wide, light world.

The next day, under the auditorium stairs, you would finally speak to Jeff, the guy you really liked. You would tell him that when he played the guitar, you trembled inside. To your astonishment, he would not make fun of you. Instead, he would give you private concerts in his parents' basement, one block away from what is now your sister's house.

Several years later, at an MIT frat party, you would initiate a ridiculous conversation with your future husband about his college major. In the early hours of that Sunday morning, you would follow him upstairs and wash his beautiful strawberry blond-ringlets with Herbal Essence shampoo. It would take four cups of an Everclear beverage concocted by one of his fratmates to give you the nerve, but you would do it.

Today in Miami, at the age of thirty-one, while your youngest three children stare at you with eyes glazed over by sleepiness, sugar, and boredom, you realize that despite the birth of these children plus their older brother back in New York, your body still retains its lushness and richness. There was a time in your early teens when it seemed like you were never going to catch up to your sister, but you have surpassed her by far. The weight of her thirty-six years has saddened and suppressed her, but you remain unscathed. You bathe in the light of your good fortune.

The following morning, before sunrise, before your husband straggles out of bed and goes for a run before heading to his dreary office, you load three sleeping children into the car and drive to Disney World. This is a four-hour drive north and east, a ridiculous round-trip for one day.

Unlike the shopping centers or alligator-ridden swamps or pastel streets of Miami Beach, your sons are not indifferent to this excursion. Everyone they've met in Florida has asked them if they are going to Disney World. They have seen ads for it on the plane, on television, on billboards. They can't wait to meet their favorite characters. Once they emerge from the fog of sleep and you hand them granola bars, they chatter excitedly all the way there.

You arrive right as the park is opening. You fork over sixty dollars for day passes, walk through the gate. The boys are already racing down a preternaturally clean path towards Cinderella's castle. You swerve around other, slower families to keep them in your sight, maneuvering the baby's elaborate stroller as if it were your rental car.

You attend Mickey Mouse's birthday party. The boys sing along, watching intently as Mickey blows out his candles and opens a large pile of presents. They pose for pictures with Mickey Mouse and Goofy. The baby looks on wide-eyed, turning her head rapidly from right to left to catch the next flash of colorful action. And you surprise yourself. You are as jittery with excitement as they are.

Despite the fact that they are tall for their age, often the boys don't measure up to the forty-five inches of height required for the most exciting rides. Or they qualify, but you can't go on with the baby, and they are scared to ride without you. No way will they enter the Haunted House. Each ride necessitates at least a half-hour's wait in line. So you ride around in boats listening to mechanical puppets sing their saccharine song about what a small world it is. And then it hits you. You rode through this very same artificial river twenty-two years ago, your bony knee vibrating against your sister's soft thigh. Disneyworld is the New York World's Fair all over again.

Wandering into Tomorrowland, you revisit more clumps of the World's Fair, transferred here in their entirety, utterly unchanged by passing years. The same moving sidewalks, the same video telephones. In the glaring light of the present these visions of the future look worn and diminished. They are a lie. Seeing them makes you think of your sister, the way she tentatively dipped her leather sandal in the water of the fountain, contemplating for a split-second joining you at its center. And then the way she pulled her sandal off and dried the leather off with the front of her new blouse from Bloomingdales. Something in the water or the leather left a brown stain on the blouse that none of Mom's miracle cleaners could extract. Mom was furious. Your sister never wore the blouse again.

You do not want to think about your sister. You do not want to follow the trail that thinking about your sister leads. You suggest to your boys that they leave Tomorrowland, and they agree readily. They find it boring. This vision of the future has come and gone before their birth.

So you wander around for a few more hours, scooting backwards down a tame roller coaster away from Norwegian trolls, and floating in a gondola through faux Venetian canals. You eat at a Mexican restaurant that serves macaroni and cheese, and then lick sloppy ice cream cones at a sidewalk cafe. At both these stops, and at a third one at a bench by the artificial beach, you feed the baby a bottle and change her diaper. Switching over to bottle feeding has relieved your guilt at transmitting drugs to your baby, but still you feel a sense of loss. Bit by bit, even your youngest, your only daughter, inevitably grows away from you.

By late afternoon she is fast asleep in her stroller and the

boys are asleep on their feet, stunned by sensation. Pluto walks
by waving his paws at them, and they barely raise their eyes.
They tell you they want to go back to the hotel and watch cartoons. The one with the sensitive stomach tells you his tummy
feels sad. You ask him if he needs to throw up and he says no,
but you can't rely on his assurance, so you duck into the nearest
lady's room, which, like the rest of the park, is sparkling clean.
You stand with him in the toilet stall for a few minutes without
incident. Slowly, color returns to his face. You make sure the
boys pee anyway, and as they play around with the soap squirter
and the electric hand dryer you realize how exhausted you are
yourself. Your two hours of sleep the night before plus all those
hours driving and walking are catching up with you. Your head
weighs heavy on your shoulders. A crevasse opens up in the
base of your belly. A feeling of dread, so at odds with the exhila-
ration that's been rippling through your bones, creeps out from
wherever it has been hiding.

You know how to make all this go away. The solution is
right there in your baby's diaper bag, hanging on the handle of
your stroller. But the opportunity isn't. You have no television to
park your boys in front of, no orange-scented showers to retreat
to. You contemplate leaving them alone briefly, as they continue
to squirt pink soap out of the dispensers, but you know that they
will sense your absence, panic and bolt or scream, or both.

A heavy woman with one platinum blond baby on her hip
and another, slightly older, one in a stroller, pushes her way into
the restroom and smiles at you empathetically. "Tired, huh?" she
says. At first you view her with scorn. She is probably younger
than you but she already looks worn out. Her pink pantsuit is
hideous. It looks like something your sister would choose if she
bought her outfits at Penney's instead of Saks. Her hair is dyed
an amalgam of three shades and has a bald spot near the crown.
Her abdomen loosely flops over her waistband, as if it bore no
relationship to her smallish saggy breasts above or her squat
legs below. Her kids are wearing cheap polyester outfits that are
miniature versions of her own. Her triceps shake as she reposi-

tions the baby and a huge sack bulging with diapers, clothes, and snacks hangs from her wrist. "What beautiful twins," she continues, and it shames you that, while you've been mentally ripping her to pieces, she's been admiring you. What a nice lady, so kind. A woman you can trust. A moment later you seize your opportunity.

"Would you mind watching them for a minute?" you ask. "I really have to go to the bathroom."

"Why sure, honey," she says. "I know how that goes."

One of your boys, the one with the sensitive stomach, reminds you that he isn't supposed to talk to strangers. You assure him that this time it is okay, that the lady is a nice mommy, the same as you.

You push open the green door to the stall, grabbing the diaper bag as you go. "I need some Tampax," you say.

"You don't have to explain nothing to me," she assures you in a silky Southern drawl. "Say hello to the nice boys, Sandra," she says as her towheaded daughter pulls at your boy's shirts.

There's something about snorting the coke behind the metal restroom stall, balancing everything on the diaper bag resting on your knee, your left thigh brushing up against the base of the toilet, that strikes you as ugly and depraved, in a way that doing the same thing in your orange-scented hotel bathroom, or your own powder room with the blue checked wallpaper, or even cross-legged on Nick Stromboli's grungy carpet, does not. For the first time the word "addict" flits across your mind, but you dismiss it. You are a very functional person. You eat (well, sometimes), you sleep (well, sometimes), you feed and clothe four children and shepherd them to all their activities and appointments, you arrange for the carpet to be cleaned, you excel at step aerobics. Your triceps muscles are firm and rounded. You feel fine. You feel finer than fine.

You feel so fine by the time you step out of that restroom stall that the kind woman asks you if you are "better" now. You assure her yes, thanking her, and she tells you how she and her husband just love Disney, they save for this trip every year.

Your boys are sucking on Mickey Mouse lollipops from her gargantuan sack and chasing her little girl around the restroom. Searching madly in your bag for some form of repayment, you uncover a box of crayons you'd brought for the airplane, forgotten, still in their wrapper. You hand them to the little girl.

"Don't forget your thank yous, Sandra," admonishes the lady, but you are already retreating.

Outside, on the paths, early evening melts into twilight. You keep walking even though the boys are on the verge of collapse and even the baby has awakened from her deep nap and started in with a low wail that neither bottle nor binky can soothe. Fireworks explode over a castle turret in streaks of purple and red. You don't want to leave until the fireworks are over, until they are locking the gates to the park. You tell yourself your mother would feel the same way. You paid sixty dollars for a pass for the whole day and you should get your money's worth. Your Mom brought you up to believe in value. You can picture her saying, if she found out about the coke: "A hundred dollars, Rikki, and poof, it's gone? A hundred dollars for only one day?"

Eventually, you follow the throngs to the parking lot. By the time you edge out onto the highway, the kids are asleep. Past Orlando, the roads are empty except for the occasional truck. Little is visible beyond the road except the shadows of buildings and the glow of neon. Out beyond the shadows, people are sleeping, snoring under the hum of their air conditioning, missing out on these clear warm nights, these unrecoverable hours of their lives. But not you. You sing along to Robert Palmer and Phil Collins. Your voice has improved, you think, tuneful and strong. Maybe you should sing with a rock band. It is not too late. Surely you are as talented as those girls with the tight black skirts on MTV. While your entire life is spent running around, all you do is run in circles. You wish you could power yourself past the inertia that glues you to the track. On nights, like this, you feel so close. Your eyes, sharp as a laser, follow the white line in front of you, extending, it seems, all the way to the Caribbean, hurtling off the edge of the earth. But try as you might, you never become one with the line. Inevitably, as you drive forward, the line recedes.

The next day is your last full one in Florida. The boys nag you to go to the pool but you call the real estate agent's number instead. You don't know exactly why. The woman who meets you in the lobby is named Constance, and she tells you in that melodic Southern drawl that she specializes in corporate relocations. She wears a pink pantsuit not unlike the lady in the bathroom at Disney World but more expensive, better fitting, and accessorized by a sapphire pendant on a gold chain.

You drive down wide flat streets smelling of freshly laid tar. The houses are spanking new and humongous, spiraling along the curves and cul-de-sacs. Every few feet, a spindly infant palm tree juts out from the rubbery grass.

Inside, the hallways are tiled with white marble. The kitchens have center islands, Sub-Zero refrigerators, and Jenn-Air grills and open up onto concrete patios with kidney-shaped pools. The master suite adjoins a bathroom the size of your childhood bedroom, with Jacuzzis and steam nozzles and plate-glass windows that overlook the neighbors' Jacuzzis. You have never seen so much luxury in a family home, not even the nouveau mansions your mother drags you to see in Old Westbury. Here, the amenities have amenities. There are home theaters and climate control and central vacuuming.

These houses do not have phones yet. They are as pristine as newborn babies. You feel like you could wander forever through their rooms, always opening a new door.

The boys tell your husband about the houses as soon as he walks into your hotel room. You are slipping on your new clingy black dress, fresh from an orange-scented shower. Over your Singapore Slings and coconut-encrusted mahimahi, he questions you about the houses, wanting your opinion of the Jenn-Air grills and entertainment centers, wondering if you've checked out the school system. You fill him in, but already the end of your vacation in Florida looms up before you like a black wall. The houses already seem unreal, like something you've

seen in a dream, and indeed, you will dream about them day
after day and question what they represent. Your handsome
husband reaches across the table and holds your hand and
looks at you with that wondrous rapt attention he bestows on
you from time to time. He is tired. His forehead is developing
thin lines you never noticed before. For some reason, this small
revelation of weakness fills you with tenderness. You squeeze his
hand back. You realize your hand is hot and sweaty and you are
dizzy, perhaps from the drinks or the accumulated fatigue of a
week of driving or simply your nerve endings firing way too fast.
You still love him with a painful intensity that feels like you've
wrapped your body around glowing coals. You wonder why you
can't speak as freely with him as you do with the slobby Nick
Stromboli, with whom stray thoughts and stories spill out of
you as you waste your mornings cross-legged on his grubby carpet. Where you have to check your watch repeatedly to remind
yourself you have to pick up your boys from school. Where your
baby daughter puts God knows what into her mouth.

Afterward you take one last, long, luxurious and fragrant
shower. You use up the rest of your Ziploc bag, so there will be
no reason to worry at the airport. There's not much left, anyway.
You lie awake next to your snoring husband—that is a new habit
of his, the snoring—and watch the sky outside your balcony
window. The hotel has turned off all the lights, so the sea turtles
can nest, and the sky is flush with stars. You slide open the
screen doors and breathe deeply. You wonder how anyone can
waste their hours sleeping in a place where the night breezes,
soft as a cashmere shawl, ripple over your skin.

You glance at the silent phone. At home the phone rings
constantly on both lines. But in the hotel, the phone has not
rung, except for nightly calls from your nine-year-old son. He
has told you about his math test, the tennis game he lost, and the
Yankees game his friend's parents are taking him to. He sounds
content. Your parents have not called, nor your sister. You are
vaguely surprised not to hear from any of them, but relieved.

If there was anything really wrong, you would know. You gave them your number. They would call.

You bask in the lies exemplified by the silent phone because maybe even then you know you are in the eye of the hurricane. In a few hours you will be sucked back into the maelstrom. You will desperately try to conjure up the slow slap of the waves on the beach, this smell of salt and diesel oil, the orange-blossom scent of your hotel bathroom, the white stripes of the empty highway, the stars and the soft breezes.

You hold your husband's hand again in the cab on the way to the airport. You lean your head against his shoulder. Tired as he might be, you are more tired. The boys are fighting in the backseat, but you don't have the energy to deal with it. Already the sun is rising high in the hazy sky.

At the airport, the flashing screens announce hundreds of possible destinations: Antigua, Rio de Janeiro, Palm Springs, Frankfurt. You could fly to any of these places. People do. All you have to is board the plane. But you are busy giving your baby a zwieback to teethe on and resolving your boys' tug-of-war over a robot Transformer. Your husband picks up a Wall Street Journal. Your head feels like sludge, and you've got weird bloating gas pains in your abdomen. Soon your options narrow down to one, the destination typed on your ticket: La Guardia Airport, New York City. You board the plane and fly home.

CHAPTER TWENTY-FOUR

"Our cabdriver was a complete space cadet," Erica told Nick, sitting cross-legged on his carpet. A yellow crust clung to one of the shaggy strands—dried cheese? She picked it off with her finger, getting flakes of the gross substance beneath her fingernail. She couldn't believe this was how she was spending her first morning back, given all the laundry and shopping to do, the mail to pick up at the post office, the phone calls to return. Yet there she was, babbling her head off.

"He said he'd never been on a plane in his life. He kept asking what it was like, way up high in the clouds. And he couldn't find the expressway. Can you believe it? How could a cabdriver not know how to get on the expressway? We ended up taking Northern Boulevard. And then he started blabbing about how Northern Boulevard was the highway to hell."

"Man, what was he on?" Nick sat across from her, on the other side of the coffee table.

"Beats me," Erica said. "His brain cells were fried." She attempted to maneuver herself into a lotus position but could only manage one leg up on her thigh. As she twisted her waist, Sophia scooted on her tummy toward Nick's kitchen, propelling herself by pushing up on her arms and then sliding forward. Erica scooped her up and attempted to interest her in Nick's telephone. Sophia poked at the buttons a few times before scooting off toward the kitchen linoleum again. Even from ten feet away, Erica could see that that floor hadn't been cleaned in months. Maybe years.

"You ever wash your kitchen floor, Nick?" she asked.

Nick looked offended. "Every few months I do a deep cleaning," he said.

"Can you turn on *Sesame Street*?" Erica waved a cloth octopus in front of Sophia's face, watching her intently track its passage from right to left.

"Sure," Nick said. "What channel?"

"How could you not know it's on PBS?"

"Because I never watch it, Mommy," Nick chortled in a tone Erica knew she should find infuriating but decided to let go. She got up and turned the television on herself. Big Bird's sunny yellow presence floated into the room, momentarily transfixing Sophia into glazed-eye immobility and freeing Erica to continue her story.

"So, anyway, I actually flagged this cabdriver down because he looked American. I figured he would be more reliable than some Russian without a license. And when we finally get home, we picked up Dylan and Sammy—God, that animal's grown into a monster—and I'm dead tired, but Ethan gets the bright idea we should all play soccer in the park. He wanted to maximize his Monday off. That's exactly how he put it. Like maximizing corporate profits or something." She picked the cheese fragments out of her nail, just as she noticed an ant scurrying along the knotted base of the carpet. She imagined how the carpet must look from an ant's perspective, all tall, waving, multicolored vines.

"You should replace this shag carpeting," she said. "It's even older than your record albums."

"Ethan's an athletic sort, is he not?" Nick asked, blowing his nose with one of the tissues that always seemed to be dangling from his pockets. "I've been running at the track myself, trying to get into shape." He patted the bulge of his belly. He was better dressed than usual: jeans, though with tissues hanging out; a tucked-in pinstripe shirt; matching socks.

"How can you be so chubby when you do coke?" Erica asked. "I've been losing weight like crazy." She patted her belly button where it poked up out of the top of her jeans, the rest of her belly hard and flat as a teenager's. She was wearing a thin cotton scoop-neck T-shirt, the first item she'd grabbed from the top of her Florida suitcase, and even in Nick's overheated living room, in the second week of June, she shivered. A flannel shirt, red-yellow-and-gray plaid, jutted out from a pile of clothes at the end of the couch. She put it on. It felt warm and soft, smelling of coffee and smoke.

"I don't do nearly as much coke as you do, honey," Nick was saying. "And I'm not nearly as urgent about it. Like, you had to come over this morning, first thing, or the world was going to end. I do have a business to run, you know."

"You can't have half as much to do as me," Erica said. "I haven't even checked my phone messages yet. We played soccer at the park yesterday, like I said, and then we came home and ordered a pizza, and by the time I'd bathed the kids, and gone over Dylan's homework with him, and done stories and bedtime, I fell sound asleep. I fell asleep in Jesse and Jake's bed, as a matter of fact. I haven't even called Debbie yet. I haven't even called my mom. Of course, nothing's stopping them from calling me. They know I'm back." She rolled back into a plough position. Thirty-one years old, and she could still touch her toes to the floor.

"Well, you know about Jared, right?" Nick asked.

She unfolded from the plough so sharply that she felt a stab of pain in her lower back. For a split second, her vision faded to black. When her sight returned, she was lying flat on the ground, and Nick's face hovered over her so closely she could see a red irritation on his upper lip. He'd slid over to her side of the table and was lying next to her, propped up on his elbows.

"You okay?" he asked. "I thought you were going to pass out. Would you like some water?"

Erica shook her head and returned to her cross-legged position. "What about Jared?" she asked.

"He's back home. Ralph Rossiter located him. The detective. They were staying with some friends of Ashley's in Philadelphia. Some former teachers of hers."

The ant skittered through the shag forest while Sophia, forgetting about Sesame Street, slithered after in pursuit. Erica stretched out her right leg, creating an obstacle for both creatures, and bent her left leg inward. She sucked in her stomach and breathed deeply.

"How did you find out?" she asked.

"One of the kids from the family clinic told me about it yesterday. You know, at drop-in."

Nick still hovered over her, way too close. His breath smelled like pizza. And where the hell was Sophia? Oh, great, she'd discovered Nick's prized record collection and was extracting a Procol Harum LP from the stack.

A vein pulsed in Erica's left eyelid. Sophia rocked the Procol Harum album back and forth. The vinyl disk slid out and landed on the carpet, making a brushing noise.

"Hey," Nick said, grabbing the album out of her hand. "Hey, that's valuable."

Erica crawled over and grabbed the baby with one arm, holding onto the turntable for purchase as she struggled to standing.

"Can I have my CDs?" she asked. "I gotta see Jared."

———

The New York air carried a bite to it that didn't exist in Florida. The sun lay closer to the horizon, and the slant of light was harsher, less forgiving. Erica buttoned Nick's flannel shirt. Nobody had called her about Jared. Not her parents, not Debbie. No attempts, not one lousy little message, as if she had no right to know.

The pulsing in her eyelid returned, soon joined by a shaking in her legs, like she was about to splinter into a thousand pieces. Sophia clawed at her shoulder. Erica zipped up her jacket and buckled the baby into her car seat and then jerked Vince out of the pet store lot so fast that his engine choked and sputtered. Bloody Tampax blared out of the speakers. No, it wasn't Bloody Tampax—it was one of Jared's other favorite bands, named, in a similarly gross vein, Barf. She figured if she listened to this music long enough, she'd acclimate to it. The slam of each dissonant chord resonated with her growing anger.

Barf hit a horrific minor chord and dissolved into an endless drum solo. A garbage truck materialized inches from her windshield, plastic bags hanging from its green teeth. Erica slid to the left and passed the ugly green thing, her driver's side tires scraping against the curb.

CHAPTER TWENTY-FIVE

Debbie's face sank when she saw Erica.

"Oh, hi, Rikki," she said. "I was going to lie down. I just got back from a doctor's appointment."

"Where's Jared?" Erica snapped.

"What do you mean?" Debbie asked, still standing at the door, as if Erica were an annoying Jehovah's Witness she wished to politely dismiss as soon as possible.

"What do I mean?" Erica's voice rose. "Do you think I'm an idiot? All week you don't call me, and then I come back and hear from—from a neighbor—that Rossiter found him and brought him home. Where is he? Is he okay?"

"He's not here," Debbie said.

"Where is he? Did he go back to school already?"

Debbie blanched. "He's at the Pritima Center," she said, looking down at the floor.

"You've got to be kidding! You promised me you wouldn't send him to that place!" Erica's voice rose higher.

"Stop screaming at me, Rikki," Debbie said, backing away.

"Only Ron's allowed to scream at you, huh? You lied to me!" Erica grabbed Debbie's hands by the wrists, the way she sometimes grabbed her children's wrists when she was angry. Debbie jumped back, skidding slightly on the polished marble tiles.

"What's wrong with you, Rikki? Get your hands off me! I never lied to you. I told you we wanted Jared home and safe. He is safe."

"You didn't call me!"

"I didn't have your phone number at the hotel." Debbie looked down at her wrists. There were red imprints right where the veins led into her palm. "I left you a message this morning." Sighing, she massaged her wrists.

"I haven't checked my messages," Erica admitted. "I didn't mean to hurt you."

"I'm sure you didn't, Rikki." Debbie put on her therapy face. "Can we sit down? I'm really exhausted." She sunk onto one of their white suede living room couches.

Erica settled into the couch opposite. "Ron's idea, huh?"

"No, we both agreed." Debbie knotted her fingers together, stroking the new bruises on her wrists.

Erica dug around her diaper bag for a bottle.

"You finally stopped nursing." Debbie nodded approvingly.

"Yep." Erica desperately missed the luscious closeness of Sophia at her breast. She fought a desire to kick her leg and knock all of Debbie's prized snow globes off the coffee table like dominoes.

"To tell the truth, I was scared to call you. I knew you wouldn't approve of our decisions about Jared." Debbie swallowed and breathed in hard, like she was about to plunge into one of her DDD slide presentations. "At first when Detective Rossiter brought Jared home, he seemed thankful to be here, but within hours it became clear he wasn't going to comply with his therapy or medication. And we had to get him away from that awful Ashley girl. They were staying in some sort of commune in Philadelphia, with two older associates of Ashley's, former middle school teachers, would you believe. They were sharing a mattress on the floor and begging for money on the streets!"

"You don't know anything about the Pritima Center except that stupid slide presentation and pamphlet." Erica's hand, holding Sophia's bottle, trembled.

"As you know, Dr. Rafferty thinks very highly of the Pritima Center, and she does have a doctorate in psychology and she is the director of the Nassau Family Clinic. They've had lots of success with boys like Jared."

"Who exactly are boys like Jared?' Erica asked. "There's only one Jared. Your son. My nephew."

"I mean boys with DDD," Debbie said. "You heard Dr. Rafferty's lecture. They all exhibit certain behavioral similarities."

"Where is this prison?" Erica asked.

Debbie swallowed again, measuring her words. "It's not a prison, Rikki—it's a school. And I can't tell you where he is. He isn't allowed to have any contact with the outside world for six weeks. That's part of his treatment protocol."

"I'm not the outside world," Erica said. "I'm his aunt."

"Those are the rules." Debbie rearranged her hands in her lap.

"Screw the rules," Erica said, her voice losing its tentative control, the pulse in her eyelid returning. Her fingers shook harder, jostling the nipple of Sophia's bottle out of its secure position between her lips. "Sorry, sweetie, sorry," Erica soothed, readjusting. "Six goddamn weeks! And then what?"

"I don't know," Debbie said. "You're screaming at me again." Her resigned and pained manner only infuriated Erica further. She wished Debbie would yell back at her so they could fight openly. She wished Debbie would grab her wrists back, scratch her, punch her, call her bluff, do anything but sit limply, injured and superior. Debbie was lying about Ron never hitting her. She'd take the punch and nurse the hurt.

Sophia guzzled the last of her bottle. Erica put her down on Debbie's white Berber carpet. No chance of her encountering mysterious indigestible substances or crawling ants here.

"You should pick the baby up," Debbie said. "The wool fibers might give her an allergic reaction."

Erica picked Sophia up. "Take your damn nap," she said. "I'm out of here."

"I knew you wouldn't understand," said Debbie, showing her the door. "You never do. You have no idea how Jared was living in Philadelphia. They were digging for food in Dumpsters. His underwear was filthy. His good leather jacket was missing; somebody probably stole it. And that awful girl. She's so much more sophisticated than him. She makes him do things he would never do himself."

Debbie watched Erica load Sophia into her car seat.

"What are you staring at?" Erica snapped. "Go take your nap!"

"I was wondering where you got that ugly flannel shirt," Debbie said. "It doesn't fit you."

⁓

At least Debbie hadn't lied about leaving a phone message; a terse "welcome back, call me" repeated itself on the answering machine along with recorded advertisements for a new cable service and a company that delivered restaurant meals to the home. Nick's flannel shirt smelled musty, disturbingly intimate, and Debbie had a point about the fit: the shoulder seams hung halfway down her arm. She tossed it in the washing machine with a load of color wash. She still felt its muskiness clinging to her, as if molecules of Nick's skin had sloughed off onto her chest.

What a fool she'd been to trust Debbie. Debbie was putty in Ron's hands.

Erica was made of stronger stuff. She would never let her children live in fear, never drive them from her home, never pack them off to thinly disguised prisons. She would stop doing drugs. She would finish her newly replenished supply of coke and then never go back to Nick again. She would eat only healthy food and never miss her aerobics class. She would clear up this mess of clothes on the floor. But first she needed to find out where Jared was.

She called Patti, who proved friendly, at least. She didn't have much positive to say about Debbie, referring to her as a Goody Two-Shoes who thought her son walked on water. Ashley drove her crazy, Patti acknowledged, but she drew the line at having her daughter referred to as a slut. She'd canceled a planned trip to St. Croix with her boyfriend and had given up on public school, enrolling Ashley in the small and expensive Pine Forest Academy in Sea Cliff. She truly had no idea where the Pritima Center was, though, and she needed to hang up, or else she'd be late picking up Ashley for her therapy appointment.

Which was just as well, because at the same moment the twins waddled sleepily into the kitchen demanding attention and Dylan burst in the door freaking out about an upcoming tennis tournament. He was beginning to resemble a miniature version of Ethan: sturdily constructed, jeans short at the ankles (add new jeans to the to-do list), broadening shoulders, a shock of curly strawberry-blond hair, a perpetual tan. He was preparing for an afternoon of tennis while Jared, no doubt, trudged on a forced march up a steep mountainside, assailed by heat and mosquitoes.

CHAPTER TWENTY-SIX

As Sophia watched from her playpen, Erica engaged in the messy task of transferring Sam from his outgrown cage to the larger one, adding a fresh supply of greens, and hooking up the heat lamps again. He stared at her with placid eyes, like two opals. She crunched up the old newspapers laden with lizard poop, stuffed them in a paper bag, and brought them out to trash can. She placed the stinky bundle in the bin, nearly stumbling over Ashley, as pale and skinny as ever, wearing designer jeans, a lacy green silk sweater, dirty running shoes, and a pair of white anklets.

"Hi, Mrs. Richards," she said.

"I just called your mother," Erica blurted.

Ashley tugged dismissively at her sweater, as if daring it to unravel. "I needed to talk to you," she said as they went inside. "I go to the most retarded school. They sent us out on a nature walk, can you believe it? We were collecting flower pollen, which I'm deathly allergic to." As if to emphasize the point, Ashley sneezed. "The teacher went in for a cup of coffee. I hitchhiked here."

"Your mother told me about your new school, but she didn't seem too keen on me talking to you." Erica scrubbed her hands at the kitchen sink.

"She probably thinks you're a bad influence," Ashley said. "Not that she hangs out with saints herself. She's always going out with her girlfriends to bars and stuff. She changes her boyfriend every five minutes, and they're all such lame disco creeps. The last one she went out with came on to me. Right in front of her. You know what he said to me?"

"What?" Erica offered Ashley coffee, but when she shook her head no, poured a cup for herself, bitter thick remnants of her morning brew.

"'Boom, boom, boom, let's go back to my room.'" Ashley grimaced. And Mrs. Lassler—I can't believe she's your sister, Mrs. Richards; you two are so different—she thinks everybody is a bad influence on her little baby boy. She treats Jared like he was two years old. And don't mention Mr. Lassler. What an asshole."

"So tell me about Philadelphia." Erica inhaled the acrid coffee. "What was it like?"

"Nothing much," Ashley said. "We watched TV. We got high with the other kids. We looked in Dumpsters for food and, boy, was that gross. We ate discarded vegetables from the supermarket bins and outdated peanut butter."

"Who are these older men you stayed with?" Erica gulped the last of the coffee and then set the mug down on the table.

"The teachers I told you about. They used to be group leaders at the Nassau Family Clinic. Like Nick Stromboli is now. Jared told me you guys know each other?"

At the mention of Nick, an electric tingle lit up Erica's body. "Yeah, Nick lives down the street from my parents," she said. "He runs an employment agency for housekeepers."

"He's actually a dope dealer," Ashley continued. "What do you think of that? And these guys in Philadelphia, well, they used to be stockbrokers. Then they had some kind of revelation or mental breakdown or something and became therapists instead. Only not real therapists. They got certified through the mail. And one of them owned this house in Philadelphia—it was a heirloom belonging to his family. They were rich, I guess, because it was a cool old house, with all these staircases going nowhere and little rooms with no purpose and these toilets with pull chains and a yard full of weeds."

"Both of them lived there together?" Erica got down on her hands and knees, picking up the puzzle pieces and random plastic objects littering the room.

"They were bisexual," Ashley said. "Roger was always walking around in his boxers, coming on to me. He was like six foot six, but he had the world's smallest penis. You wouldn't think someone that tall could have such a tiny penis."

Erica couldn't help laughing, though she also recalled Debbie's comment about AIDS. She continued picking up toys, sorting them into appropriate piles to put away later.

"He had this wife, but she ran away to Fiji with the contractor on their house and left him with their kid. A retarded kid, about seven years old. I felt kind of bad for him, about the kid."

Something about the retarded child brought Ashley up short. A rustling and cooing came from the playpen, and they turned to see Sophia pulling herself up against the fabric diamonds of the sides, uttering ma-ma sounds.

"My God, that's the first time she's done that," said Erica. "Stood up and said Mama, both. She's so precocious. Maybe it's because she's the youngest."

"She is so adorable," Ashley said. "I love that little lavender dress." Her voice cracked and then her face collapsed, flooding with tears.

"What's the matter, honey?" Erica said, balancing Sophia on her hip.

Ashley wiped her nose on her sweater, a sweater that Erica recognized as one she'd seen in the window of the Ziggy Boutique, at Westbury Mall, for $250.

"Careful, you're ruining that pretty sweater. It looks expensive." Erica knew she sounded like her mother. As if, with Ethan's recent bonus, she couldn't buy that sweater, in every color, many times over.

"They killed my baby!" Ashley choked out. "They made me have an abortion. My mom and those assholes at the clinic. And don't you think Mr. and Mrs. Lassler don't know. 'Cause they do."

"You were pregnant? You were pregnant with Jared's baby?" Erica tried to picture Jared, her smooth-chested baby-faced nephew, as a father.

Ashley nodded. "Even after they found us, I wasn't going to tell them until it was too late. Until they couldn't do anything about it. But my mother notices everything about your looks, if you haven't figured that out yet. She took me shopping—see this sweater—and she noticed I had a little tummy bulge I didn't have before. At first she thought I needed a diet. So she took me to her diet doctor, she said to make sure I was eating right, because, you know, I ate lots of hot dogs and junk in Philadelphia. But the doctor, he figured out what was going on and told her."

"So, did you change your mind? I mean, about having the baby?"

"Yeah, right. Like, you assume I had a choice; like, you know how they say right to choice. They took me to Planned Parenthood in Port Washington, and this counselor told me why what they'd already decided to do was the only thing I could do."

Erica knew that Planned Parenthood clinic. She'd been there herself, in 1973. It was a brand-new proposition then, freshly legal, the chemical off-gassing of the new paint and carpeting blending with the antiseptic medical smell to intensify her vague nausea. Her mother had nothing to do with it, didn't know a thing. She went with her friend Lane, who assured her that the procedure would be no worse than having her tonsils out.

"I'm so sorry, Ashley," Erica said.

"Do you mind if I have something to drink, other than that coffee? Maybe something with real sugar in it?"

Erica poured Ashley a glass of lemonade and filled up a bottle of formula for Sophia. In 1973, she'd also listened to the routine script from the counselor, who never dared raise any questions, who assumed the session would end as it did, holding Erica's hand as a nice, clean, efficient doctor sucked Jeff's baby out. Or maybe it wasn't Jeff's baby; that had been part of the problem. If she had been certain it was Jeff's, surely she would have told him, and then? Well, who could possibly know? Maybe they would have run off to California and lived in a tent on the beach while Jeff strummed his guitar to the rhythm of the Pacific Ocean. Or maybe not.

"Want to feed Sophia?" Erica asked. "She's on the bottle now."

"Oh yes, please," Ashley said. She positioned Sophia carefully, head on forearm. "And they fed me all this bullshit, like, now I have the opportunity to go to this great school, my third school in three years, and I have all my life ahead of me, and I'm too young to have a baby, and blah, blah, blah. Like my life was that exciting? I've never been a good student, I've got dyslexia and ADD, and you know, I was all into partying and drugs and stuff, but then I thought, I'm going to be a mother, and it was all different, like I could do something useful in my life for once. And now that's all over. And I miss Jared. I miss him so bad."

Lane was mistaken. Erica's tonsils were a mass of tissue, without meaning once separated from the rest of her body. But having her almost-but-not quite theoretical baby torn from her, that was a different scale of injury. She'd thought about that child, or the possibility of that child, every single day, as she went on with the rest of her life, as she graduated high school, and studied in college, as she babysat her nephew Jared, as she married Ethan, as she gave birth to Dylan, and Jake and Jesse, and Sophia. She'd never forgotten the due date for her child that never got a chance to be born.

Ashley leaned forward, positioning the bottle nipple between Sophia's lips, periodically readjusting her supporting arm. Sophia's bootied feet hung over her knees. Her scraggly blond hair fell over her forehead. Erica could see brownish roots at the scalp. A tendril of hair brushed Sophia's face, and Ashley flicked it away.

"Mom hates my hair," Ashley said. She thinks I should grow it out into its natural color and then cut it short, layered, you know, because it's so fine. She told me I could have a day of beauty at her spa." She burst into a fresh round of tears, allowing Sophia to dangle a little too loosely off her lap.

"We should burp her," Erica said. "You put her up over your shoulder, like this." Ashley patted Sophia's shoulder and the baby promptly emitted a loud burp, depositing curds of formula on Ashley's silk sweater.

"Screw the sweater," Ashley said. " My Mom's so maxed out on her credit cards. Half of them are still my Dad's, but he's going to stop payment. He filed a lawsuit. He's, like, this big-shot lawyer jerk."

Jeff never knew he was the father of her child, if indeed that was the case. He'd broken up with her two weeks before she found out: she wasn't intellectual enough, or her hair didn't part neatly enough in the middle , or her butt was too fat, or a combination of all three. Plus he found out about Bernie, with the greasy hair and the awful imitations of Jethro Tull but those strangely magnetic eyes. Or Rob, it was Rob, right? Rob from Algebra II—try as she might, she couldn't remember what he looked like.

"Did Jared know about the baby?" she asked.

"Yeah," Ashley said. "He did. We took a test that, you know, you could get in a drugstore. He was kinda scared, but I knew he'd get used to the idea. He's really smart—his stupid parents just don't see it. If we'd only stayed in Philadelphia. If they'd only left us alone." Ashley's tears flowed with renewed vigor, staining Sophia's lavender dress. "He's gonna be so devastated when he finds out."

Erica had confided her pregnancy only to Lane, who wasn't even a close friend but who was notorious at school for her D&C sophomore year. Lane's overnight stay in the hospital, prior to *Roe v. Wade,* had required multiple deceptions and contortions, while Erica's afternoon at Planned Parenthood was simple to arrange. She'd told her mother she was shopping at Roosevelt Field.

"You know," Erica said, "I understand how sad you feel, but you are awfully young to have a baby."

Her words sounded hollow and false; the kind of platitudes adults blurt out when they don't respect kids enough to speak from the heart. Ashley repositioned Sophia, who lay across her bony knees, sleeping. "There's a girl in my therapy group who had a baby, and she's only fourteen," she said after a few minutes.

"You know," Erica dutifully tried again, "you and Jared—if you're still together—can have another baby when you're older, out of high school, on your own."

Ashley looked her straight in the eye. "That would be a different baby," she said. "This one is dead."

After her abortion, Erica had dreamed of babies, babies in the abstract, creatures who would lift her to another, more deeply essential plane, who would anchor her and justify her existence. She'd felt like an inconsequential bouncing atom until the day Dylan was born, healthy and whole, binding her to the world with blood and tissue.

All these years, she'd considered tracking Lane down—she'd heard that she lived in Brooklyn, worked in advertising—and telling her she was wrong, an abortion was nothing like having your tonsils out. She'd given her baby a name, and maybe that was her biggest mistake, lumps of tissue don't have names. It was an ordinary name and a secret one; she'd not given it to any of her other children nor ever spoken it out loud. But ultimately she couldn't muster the will it would have required to choose having that baby: to tell her parents; to tell her sister; to discover Jeff would not run away with her to California; to walk down the halls of her high school in West Meadow where things like this did not happen; to be the academic one and not even attend a second-rate college. She never made a choice. She made an accommodation. Her baby left its trace anyway. Out of all the decisions you make in life, you don't know which ones are irrevocable until it's too late. The secret name bubbled to the surface, Aaron Charles, and she spoke it out loud.

Big bulbous sobs cascaded out of her. The ferocity of her tears shocked her, huge racking convulsions. Sophia responded with screams of her own, and the three of them rocked together on the couch, surrounded by plastic action figures and Sophia's pink teddy bear smiling innocently at them with his yarn mouth.

Sophia's damp cheek rested against her shoulder, her eyes closed, her lashes long against the faint red blotches on her cheeks, her heart beating so fast she hiccupped. Erica could hear Ashley's heart beat too and feel the boniness of her ribs jutting through her sweater, pressing into her side.

Ashley lifted her head up, blinking her eyes, mascara running down her cheeks. "Jared's at Dr. Rafferty's stupid Pritima Center. They don't let you know the address or the phone."

After her abortion she'd listened to Debbie bitch about pregnancy and infant care, her exhaustion, her weight gain, her never-ending laundry. Debbie and Mom would sit over coffee, bitching together, ungrateful members of the sorority of motherhood. Meanwhile, while they weren't looking, Jared wiggled his perfect fingers and toes, soft as butter, grinning his radiant, toothless smile. Erica restrained herself from clutching him to her chest, whisking him swiftly and quietly out the door, and never coming back.

"They hide him away like he's a prisoner of war. . ." Ashley moaned.

"Let's break him out of there." Erica blotted her face with the hem of her sweatshirt.

"Are you crazy?" Ashley said. And then in the next moment, sucking up possibility like Sophia sucked up milk, she asked, "How could we do that?"

CHAPTER TWENTY-SEVEN

The prospect of rescuing Jared made Erica feel dizzy and light, like peppermint flooding her brain. The vision floated before her, a cop show for which they could write the script. They would break down the walls and, in a flash of decisive action, free him.

"Like a prison break," she said. "We'll save him."

"Gosh, I don't know how," Ashley said. " I think he's somewhere down South."

"Let's do it!"

"Well, uh, I can't at this precise moment in time. I have to find out where he is. It might take a little while." Ashley sat up straighter, wiped her eyes with her silk sweater, pushed back her hair, and opened her purse to apply pale pink lip gloss. "Can you give me a ride back to school, Mrs. Richards? I'd better get back before my mom tries to pick me up."

———

Upon her return home, Erica discovered Ethan rummaging noisily around the basement for a particular brand of tennis ball. Apparently he'd flown into La Guardia that afternoon and, not seeing much point in fighting the traffic into Manhattan for only a couple hours of work, had arranged a tennis game. His presence in the house during the weekday, at such an early hour, unsettled her. She slathered barbeque sauce on a tray of chicken, listening to him clatter about.

"Erica, have you seen my Penn ATPs?"

"Nope, I don't even know what they look like," she called down the stairs.

"Well, I need them. I have a match at the club in half an hour. How many toys can our kids possibly own, anyway?" More rustling and shuffling ensued, followed by silence. After a few minutes, Ethan trotted up the stairs carrying the plastic baggie of pot she'd forgotten about, the one in the crayon carrier.

"I think Dylan's been holding out on us," he said in a serious tone that struck Erica as peculiar, since he'd smoked his first joint on his twelfth birthday with his father, on the peak of Mt. Tamalpais.

"It's not Dylan's," Erica said. "It's mine."

"Well, what do you know," said Ethan, clearly relieved. "Don't you share?"

That evening, after Ethan's tennis match and after all the kids were sleeping, they smoked the rest of the baggie on the balcony off their bedroom.

"Why didn't you tell me about your little secret?" Ethan asked.

"Because if I told you little secrets, I might tell you big ones," she thought. "I don't know," she said. "I didn't think you'd approve. Your Wall Street job and your golf and tennis and marathon training and all."

"I'm still me." Ethan edged closer to her. "And I think I'm giving up on that marathon. Can't get up the discipline." His thighs pressed into her, itchy and sweaty. As the distance between them shrunk, her sense of exposure grew.

"Look at Harry Crabtree's hideous pants," she said. From their balcony, they could see directly into the Crabtree's family room. Harry was sitting on the couch with a bowl of chips, wearing purple-and-yellow-plaid pants and a bright-yellow shirt.

"He's making me hungry," Ethan said. He ran down to the kitchen and returned with two Three Musketeer bars that had been lost in the freezer since Halloween. They nibbled on the bars, Ethan's left hand stroking Erica's thigh.

"It looks like Harry's watching *ALF*," she said.

"What do you care about his television habits? I doubt I've ever exchanged two words with Harry Crabtree." Ethan swallowed the last of his chocolate and carefully smoothed out the wrapper. "I should have stayed with my dad, with Apple," he said, apropos of nothing. "He offered me a programming job, back when we lived in Boston."

"You never told me that," Erica said. Mosquitoes settled in with dusk. She scratched her arm.

"Yeah, I'm sure I did," Ethan said. "But then the Grant Fishel offer came in, and besides, you were pregnant." He folded the Three Musketeers wrapper into an intricate pattern.

"You could still do it, I guess," said Erica.

"No, it's too late. Way too late." He folded the candy wrapper one more time, into a tight rectangle, and then pulled the two opposing edges apart. "Look, a boat," Ethan said, handing the folded wrapper to Erica.

Their thighs separated with a damp squeak. He stretched his long legs between the rails of the balcony and leaned the back of his head against the sill of the bedroom window.

⌒

Erica stopped by Nick's the following morning, but he wasn't particularly friendly.

"I said Thursday. Today is Wednesday."

She'd been under the apparently mistaken impression that Nick had a crush on her, which grossed her out on one level but flattered her more than she cared to admit. Surely she looked good enough, with a new summer tan settling in over the residual tan from Florida, lean and tight in jean shorts and a stretchy T-back tank top. She emanated a degrading neediness, she realized, that frightened her and no doubt turned him off. What was that word he'd used to refer to her last week? Urgent.

She tried to diffuse the urgency. "I'm sorry," she said. "I could swear you said Wednesday."

"You should have called." Nick's dress was regressing. He wore a pair of horrific plaid pants and a rumpled T-shirt announcing, "Run for Families, Family Clinic 1985." Continuing the fashion mistake, he'd tucked the shirt into the strained waistband of his pants and locked it in with a braided macramé belt. He'd caught his thinning black hair in a rubber band to make a stringy ponytail.

"You don't like it when I call you," she reminded him. "Plus, I tried your business phone, and it was disconnected. What's going on?"

"I've got all kinds of problems," Nick said. "The INS is up my ass."

Erica tended to forget about Housemates, the presumably legitimate aspect of Nick's business life. Perhaps this INS investigation explained Nick's uptightness, though. Maybe it had nothing to do with her.

As if reading her mind, Nick's face lapsed into an expression both friendly and rueful. "Everything sucks," he said. "Want to get high?"

Erica nodded, settling in against the ripped leather of his ottoman. A cooling breeze from an air-conditioning vent ruffled the pile of old magazines at her side. Sophia commenced ripping the pages of out of last October's issue of People.

"So, that Pritima Center, is that down South somewhere? I've heard it's got a religious orientation." Erica extracted a wet strand of paper out of Sophia's mouth.

"Yeah, yeah, the power of prayer." Nick turned up the volume on the Aerosmith album he was playing. "Dream On" blared out from the loudspeakers. Nick rocked back on his hands and closed his eyes. "I never get tired of this song," he said.

"Do you happen to have their address?" Erica asked.

Nick abruptly dropped back to earth from the cloudy region he so often inhabited. He looked sweet up in the mist; back on the ground, he assumed a shiftier expression.

He dumped out more coke onto the ceramic serving tray he used—it reminded her of a wedding present she'd returned—but Erica, for once, felt like she'd had enough. She shook her head. "No one will tell me where it is, and I'd like to write Jared a letter."

Nick finished up the coke himself. He fiddled with the waistband of his pants, releasing the hem of his T-shirt from its prison, letting it flop over his belt. "Even if I knew the address of the Pritima Center, I couldn't legally tell you," he said. "I'm an employee of the Nassau Family Clinic. I had to sign all kinds of privacy documents."

Nick's face tightened officiously, but what was appealing about him was his lazy looseness—the way when she walked through his warped pine door with the ripped screen the rest of the world fell away.

"I didn't realize you were so much on the straight and narrow." Erica shifted into a cross-legged position, sucking in her newly ripped belly and throwing back her naturally sexy shoulders.

"I can be. I've been a neighborhood counselor there ten years."

"Well, it seems like a mighty odd combination of activities to me." Erica pulled a damp photo of Michael Jackson out of Sophia's mouth. "Say, I was wondering, when you run out of coke, where do you buy more? Like, who do you hang out with when you're not hanging with Dr. Rafferty or West Meadow teenagers?"

"That," Nick said, in the same bristly, officious voice, "is none of your business."

"Why not?" Erica asked. "Curious minds want to know."

"You are so far over your head," Nick said. "You might like to fantasize otherwise, but you are a nice wifey-poo from the suburbs. There's a lot you don't know, sweetie." Nick straightened the piles of paper on the tile table in the center of the room, positioning a stack of mail over a particularly gooey juice stain, as if to indicate he was an upstanding citizen.

"You're from the suburbs too," Erica said.

Nick dumped a clutch of dirty mugs in the kitchen sink.

"You better go about your wifey-poo business. I told you, I'm busy."

"Suit yourself," Erica said.

The heavy gray clouds of early morning had dissolved into pouring rain. After buckling Sophia into her car seat and blotting her dry with a towel, she turned Vince's ignition key, and got silence in return. Just like Vince, to choose a day like this to break down again. She needed to take Sophia for her eighth month checkup, and pick up Ethan's shirts at the cleaners, and buy milk and mayonnaise. She tried again: no sound but the beating rain on the windshield and Sophia's irritated whimpers. Pressure rose up on the back of her neck, spiking into a pain burst on the right side of her head. She tried Vince a third time. He gave a chug chug noise that with gentle pressure on the accelerator gradually shifted into a solid hum. His windshield wipers beat rapidly, transforming the street into an impressionistic blur. Her tape deck blared out another one of Jared's selections, Rat Debris, a cacophony of drums, squealing guitar, and unintelligible lyrics. At the Pritima Center he was probably forced to chant some paramilitary incantation, or maybe sing gospel tunes.

CHAPTER TWENTY-EIGHT

On Saturday Ethan and Erica drove with Lisa and Les to Long Island City, where they put their respective nine-year olds on a bus for Camp Whispering Wind in the Poconos. Monday, a small yellow bus picked the twins up for their first day at Sandy Hollow Day Camp. They hugged her hard, grabbed their water bottles, swung their sturdy little brave selves up onto the bus, and waved out the window. For the next seven hours, Erica and Sophia would be alone.

The morning was already blisteringly hot. She could take Sophia to the pool club and walk back and forth with her in the icy blue water, even though theoretically she wasn't allowed there in diapers, and they might be exiled to the awful pee-stinking wading pool to exchange desultory conversation with Jamaican nannies, probably employed via Housemates.

Or she could stop by Nick's again. The spot right in front of his window air conditioner always felt deliciously icy. No, she convinced herself. She mustn't look urgent.

She could call Ashley, who had disappeared from her life as abruptly as she'd entered it. But that would require potentially risky interaction with Patti or, at the very least, leaving a message with the housekeeper.

Or she could call Debbie. With Jared neatly filed away, she seemed more her typical self, no desperation seeping out at the corners. Now that she no longer needed to roam all corners of the New York City metro area searching for Jared, she'd returned to work. But she never initiated contact with Erica and, when faced with her, shied away like a timid kitten. They'd brushed up against each other gingerly at her parents' supper Sunday night, clearing platters of chicken and loading the dishwasher. That whole long evening, no one mentioned the Pritima Center. When Erica threw Jared's name out into the conversational void, just to hear it spoken, just to validate his existence, the syllables simply hung there, echoed, and dropped. Separated from Erica by the width of the dining room table, holding Ron's hand between turns, Debbie beat everyone at backgammon. Dad chattered on about Budapest and Prague.

Today, Monday, was Debbie's day off. Erica briefly considered inviting her to the club. Perhaps, lounging by the pool, she could worm some information about the Pritima Center out of her. But, even under the best of circumstances, Debbie disliked swimming and lying in the sun.

Erica called Justine instead, who accepted Erica's invitation with genuine enthusiasm. Her husband was away on a golf boondoggle with some doctor buddies and her children away at sleep away camp. They ate chips from the snack bar and flirted with the gross lifeguard in his zebra-striped Speedo. Erica produced a metal flask filled with Jamaican rum.

"You sure are a character, Erica," Justine enthused, glugging a shot. "A real individual."

"I try," Erica said.

Justine sighed, readjusting her bikini top. "Life is so monotonous," she said. "When's the last time you did anything really exciting?"

Erica thought back to Josh Hendrie's apartment. That seemed pathetic; plus, she wasn't about to share it with Justine. She thought back farther.

"Childbirth," she said. "Childbirth is the best rush ever." She remembered how the pain, and all the memory of the pain, vanished at the moment of each of her children's births, leaving her only a light sensation in her body like she'd run a marathon: a soft elation, a desire to do it all over again.

"Childbirth is agony, Erica," Justine said. "I wish they could have knocked me out. I suppose you were one of those all-natural women? No epidural for you?"

"No epidural for me." Erica finished off most of the rum and handed the last driblet to Justine. "I'm tough."

"Four times tough, huh? I gotta say, I've never met anyone like you." Justine tossed her hair back in full view of Mr. Speedo. By early afternoon, sunburnt and giggly, they retreated to Erica's house for tuna salad and more rum cocktails.

That night, Erica lay on her bed, hot and headachy, wearing only a pair of panties and supporting a can of lemon soda on her tummy. Ethan, the paycheck that occasionally materialized in human form, made a rare phone call. He was feeling lonely. He'd attended a barbeque at his boss's house, in some gated luxury development in Boca, but everyone else attending had come with their wives and families, so he felt awkward. The weather in Florida had turned uncomfortably steamy, with swarms of mosquitoes and humid air that stuck to him like paste. He would return in a week and a half.

"Why not earlier?" Erica asked.

Believe him, he wanted to come home earlier, he said. But he couldn't swing it—there was a lot going on he didn't want to talk about; he was under pressure; he was working eighteen-hour days; something about the SEC.

"I should have gone back to the Bay Area and worked at Apple with my father," he repeated.

"What's the point of regrets?" asked Erica.

"Not much," Ethan said. He was sorry about his mood. He was tired. He was going to bed.

A cascade of crickets chirped in the backyard; tires squealed down the street. The night was still young. Talk about regret. Summer had always been her favorite season, but now, the season in only its second week, she could already sense the fading of its heavy light.

The phone rang: Amelia.

"I'm sorry to call so late," Amelia said, "But I'm freaked. I had to let Dahlia go. I couldn't take a chance, with Jason's county job and all. And here I just started my interior decorating business. I don't know what on earth I'm going to do."

"Can't you hire a replacement?" Erica guzzled the last of her soda.

"You didn't hear? I thought you were friends with Nick Strom- boli. An old high school buddy or something."

Muscles tightened across Erica's skull. Her right eyelid twitched. She forced herself to sound casual. "We did go to high school together. He owns Housemates, right?"

"You never did follow up on Housemates, did you?"

The air-conditioning didn't seem to be working right. Erica opened the bedroom window for air. A sultry, rich fragrance drifted in from the yard.

"Are you listening to me, Rikki?" said Amelia, sounding agi- tated.

"Yes. No. I decided I didn't want some strange girl living in the house. Isabella comes once a week, and she keeps things clean enough, I think." Erica pressed the can of soda, still retaining some residual cool from the refrigerator, into her sweaty forehead.

"Well, it's just as well. They closed the whole operation down. It's been in the works for weeks, I guess, but it all blew up a couple of days ago. Seems like none of Nick's housekeepers had green cards. He had shady connections funneling them in from the Caribbean or something. He's in major trouble. I always thought he seemed a little slippery, you know. I'm sorry—I realize you're friends."

"He's not my friend. I hardly know him." Erica's knees vibrated of their own volition.

"Well, whatever."

"Hang on for a sec—it's call-waiting," said Amelia. Erica wait- ed through several minutes of silences, wondering if her phone was tapped. "It could be," she thought. There were so many suspects: Ralph Rossiter the private eye; the SEC; the DEA.

Amelia's breathless voice returned. "Gotta go," she said.

So that was why Nick had been so distant and distracted, so testy. It had nothing to do with her looks or her urgency. The thick air closed in like a wall, pressing on Erica's chest. She sank down onto her Pakistani cream wool carpet. It smelled of lanolin and dust.

CHAPTER TWENTY-NINE

Tuesday morning's air bristled electric, rife with unfinished business. She needed to go somewhere, if only there was anywhere worth going. She couldn't return to the pool; it was closed for a swim team competition. Once again, she fought the desire to stop by Nick's. She was too dependent on him. Plus, she didn't trust him. Now that the authorities had discovered the INS scam in his "legitimate" operations, surely they'd dig further into his activities. Maybe she should buy her drugs from someone else. She still had Stephan Langston's number written right there in her phone book. Or maybe she could cut down. She could save it for the morning, as a supplement to her coffee. She would start that afternoon. Or better yet, tomorrow afternoon, after she used up the stuff, right there in the car, right there in her diaper bag.

She called Stephan's number and left a message. He was at work, no doubt. For all she knew, he was in Florida holding mysterious meetings with Ethan. She called Nick, despite her misgivings, and to her surprise, he answered and tersely suggested she try him late afternoon. Late afternoon seemed eons away.

And what was the deal with Ashley? She'd barged into Erica's house, breaking scars off her heart, and then vanished, la-de-da, into the ether. Erica ran through Jared rescue scenarios in her head: scaling a brick wall, dropping into the ivy on the other side, charging toward a gothic bricked structure with barred windows, breaking the glass, shoving away orderlies. The scenarios grew ever more ornate, but she needed Ashley's assistance to enact them.

Her heart beating way too fast, Erica drove to Kiddie Warehouse in Mineola and bought Sophia a new bathing suit. All around them shoppers buzzed like ravenous flies, sucking up bargains under the fluorescent lights. On the way home, she listened to yet another one of Jared's atrocious tapes, an LA-based band called Roach. Thrash metal, that's what Jared had termed this noise. She figured the term itself was a significant part of the appeal; it reminded her of the way her boys thrashed their legs all over the bed when they slept.

She found herself pulling into Debbie's driveway. Debbie opened the door, smiling tentatively. She was wearing her work clothes: crisp white shirt, navy slacks. Her wrists still looked pinkish and irritated where Erica had grabbed them, even after all this time.

"Oh, hi, Rikki," she said. "You look bleary. Allergies or a cold?"

"I'm fine," Erica said.

"You're flushed. Your nose is running." Debbie pressed her lips to Erica's forehead. "Are you sure you don't have a fever?"

"It's just so sticky outside," Erica said.

"Do you want some iced tea or something? I can't sit long. I just got home from work, and I promised Ron I'd make pot roast for dinner."

Erica sank down onto the couch, placing Sophia's baby seat on the carpet. The baby's fingers played against her seat buckle, attempting to penetrate its mysteries and unlock it.

Debbie brought Erica a glass of iced tea, the powdered kind with Sweet'N Low.

"I'm sorry I scratched you," Erica said. Cool liquid sweetness slid down her throat. "It was an accident."

Debbie nodded, maintaining careful distance.

"Are you still making DDD presentations with Patti?" Erica asked.

"Not so much since I'm back at the salon. And not with Patti. Patti's taking psychology classes. She wants to go back to college and get a degree as a therapist. To tell you the truth, I'm relieved. We never had much in common, and the less contact I have with that daughter of hers, the better."

Silence hung thickly in the air. Erica closed her eyes and leaned against the cushions. She could either fall asleep or punch through walls.

"I wish we could be closer, Rikki," she said. "We were discussing the importance of sibling support in therapy. But you're so inconsiderate and impulsive, and you always have been. You don't care if I hurt, you don't care if I'm in pain, and it's always been that way."

"Always?" Despite the tea and the air-conditioning, sweat beaded on Erica's forehead.

"Yes. Since we were kids together. Remember my elbow fracture?"

"Of course I remember your elbow. I cared about your elbow."

"I wouldn't have broken it if it wasn't for you." Debbie stroked the faint scar on her arm as if it still hurt.

"It wasn't my fault. I was seven." Debbie had fallen, in slow motion like in the movies, crashing down on her arm, the arm splaying out against the concrete like it wasn't part of her body. It wasn't Erica's fault she kept swinging. She kept trying to slow her swing down, but it kept going. She'd swung so high, and it took so long to come down to where she could put her feet on the ground.

"That wasn't the only thing. You were always running away and terrifying everybody, like that day at the World's Fair. What were you thinking?"

"I was thinking about the light. How when I opened my eyes and looked straight through the water, all the buildings and people broke down, and all I could see was rivers of colored light."

Debbie snorted. "And what were you thinking about when you convinced my son to run away? Sparkles and fairy dust?"

"I didn't convince Jared to run away. He decided that all on his own." Erica's legs shook of her own accord, and she expected Debbie to diagnose her with a terminal muscular disease. But Debbie wasn't looking at her, only down at the silver bracelet on her fragile wrist.

"Well, Ron doesn't think so. And that's another thing we discussed in therapy. How you disrespect my husband. You and Ethan both. You treat him like he's beneath you."

"I didn't come here to be insulted." Erica put her leg up on the coffee table, in full defiance of Debbie's rules.

Debbie pointedly said nothing but stood up and walked into

the kitchen. Erica heard the sound of stirring, and the refrigerator door opening and closing. A scent of seared meat and onions drifted in. Erica wiggled her leg. One swipe of her foot and all those paperweights would come tumbling down.

"Rikki, I needed a moment to think," Debbie said, returning to the living room. "Things have gotten out of hand again. If you take your foot off my furniture, perhaps we could have a few minutes of civilized conversation."

Erica moved her foot. She felt dizzy. She forced herself to look into her sister's eyes as if she was a normal human being.

Debbie sighed and sat down again. "Ron and I are visiting Elyse and Martin in Albany next weekend." Elyse was an old friend of Debbie's from beauty school. "We're finally finding some time to get away and share some fun times together ."

"Great," Erica said. Now her right hand was shaking. It wanted to take action.

"Did you hear about Nick Stromboli and Housemates?" Debbie asked, leaning across the table confidentially. "Mom told me all about it."

She could punch her hand right through the glass cabinet on the opposing wall, housing Debbie's insipid collection of ceramic bunnies, if only Debbie herself wasn't in the way. She picked some peeling skin off her knee instead. "Yeah, Amelia told me. She was freaking out."

"You never did contact him about a housekeeper, did you?"

"I changed my mind." Erica put her ice tea directly down on the glass.

"Well, good thing," said Debbie, discreetly sliding a coaster under the glass. "I'd never trust a stranger to clean my house. And Ron is so particular. He used to fight so with Jared, the way he kept his room, with books and records and clothes all over the place."

Jared. The forbidden name had been spoken. Erica took the opening.

"How is Jared?"

"He's doing well," Debbie said. "He calls from a supervised situation."

"Can you give out his address now? Can we write him let-ters and stuff?"

"No, Rikki." Debbie sighed, as if addressing a nagging two year old. "I've told you a thousand times, outside contact is forbid-den right now. When he progresses further in the program he'll be granted more privileges. Excuse me, I have to check the roast."

"I have to go anyway," Erica said, rising from the couch. She picked up Sophia's baby seat. Her limbs shook, both from nerves and effort; still way too much flab jiggling around her triceps. "Are you sure you don't want the name of my ear, nose and throat doctor before you go?" Debbie asked, pouring a can of stewed tomatoes into the roasting pan. "You look funky and you sound congested."

"Nah," Erica said.

"You want this sandwich?" Debbie pulled a styrofoam con-tainer out of the refrigerator. "It's a chicken teriyaki from Buck-man's. I think I'm allergic to the wheat in the soy sauce."

"No thanks." Erica shifted Sophia's seat to the other arm.

Debbie looked hurt. "I'll throw it out then," she said. "Ron hates leftovers."

———

Erica set up the wading pool at home but couldn't interest Sophia in splashing around in it. Her face looked flushed and she whim-pered irritably. Erica gave her a dose of Infant Tylenol and drove around the neighborhood in her damp swimsuit, listening to Peter Gabriel, hoping the ride and the tamer music might lull Sophia to sleep. Her neighborhood looked empty: squares of green lawn; a few wilted impatiens here and there; Hispanic gardeners blowing debris off a curb. She rounded a corner past a farmhouse colonial her mother had sold the previous year to a family with three boys, one in Dylan's class, the others in middle and high school. A wood refinishing truck was parked in their driveway and the whine of their equipment echoed on the empty street. The ride, or maybe the Tylenol, didn't put Sophia to sleep, but her color went down and her mood cheered up. She chattered away and pointed at the truck, but now Erica fought to keep her eyes open. The easiest thing in the world was to do nothing; to drown in her ennui. Crossing the railroad tracks, she saw that her parent's lawn sprinklers were running full blast, popping up and down between the perennial beds, but neither her Dad's Honda Accord nor her mother's Mercury Sable were in the driveway.

Nick's brown Acura was, though, and it was already afternoon, albeit not late. He met her at the door with her stuff—twice her usual order, this time, she wasn't taking any chances—and Erica handed over a big lump of cash. Today there clearly would be no lazy conversations, no lounging on his sticky rug. She lingered on his stoop, fingering the metal doorknob, tracing the wrought iron vines fronting the screen. A few weeks before, recalling third grade math night, they'd estimated the number of metal holes in that screen. They'd counted the number horizontally (150) then vertically (324). There was a ragged tear, though, about two inches in diameter, that they couldn't account for. The whole attempt had collapsed in hilarity. For Ethan, Erica noted, solving a problem like that would be as simple as breathing. Then Nick had asked, "Are you sure breathing is simple?"

Erica crossed the street back to her car and picked up a high intensity lamp at the pet store.

———

As she was installing it, Stephan Langston returned her call. He was on his way to California but checking phone messages. He was sorry, but he didn't recall her name, what firm was she with?

She wasn't with any firm, she told him.

Was she a journalist? Because if she was, he wasn't speaking to the press.

When she assured him she wasn't; he grew friendlier. When she reminded him of where they'd last met he said that Ethan had mentioned something about a hotel they liked in Jamaica. Was that was she was calling about? Because surely Ethan had told her, things had come up, he couldn't get away.

"Well, no," Erica said, taking a deep breath. "Remember that coke we shared in the bathroom? I was wondering if you could tell me where to buy some."

He didn't sound so friendly anymore, but he did give her the number of a guy named Anders. Her call waiting beeped, allowing her a graceful exit from the conversation.

It was Ethan, terribly distracted. He wouldn't be home for at least another week. Problems. Meetings. A trip to California without mention of visiting his parents or sister Pauline or getting some surfing in.

"I'm bummed," Erica said. "I miss you."

"So am I, " Ethan said. "This is not my idea, believe me. Gotta go. Talk to you later."

She and the twins watched reruns of The Brady Bunch. While Erica's face was turned, Sophia grabbed a Transformer toy and brought it to her lips. The head broke off, rolling to the back of her little pink mouth. Quickly, instinctively, Erica extracted it from her throat, then threw the Transformer into a bin on the wall unit. She placed the Legos and puzzles out of reach too. She'd clearly reached that stage of life with Sophia where nowhere in the house was safe. She put her in her playpen and sank back on the couch, closing her eyes, imagining running down a road with Jared, downhill, their speed steadily increasing, leaping, soaring through the landscape.

Someone tapped her on the head.

"Mommy, where are you? Pay attention."

"Huh?" She raised herself up on her arms. Sophia was dumping all her toys out of the playpen.

"Mommy, we're hungry," said Jesse.

She pulled a bag of chicken nuggets out of the freezer. The stupid phone rang again.

"Are you sitting down?" Amelia asked.

"I'm making dinner."

"You know Nick Stromboli?" she asked. "Housemates?"

"Of course I do, Erica thought. Get to the point."

"Well, he got busted a couple hours ago. By the state narcotics commission or something. Apparently once they started looking into the immigration fraud, they discovered he was a coke dealer. Like, a big one. He had cash stuffed all over his house, in the mattresses, in his Tupperware, you wouldn't believe it. I just heard it on the evening news."

"Oh my God," Erica said. She put her head in her hands, upending the plastic bag of breaded chicken.

"Rikki?" Amelia asked. Her voice sounded thin and distant.

"Yeah, sorry, I dropped chicken all over the floor."

"Brilliant, Rikki. But you never know about people, do you? Nick seemed like such a dork. And Debbie told me he was a counselor at the Nassau Family Clinic."

"Good grief," Erica said. "Look, I'm sorry, but I have to pick up this chicken. It's under the dishwasher."

"One more thing," said Amelia. "He had this notebook on him? A notebook that listed all these people he sold drugs to? All these people right in the neighborhood, big shots like lawyers and doctors and stuff. Of course, they're not releasing any names, but I can't believe you haven't heard any of this. Don't you listen to the news?"

"You're my personal anchorwoman," Erica said, both her eyebrows pulsing as if they had a mind of their own, her hand on the telephone slick with sweat. She carried it into the bathroom and shoved her little Ziploc baggie farther back in the cabinet, behind the Drano.

"Want to get together tomorrow morning for coffee?"

"I have to go to aerobics."

"Are you sure you should be working out?" Amelia asked. "You sound congested. "Do you have a chest cold? One's going around now, you know."

"If I don't exercise, I'll go crazy," Erica said. "I really gotta get this chicken off the floor."

CHAPTER THIRTY

When Erica worked as a nurse in South Boston, in the outpatient clinic, they sometimes brought in convicts from the nearby high-security prison for medical attention. They were leathery men, with track marks and scabs and hard eyes, who endured her with a weary tolerance as she clasped blood pressure cuffs on their arms or explained the protocol of diabetes treatment. They bore no relation to her friend Nick with his flabby stomach and soft hands, who, like her, still lived within a mile of his mother, on their manicured island, apart from the grime and chaos of the city.

She forced herself up from the bed the morning after Amelia's call, wiping her sweaty palms against her mouthwash-stained nightgown. She woke up Jesse and Jake and gave them Cinnamon Toasties and orange juice, remembering to tuck their swimsuits and tennis rackets into their camp bags. She fed and changed Sophia and waited outside with the boys for the camp bus. Once the bus left, she loaded the dishwasher. She drove to the gym and did V-steps and A-steps and bicep curls, avoiding conversation with Lisa and Justine, and then drove home. There were no police at the door and no messages on the answering machine. She didn't know what to do next. She called Anders. He agreed to meet her in an hour in a park off of Utopia Boulevard.

She drove south down Utopia Boulevard, passing a multitude of stoplights, body shops, sad-looking brick garden-apartment complexes with patches of limp pansies, and a lawn warehouse store she'd shopped at once. She found the intersection scribbled on the back of her shopping list and, after a fruitless several-block search for a space, parked Vince Volvo illegally in front of a fire hydrant.

A couple of young mothers watched their toddlers play in the dirt by a metal jungle gym that reminded her of the old-fashioned unsafe one she used to climb in elementary school. At one bench, a couple of old men played cards; on another, a homeless man snored under a ripped black blanket. She saw no one who might possibly be Anders. She double-checked Vince Volvo's locked doors. The sky pressed in on her, ozone-yellow. She had a splitting headache.

After Erica walked Sophia's stroller up and down the path between the playground and the benches numerous times, a skinny guy in his twenties, with tight jeans hugging his hips and a thick shock of straight dark hair, sidled up to her and asked her if she wanted any T-shirts. Startled, she shook her head no, and then got it. "You bet," she said. "White."

He didn't smile. He handed her a bag; she handed him the money he'd requested over the phone: $300, way more than Nick. He seemed put off by Sophia and not particularly friendly. The whole interaction took no more than two minutes. She scrambled back to Vince and turned on the air-conditioning, even though it made the engine hesitate unnervingly, and blew through a few red lights as she motored down Utopia Boulevard back to the expressway.

Throughout the hot, empty middle of the day, Erica followed Sophia around. She circled the first floor of the house, hallway to kitchen to family room to living room and back to the hallway, meandered around the backyard; dodged duck poop at the town pond; climbed through the ladders and tubes of the West Meadow Elementary play structure. The parks were deserted: the children away at camp; their parents scampering about like hamsters on a wheel; everything suspended, about to crash and break.

The twins were eating macaroni and cheese for dinner, Erica hovering over them playing with a plate of salad, when Ethan called from California.

"I wanted you to hear from me, before you heard it on the news," Ethan said.

"About Nick Stromboli?" she asked.

"Nick who? No. They've indicted several Grant Fishel executives on securities fraud. Insider trading. Manipulation of markets.

All kinds of bullshit. I don't know how far this is going to go." Ethan mentioned several names, the only familiar one being Stephan Langston.

"I can make markets move," Ethan had told her excitedly, a couple of years before, when the big money started coming. "It's just a matter of figuring out the system. It's just a matter of math and staying a step ahead of everybody else."

The idea of markets moving had tickled Erica's fancy. She pictured Pathmark growing legs and walking down Northern Boulevard. She didn't mention this vision to Ethan; he would have thought her stupid and frivolous. He would have sat her down and explained the difference between the Dow Jones and the NASDAQ.

"This isn't going to affect you in any way is it?" Erica asked.

"Well," Ethan said. "Well. It involves a lot of people I know. That I've worked with. I'm sure they're going to want to question me."

"Is that what the meetings in California are about?" Erica scraped uneaten noodles into the garbage.

"Well. Yes and no. Events have overtaken us, if you know what I mean. Listen, Erica, I have to go. I'll call back when I can. I just wanted you to know. Is everyone all right? All the kids all right?"

"Yeah, sure," said Erica. "Dylan is playing a magician in the summer performance at Whispering Wind.'"

"Cool," Ethan said. "Take care, okay? Don't worry."

New York was closing in on both of them like an iron claw. And even though the boys needed baths, and the diaper pail needed emptying and the clean dishes needed to be unloaded from the dishwasher and replaced with dirty ones, Erica paced around the kitchen, watching Sophia gurgle in her swing and a butterfly land on the zinnias outside the kitchen window.

The phone rang.

"Rikki, I just heard the news about Grant Fishel. Is it going to affect Ethan?" Debbie gushed concern, but Erica also detected a faint tone of satisfied suspicion. Debbie had always thought Ethan's income was too mysterious in origin and too generous in amount to be trusted.

"No, no, it's got nothing to do with his department." Erica's phone beeped. "Oops, I gotta go. Call-waiting."

"Hey, Mrs. Richards, great news!" Ashley announced cheerily.

"Great news?"

"Jared's address! I was at group therapy, and this kid Hayden, he was at the Pritima Center until two weeks ago, and he started talking about it. Usually people who've been there don't talk about it. It's like they're under a conspiracy of silence, you know?"

"What did he say?"

"Well, he said it's really horrible. They take these long hikes, out into the country, where it's really hot, and they don't bring nearly enough water or anything to eat, and they have to go to the bathroom in the woods. They don't bring toilet paper. You have to use leaves. And they have to do these farm chores. They make everyone work like slaves. He said he passed out once, and he lost a ton of weight, and he's still feeling really weak, and his parents are thinking of suing them."

"But what about Jared?"

"Well, yeah. They weren't in the same group, but he saw him on some of the hikes and at meals. He said the food is awful, all greasy, and that Jared looked real skinny and kinda sick. But, and this is the point, Mrs. Richards, I asked him, 'Say, where is this Pritima Center?' and he said that was confidential information, but then he cornered me while we were waiting for our parents in the parking lot, and he told me! It's in a town called Burkittsville, South Carolina!"

CHAPTER **THIRTY-ONE**

Anonymity might seem an alien concept when you lived in the same neighborhood where you'd grown up, surrounded by people you'd known your whole life, but the fact was, all anyone noticed was surfaces. Did your eyes look bleary, had you put on any weight, did you add a new bathroom on your house, did you sound congested? All you needed to do was put up the thinnest of veneers, and no one dared peek behind. You didn't need to be a good liar. Just a consistent one.

Ashley didn't have any problem getting away. Her mother wouldn't pose a problem because she had left on a weeklong yoga retreat in the Berkshires with her new boyfriend, leaving Ashley to rattle around in their six-thousand-square-foot contemporary house in Old Westbury. Erica's parents were zipping around their house like twittering birds, packing and repacking their overstuffed suitcases. Their flight to Amsterdam left Saturday morning.

Debbie and Ron were visiting their boring friends in Albany, planning a stop at an outlet mall along the way. She'd called to ask Erica to pick up the newspaper. "They've sold WBEZ to some giant conglomerate," Debbie said. "Ron's scared he might get laid off."

"Most likely he won't," Erica said. Debbie and Ron's troubles seemed very small. "Say, I meant to tell you I'm going to the Hamptons this weekend. Some friends of Ethan's from work invited us to their summer rental."

"Sounds ritzy," Debbie said. "Some of his Wall Street buddies, huh? Even with the Grant Fishel trouble?"

"It's overblown," Erica reassured her.

She arranged for the twins to spend the weekend with loyal Lisa, who chattered excitedly about an idea she had for starting a dog-friendly bed and breakfast. "I can't bear the thought of going away without Penny and a lot of the girls in my spaniel club feel the same way," she enthused. "So where are you going?"

"I'm visiting some coworkers of Ethan's in the Hamptons."

"You're not!" Lisa's transparent voice dripped with envy. "Tell me more."

"I met them at that Don Johnson party, they've got a big house overlooking the beach, in, I don't know, Amagansett? I gotta check the address."

She enhanced the Amagansett story when Justine called, describing a ten thousand square foot beachfront Spanish-style hacienda with a firepit. It served as a good way to change the subject when Justine inquired about Ethan and Grant Fishel and, when that didn't get anywhere, yammered on about Nick. "I haven't fired Needa yet," she said. "I think she's legal. I don't ask. But I'm wondering if my plastic surgeon, you know, Carl Donsky? Is one of his coke customers? He gives these wild parties, not that I've been to one—but he strikes me as the cokehead type."

"I've never met him," Erica said.

"Well, have a super time," Justine said. "I want to know every detail."

Erica could not sleep. At three in the morning she began throwing items willy-nilly in Vince's backseat.

She remembered how she used to swing higher than even the boys at West Meadow Elementary, pumping until her legs came parallel with the top bar, till the whole metal frame tipped back and the concrete bases rocked in their sockets. She kept trying to swing above the bar, all the way around, but as hard as she pumped, she could never break past that level spot, sandwiched flat between the sky and the blacktop.

One day she challenged Debbie to a swinging match, which shouldn't have even been a fair contest, given that she was seven and Debbie almost twelve. They hit the top point, and the concrete base rocked back extra far because there were two of them. "Whee," said Erica, giving just a little extra push and raising her legs high in the air. Her toes touched the edge of the bar. The swingset creaked and shook.

"Rikki, stop!" Debbie shouted.

Erica pushed harder and took her hands off the chain. "Look, Debbie, no hands. You try it."

"Stop, Rikki. I mean it." A high note of panic entered Debbie's voice.

"Chicken, chicken!" Erica flapped her hands in the air like a bird.

"I'll tell Mom," Debbie said, but she let go of the chains, looking down as she did so, sliding out of her seat, screaming all the way down to the blacktop, which was concrete then, no bark dust to cushion her fall. Mrs. Sheldon from down the block was playing with her toddler on the seesaw; she called an ambulance. By the time the ambulance came, Debbie was sitting up and screaming, her elbow bent out at an unnatural angle. She'd broken her elbow socket in two places. The elbow had to get put back together with metal pins that were still there to this day.

"Rikki made me do it," Debbie told her mother, who believed her without question, banning Erica from the playground for six long antsy months. Everyone signed Debbie's cast. She got a $200 playhouse and chose the ice cream flavor every time they went to the supermarket, inevitably a gag-worthy butter pecan.

If Erica could have flown through the air and caught Debbie, she would have, but she wasn't a bird, just a little girl, and it took so long for her swing to slow and come to the ground. Debbie stopped and looked down—that was the problem. Only then did she slip. Even at seven Erica knew never to look down. You look straight ahead and keep on swinging.

———

Ashley waited for Erica at Pathmark, by the shopping carts. Her hair was freshly frosted and curled around her ears. She wore big silver hoop earrings, jean cutoffs, and a blue top that initially appeared worn and faded but upon closer observation was actually washed silk. Before she climbed into Erica's car, she stubbed out a cigarette on the sidewalk. She stuffed a small backpack, covered in embroidered flowers and butterflies, under her legs.

"I know I shouldn't smoke," she said.

"Don't worry about it." Erica turned around, handing Sophia her pacifier. She was kvetchy this morning, pulling at her ear, slightly warm.

"You brought Sophia?" Ashley looked surprised.

"What else was I going to do?" Erica said. "She's my buddy. She comes everywhere with me. What kind of music do you want to listen to?"

Ashley shifted Ethan's geeky atlas, a deluxe model sporting detachable maps of all fifty states, around the center console, and riffled through the large stack of tapes wobbling below. "How about Billy Joel?" she asked.

"Okay," Erica agreed, sticking in the tape though it hardly fit her mood. "Do you like Rat Debris or Bloody Tampax? Or Barf?"

"Oh no, yuck!" Ashley said, pushing back her curls. "That's Jared's thing. He knows I hate that type of bands. Do you like heavy metal, honestly?"

"Kind of," Erica said, realizing that was true, that she'd acquired a taste for heavy metal like one might a tannic wine, through a combination of desire and numbing repetition.

Despite the midmorning hour, they hit all the usual traffic snags: the hill between Douglaston and Little Neck, the merger with the Cross-Island Parkway, the inevitable clog by the Shelby Manor Assisted Living Center. Erica kept switching lanes while accomplishing little forward motion.

"How convenient," Erica muttered to herself. "A nursing home next to a cemetery." Even after they merged onto the Brooklyn-Queens Expressway, the gravestones continued for mile after tortuously slow mile. As many live people as there were in New York, there seemed to be more dead ones. She wiped her sweaty hands off on her shorts and scratched the spot at the top of her head where it felt like an artery was pulsing and bulging out. How did that song go from the seventies, was it Art Garfunkel? "Nothing but the dead or dying back in my hometown"? A tractor-trailer backfired, spewing a waft of black smoke through the front windows of the car. Despite the thick, hot stink, Erica breathed in rapid bursts, the air muddy against her throat.

They joined the slow crawl over the Verrazano Bridge. Below them, whitecaps rustled in a soft, sour-smelling wind, frothing over the brown water like a cappuccino. To their right, they lapped against the towers of lower Manhattan. A few months ago, she'd looked out at this same view from the opposite perspective, at night, and it had all seemed magical and limitless. What an illusion.

"Mrs. Richards, are you okay?" Ashley glugged a bottle of Evian water.

"Yeah, why?" Erica asked, blowing her nose into a crumpled tissue. She made the mistake of looking at it, spattered with drops of blood. She squished it into her pocket.

"You scratched the back of your head." Ashley twisted the bottle cap closed and returned it to her bag.

Great, she was starting to scratch the back of her head when she got nervous, like her mother. She wondered if her mother ever felt that tangible increase in arterial pressure, the sensation as if something was about to burst. "I hate this traffic," she said.

The truck in front of them stopped suddenly, forcing Erica to brake in order to avoid hitting his flatbed. They stood still on the downslope of the bridge for a second before the traffic jounced forward onto Staten Island, which, as Ethan had noted so long ago on Josh Hendrie's balcony, was quite unremarkable in the morning. On one side of the highway stood dingy rows of worn-out houses with aluminum siding and dingy pizza shops; on the other side equally dingy water slapped against a trash-strewn beach. At one spot, the trash accumulated into an honest-to-God landfill. Seagulls shrieked around the sulfurous mound, while across four lanes of heavy traffic, an elderly lady hung out her laundry. Everywhere was in reach of a grabbing hand, a ceaselessly ringing phone, an ominous knock on the door.

Ashley's fingers danced across her backpack. "Mrs. Richards," she said, "what are we going to do when we get to South Carolina? "

"I figure we'll get down there and play it by ear. Scope it out, figure out what we're up against."

"Wow," Ashley said. "That makes me nervous."

The centipede of traffic crawled over the Goethals Bridge. On family trips, her father had always referred to this span as the

Goebbels Bridge, giggling under his breath at his own black humor. As a child, she'd never had any difficulty imagining Elizabeth, New Jersey, the wasteland of oil refineries beyond the bridge, as a concentration camp—all those foul vapors arising from bodies burning in the chimneys. But today she thought of it simply as not New York. She put on a Bruce Springsteen tape in celebration.

"'Sometimes it's like someone took a knife, baby, edgy and dull, and cut a valley through the middle of my soul,'" Erica sang along with Bruce. The industrial moonscape gave way to dull farm fields and big-box stores. Erica pulled off the parkway at the Walt Whitman rest stop. Her father used to obsess about that too: why a highway rest stop in dreary New Jersey was named after a famous Long Island poet. They sat on a picnic bench near a strip of anemic oak trees while Erica fished out formula and diaper-changing supplies. Sophia's bowels were loose and her cheeks flushed. She didn't seem much interested in her formula and after half a bottle turned her head away and whimpered.

"Is she all right, Mrs. Richards?" asked Ashley. She fumbled in her pocketbook. "Drat. I need more cigarettes."

"I think so," said Erica. It figured Sophia would pick this time to get sick. She gave her a dose of infant Tylenol. "Let's go inside where it's air-conditioned and get something to eat," she said. She wasn't very hungry, but coffee sounded good. And something sweet.

A poodle walked by. "Doggie, doggie!" Sophia cried, reassuring Erica of her health. In the midst of the frenzy of the previous week Sophia had uttered her first word other than "mama," a distinct "dog-gie," which turned out to apply to any animal, be it Lisa's cocker spaniel or Sam the iguana.

In the cafeteria, they got in line behind a flotilla of families that reminded her of the ones at Disney World: overweight, blond, and dressed in polyester primary colors. Like a herd of colorful elephants, they stomped to a counter where slimy chicken a la king and overcooked broccoli steamed sulfurously from metal pans.

They slid their trays down the metal rods to a cold case, where, for lack of any better option, Erica chose a wedge of lemon meringue pie.

"I'm a vegetarian," Ashley informed her, grabbing a mound of cottage cheese garnished with a canned peach. "Hayden told me more stuff," she said.

"What?" Erica searched for a high chair. They were all taken, and the yellowish linoleum beneath their feet was punctuated every few inches by a squashed french fry, crumpled napkin, or blot of ketchup.

"They have to eat this crazy diet to balance their blood enzymes or something. Some concoction with cider vinegar for breakfast and raw milk from the cows on the farm. All this gross stuff, but there's never enough to eat. Their showers are cold, and they have to wash their laundry in a bucket. And they have to watch these stupid inspirational videos all the time, and if they don't toe the line, they'll get demoted and sent to solitary. Like in Alcatraz or something."

"God," Erica said. "That's disgusting."

They ate their snacks as Sophia lay quietly in Erica's lap. Afterward, Erica asked Ashley if she could watch the baby while she went to the ladies' room, promising her an opportunity to buy cigarettes afterwards.

Like in Disney World, she performed the same grotty act in a comparable bathroom stall, snorting her diminishing coke store with one leg on the toilet seat. By the time she slid the metal lock open, her perspective felt totally refreshed. The patina on the tilework shimmered luminously. All those fat folks whose clothes she had scorned before looked purposeful and beautiful in a distant sort of way, a mass of migrating humanity, dappled with light. As she reached the bench where Ashley sat cradling Sophia, the chorus of the pop song on the loudspeaker, which she vaguely recognized but didn't recall the title of, swelled to such a peak of poignancy that tears came to her eyes. She reached down and gathered the baby onto her shoulder, Sophia's mouth dribbling a dot of curdly spit-up onto her neck. She touched Sophia's forehead with her lips. Cooler. Everything was going to be all right.

Ashley kept up a steady burble of chatter, mainly regarding cloth-ing bargains she'd found with her mother on the Lower East Side, in between applying various makeup items and drawing intricate designs on the back of her hand with a ballpoint pen.

They drove through eighteen miles of spewing smokestacks in Delaware. When they reached the Baltimore tunnel, rush hour traffic slowed their progress. Erica imagined the fierce pressure of the water against the walls of the tunnel and all the ways they could be crushed and inundated. Her heart fluttered. Sophia began to cry, a snuffly, weak sort of whimper.

"Are you sure the baby's okay, Erica?" Ashley asked. "She's not usually so irritable."

"Yeah, I think it's the long car ride. We'll make a quick stop as soon as we get out of this tunnel." Erica wiped her sweaty hand on her thigh.

At the J. Millard Tawes Rest Area in Maryland, the midsum-mer sun still lay high on the horizon. A sea of gnats orbited their heads.

"Who the hell is J. Millard Tawes, I wonder?" Erica asked, shielding Sophia's body with her arms. With coaxing, she took a little milk but refused both cereal and applesauce.

"I dunno," Ashley said. "Maybe he's another poet?"

Erica changed Sophia's diaper and wiped her runny nose. Her forehead felt warm again. She gave her another dose of Tyle-nol, even though you were supposed to give it every four hours and only three hours had elapsed. But they couldn't afford to stop again, in another hour, just for that. Plus, Sophia was feverish now, so why wait.

"When I think about what we're doing, I get scared," said Ashley.

"Try not to think," said Erica.

———

By early evening, they had cleared the clot of the Washington, DC, metro area, passing the exit for Dulles Airport, passing the suburbs and exurbs until the buildings thinned out, hills mounded greenly, and horses nibbled grass behind white fences. They drove west, into a setting sun so glaring that Erica kept adjusting her position so as not to be blinded. Rounded violet shadows of mountains rose in the distance, and then they were upon them, climbing up forested roads. High wispy clouds sailed through the darkening sky. The oppressive heat in the car lifted, and a pine-scented breeze drifted in. They turned right on a Route 81, which looked correct, according to Ethan's atlas, and drove south, bracketed by trucks. Sophia slept so soundly that Erica sometimes forgot she was there; then she would remember with a start and turn to the back and check, yes, there she was, her breathing congested but steady, her fists knotted, her chubby thighs poking out of her seersucker onesie.

"D'you think we should find a motel, Mrs. Richards?" When she was nervous, Erica noted, Ashley reverted to Mrs. Richards.

"No, I can keep driving through the night," Erica said.

"I wish I had my license; then I could help you drive."

"No, don't worry about it." Night was her favorite time to drive, just her and the ribbon of road, her radio and tape deck.

Soon Ashley fell asleep, her stream of chatter replaced by a lolling head and a heavy, nasal breath. Her belly button peeked out from beneath her silk top. There were a few downy hairs on it. Her belly looked blank and innocent, like a child's. Up ahead, the road split. Any signage was obscured by the high truck bed in front of her. She took her chances and bore to the right.

The trucks disappeared. The mountain road twisted. Here and there she could see a long driveway or a trailer set among the trees. Road signs pointed their way to unknown locales: Harrisonburg, Elkton, Staunton, Clarksburg, West Virginia. The people she loved still tugged at her with insistent tendrils: Ashley and Sophia asleep in her car; Ethan in Florida; Jared in South Carolina; the twins at Lisa's; Dylan in the Poconos; her parents in Bucharest; hell, even Debbie in Albany. If it weren't for all these attachments and responsibilities weighing her down, she would float like a dandelion seed. She would fly up into these black mountains.

She chose turnoffs at random. A deer skittered across the road, right in front of her car. She plugged in Robert Palmer and drove deeper into the mountains, deeper into the night.

CHAPTER THIRTY-TWO

The near-absolute darkness comforted her at one level; at another, it terrified her. What it did primarily was focus her attention. The narrow road rose higher and higher into the mountains, curving in corkscrews, and it took all her concentration to determine where the road ended and something else began, and she couldn't be sure whether it was forest or empty air. Apart from her headlights, the sky, milky with stars, provided the only illumination. There were no gas stations, no rest stops. Every now and then a series of boxy shadows, perhaps a cross rising from the triangular roof of a church, indicated human habitation. More deer crossed the road, and once, a lower, longer animal with a long tail, his fierce eyes glowing in the darkness. Occasionally a car passed her going in the opposite direction, blinding her with its headlights.

In what passed for a turnout, she stopped for about twenty minutes and fed Sophia, glancing about nervously for bears or whatever else might swoop out of the darkness. Sophia drank about half of her bottle and then lost interest. Erica bounced her about on her knees, hoping to generate her usual energetic curiosity. The dark seemed to scare her; she snuggled into Erica's armpit. Her forehead was hot. She coughed, a dry cracking heave that shook her chest. Erica gave Sophia a sweater, more Tylenol. She fell back asleep.

Erica drank her gallon of coffee and munched through her bag of potato chips. She slid in tapes one after the other—Steve Winwood, Peter Gabriel, Jefferson Starship, Bon Jovi, Cyndi Lauper, John Cougar Mellencamp, Phil Collins—avoiding the heavy metal so as not to wake Ashley and Sophia. A couple of times she stopped to pee, squatting on the narrow shoulder between Vince and the edge, where the land fell away down a sharp slope. She snorted several lines of coke right there in the car, driving very slowly, one hand on the wheel. Ashley slumped against the passenger door, breathing softly, her sweater bunched up against her ear, a blotch of eyeliner on her closed lids.

Eventually, a faint line of light appeared on the horizon. She was driving down out of the mountains into land somewhere flatter and greener, dotted with pine trees and ranch houses.

At a gas station with a neon dinosaur sign and a couple of freestanding pumps, Erica leaned back and felt Sophia's head. Cooler again, and she wasn't coughing so much. Maybe she was on the mend. These viruses didn't usually last very long.

"Erica, I gotta pee!" Ashley rolled and stretched and yawned. "And I gotta brush my teeth. My mouth tastes like a sewer." She dashed indoors.

As Erica unlocked her gas cap, shaking her left foot, which had fallen asleep, an attendant emerged. He stared at Vince's New York plates. "Y'all aren't from these parts," he observed. "Where y'all headed?"

"Burkittsville," she blurted, her voice sounding foreign to her ears, harsh and nasal. "Is it far from here?"

"'Bout fifty miles down the road, give or take a few. Take a right on Route 40. Don't tell me—you've got family in the penitentiary?"

"Why do you ask?" Erica said.

"Can't think of any other reason why folks would want to go to Burkittsville."

The boy, Erica noted, was rather attractive, with longish strawberry-blond hair, an open face, full lips, well-defined arm muscles. "You're frownin'," he continued. "You're hidin' somethin', I can tell. Is it your husband in the pen? Your boyfriend? The father of that cute li'l baby back there?"

Sophia's eyes fluttered open. "Dog-gie!" she said, pointing at a black lab sniffing the base of a tree.

Ashley emerged from the bathroom, holding her nose.

"That guy was gross," she said as they pulled back on the road. "Did you see that one tooth he had that was totally black?"

"I thought he was kind of cute," Erica said.

"Sometimes you're very strange, Erica." Ashley sprayed her face with rosewater. "Are you sure you're okay? You look kind of flushed."

"I'm fine," Erica said, though her face did feel bright and hot, her eyes dry, her nose congested and dripping. Her right calf ached from pressing on the accelerator. When she glanced down at the leg, she noticed a long scratch on her thigh that she didn't remember getting. Perhaps she'd scratched herself on the spiky weeds by the gas station. "I think I'm allergic to something around here," she said, inserting REM in her tape deck in honor of the South.

They ate at the Pine Cabin Cafe, which smelled of grease and coffee. The place was full, despite the early hour, everyone chatting like they were best friends, all turning to stare suspiciously at the newcomers, their gazes turning friendly as soon as they saw Sophia. Babies. Erica could not get over their power, how they rendered their caretakers harmless.

She rolled out Sophia's changing pad on the floor tile of the ladies' room. Sophia's diaper wasn't dirty, like it usually was every morning. It wasn't even very wet. Unsurprising, Erica supposed, as Sophia had eaten virtually nothing since the start of their trip. She lay there, casting her eyes listlessly about, allowing Erica to give her a fresh diaper, powder, and a pink stripy sundress. Erica dabbed water on the gash on her leg, brushed her teeth, splashed her face, redid her banana clip, and did a couple of lines off the changing pad.

A middle-aged waitress sporting a beehive hairdo so out of style Erica was stunned to see it existing in the real world, poured Erica and Ashley big mugs of coffee. "What can I get you folks?" she asked.

Erica studied her laminated menu, sticky with syrup. "I'll have the biscuits and gravy with a side of bacon," she said. "And can I get a chopped up banana for the baby?"

"Sure thang," the waitress said. "Such a sweet little girl."

"Can I have an egg white omelet?" asked Ashley.

"Can't be just the whites—it's all mixed together," replied the waitress, perplexed.

"Oh, forget it, just scrambled eggs and toast." Ashley patted her belly as if preparing it for the extra calories.

Erica plowed into two biscuits as big as baseballs drenched in a plaster-like white substance studded with sausage chunks. She chugged down her third mug of coffee. The biscuits tasted like greasy sheet rock. Her stomach was so uncharacteristically full that she felt leaden and exhausted, as if she could put her head down on her elbows and fall asleep, right there at the table. Which was exactly what Sophia did, her cheek flat against a slippery slice of banana. Erica left her with Ashley for a few minutes while she did a few more lines of coke in the bathroom stall, which made her feel like a rubber doll, her mouth speaking, her limbs moving, everything functioning basically as it should, but not necessarily connected to her conscious brain.

She emerged to find Ashley wiping off Sophia's cheek and coaxing her to drink a little milk.

"Such an adorable baby," the waitress cooed as Erica paid the bill. "Poor thang. Does she have a summer cold?"

"Yeah, "Erica said.

"Maybe you should put a heavier sweater on her," the waitress suggested.

"In this weather?" Erica fidgeted, eager to get going.

"Where y'all from?" asked the waitress.

Erica pressed her lips against Sophia's warm, moist forehead. The last thing she needed was more clothing.

"New York," Ashley answered.

"New Yawk?" the waitress said, handing over their change. "I should have figured from your accents. My son wanted to go to New Yawk. He got into NYU, into their film school there."

"Did he go?" asked Ashley.

"No, it would have cost a fortune," the waitress said, handing over their change. "He ended up going to the state university. He owns his own photo shop in Charleston. Where are you folks headed?"

"Burkittsville," she answered. "I have relatives there," she explained. Sophia leaned heavily against her shoulder. The incessant necessity to engage in polite conversation, plus the thick air, smelling of burnt coffee and scrambled eggs, pressed in on Erica. Her veins swelled against her thin skin, all that blood roiling, that air sharp in her lungs. Her body struggled to contain it.

"All the way from New Yawk?" exclaimed the waitress. Have you got family in the penitentiary?"

"My nephew," Erica said.

"What's he in for? Drugs?"

"Clarissa, there's folks here needing their breakfasts," a man called from a nearby table.

"Well, I won't keep you any longer," said Clarissa. "Have a nice day now."

Outside, the dense air smelled of grass and cow manure and something industrial Erica couldn't identify. She didn't turn on the air-conditioning, for fear of Vince overheating. She couldn't take a chance of him breaking down on these strange roads. The Tylenol seemed to be helping Sophia. She was babbling, pointing at cows. Erica's stomach hurt. She shifted in her seat, ejecting the REM tape and scanning the radio, finding nothing except dreadful country music stations and a couple of preachers blathering on about how the end of the world was coming. Ashley drew elaborate spirals on the backs of her hands.

They passed a sign that read, "Burkittsville, population 3100, Home of the Panthers." To their right stood a series of barracks-like buildings set far behind a wall of barbed wire.

"That must be the penitentiary everyone's talking about," Erica said. Which made it seem like it might be exactly the place they were looking for.

"Excuse me—is this the Pritima Center?" she asked a sullen fat guy reading a paperback in a booth adjoining a locked iron gate.

"No, ma'am," the guy drawled. "This here is Burkittsville State Penitentiary".

"Do you know where the Pritima Center might be located?" She stuck her head out into the dense air, radiating what she hoped was an ingratiating smile.

He scratched his head. "Do you mean that private school?

There's a school. Down the road a ways. In the old plantation house, lots of gardens."

"How do I get there?"

"Turn left by the motel, then down Main Street, past the courthouse, and then past the gun club and the rib shack, make a right, you'll see a fancy white house with columns and rose-bushes—that's it."

"Thanks," Erica said. When they passed the motel, she pulled in and parked. Her eyes were closing. Even her rubber doll arms were failing.

She felt Sophia's forehead. It was still warm and sticky. She opened her eyes, blearily, and then shut them again. "Can you try giving her some apple juice, Ashley?" Erica asked. "I'm going to head on in here and change my Tampax."

"It's only nine in the mornin. The rooms aren't cleaned yet," said the motel clerk. He was bug-eyed and unusually short; Erica couldn't decide whether he was a dwarf or just really ugly.

"Doesn't matter." Erica yawned. "May I use the rest room?"

The troll-like clerk handed over a key and sent her around the side of the building. She stretched out Sophia's changing pad over a sink the size of a mixing bowl and snorted a few lines. She was running way too low. She should have brought all of Anders's stuff instead of leaving it behind, flattened under a jug of fabric softener.

"Have a nice day now," she told the troll as she handed back the key.

"She took a little of the juice," Ashley reported when she returned. "And I gave her a couple animal crackers."

They passed what Erica assumed was Main Street: the rib shack; a small grocery; a drugstore; Felicia's Cafe (closed); a Laundromat; a resale shop; and something called Feed and Seed. Main Street ended at the courthouse, an imposing-looking white building set back on a dusty lawn. She turned right again, on what seemed to be the only valid road, and passed an elementary school, a couple of churches, and a pawn-and-gun shop, ending up at a T intersection with no indication where to go.

She turned right again—right seemed to be the order of the

day—passing small houses, little more than shacks, that seemed to shrink in size the farther she drove from the town center. Chickens pecked and clucked in the yards.

The road narrowed, became gravel, and a few miles down was blocked by a wooden gate. A mild retching sound came from the backseat. Erica turned around; a spatter of spit-up juice and cookies littered Sophia's chin and pretty pink dress. "Are you okay, honey?" Erica asked, wiping the baby's chin.

"Mama," Sophia said. Her face was flushed and hot.

She wiped it with a cloth dumped in some of Ashley's Evian water and then stood at the side of the car and looked around. An overgrown path led off into a strand of woods. Erica got out of the car and peered around the gate, looking in vain for a big white house. A posted sign warned, "No Trespassing."

"Mrs. Richards, is this it? 'Cause all this is giving me the creeps, and I'm sweating like hell. And it smells like barf in here." Ashley spritzed rosewater about.

"I'm checking, I'm checking." Clusters of mosquitoes buzzed around Erica's face. Beer cans and piles of cigarette butts littered the adjoining weeds. From the distance, she heard what sounded like a rifle shot. Behind her, she heard a screech of wheels.

A man wearing dirty blue jeans and a T-shirt emerged from a wobbly flatbed truck, hauling piping. He reached in his pocket, and she fell to the ground for protection, like she'd seen on so many cop shows, covering her head with her arms. They'd find hers and Ashley's and Sophia's bodies rotting in the sweltering heat.

"Ma'am, can I help you?" the man asked.

"No," she gasped.

"You sure?" he asked, extracting what was in his pocket, a bandana to wipe his perspiring forehead. "'Cause I see those kids and those New Yawk plates."

"We're okay," she said, breathing heavily, rising to her knees. "Thanks."

The man was middle-aged, broad faced, wearing an orange vest. He helped her to her feet. His breath smelled like tobacco. "Better be careful around here," he said. "It's pheasant season."

"D'you know where the Pritima Center is?" Erica asked.

"The reform school place?"

Erica nodded.

"I had a feeling," he said, looking knowingly at Ashley huddled miserably in the car. "Turn around, go back to town, take your first right past the courthouse and then the next right by the Foursquare Church. It's about ten miles down the road. You have a good day now."

Pheasant season. Erica had been served pheasant once, at a Grant Fishel dinner. It arrived on a bed of wild rice, with its little beady-eyed head wobbling about. She couldn't eat it. The man's directions were correct, though. She passed a church with a billboard pronouncing, "In the gym meet of life, Lord, please give me a perfect ten," turned right, and a large white mansion, like the courthouse but bigger, materialized on Erica's left. It was set well back from the road, behind a gate almost as large and imposing as at the penitentiary. Paved paths threaded through past a center circle, landscaped with magnolia trees, gladioli, and roses. A bench sat under a large oak tree. Outside of the circle, off a ways, she saw tennis courts, a swimming pool, and what looked to be vegetable beds. In front of the gate was one of those telephone gizmos where someone could buzz you in.

"Listen, you can't come in with me, but I can't leave you here, Ashley," Erica said. "Someone's bound to come out and ask you what you're doing."

"I lie real well." Ashley twisted her silver ring. "I've run away twice."

"Doesn't matter," Erica said. She drove down the road a half-mile or so, turned down a dirt track, and parked by a desultory creek, where a thin trickle of water dribbled over mossy rocks.

"Wait here by this stream," she said, handing Ashley the last of the boxed drinks.

"I hope no one is going to shoot at me thinking I'm a pheasant or squirrel or something." Ashley shifted from side to side on the uneven ground, flicking away gnats. She'd changed in the cafe restroom and was wearing a silk tank top with a crocheted lace edge, distressed jean cutoffs, and sandals with two-inch heels. "I'm scared," she said.

"I'll come back with Jared," Erica assured her.

She drove back to the gate, and despite the oppressive heat, put Sophia into the front carrier. She couldn't see breaking Jared free while pushing a stroller. She stripped Sophia down to her diaper, tied a ruffled pink hat on her head, gave her a bottle of apple juice, hoping she would keep it down, and pressed zero on the keypad. "Pritima Center," answered a voice with the same drawl she was becoming accustomed to but a little more clipped, a little less friendly. "Who is this?"

In answering, Erica took a cue from her mother. "Sound authoritative," her mother had told her since she was a child. "Sound like you know what you are talking about, and people will assume you do." This approach had allowed her mother to return a year-old white couch because of stains, exchange pants that had already been hemmed, and no doubt earn her commissions on many West Meadow houses.

"Mrs. Mary Brittaca," Erica pronounced. Mary Brittaca was Dylan's fifth-grade teacher.

A buzzer sounded, and the metal gate swung open. Erica walked up the long path, her dress already damp at the underarms, Sophia's cheeks flushed with heat and fever. A swarm of gnats buzzed about her tender neck, undeterred by Erica's ineffectual swatting. Both sides of the path were lined with beds of brightly colored zinnias and geraniums, all carefully weeded and watered. She passed a group of teenagers and a man in his early twenties sitting cross-legged under a magnolia, apparently engaged in a class of some sort. They looked at her curiously as she passed by. None of them were Jared.

She walked up a flight of wide white steps and onto a covered porch and rang another doorbell.

"Who is this?" came the same voice through the loudspeaker.

"Mrs. Mary Brittaca," Erica repeated.

There followed a slight hesitation and then another buzzer. Erica opened the door. Sweat dripped like raindrops from the tops of her breasts down to her belly, soaking her chest under the baby carrier.

Once inside, a waft of air-conditioning sent chills down her body. She walked down an imposing marble hallway. At the end of this hallway an office opened up, with a big-breasted fiftyish woman sitting at a desk, and, standing, a younger, harder looking woman with pixie-cut blond hair, whom Erica immediately termed Miss Peroxide. As Erica entered the office, it became clear that the woman at the desk had buzzed her in and Miss Peroxide wasn't any too happy about it.

"I'm Mrs. Mary Brittaca, and this is my little daughter, Sophia." Erica extended her arm.

The woman accepted her hand with a firm grip. "And what agency are you with, Mrs. Brittaca? We don't typically admit visitors without documentation. Mrs. Lagore here is new and was a little forward in buzzing you in."

"Oh, I'm not with an agency, Miss Pero—your name?" Erica continued smiling, attempting to channel not only her mother but Jeff Russell, who'd once weaseled their way into a Steppenwolf concert without any tickets.

"Mrs. Olney." Her voice dripped poisoned honey.

"Mrs. Olney, I'm here to see Jared Lassler. I'm his big cousin, and I'm on my way to visit relatives in Atlanta, and I know he's been, uh, going to school here, so I couldn't pass by without visiting him." Erica gave her best attempt at what she hoped was an ingratiating smile. She wrapped her arms around Sophia, claiming possession.

"What a darling little girl." Mrs. Olney oozed more honey, and Erica hoped against hope that once again Sophia had rendered her harmless.

"Jared Lassler is on schedule F," Mrs. Lagore said, consulting a list on her desk.

"I can't imagine how you got our address. Someone must have broken confidentiality," said Mrs. Olney. "I'm sorry you've driven out of your way, Mrs. Brittaca, especially with a young child in this heat, but I can't allow you to see Jared."

"Why not?" Erica tried, unsuccessfully, to keep an edge out

of her voice, which sounded harsh and foreign in South Carolina under the best of circumstances. "Actually, his mother hasn't been well. She's had problems, as you might know, with a blood condition, and I know Jared is concerned. I could reassure him she's all right."

"We have a very well-planned, gradated program here at the Pritima Center. Jared has regular phone contact with his mother, and I'm sure she would share with us any changes in her condition." Mrs. Olney's voice was clear and measured. "Visitors are a privilege accorded only to our very highest level students, those who are almost ready to graduate. Jared is nowhere near that level at this time."

"He's on schedule F," echoed Mrs. Lagore.

Sophia reached her sticky fingers onto Erica's neck and coughed. Erica looked away from the four eyes fixed on her, to a rack of pamphlets. Above them hung a poster featuring a child leaping through a field of daisies. Superimposed over the flowers were the words "Home. Faith. Family."

"We're a very close family," Erica tried again. "Are you sure I couldn't just say a little hello to Jared?"

"As I've made eminently clear, Mrs. Brittaca, that would be in violation of our rules," said Mrs. Olney, her voice brittle. "Now, if you don't leave, I'm going to have to escort you out of here." Mrs. Lagore rose unsteadily from her seat, the shelf of her bosom wobbling. The two women closed in on Erica. She breathed heavily. Sweat trickled down her belly, below the elastic ridge of her underpants.

"Let me escort you out," said Mrs. Olney and then led her down the hall and down the stone path to the gate.

"I'm sorry to have wasted your time, Mrs. Brittaca," she said as the metal clanged shut. "Why don't you and your little girl go get some sweet tea in town? You both look tuckered out."

Erica watched Mrs. Olney walk up the path and back into the big white house. The group under the magnolia tree had left. Erica walked down the fence a ways, noting that it was just an ordinary wrought-iron fence, not that high, without spikes or barbed wire.

At one spot a thick limbed tree abutted the fence. She clambered up the branches like she used to do as a kid, balancing Sophia in the baby carrier. "In the gym meet of life, Lord, give me a perfect ten," she muttered to herself as she clutched Sophia's carrier tight, straddled the top of the fence, and swung her way down onto the thick, flat top of a well-groomed azalea bush. She jumped down onto the grass. Brushing off leaves and twigs from her dress, the baby carrier, and Sophia's hair, with the full assurance of someone who knew where she was and what she was doing, she cut across the lawn to the back of the big white house and kept on going.

Behind the pretty house, the landscape looked shadier and shabbier. The buildings hidden from outside view were barracks not dissimilar from the penitentiary. The grass was shaggier, the flowers limited to dandelions, the paths dustier. She passed an outdoor shower and a collection of buckets. At one of the buckets, true to Hayden's tale, a girl scrubbed clothes on an old-fashioned washboard. Past the barracks lay rows of limp vegetables, a pen with goats, a chicken coop, a field of grazing cows, and a series of sheds. She passed teenagers picking beans, doing something unpleasant with the chickens, painting a shed, even dumping lime down an outhouse toilet. All of them looked limp, skinny, sullen, and deeply tanned. None of them were Jared.

"May I help you, ma'am?" asked a tall boy hauling a sack of fertilizer. "No, no, I'm Mrs. Brittaca," she said, wary of any attention. A group of kids emerged from one of the sheds, holding garden implements, led by a man hauling a wheelbarrow. One of the teenagers had a familiarly shaped head, albeit shaved; a familiar long, angular body, albeit painfully thin; and a familiar languid slope of the shoulders. "No, no, no, I see the group I'm looking for," she assured the boy, who was still lingering at her side. She brushed past him, almost stepping into a cow pie as she lengthened her stride, catching up with the group, gently tapping Jared on the shoulder.

He turned around, his pale face burnt red as an apple. His eyes opened wide. "Aunt Rikki," he mouthed. "What are— How did you—"

"Shh," she mouthed back, following the group to the front of the white house and into the rose beds.

"Pull out everything that don't look like a flower," their leader commanded. He walked down the line with his wheelbarrow, passing out trowels and hoes.

"Excuse me—I don't know you," he said when he got to Erica. He didn't look any older than Jared. Maybe he was on schedule A.

"I'm Mrs. Mary Brittaca," she said, reaching for a hoe. "With the Agricultural Extension Service. I'm looking for invasive species."

"They didn't say nothing about that at the office," the boy said, but his manner indicated he didn't care much about what the office said. "The baby?" he inquired. "She looks like she's boiling to death in there."

"She's all right. My childcare fell through." Erica stroked Sophia, asleep under her sun hat.

"It's all the same to me," said the boy, shrugging. He continued down the line, giving instructions on how to effectively weed the flowers and plant a new set of dahlias.

Erica and Jared weeded for twenty minutes or so. The air smelled wet and rotting. Frogs ribbeted in a nearby pond. Gnats buzzed. She made a few perfunctory stabs with the hoe. Mainly she watched the kids listlessly raking their trowels along the red dirt, scraping up a dandelion or a blade of grass, exhibiting the minimum animation needed to avoid prodding by the boy supervisor, who periodically strolled down the line, muttering, "C'mon, look alive!" Sweat dripped into Erica's eyes, creating a glazed tableau of dust and grass and flowers and bent backs. Sophia's head lolled to the right. Her cheeks were bright red; a green clot of mucus smeared the corner of her right eye. As Erica wiped the mucus with the sleeve of her dress, Sophia opened her eyes and then turned her head, distracted by a sound in the distance. The boy supervisor stood up from his squat, also looking toward the source of the sound, and then Erica heard it too: gravel crunching. A garbage truck was driving up the road, spraying up dust. The driver got out and buzzed at the gate. Jared pawed at the dirt with his hoe . He looked exhausted. His allergies were obviously acting up; he sneezed and coughed and gagged. He had always detested yard work.

"Follow me," Erica whispered, and because Jared had been raised to follow the rules, because he had been spending weeks taking orders in the extreme, he followed her without question.

"Ma'am, where are you headed?" called the boy supervisor.

"I'll be right back," Erica said.

"You're not allowed to take residents away from the work area," the kid said.

"I'll be right back," she repeated, grabbing hard onto Jared's arm. The supervisory boy lunged at them, but them stalled, perhaps unwilling to leave his charges, perhaps disinclined to make unnecessary motion in the heat. His footsteps started up again, but then there was a sound, and Erica turned to see him brushing off his skinned knee—he might have tripped over a shovel handle— but after that she didn't see anything else because, walking with assurance, like she deserved to be there, like she was Mrs. Mary Brittaca, of the Agricultural Extension Service, on official business, removing invasive species, she walked with Jared straight toward the metal gate as it opened and the garbage truck barreled in, sending up a spray of dust and pebbles.

She didn't look down. She didn't look back. Hidden by the shadow of the truck, she led Jared out of the gate and into the car. "Get down," she told Jared, and he too had seen a lot of cop shows and obediently kneeled on the floor of the rear seat. Erica snapped Sophia into her car seat. Without removing the empty baby carrier from her chest or opening so much as a window to freshen the stultifying air, she floored the engine and fled down the gravel road to the turnoff by the creek.

CHAPTER THIRTY-THREE

Ashley scrambled up the hill, sticking her thumb out like a hitch-hiker. Erica opened the door, leaving Vince's engine running. The minute Ashley climbed in, Erica gunned the accelerator again.

"Jared!" Ashley shrieked, swinging her backpack over onto the floor of the car, covering his face with kisses.

"God, this is all so weird," Jared said.

"It was sweltering by that stream. I thought I was going to pass out if you didn't come back soon. And the bugs! Look at my face, Jared!"

"You're all bitten up," he agreed.

"There must be a zillion of these itchy monsters all over my face," Ashley continued. Erica flashed on Debbie and her twenty-two mosquito bites at the New York World's Fair. Ashley did look the worse for wear, swollen faced, with a smear of mud across her silk shirt.

"Where are we going?" Jared asked. His voice was oddly flat, as if Erica could have answered anything, like Houston or Tierra del Fuego, and he would have just sat in the back of the car and gone along for the ride.

"Out of here," said Erica, making turns at random, passing endless churches and cows and gun stores and Feed and Seeds.

"My mom made me have an abortion, Jared," Ashley said. "They killed our baby."

"Huh?" Jared stared dazedly out the window.

"I said, they killed our baby."

"It's okay, Ash. It wasn't really a baby yet. Just a clump of cells or something."

Ashley uttered an odd sound, somewhere between a squeak

and a cry. Erica expected her to pummel Jared in the face, or lapse into hysteria, or both. Instead, after a few moments of silence, she went into default chatter mode, filling Jared in on her boring summer school, her mother's Buddhist conversion, and Hayden's horror stories about the Pritima Center.

Erica kept looking in her rearview mirror, expecting to see Miss Peroxide barreling after her or, worse, security guards or cops. She turned onto a larger, two-lane highway. The land grew flatter, the trees scrubbier. They entered a more populous area, with townhome complexes and stoplights. At an antiques mall on her right, a pack of obese women waddled out of a minivan. She sensed they must be getting closer to the ocean. The air smelled like mud and salt.

"I can't believe what's happening," Jared said, breaking his silence. "How did you get into the Pritima Center?"

"I pretended I knew what I was doing," Erica said.

"Is my mom feeling all right?"

"Yeah, she's okay, I guess. Same as ever."

"Does she know you're doing this?"

"Of course not."

Stalled at one endless red light, they noticed a large wooden building with a wraparound porch and a neon sign blinking, "BBQ." Shaded by canvas awnings, people sat at picnic tables, eating large plates of food.

"Can we stop here and eat?" Jared asked. "I'm starving. I haven't eaten meat in weeks."

Erica twisted her neck around, looking at Jared's bony body, the way it looked like it had had all the air squished out of it.

"We can't stay, but we can run in and get some sandwiches," she said.

The restaurant was stuffed with families, hefty men and women accompanied by equally hefty red-faced offspring, all avidly chowing down on hearty plates of barbequed meat, macaroni and cheese, baked beans, and coleslaw. Jared ordered a super deluxe barbequed pork with two sides; Erica and Ashley were more circumspect. Ashley thought the food looked too fattening, and Erica wasn't hungry. She wasn't unhungry, just like she wasn't untired. She'd entered a detached space where these physical needs were irrelevant. Nevertheless, her eyes were dry, and her butt ached. It felt good to be out of the car. The ceiling fan rotating directly above her sent a cooling waft of air directly down the back of her tank top. She imagined the four of them in the tropics, three rebels and a baby on the run from the law.

She sat Sophia in her lap and fed her a french fry, which she rejected, swatting it and sending it tumbling toward Erica's crotch. Erica opened a can of Enfamil and poured it into a bottle. Sophia took a few dispirited sips and turned her head away. Erica didn't remember when she'd last drunk a full bottle. She didn't remember when she'd last changed her diaper, either. She felt under Sophia's flouncy shorts—not too wet, but she may as well change it. She needed a little visit to the restroom for her own purposes, anyway.

She transferred the last of the coke from her diaper bag to her purse. As a diminishing resource, it felt like a fine line standing between her and something unbelievably terrifying. She washed her hands, blotting some cool water on Sophia's face and giving her another dose of baby Tylenol. As she tossed her paper towel in the trash, a woman, fortyish, well put together, blond, very much like Miss Peroxide, approached them, smiling tentatively. Erica ceased imagining herself in Barbados or Bali. Her legs shook of their own accord. Her eyebrow twitched. Her vision narrowed. Feeling unsteady on her feet, she leaned against the towel dispenser. The woman spoke to her in a thick yet aristocratic Southern drawl.

"Excuse me, ma'am, but you wouldn't be from Wilton Acres, would you? Near Myrtle Beach?"

"No," replied Erica, her voice trembling.

"No?" the woman answered. "Because you look just like a woman I know, from the garden club down there. She was from New Jersey, never quite got used to the pace of life down here. I thought she'd moved back, but then when I saw you, I thought, well, I may as well take a chance and ask."

"It wasn't me," Erica said, managing a faint smile. "We're on vacation."

"Well, have a lovely time now," the woman said, tweaking Sophia's fingers. "Are you going to swim with the dolphins?"

"Maybe," Erica said, extricating herself from the restroom. What was it with these folks around here always inserting themselves into your business? Always wanting to know your destination, where you ate, where you slept, how often you brushed your teeth? She picked up an extra large coffee on the way to the car.

———

"Thank you, Aunt Rikki," Jared enthused through a mouthful of pulled pork. "This tastes so good! You wouldn't believe the crap they gave us to eat at the center. Lots of beans, and white bread, and weird apple cider vinegar shakes every morning."

"The central office looked pretty fancy," Erica said. "The office manager was munching on a bowlful of chocolate mints."

"They keep the central house looking nice for visitors," Jared said. "I should know. They made me mop it and take out the garbage. They don't let anyone back where we stayed. It's disgusting. The roof leaks. There's ants. The place where we slept, they don't even have electric lights." He hesitated. "Aren't they going to come after us?"'

"I doubt it," Erica said. "I think we eluded them. I made a lot of turns. Tell me more about what the place was like."

"There's not much to say," Jared said, but the words poured out of him. "We had to do all kinds of chores. Gardening, like you saw. We had to clean out the chicken coop—gross—and clip the chicken's nails, even grosser. Every morning they made us do calisthenics, and we'd go on character-building hikes. Mom never let me go hiking because of my asthma, you know, but here, they made us keep walking, all these horrible walks, and not enough water. I had a couple asthma attacks, and my inhaler ran out, though they told me Mom was sending another one. Want some of this bread with sauce on it?"

"God, no." Erica followed signs to North Carolina.

Jared chewed intently for a few minutes before continuing.

"Plus, it wasn't all exercise. There was lots of sitting around too. There were regular school subjects, like biology and math, all these worksheets and multiple choice tests but it wasn't any more boring than regular school."

"Didn't you have therapy?" Ashley asked. "Hayden said there was tons of therapy."

"Oh yeah." Jared grabbed the last of Ashley's broasted chicken. "Tons of therapy. Everybody laying into everybody else about their inadequacies. And these instructional films, like why you shouldn't take drugs and shouldn't talk back to your parents and all that crap. You had to take tests on them afterward, and if you didn't pass, you had to watch them again. Oh yeah, and prayers in the morning and before therapy group and before meals. Plus hours of contemplation when you had to sit in a dark room and not say anything."

"What kind of prayers?" The traffic thickened around them— rush hour in some strange town. On the ride south, she'd veered into the Smoky Mountains as the result of one wrong turn or many. Now they were driving north through rolling hills, populated with the familiar landmarks of garden apartments, office parks, and fast food restaurants. Still, their specific geography remained unfamiliar—each highway exit sign an invitation to a potential locale for living one's life.

"It was all this junk about putting your life in the hands of a higher power," Jared was saying. "It wasn't any stupider than Hebrew school. Religion's a scam. Say, do you want that pie?"

Erica's banana cream pie, neon-yellow custard topped with several inches of whipped cream, sat half eaten on the center console.

"Man, this is good," Jared said. "We weren't allowed sweets." He spoke rapidly, apparently gaining energy from each calorie ingested. "Oh man, all the rules. Rules about when you could eat, when you could sleep, when you could socialize with other kids in your pod."

"Pod?" Erica asked. Nick had used that term in reference to the Pritima Center.

"Yeah, it was their dorky name for the kids in your group. The ones you saw. We were all gardening together. The guy in charge, he was on schedule A. Scheduled to be released in a few weeks. Do you have a cold, Aunt Rikki?"

"Oh no," Erica said, blowing her nose with a napkin. "Allergies." She scratched at her mosquito bites, all those blood-streaked scabs. She was feeling lightheaded and sweaty again.

"You look like you've lost weight too," Jared said.

"Don't I look better?" Erica asked, pleased that he noticed.

"Not really," Jared said. "You look like you've been sick. Have you been to your doctor, for, I don't know, tests?"

"I don't do tests," Erica said. "I leave that to your mother."

"Are we driving back to New York now, Mrs. Richards?" Ashley asked.

"No way!" said Erica, startled, but she realized she was driving directly north, all journey and no destination. "Where to, Jared?"

"Someplace nowhere near New York. Someplace no one can find me, none of Dad's private detectives, nobody," Jared said. "And nowhere even resembling a farm."

Erica wished she could magically transport him to that tropical place of her fantasies, one of those destinations on the airport screens: Rio de Janeiro, Casablanca, Sardinia.

"I have an aunt in Baltimore," Ashley offered. She'd unbuttoned her seatbelt and was waggling the toy octopus in Sophia's droopy face.

"Are you crazy?" Jared asked. "Like we're really going to stay with your aunt."

"We could stay somewhere else in Baltimore," Ashley said. "It's a pretty big city."

"Maybe somewhere else in Maryland?" Erica suggested. Maryland sounded like a safe proposition, equidistant from South Carolina and New York.

"I know!" Ashley said. "How about Ocean City, Maryland? I've been there on vacation with my aunt. There's a really cool boardwalk, and wild horses run free on the beach. Well, not exactly on the beach, but close to there."

"That sounds kind of fun," Jared agreed.

"Then we're settled." With one hand on the wheel and one eye on the road, Erica rummaged through Ethan's atlas, looking for Maryland.

"I think I'm getting over the baby," Ashley said.

———

Eventually, Jared, Ashley, and Sophia dozed off, while Erica kept driving. Unlike in the lonely Appalachians, many vehicles traveled this highway, even in the wee hours of the night, requiring plenty of lane changing and the occasional sudden slowdown. She'd played all her tapes at least twice through, and they bored her to distraction. To keep herself focused, she took note of the anonymous figures sharing the road with her: the twentysomething girl curling her eyelashes as she drove; the woman with the dog in her lap; the minivan with the "When the rapture comes, this car will be driverless" sticker. Gulls shrieked, and the wind rattled as she drove over the Bay Bridge.

The Eastern Shore of Maryland resembled South Carolina. The gray dawn light revealed clapboard houses, barbeque shacks, and evangelical churches with billboards warning the end was near. Her body felt as if it could go on forever, but her mind was numb and her eyes dry and burning. Her thighs ached. Sophia whimpered—maybe she was hungry. When had she last eaten? Erica didn't remember. Erica was out of baby food, out of formula, almost out of diapers, but it was early Sunday morning, and the few stores she passed were closed. Ahead of them, a chain of cars turned right into a monstrously huge church, the size of West Meadow High School. A boy with an abnormally large head emerged from a car in the parking lot and swayed his awkwardly shaped body in the direction of the church, gesticulating at the sky.

"Remember that kid in Philadelphia with Down syndrome?" Jared asked, yawning. "Remember, Ash? He was on a stupid wheat-free diet like the one Mom put me on, but it wasn't doing much good because the kid walked weird and kept wetting his pants."

"Yeah, remember how Roger and Griffin made us entertain him for days at a time?" Ashley brushed back her hair and splashed toner on her face.

"Say," Jared smiled slyly. "Have you seen Nick Stromboli lately?"

"He got busted." Erica tightened her grip on the wheel.

"You're kidding!" Jared said. "Is he in jail?"

"No." Erica passed a poky RV on the right. "I guess there's going to be a trial."

"Wow," Jared said. "Mr. Safe House. Mom really liked him, you know. She told me what a sweet man he was. How he really cared about young people. She's so clueless."

"Unfortunately," Erica said.

"Say, Aunt Rikki." He sounded very young, anything sly vanished from his tone. "Are you going to tell Mom where I am?"

"I thought you didn't want to be anywhere near New York."

"Well, yeah, but I don't want Mom to worry, you know? You could tell her and not Dad."

"She tells your father everything, Jared, you know that. I would if I could, but I can't. You don't want me to tell her, believe me."

All that teenage bluster—it was such a lie, a lie much easier to profess when you were securely in the grasp of those you pretended to hate. Erica thought back on all the fun they'd had that spring: Lauren's bat mitzvah, up until Ron's food fight anyway; listening to REM; feeding Porky the Litter Eater; giggling through Sunday night family dinners; even the morning she'd found Jared and Ashley sleeping on her patio. It had been fun then because it was all a game, theoretical revolt. This adventure, this authentic revolt, was wearing thin; it had a script whose beginning she could no longer precisely recall, whose purpose she could not precisely delineate. All she knew was that she urgently needed to see it through.

She gave up looking for a store. The slate blanket of metallic clouds above them exploded into thunder. Heavy rain beat across the windows in sheets. The road, thankfully, stayed free and clear, save the occasional eighteen-wheeler or station wagon crowded with kids and vacation paraphernalia. She played Bloody Tampax and Barf to block out Sophia's insistent whimpering and gloppy coughing. She passed every vehicle she encountered, speeding up to eighty, ninety, ninety-five. She hadn't realized cranky Vince was capable of such speed. He made no choking noises at all. The road looked like a blur of water and lights, beautiful, in its fashion. Ahead, a flash of lightning streaked down like the sky was splitting.

CHAPTER **THIRTY-FOUR**

By the time they reached Ocean City, the rain had stopped, leaving a steamy haze in its wake. Erica pulled into an angled space by the boardwalk. High, unbroken waves rolled onto a broad white beach, as tubular as a roll of paper towels. A few couples strolled along the storm-pounded sands, and families were tentatively setting up umbrellas and blankets. A teenage boy, around Jared's age, ran into the water. You could see him framed in the wave, as if encased in glass, before the top of the wave curled over him and washed him ashore, leaving him gasping in the sand.

"I wish we could go swimming," Ashley said.

"The water looks awfully rough," said Jared. "Besides, we don't have bathing suits. I don't even have a change of clothes."

While the beach slowly filled up, the main action was taking place on the boardwalk where crowds of people drifted, licking snow cones, drinking beer even this early in the morning, shouting, laughing, visiting the arcades and salt water taffy stands. The town radiated a cheesy, cheery mood.

Jared's eyes darted around uncomfortably, as if he still expected Dr. Rafferty's minions to swoop down and capture him; Ashley bounced about the boardwalk. Both seemed expectant, waiting for Erica to detail the next step in a plan she hadn't formulated. Sophia had worn herself out from crying and slept slumped over in her stroller, waking only to cough up gooey green mucus. She couldn't seem to shake whatever was ailing her. She perked up every time she took the Tylenol and then deteriorated again. It unnerved Erica to see her looking like this, without enough spirit to even cry. She stopped at a convenience store and bought more

baby Tylenol, some sort of baby cold formulation, overpriced diapers, formula, and strained apricots and green beans.

"Ooh, food," Jared said, looking around at the elephant ear
and salt water taffy stands. "I'm still starving."

They settled on fried shrimp baskets and then sat at the edge
of the boardwalk, dangling their legs in the sand, eating the greasy
food. Sophia ate a few bites of apricots but refused her formula.
She spit back half her medicine but took in enough to do the job,
Erica figured. The soft fishy breeze off the ocean mingled with a
sweet scent of spun sugar and a faint overlay of rot.

"You see all these restaurants?" Ashley pointed to a huge
seafood emporium about five hundred feet down the walkway,
complete with a blinking neon crab. "And the video arcades and
everything. It'll be easy to get a job."

"It's already the middle of the summer," Jared pointed out.

"People quit all the time," Ashley said. "I had this babysitter
once, when I came here as a kid with my aunt, and she got a job at
O'Donnell's over there, right in the middle of July."

"Where will we stay?" Jared asked.

"We can sleep on the beach," Ashley said.

"That sounds about as comfortable as the Pritima Center."
Jared traced his toe around a shard of glass on the sand.

"Let's go swimming," said Ashley.

"I told you, no suit." Jared said.

"I'll buy us some," Erica said, pointing to a swimwear and
T-shirt store adjoining the salt water taffy stand.

They changed into the suits right in the store. In the changing area, Erica pulled the cotton curtain around on its metal rod.
Sophia's stroller jutted out, making it impossible for the curtain to
close completely. She'd bought a peach bikini, which, at least in the
fluorescent light of the store, appeared to be a mistake. She looked
thin, indeed, but also stretched and worn out, like the cashiers at
Pathmark. Her hair was a grease fest. Her nose was swollen and
red; there were blotches under her eyes. Her arms and neck were
covered in picked mosquito scabs, and her weirdo rash seemed

to have spread. She looked very, very, tired. She looked nothing like she had that day in South Beach. Maybe it was the light. She turned away from the mirror.

Ashley dove headfirst into the waves while Jared hesitantly let the water wash over his ankles. Erica, clutching Sophia, waded out past him. The surf splashed up to her waist and onto Sophia's legs, sharp and cold, with considerable force. Sophia squealed in fear, clinging to Erica's shoulder. Her skin felt hot against Erica's body. Maybe it was a mistake, taking her in the ocean. Erica retreated to where she'd put Sophia's stroller and lay down in the sand.

Now that she was no longer driving or walking, a deep weariness suffused her. She closed her eyes and, half asleep, caressed by the steamy breeze, dreamed soft swirly visions of the stuffed animals lining Sophia's crib: the pink wooly hippopotamus, the bear with the heart embroidered on its chest, the lamb that played lullabies when you wound it. On the screen of her shut eyelids, she could see Sophia's bird mobile of parrots and bluebirds jiggling gently up and down. She wondered what it would be like to be a baby, with nothing more pressing to do than lie there and watch the flickering of shapes. She missed nursing Sophia like a vacancy at her very heart. She missed her twins, the way they grabbed at her knees and pulled at her arms, filling her with questions and the sweet endlessness of their need. She missed Dylan, his intent intelligence, his nerdy enthusiasms, his sloppy, barely readable weekly letters from camp. She missed Ethan, viscerally, and longed to curve her body around him and press her breasts into his back. She wanted to lie in bed with her eyes closed and hear the gentle buzz of his morning sounds as he shaved and poured coffee out of his thermos. She wanted the soft brush of the cream carpet in their bedroom. She wanted her comfortable beautiful house, yet she wanted to stay in Ocean City and waitress at O'Donnell's. She wanted Jared and Ashley's baby to come back to life. She wanted to take Jared back in time, to somewhere sunny and safe. She wanted to walk down this broad white beach all the way to where the wild horses ran and run and run and run with them, the wet sand squishing between her toes and her lungs gasping for air if she could only transcend the limits of her fallible body. She wanted all these things at once.

A spray of sand jolted her awake. Jared, his new swim shorts barely damp, plopped down beside her.

"The water is rough, like I thought." He glanced over at Sophia, sleeping in an awkward position in her stroller, which Erica had forgotten to shift from the upright position. Her head hung down over her chest, one of her legs caught in the strap. Milky spittle, dotted with apricot, dripped from her mouth. "Is Sophia all right, Aunt Rikki?" he asked.

Erica took a closer look, and no, Sophia was not all right. She was burning hot. She was sunburnt, mosquito-bitten, and caked in damp sand—sand in the corners of her eyes, between her toes, between the folds of her chubby thighs. She wasn't totally asleep, but she wasn't truly awake either. "Sophia! Sophie!" Erica jiggled her, trying to trigger a reaction, brushing a bottle of juice against her hot, dry lips. Sophia opened her eyes as if it took great effort, managing only a slitted, dull gaze. A giant black-and-white New-foundland walked up, wagging his tail and then sniffing at Sophia.

"Look, Sophie, doggie! Doggie! You love doggies!" Erica shook Sophia's shoulders.

Sophia did not respond. Her slitted eyes closed again. She breathed heavily.

"Don't you see the doggie, Sophia?"

But Sophia lay there blankly, indifferent to the dog's gentle tongue on her leg.

"My God," Erica cried softly. She'd been carrying around her precious little girl like she was so much luggage.

"No, she's sick, Jared. I have to take her to the doctor. I have to go home. I have to go home right now."

"But what about me?" Jared didn't look so good himself, skinny, heavy lidded and grungy, blinking back the sun. Down the beach, Ashley was standing with a group of kids holding boogie boards and passing what appeared to be a jug of cheap wine. She seemed to have forgotten about her dead baby. Maybe Ashley had decided having an abortion was really like having her tonsils taken out. The wound bled for a while but healed quickly, allowing her to get on with the rest of her life. Erica didn't doubt that Ashley's sadness would catch up with her years later, when she'd long forgotten about it. Her submerged scars, visible to no one but her, would rip open, leaving a gaping, unfillable hole.

But screw Ashley. Ashley wasn't Erica's problem anymore. Erica kept trying to get a reassuring reaction out of Sophia. She bounced her and tickled her. All she did in response was wiggle and moan a little without opening her eyes. Erica pried open her mouth and dropped apple juice on her tongue while Jared hovered foolishly over the two of them. She was tired of Jared being her problem too.

"Why don't you go join your girlfriend, Jared?" Erica said.

Jared's eyes filled with tears. "Aunt Rikki, please take me home, and I'll face the music, whatever it is. At least I'll see Mom."

"Jared, listen to me." Erica tightened her free hand around his wrist. "You can't go back to things the way they are. I rescued you from that boot camp, didn't I? You're free now."

"I know you love me, Aunt Rikki, but I'm scared."

Erica pressed Jared's bony knuckles into her palm. "Listen to me. Stay here in Ocean City. Ashley's right: it's the middle of the summer, there's tons of people, you'll get a job."

Jared nodded assent, his wide, deep-set hazel eyes blinking, as Ashley ran toward them, dripping water. Alone among the four of them, she appeared physically untouched by the previous three days, sparkling in her new striped bikini, her hair hanging damp down the center of her back, her hands fluttering excitedly.

"Hey, Jared," Ashley said, "I found a place to crash." She pointed to the circle of kids with the wine. "And leads on a job too. They need people at this fried fish place; they're always looking for help. And Alvin over there"—she pointed at a tall boy with curly brown hair wearing an oversize pair of board shorts—"says I can use my fake ID and maybe get a job as a cocktail waitress. He says I could pass as twenty-one for sure. What do you think, Jared?" She struck a swimsuit model pose.

"All right," Jared said. "Ashley, Aunt Rikki has to leave. Sophia is sick."

Ashley looked at Sophia, lying limply against Erica's damp and sandy breasts. "Oh, the poor little thing," she said. "Well, I guess we'll be okay, won't we, Jared?"

Jared swallowed and bit his lip like Dylan always did standing at home plate in Little League. "Yep," he said.

The late-afternoon sun, still strong, beat down on Erica's head. She imagined it drilling down into Sophia's fevered skull. All she could think of was getting her off the beach, sheltering her from that harsh sky.

She pressed $500 into Jared's hand and left them there, standing in the sand.

Back at the car she forced another dose of Tylenol plus the cold medicine down Sophia's throat, taking consolation in the fact that she swallowed the syrupy liquid rather than throwing it back up. Not that the Tylenol was doing any good anymore. Sophia felt hotter than ever. Her diaper was barely wet, even though she hadn't changed it in, well, she didn't remember. She didn't think she'd changed it back on the boardwalk. Oh yeah, in the restaurant of that barbeque place with the nosy lady, way back in South Carolina. Surely a baby's diaper typically needed changing more often, but she couldn't recall precisely how often—she really wasn't thinking straight.

She turned on the air-conditioning. Vince's engine knocked but, thankfully, still functioned. The traffic crept all the way to the Bay Bridge and beyond—hordes of oblivious vacationers crawling home to the DC area after the weekend. At every stall she turned her head to the backseat, rolled up on one knee to touch Sophia's chest, to reassure herself with the soft in and out of her breath. She did not seem to be coughing as much, but Erica could not rouse her from sleep. By the time she reached the J. Millard Tawes Rest Area the sun was setting. She filled one of Sophia's bottles at the water fountain, forcing lukewarm water between her parched lips. Sophia's eyes opened, briefly, dully; she turned her head, and half the water dribbled out of her mouth. Erica took her into the restroom where she changed her diaper, even though it was only slightly wet with what looked to be fluorescent-yellow pee, almost orange. Every inch of her body was ablaze. The Tylenol wasn't doing any good, but Erica forced some more down anyway. She splashed her all over with cool water in the bathroom sink, her naked tush bumping up against the metal faucet. She washed off the sand, revealing more bright-red mosquito bites with spreading round circles around them, but thank goodness, the coolness, or maybe the discomfort, made her open her eyes for a couple minutes. "Sophie, Sophie," Erica murmured. She changed her into the last of the clean clothes she'd brought, a pastel-green stretchie with zebra appliques. She snorted the last of her coke, right there in the parking lot; it was dark and filled with oblivious truckers. Her rag doll arms steered her back on to the turnpike; her rag doll legs worked the accelerator. Her robot eyes guided her past the eighteen-wheelers, whipping in and out of the lanes with instinctive precision. The throb at the base of her head provided a bass line for Robert Palmer, the Clash, Barf, Bloody Tampax. Sophia slept through it all. Erica drove with her right hand on Sophia's little chest, feeling her little heart pumping rapidly, her little chest rising and sinking. She kept her left hand on the wheel except once, when Sophia made a gravelly, choking noise, and Erica turned to check her throat with both hands, steering the car with her sandaled foot. The familiar moonscape of Elizabeth, New Jersey, shone metallic and incandescent. Through the mustard-yellow miasma, she made out the neon lights of a hospital emergency room and briefly considered stopping. But she couldn't, because everything was crashing in on her, not just Sophia but also Jesse and Jake, due back from Lisa's in less than half a day and everyone else returning from where they'd gone, everyone looking for her. She drove over the Goebbels Bridge and through Staten Island and over the Verrazano in the waning hours of the perpetually lit New York night, down the Brooklyn Queens Expressway and past the graveyards and down the Grand Central to Northern Parkway. To the accompaniment of Dire Straits playing "Money for Nothing," she roared into the North Shore Hospital parking lot, slammed on the brakes, and opened herself up to the mercy of the emergency room staff.

Sophia looked tiny in the midst of the white-sheeted ER bed. Her heart beat visibly in her sunken chest, her breath short and fast. The nurse poked her all over with needles, trying to locate a vein robust enough to insert an IV catheter. All Sophia's veins were thin and flat, blue streaks dotting her translucent infant skin. Finally the nurse plunged a needle into her carotid artery, in the hollow of her fragile neck.

"You got her here just in time," said the doctor. "Her kidneys were on the verge of shutting down. And her heart."

Erica watched the fluid flow into Sophia's veins. She'd carted her baby around like baggage. She tried to answer the doctor's questions.

Her husband was away on a business trip. They'd been traveling, visiting relatives in Virginia. Sophia caught what she assumed was a cold: a stuffy nose, mild fever, poor appetite. She supposed she should have taken her to a doctor down there, but she kept figuring she would get better. And in fact her nasal congestion and coughing had almost disappeared, but she was so hot, so difficult to rouse. Yes, agreed the doctor, a 105 fever. When had she last eaten? Peed? Pooped? Erica couldn't quite recall. She didn't understand what possibly could have happened.

Lots of potential things could be wrong, said the doctor. Meningitis, for one, given Sophia's unresponsiveness and that puffy mosquito bite underneath her eye. They inserted another needle into the vulnerable hollow underneath her curls and took a spinal tap. Or she could have sunstroke, given her high fever and all those hours in ninety degree weather and on the beach. Or perhaps acetaminophen poisoning. How many doses of Tylenol had Erica given her over the past seventy-two hours? About every four hours, she guessed. She couldn't precisely recall. Plus that cold medicine stuff. Or maybe pneumonia, added the doctor, though he couldn't detect water in Sophia's lungs. But sometimes pneumonia in babies could be deceptive.

How old were her other children? Was she feeling overwhelmed? Did she need help? The hospital had social workers on staff.

No, no, Erica assured him. She paced about the small parcel of linoleum allotted her, never averting her gaze from the life-giving tube inserted into Sophia's artery. She was wearing cutoffs and the bathing suit she'd bought in Ocean City, stiff with salt water and smelling of seaweed and coffee. She tapped her fingers on the sides of her thighs, sweaty and sticky from the car, clumps of sand still stuck to the sides of her knee. She'd stumbled into a nightmare and prayed for release.

The spinal tap came in negative. No meningitis. The chest X-ray came in negative too. No pneumonia. Blood tests indicated Sophia's liver was stressed but not beyond easy repair.

Slowly, Erica watched Sophia return to herself. She opened her eyes. Her breathing became regular. Her cheeks filled out; her body grew more substantive, more settled. She kicked her legs, unballed her fists. She drank a bottle of apple juice. "Mama, mama," she murmured. A hesitant smile revealed her two new teeth. One of the nurses pranced an elephant puppet in front of her face. "Doggie," she gurgled weakly, her smile radiating and encompassing the world.

"It appears she was basically suffering from severe dehydration," said the doctor. "Maybe complicated by sunstroke." The fever might have burned the enamel off her baby teeth. Whatever respiratory infection that had originally caused the problem was almost gone. She needed more juice, more formula, a few quiet days. They could keep her overnight for observation, but given her quick recovery with the IV fluids, they were willing to send her home.

"The upshot is that she's going to be okay," said the doctor.

Darkness closed in on Erica, and she crumpled to the floor. She came to on the same bed where Sophia had lain. The nurse with the elephant puppet, now cradling Sophia, offered her water.

Erica sipped the water. She was soaked in sweat. Her body felt trembly and light, almost airborne. "I'd rather take her home," she said.

"Are you sure?" said the nurse.

"Yes," said Erica. "I feel fine now."

"We have a parenting class on Thursday nights," noted the nurse, as she accompanied them unnecessarily to the checkout desk to fill out dismissal papers, handing Sophia back to Erica only at the last, unavoidable instant.

"I used to be a nurse, you know," Erica told her, as ambulance sirens shrieked, the doors to the emergency room burst open, and paramedics rushed in bearing an unconscious man on a stretcher. Attentions turned to saving another life. Erica and Sophia walked out into the New York morning and drove home.

Erica's house enclosed her in its warm and stuffy embrace: the shiny white mica cabinets spilling over with board games and plastic figurines; the refrigerator stuffed with cheese sticks, rotting cherries, and an economy jug of lemonade; the mail scattered all over the hallway tile; the blinking answering machine. The beauty of it all staggered her. It may have been a mess, but to her it looked washed clean.

She bathed Sophia. She seemed subdued but still chuckled with delight, pushing her plastic duckies around. Erica changed her into a fresh diaper, reveling in the overflowing pile of them, and the giant box of wipes and new canister of powder. She dressed her in a seersucker stretchie painted with lilac flowers. After putting Sophia into her crib, where she chortled and shook her legs to the musical mobile, Erica luxuriated in a long, hot shower, pulling brambles and sand out of her hair, washing out geological layers of filth. She put on fresh underwear and one of Ethan's favorite T-shirts, one with a picture of Albert Einstein in a police cap saying, "E = MC squared—that's the law." It was the middle of the day, Jesse and Jake due home soon, but Erica did not think to check the clock. She was beyond time. She took Sophia out of her crib. She lay down on her bed, offering her daughter her breast. She craved the pressure of Sophia's soft sweet skin against hers. She would never, ever have enough of it. Sophia accepted her nipple as if she'd never been on the bottle, sucking madly. After a couple of minutes, Erica felt the familiar tingle, the ripe fullness. She gave into her absolute exhaustion and fell asleep like that, Ethan's shirt tucked up around her shoulders, Sophia sucking at her breast. Back in the trap, in the salivating mouth of the beast, she held her daughter, returned to her from the depths of terror. She sank into the comforts of her home and allowed herself to believe it was a refuge.

CHAPTER THIRTY-FIVE

Sophia whimpered and rooted against her breast, and Erica woke in a haze, conscious but not fully present. She'd dreamed in vivid colors: oceanic blues, velvet purples, and an orange-yellow rich as an egg yolk. She'd been cruising down a river with Ethan, Debbie, Ron, and her cousin Amelia, somewhere steamy hot filled with the loud chatter of parrots. She'd spilled her wine, and it had streamed, deep burgundy, all over her napkin and her low-cut dress where her breasts swelled out of the lacy top, engorged with milk, until the captain came out and officiously informed her she must leave the ship.

Lines of white light crisscrossed the crumpled sheets, silky and patterned with yellow tulips. She hoisted herself onto her elbows and, lifting Sophia onto her lap, swung her legs over the side of the bed. She felt as if she were floating over the bed in a balloon, like the time she'd floated over date palms with Ethan on one of his business trips. She closed her eyes momentarily, breathed deeply, and clutching Sophia tightly, rose to standing. In contrast to the fog in her brain, her leg muscles tensed, all the way down to the arch of her foot, like they were about to pop out of her skin. The scratches on her legs throbbed, pink and hot.

She wandered through her house, replete with every toy she'd ever wanted, from the embroidered summer quilt to the hand-cut tile to Sophia's dresses hanging in pink and lacy rows. All these lovely possessions shone bright and crystalline in captured light. She rooted around the refrigerator for food, rolling cool and creamy spoonfuls of raspberry yogurt around her mouth as she fed Sophia strained peaches. She tore off the chocolate wafers from a box of Oreos, saving the sugary insides for last. The throbbing at the base of her neck shattered into sparkles of pain.

She turned her head to see her message machine blinking its customary angry red. The lovely light slipped from her grasp. She breathed hard, deep, ragged breaths that hurt her lungs, her heart racing, her stomach jumping, stinky sweat soaking her panties and Ethan's T-shirt. Faint again, she put her head between her knees, reaching and stretching her arms down her calves. The ER doctor had told her that he'd saved Sophia's life. It was only a matter of hours, he'd emphasized; a tiny infant body runs out of water very quickly. Sophia had been burning up, drying out, fading away while she'd raced up one road and down another, while she'd lain on the beach soaking up the sun, while she tried to save someone who was not her child. The last few days were a blur, but at the fringes of her consciousness, she still saw Jared, standing on the beach, eyes moist, biting his lip. She should have hugged him good-bye.

"Mama?" asked Sophia from her high chair.

Erica called Anders to ask if she could meet him that day.

"I'm busy," he said. Anders was not one for explication. "See you tomorrow morning at ten."

Call waiting beeped.

"It's Lisa, hon," said the voice at the other end. "I kept calling you, but you didn't answer. You didn't answer my messages either. Can I return your little boys? I have a tennis game at the club. I hope you don't mind—we stopped for dinner already."

Dinner? Erica looked for the first time at the clock; it was almost seven. "I just got in," she said. "How did everything go?"

"Oh, fine," Lisa said. "They're darlings, though I think they got a little homesick at the end."

In the hallway mirror, she caught a glimpse of herself, tan and scraggly, sun-bleached auburn hair with raggedy split ends, limbs studded with scratches and mosquito bites. At least she'd changed into a cute flowered sundress. The light was more forgiving than in the changing room in Ocean City, and she couldn't decide whether she looked good or bad. Jesse and Jake ran in, dragging their tote bags and the remnants of Happy Meals.

"I hope you don't mind the fast food, but I'm beat," Lisa said, shaking her streaked-blond head. "I don't know how you do it with four kids."

"Thanks again," said Erica. "I'm sorry I didn't get your calls. Would you like a cold drink or something?"

"Oh no, I'm in a rush." Lisa put her hand on her hip. "Don't get me wrong—the weekend was a blast. So, tell me, how was yours? You're looking tan and model thin, my friend."

"Great," Erica said. "The beach was gorgeous. We ate lobster."

"Did you party with Christie Brinkley or anything?"

"No, no. Just Ethan's friends." Erica hoped Lisa wouldn't press her for any more details she lacked the wherewithal to invent.

"Well, my court time is in five minutes. You fill me in later on all the beautiful people, okay?" With a squeaky turn of her tennis sneaker Lisa bounced down the steps to her Saab.

Back in the family room, Sophia was pulling records out of their jackets. Now that they'd bought a CD player, Ethan's once top-of-the-line prize stereo was gathering dust, but their shelves of LPs still lined the wall. Erica watched the quick flick of Sophia's wrists as she grasped the end of each disc and pushed it along the rug. Inspired, the twins pulled down the crates of Legos from their shelf and overturned them, dropping ketchup-smudged potatoes in their wake.

Her back hurt from all those hours driving. Her head was hurting so much it made her dizzy and nauseous. Maybe she had a brain tumor. She rolled back onto the carpet, kicking her legs up in the air and then over into a plough position. Maybe being upside down would send needed blood to her brain, though in reality her arteries felt on overdrive, all that blood rushing about under her skin. Maybe there was something amiss with her heart rhythm. Tachycardia, that was the term, right. Yep. Tachycardia. Rapid heartbeat. She didn't want to think about hearts or blood. The air was stale and warm; she hadn't opened the windows since the weekend. The limp french fries under her fingertips reminded her of hazy mornings at Nick's house.

"We took Penny for a walk." Jake stuck his head between her

legs and belly. "We took a walk with a lot of other dogs just like her. The dogs are in a club. A spaniel club."

"That's nice," Erica said, uncurling from the plough and stretching her legs out long and wide, stretching her upper body over her right knee, laying her forehead down on its rough surface.

"I missed you, Mommy," said Jesse, sprawling over her exposed left leg.

"I love you, Mommy," said Jake. They all snuggled together on the rug.

The phone rang: Dylan, making his weekly call from camp. In his sweet voice, he filled her in on a swim meet and the homemade strawberry ice cream they'd made after dinner and reminded her he was playing a wizard in the Parents' Day play.

The phone rang again.

"Hello, stranger," said Ethan.

"You sound tired," said Erica.

"So do you," he said. "How was your weekend?"

"My weekend?" she asked, thrown off balance for a moment.

"Weren't you going to the Hamptons or something? I didn't call last night because I figured you'd be stuck in traffic until late."

"Oh yeah, it was great. The beach was beautiful. We ate lobster," she said.

"How are the kids?" he asked.

"Good."

"I'll be home Wednesday." Ethan sighed. "Everything is such a disaster."

"No," Erica massaged a raw tender spot at the base of her neck.

"Unfortunately, yes."

Erica's index finger touched a crusty scab oozing a slick fluid. She pulled it off and rolled it between her thumb and finger. Once Sophia fell asleep, she'd take a nice long bath, with lavender bubbles, soak herself clean again. She heard a faint beeping.

"I think it's my call waiting but I can ignore it," she said.

"Go ahead and answer it," Ethan said. "I don't want to talk about this whole disaster on the phone anyway. I'm exhausted. I think I'm going to take a shower and watch a little TV."

Erica could wait on Ethan's bad news. She could wait on all bad news. She thought of soap bubbles. She thought of Ethan washing his body with the orange-scented hotel soap and the way she used to wash every inch of his body in the communal showers of his MIT dorm, when he was her new possession, all hers to explore. They'd used a scented soap that smelled like apples, though it was no doubt something cheap and synthetic. She visualized Ethan's skin, shimmering iridescently under the bubbles, as she heard Debbie's irate and panicked voice.

"You never pick up your messages, do you, Rikki? Or maybe you do, but you don't concern yourself enough to call?"

"I told you I was going to the Hamptons for the weekend." Erica pictured bubbles, shimmering like prisms, bursting. "I was just about to call you. How was your weekend in Albany?"

"Jared's run away from the Pritima Center! We got home from upstate, all exhausted from the drive, to find this news waiting for us."

"Oh my," Erica managed, her voice thin and flat. The weekend felt like such a disconnected dream that she could almost convince herself Debbie was relating fresh news. "That's terrible," she said.

"Is that all you have to say?" snapped Debbie. "You don't sound overly concerned. Are you too busy hanging out with your new rich friends at the beach?"

Erica watched as Sophia crawled up on a low shelf, reaching for more records, and slipped, falling to the carpet, screaming. Erica dropped the phone and grabbed her, investigating every inch of her body. No cuts. No blood. No bruises. No trips to the emergency room.

"Rikki, are you still there?" Debbie asked.

Erica almost gave into to an impulse to tell Debbie about Sophia's illness. Of all the people she knew, Debbie would most understand the helpless sensation of watching your child lying in a hospital bed. She'd remember how the whole big wide world ceased to matter and your world shrunk to that tiny space, with its horrible noisy machines and artificial, overly bright light. When Jared had been in the ICU, all Erica did was listen to Debbie babble;

she did not possess the breadth of understanding to know what to say in return. Now she understood, but they could no longer talk. Sophia nuzzled her teary face into Erica's neck as she picked up the phone again.

"Sorry," she said. "Sophia fell."

"Speaking of babies," Debbie said, "about an hour before Jared ran away, some woman came into the center claiming she was a relative of his. They didn't allow her to visit him, of course—that's not protocol. But then this same woman joined his work pod, claiming she was from the agriculture department. Then he walks off the grounds with this mysterious woman."

"How strange."

Sophia, recovered, rooted around Erica's shirt for milk.

"The woman was carrying a baby girl," Debbie said, sounding eerily calmer now, "and the description they gave me sounded a lot like you."

"How could it possibly be me?" Erica squealed. "I was in the Hamptons. How could I be in South Carolina at the same time?"

"Of course it wasn't you," Debbie continued, deliberately drawing out the length of each word, calm, yes, but, Erica thought, artificially so: the calm tone you might use if someone was pointing a gun at your back. "I said the description sounded a lot like you. How did you know Jared was in South Carolina, anyway? The center's location is confidential."

Erica placed Sophia, down to residual tears, in her high chair with the box of animal crackers. She'd lost weight over the weekend, all the chubby folds in her thighs flattened out.

"Of course," said Debbie. "Your good buddy Nick must have told you. That man sure had me fooled. "

"What makes you think he's my good buddy?" asked Erica.

"Oh, Mom told me you guys had become friends. Like you knew each other in school but never really liked each other, but lately she'd seen you chatting in the neighborhood. You've got odd taste in friends. You know how he got out on bail? Ron thinks he made some sort of deal."

"What would Ron know about a deal?" Erica asked. Jesse

wandered into the kitchen, intertwining his fingers with Erica's, smelling of french fries and chlorine. Golden dog hairs stuck to his shirt.

"Oh, you know Ron," said Debbie. "He's friends with everybody. He's got buddies down at the police station—they know him from the military or from his Paul Anka fan club or something."

Jesse pulled at her fingers insistently. Sophia tossed a lion cookie onto the kitchen floor. In the family room, Jake rammed a toy truck into a Lego tower.

She'd run off and left Jared standing in the sand, clutching a few hundred-dollar bills. Where was he sleeping? Had Ashley left him for one of the boys on the beach, one who hadn't fathered the baby she never truly wanted, one who wasn't scared of rough water—maybe Alvin? Had Jared found a job? Was he serving fried fish? Frozen custard? Begging on the streets? He'd run out of inhalers at the Pritima Center. He missed his mother.

"Hell is breaking loose here," she said. "I better give the boys a bath."

"I really need to talk to you more, Rikki," Debbie said. "There are a lot of unanswered questions here."

"How about tomorrow? I've got little kids to attend to, you know."

———

Erica's head ached even more the next morning, a wracking heavy pain unalleviated by five cups of coffee. Clouds of amorphous fear pressed upon her like an infection. She got Jesse and Jake off to camp with clean towels and bathing suits and then plodded through putrid LIE traffic to meet Anders. She didn't like him. He was a sullen, scowly sort with greasy hair and pimples across the bridge of his nose. She didn't know him: whether he had a wife or girlfriend, what kind of music he liked or how he spent his days when he wasn't hanging out in this godforsaken park that even the teenage moms and the old men seemed to have abandoned. She joked with him about the T-shirts, asking whether they were tie-dyed, or pastel green, or bearing Columbia logos. He stared at her blankly and handed her a paper bag. She handed over her money. "Have a good one," he muttered and left.

Her skin hung loose over her bones, and her limbs were antsy, anxious to move. She didn't feel like driving home yet, where the walls closed in on her, where Sam's grotty cage awaited, lacking water and greens, where there was fetid laundry, mail to sort, bills to pay, and phone messages to listen to. Most particularly the phone. One only needed to wait for more bad news to arrive.

Sophia struggled with the stroller seatbelt, attempting valiantly but unsuccessfully to master its mysteries. She chewed on the strap and then fell asleep. Erica wandered past gas stations and auto repair shops.

The air lay dank and thick. Really, what was she thinking, raising her children on this tapped-out chunk of earth, between two highways spewing benzene, bordered by an oily ocean? Bloody Tampax, Jared had told her, was a punk band from Hicksville who had gone to the beach one day and found a raft of plastic Tampax holders washed up on the litter-strewn sand like scallop shells. What did it matter if she poisoned her body? The air and the water were doing a good enough job on their own, even without her assistance. She dreamed of distant, unattainable places: Ethan's parents' wooden A-frame bungalow, surrounded by beds of fiery nasturtiums, framed in the cool mist like it was behind etched glass; the night air in the Smoky Mountains, moist and piney.

She was out of breath; her chest ached. She walked the many hot smelly blocks back to the car and drove home, where the phone machine was, of course, blinking. She put Sophia in her playpen. She promptly clambered up the fabric diamonds of the wall, perched herself on the rim, and jumped off. She did this several times in a row. Erica folded up the clearly pointless playpen and stuck it in the basement. Untethered, Sophia wandered through the house like a miniature Godzilla, dislodging everything within reach.

The phone rang.

"Where have you been, Rikki?" Debbie asked. "I called you

several times this morning. I should stop leaving you messages. You never answer them."

"I took Sophia for a walk."

"You shouldn't have taken her outside. Don't you know there's an ozone alert?"

"I haven't read the paper," Erica said, pulling a Happy Meal action figure out of Sophia's mouth.

"Ron thinks it might be a kidnapping, though deep in my heart, Rikki, I fear he's run away again. That little bitch Ashley is missing too. Why on earth, really, would anyone want to kidnap my Jared? What kind of security do they have at that Pritima Center? How much more of this can I take? My stomach is in such pain, Rikki. I've run to the bathroom ten times this morning."

"My stomach doesn't feel so great either," Erica said.

"By any chance, if you speak to Mom and Dad, please don't tell them anything about this," Debbie continued.

"How could I speak to them?" Erica asked. "They're in Eastern Europe."

"Well, if they call. They called me collect from Vienna, though God knows what the phone bill's going to be." Debbie paused and then spoke in a breathy whisper she reserved for disturbing medical information. "Dad has angina, you know," she said. "Or didn't Mom tell you?"

"No," Erica said. The phone slipped through her sweaty hands. A spasm rippled through her belly. "I really gotta go, Debbie," she said. "I have to go to the bathroom really bad." Somehow her robot self still managed to utter coherent sentences. "Keep me posted, okay?"

CHAPTER THIRTY-SIX

Erica followed Sophia around as she marched through the house like a drunk windup doll, into the kitchen, out to the hallway, around to the living room, through to the family room, back into the kitchen again. For variety, they marched back and forth across the backyard, in and out of the play castle. Sophia stuffed wood chips in her mouth. Erica liked the smooth feel of the inside of Sophia's mouth, the sensation of her saliva on her finger. She could follow Sophia about endlessly, dumbly. Her diapered tush rounded out her yellow polka-dotted sundress, and the ringlets of her hair covered the bandage on her neck. She probably didn't need that bandage anymore. Erica gently ripped it off, spitting on her finger and wiping off some gooey residue and a drop of dried blood. The IV insertion site was barely visible, a faint mark at Sophia's throat. The grass felt wet and sticky under Erica's feet, despite the fact it hadn't rained for days. The sprinkler must be malfunctioning. She should call the sprinkler people, but she didn't feel like facing the phone again.

To satisfy Lisa and Justine, she'd elaborated details of her fictitious Hamptons weekend: the Bulgari choker worn by her hostess, the $300 bottle of wine served at dinner, the sighting of Billy Joel at the East Hampton ice cream parlor. Justine demanded details of the Grant Fishel debacle too, in that it was splashed all over the paper, but there Erica brushed her off, changed the subject. She couldn't fabricate anything credible about that.

Ethan was due home in two hours.

Sophia refused to nap, allowing Erica no opportunity to wash her hair, which hung limply about her face but frizzed untidily at her shoulders. She sprayed hair glop on it to no avail, finally pulling the unruly mass back with a banana clip. She splashed her face with cold water and rubbed toner on her cheeks and the back of her neck and put on a lime-green sundress she'd bought in Florida. It gaped unflatteringly at her shoulder blades, so she changed into shorts and a tight Benetton top. She ate a few spoonfuls of tuna fish as she followed Sophia around the house once more, picking up toys in her wake.

She heard Ethan's key in the lock.

Ethan lugged in a set of golf clubs and a duffel bag, wearing wrinkled khakis and his scoop-neck peach T shirt. They hugged.

There had been a period when she told Ethan everything. On the upper tier of his dorm room bunk and along the banks of the Charles River, washed of inhibition by too much pot and cheap wine, she shared all her secrets stored up over a childhood and adolescence. Ethan knew all about the World's Fair, about the parties at the Mackay estate, about the time she drank her parents' tequila and replaced it with water. He was the only person she'd ever told about her abortion. At the time, these had seemed like the keys to her private self, the biggest secrets she could ever imagine she might own. She felt they scarred her just enough to render her cool and edgy. By releasing them, she freed herself, merging herself with Ethan in the clear and clean and limitless universe of adulthood.

As Jackson Browne said, hold on to your illusions until they shatter.

Sophia toddled up to greet Ethan, and he flung her high into the air. "She's so big," he said. "I feel like I've been away forever." He took a closer look at Erica. "You look washed out," he said.

"Just tired, I guess." Erica pulled up her loose shorts and hid her flyaway hair behind her ears. "So, how's everything been going?" she asked.

"Okay." Ethan jiggled Sophia about, making razzberry noises.

Erica poured them each a glass of ginger ale. "What's going on with Grant Fishel?"

"I'll tell you. I've got lots of stuff to tell you."

"Let's go outside," Erica said, but as she opened the patio doors, thunder rumbled. The arborvitae rustled in a sudden wind.

They sat down in the family room instead. Sophia pulled more records out of their jackets and rolled them over the carpet.

"I think we should put those away and get some CD storage," Erica said.

"Whatever you like," Ethan said absently, setting his glass down. "Say, Erica, what would you think about seriously moving to Florida?"

Erica imagined leaving the toxic air, the oily ocean, Debbie, Ron, Nick, and Anders behind, living safe within a flower-scented paradise with turquoise water where palm trees waved their wide funny leaves to the sky.

"I'd like it," she said. "But why? Did you do that insider trading or whatever it is they're accusing Grant Fishel of doing?"

"No, I didn't," Ethan said, his voice flat and frustrated. "I make a product—that's all. I got carried away with the elegance of the product, I guess. I couldn't predict all the possible uses people would put it to."

"What are those uses?" Erica asked.

"You wouldn't understand," Ethan said.

"Do you think I'm an idiot?"

"It's not that you're an idiot, Erica. It's that you've never expressed the slightest interest in what I do for a living." Ethan sighed and looked out the patio doors, where a heavy rain beat down on the open patio umbrella. "You should close that umbrella. The table could fly away in that wind."

Erica got up to close the umbrella, stomping her bare feet on the ground. She walked back in, chilly and soaked. "So, is somebody going to be asking you questions? The FBI or the SEC or whatever? I mean, are you in trouble?" She wrapped herself in an afghan.

"After a fashion," Ethan said, tickling Sophia on her tummy. "I don't believe they care about me, but they care about people I know."

"Like Stephan Langston?"

"Yeah, like him." A sour smirk crossed Ethan's face. "Did you ever call him about our Jamaica hotel?"

"Yeah, I did, actually."

"Well, he's not going to the Caribbean anytime soon, because he's going to jail."

Erica cast her eye possessively about the surroundings they'd built with Ethan's paychecks and her taste: the leaf-green shag rug; the TV and Nintendo console; the flower-tiled kitchen at ten dollars a tile; even immense Sam the iguana, lolling in his cage with those impervious eyes. She stored it all in her mind for future sustenance. The world was closing in on both of them. She couldn't figure out why she kept looking at the stuff, kept focusing on the stuff, but maybe it both symbolized and hid the things that really mattered. She edged closer to Ethan and curled her right hand around the tips of Ethan's fingers.

"So why move to Florida?" she asked. "We could move to California like you keep talking about."

"Well, there are various things—various things with the securities laws. It's a more expeditious place to be." Ethan hedged.

Erica couldn't figure out whether he was being purposely obtuse or whether all this skirting around was a consequence of the abstractions that constituted his work, in deference to all the complexities she evidently didn't understand.

"Grant Fishel wants me out of the New York office," he said finally, spitting out the words like they were a chunk of steak he'd been choking on.

"You mean we have to move?" she asked. "We have no choice?"

"Well, yeah," Ethan said. "If I want to keep my job."

Outside, lightning flashed, and rain poured down. Everything within her line of vision appeared bleached of color, solid and still. Once, at a college party, extremely stoned, she'd experienced a similar sensation, uncertain whether she was actually living her life or floating somewhere above, watching it. So many years had gone by since then, and she could see them stretched out like a roll of film negatives. One moment followed upon another, and she could zoom in on any of those moments in fine relief: the expressions on people's faces, the way light fell across their bodies, the split-second gap before things changed again. For a few minutes—she couldn't say how long—she felt a strange clarity, a heavy calm.

———

The phone rang, jerking her out of her stupor.

"You'd better come over here right now, Rikki," Debbie said, her voice short and breathy, uneasy. In the background, Ron hissed remarks she couldn't decipher.

"I can't come over now," Erica said. "Ethan just got home, and he hasn't been home in almost three weeks. Plus the boys are coming back from camp soon."

She heard another sharp imprecation from Ron and rustling in the background.

"You'd better come now," Debbie repeated softly. "It's about Jared."

Erica's mind flooded with horrifying scenarios featuring Jared murdered by a narrow-eyed redneck, smashed by a truck, thrown in a ditch by the side of the highway. She shouldn't have run out on him the way she did, leaving him standing on the beach without so much as a hug, biting his lip and crunching her hundred-dollar bills.

"Get over here now," Ron barked.

"What is going on? Where is Jared?"

"Get over here right now, you bitch!"

All Erica's free-floating dread congealed into one black knot. She was not a bad person. She could explain. Let Jared be alive.

"You get your sorry ass over here, Rikki, or I'm going to break your door down!"

Debbie should never have married Ron. When he asked her out for drinks at the Williston Diner that first day she cut his hair—that alone should have been a warning sign; who with any taste would invite a girl to a dump like that?—she should have run like hell. She remembered the night they announced their engagement at Sunday family dinner, Ron's long, knotty white arm twisted around her like a possessive eel, Debbie beaming with a settled pleasure, as if marriage to Ron would answer any open questions she had about her life and guarantee her smooth sailing forevermore. Erica should have talked her out of it right then and there, but the thought didn't even occur to her. She was too intent on escaping Sunday family dinner and getting high with her friends at the Mackay estate. Besides, at that time, Ron didn't seem significantly more odious than any of the other dull, blustery jocks Debbie seemed attracted to. Debbie wouldn't have listened to her wayward sister anyway. Unbeknownst to Erica, she was already pregnant with Jared. Perhaps that was another reason behind her sated smile. No trips to Planned Parenthood for her. Debbie was marrying the father of her child. Fait accompli.

Erica felt the pull of Debbie's soft dry palm, holding her back at the curb until the yellow-sashed patrol guard waved them across. Debbie's hand grasping her tight and pulling her into the black murk.

Just let Jared be alive.

"Okay, okay, I'm coming," she said.

Ethan insisted on going, saying he could hear Ron screaming all the way from the couch. They buckled Sophia into Vince Volvo and drove the three blocks to Debbie and Ron's house. Rain gushed down the curbsides and pooled in the gutters.

The door stood ajar. The first thing Erica saw was Jared, alive and presumably intact. Then she noticed that he was standing in an odd formation with Ron and Debbie between the living room couch and the coffee table, as if they were practicing a skit.

"What the hell is going on here?" blurted Ethan.

"You should know," said Ron.

Clinging together in their own family unit, Erica, Ethan, and Sophia faced Ron, Debbie, and Jared from the opposite side of the coffee table, where Debbie's snow globes lay arranged in a flawless semicircle. Sophia buried her head in Erica's shoulder, whimpering.

Jared shuffled his feet awkwardly, looking down at the carpet.

"You asked why we're all standing here like this." Ron was swaying his upper body like a stiff and stringy rubber band, speaking in his soothing radio voice, all puffed up with the power that comes from the safety of your own territory. Debbie clasped her hands, smiling stiffly like a political wife.

"Yeah, I just might ask that," Ethan said, exuding his own brand of languid confidence.

"I would have gone directly to the cops, but Debbie prefers to avoid the embarrassment and the consequences. She prefers to handle this matter privately if at all possible, so, against my better judgment, I'm deferring to her feelings."

"And may I ask you what matter this is?" Ethan asked, still calm, still confident. He'd be like this facing a lawyer or judge, Erica knew.

"My private detective, Ralph Rossiter, picked up Jared in Ocean City, Maryland," Ron pronounced, "with his friend Ashley. They were staying in a house with extremely shabby sanitary conditions where illegal drugs were openly used."

Erica tried to catch Jared's attention, but he only stared at the floor.

"Jared denies this," Ron continued, and at this comment Jared did look up, shooting a defiant, pained look at his father, "but the Pritima Center tells us that Erica impersonated a nonexistent relative and also claimed to be a representative of the state agricultural department. That Erica kidnapped him from the Pritima Center."

"I was in the Hamptons," Erica said. "How could I be in South Carolina?"

"Yeah," Jared said.

"Well, that's not what Rossiter and the Pritima Center say. Their security cameras were fuzzy, but they indicate a woman who looked an awful lot like you, carrying a baby who looked an awful lot like Sophia. And Jared—this comes directly from Jared's mouth, mind you—Jared told me you've smoked marijuana with him on numerous occasions. He told me you let him and his little girlfriend sleep together on your property. He told me you gave him money for their little adventure in Philadelphia." Ron stopped his tirade for a moment, draping his arm around Jared. Jared fidgeted under his touch, looking at the snow globes, at the thick navy-blue drapes, at the blank television screen, at Ron's shuddering chin and furious eyes, everywhere but at Erica.

Erica shook her head firmly.

"Debbie tells me your mother saw you with Nick Stromboli, the cocaine dealer," Ron continued. "That you've visited him at his house."

"Nick Stromboli!" Erica said. "Jared's visited him in his house. Many times. With your approval. He worked for the Nassau Family Clinic, remember? He ran a Safe House."

"Yeah, my mistake," Ron said. "But what's your excuse?"

"Debbie?" Erica said. "Let me explain."

Debbie stared at her with an expression she couldn't quite categorize: disappointment, perhaps, sadness, fear, and a touch of sanctimony. "You've lied to us, Rikki," she said.

Anger coursed through Erica, lightning bright. Forget about explanations. She wanted to spit on their white linen upholstery, their matching rug stiff with vacuuming, their glass table without so much as a water stain marring it, the thick blue drapes hiding the sky, the snow globes enclosing their imaginary landscape. Possessions did speak—they did have meaning—and these possessions spoke a lie.

"How can you talk to me about lying!' she screamed. "Both of you! You lie all the time. You lie about your saintly lives. So I've smoked pot with Jared—so what? We were just having a good time. I was just trying to be his friend."

"We're not his friends. We're his parents. You have four children. You should know the difference," said Debbie, in her prim PTA-presentation voice.

"What kind of parents are you? You send him to a zillion stupid doctors. You make him carry a green sheet around in school. You give him all kinds of drugs prescribed by doctors, but you hassle him about smoking pot. You send him to a school in the middle of nowhere that you don't know anything about, that you read about in a pamphlet, because the director of a clinic who employs a coke dealer as a teen counselor thinks it's a good idea. "

Erica paused for a ragged breath. Sophia clung to her shoulder, screaming.

"The baby," Ethan muttered. "I'm telling you—hand me the baby."

Erica handed her over, and Ethan stepped back toward the glassed cabinet where Debbie kept her ceramic bunny collection. Debbie's eyes grew wide, moist with tears, her well-tweezed eyebrows faintly lifted, her fine hair curling softly around her shoulders, her feet in black pumps and nylon peds, pinned to the carpet, unable to move. She reminded Erica of one of the bunnies.

"Don't tell me how to be a parent," Erica continued. "I'd risk everything for my kids. I'd lay down my life for my kids. I'd lay down my life for Jared." She paused, her breath painful in her chest. She scratched her neck, reinflaming the scabs that were there. She looked down at her nails, chewed and bloodstained.

"Done ranting, Rikki?' Ron asked.

"I'm sure we can discuss all this reasonably like rational human beings," Ethan said, cradling Sophia protectively.

Ron cleared his throat, commander of the room. "It depends on the terms, Mr. Wall Street," he said. "I think Rikki's gone way beyond rational."

"Now you just wait a minute," Ethan said.

"Now you just wait a minute, Mr. Wall Street, for a change. You aren't the know-it-all here. I wanted to bring legal charges against Rikki, and I can readily do so. Kidnapping is a federal crime. She traveled across state lines with a minor."

"I told you she didn't do it, Dad," Jared said softly, scuffing his heels on the carpet.

"Why don't you listen to Jared?" Erica pressed her shaking knees against the hard edge of the coffee table.

"I think I'll stick with Mr. Rossiter's version, thank you. Jared's told us quite a few stories in the past few months, haven't you, young man?" He ruffled Jared's hair. Jared scowled and shifted away.

"Plus, the drug charges alone are not insignificant," Ron concluded. He paused for dramatic effect. "But as I said, Debbie convinced me not to involve the cops. She insisted I have this family conference with you. As a preliminary."

"Now, I'm not sure we have all the facts here." Ethan tried again. "I think we should all calm down and sit down and talk together on an equal footing. And I think you can stop calling me insulting names. I've done pretty well for myself and my family on Wall Street, Mr. DJ."

Ron pulled up to his full Marine bearing. "That all depends on your perspective," he said.

Erica swept her right hand along the coffee table, knocking snow globes over like dominoes. They toppled onto the table's brass leg, shattering into thousands of shards of glass, fragments of plastic, and colored water.

"How dare you threaten us!" she screamed. "How dare you! Jared's told me some things too, you know. Some things that I could tell the cops. Like how you've beaten him up for years. You think I didn't see you throw that plate of food at him at Lauren's bat mitzvah?"

Ron growled like an angry German shepherd.

"And that's not all," said Erica. "You beat my sister too. Jared didn't have to tell me that, although he did. You think I don't see those bruises she hides under her clothing? You think I believed her cockamamie story about that blood disease? Who the hell do you think you are? Debbie should have left you a long time ago."

"Ron, honey." Debbie disengaged herself from Ron's grasp enough to stroke his cheek. He pushed her away, gruffly. She shifted to Erica's side of the coffee table.

"You don't even love her," Erica continued, close enough to her sister that their hips brushed. She placed her hand tentatively on Debbie's back. Ethan, cradling Sophia, leaned against the glass-fronted cabinet with the ceramic bunnies. Jared sidled toward the dining room. That left just her and Debbie, facing down Ron.

Erica raised herself on her tiptoes, staring directly into his yellow-flecked, enraged eyes. "You think I don't see the way you look down my chest, you lecherous creep! I don't know how Debbie lets you touch her. I wouldn't sleep with you if my life depended on it. You look like an emaciated weasel, you, you and your sucky music and sucky Mets!"

Ron's face swelled up, red and bulbous, like a perverted balloon. Guttural noises emerged from his throat. He leaned over the coffee table, six inches away. Erica leaned her face into his, so close she could feel his breath.

"You don't scare me, you stupid asshole," she said.

Ron's arm lashed out, his tight fist headed directly for her face. Erica leaped away, a strong, agile bound, a leap she'd known since she was a little girl springing across the playground, a leap honed by track team and step aerobics, and smashed into Ron's La-Z-Boy armchair.

At that instant, there were only the two of them in the room. She grabbed a cracked snow globe from the floor and aimed it at his cheek. It missed. She heard it crash against the wall unit. Ron fell over the table, stretched long like a cobra, and slithered toward her. She lunged after his stupid ugly mug again, connecting, hearing his skin split, his cartilage bend.

An odd alarmed noise rose from Ethan: somewhere between a moan and a shriek. Erica turned to see her sister Debbie lying still on the ground, Ethan leaning over her, and Sophia opening the glass case of ceramic bunnies.

Jared's face collapsed as if it had been punctured. "Mommy!" he cried.

"Deb?" croaked Ron, in a tone Erica had never heard before. "Deb?"

And even though Erica was the CPR-trained nurse and Ethan plugged numbers into computers for a living, it was Ethan who opened her mouth, checked her tongue for obstructions, pressed her chest, and breathed air between her lips.

"Call 911," he gasped.

CHAPTER THIRTY-SEVEN

The 911 operator kept asking Erica questions whose answers were obvious or irrelevant. The address. Her name. The injured party's name. The injured party's age, her relationship to Erica. When Erica finally broke through with the reason for her call, she phrased it clumsily. "My sister fell. She's unconscious. I'm not sure she's breathing. There's blood on the side of her head."

"Has she been ill?" asked the operator.

"I don't know," snapped Erica. "Just send someone! This is an emergency!"

"They're on their way," said the operator.

When she returned to the living room, Ron and Jared were also kneeling over Debbie, though Ethan was still doing the compressing and the breathing.

Debbie's pupils floated about her irises, uneven and murky, like the triangle inside of an eight ball. Her neck lay at an angle. Her arms and legs flopped limply. Blood dripped down her pale cheek. Erica searched her rusty nurse's brain: it looked like a head injury. She was breathing, though. Erica took her pulse: rapid but steady.

"I think you can stop the CPR," she told Ethan. "Get her a blanket. They're in the linen closet." Ethan rose to a standing position, cutting his thumb on a shard of snow globe.

"Fuck a duck," he mumbled.

"Mommy, Mommy!" Jared cried, collapsing like a toddler in tears on the floor.

"She's had some sort of attack," Ron croaked. "It must be that blood disease."

The bogus blood disease could not be the truth, but the truth was lost in a fog of rage and panic, and try as she might, Erica could not bring it into the light of day. She'd connected with Ron's nose with a satisfying crack. She'd always hated his piggy little nose.

Debbie's chest rose and fell in short shallow breaths. There was a gash at her left temple. She'd evidently hit her head on the sharp metal corner of the coffee table, corners that Erica had always resented out of fear that one of her children would split their heads open on it, and Debbie's main concern would be the resultant bloodstains. But it was droplets of Debbie's blood that puddled like polka dots on the white carpet.

Maybe when Erica leaped out of his way, Ron's fist had missed its mark and hit Debbie instead, just enough to make her wobble. Maybe her heel had caught on a strand of carpet. Maybe Erica, leaping, had banged her ankle into Debbie, knocking her completely off balance. Erica's package of Kleenex lay on the floor by Debbie's feet, along with her bottle of nasal spray. She should have kept her hand on Debbie's back; she should never have let go of her.

Erica replaced the ceramic figurines that Sophia was methodically pulling from their glass case, turning the chipped part of a rabbit's ruffled underpants discreetly to the other side.

"Wake up, Deb," Ron pleaded.

———

The shrieking of fire sirens tore through the air, soon followed by the eerie squeal of an ambulance, and suddenly the house was flooded with people in uniforms tramping mud across Debbie's spotless living room.

"She collapsed," Ron told a tall, blond paramedic with a bowl cut as he checked her vitals. "She's been ill. There's something wrong with her blood."

"Did she hit her head?" he asked, taking note of the spreading bruise on her left temple.

"She must have hit her head on the coffee table when she fell," said Ron.

"No, no, she fell after he hit her," Erica said, pointing at Ron.

"My brother-in-law here threw a punch," Ethan said. "I think he was aiming at my wife, but he missed."

"She has a blood disease, I told you," said Ron.

"What disease?" the paramedic asked.

"They were still doing tests," Ron said.

"I'm a nurse, and I can tell you she doesn't have any disease," Erica said.

"What happened to your nose, sir?" asked a different paramedic, a short, fat one with a bald spot.

"This crazy woman hit me," said Ron, pointing at Erica.

"Self-defense," Erica said.

"Can you tell me what happened, young man?" the tall, blond one asked Jared.

"I don't know!' Jared wailed. "It all happened so suddenly."

"Call the police," Tall Blond said to Short-and-Fat. "Then let's get this lady to the hospital."

"What the hell," said Ethan. "What a horror story."

"Ethan," Erica said. "You gotta get the twins. The bus must have dropped them off a while ago."

"Don't I have to wait for the police?" Ethan asked.

"The camp bus came at least half an hour ago! For all I know, Jesse and Jake are wandering around the neighborhood. They're just five-year-old boys! You gotta get them, okay? I'll meet you at home. Take Sophia."

"All right, all right," Ethan said.

It took a long time to position Debbie on the stretcher. She was still unconscious. Erica couldn't bear to look at her dilated pupils, black and bobbling. Her limbs hung limply, occasionally vibrating like the spring of a broken toy. The paramedics were preparing to carry her to the ambulance when the police arrived. Ron was following them out the front door when Tall Blond waved him off.

"You gotta stay and talk to the police, sir."

Ron tried to regain his former authoritative bearing and sway, but his body refused to obey. "I need to be with my wife," he said.

"You talk to the police here and answer anything they ask you, sir, and then you're free to join your wife at the hospital. Tall Blond and Short-and-Fat maneuvered Debbie out the door. The ambulance sped off, sirens wailing.

"We've had the report of an incident," one of the police said, staring at the blood spots on the floor. He pulled out a notebook while his partner strolled around the living room, peering behind the furniture and photographing the blood stains. "Can I have your full names, please?"

They gave their names, their addresses, their phone numbers, their dates of birth.

"What are you wasting your time with this claptrap for?" Ron barked.

"Just necessary information," the officer said. "Can you tell me what happened here?"

"My wife collapsed. She had some sort of blood attack," Ron said. In the presence of the law, he regained a modicum of equanimity. "An ambulance took her to the hospital, and I need to join her there."

"And what happened to you?"

Ron's nose was swollen and red, with drops of blood crusted below the nostrils. "She hit me!" Ron pointed his index finger in Erica's direction.

"Is this true?" asked the officer

"Yeah, it is," Erica said, and briefly that angry pride rose in her again. "It was self-defense. He knocked my sister into the coffee table."

"Is this true? Did you hit your wife?'

"Of course not," said Ron, radio voice back in full swing. "My sister-in-law, Rikki, has a very bad temper. We got into a little"—he paused, like a military spokesman struggling to come up with the proper term for the latest carnage—"altercation."

"It's Ron who has the bad temper," Erica said. "He's beaten up his son, Jared, here, for years. He's beaten Debbie too. I can prove it."

"Come with me into the kitchen," the notebook officer said to Erica.

"Did Mr. Lassler hit his wife this afternoon?" he asked Erica, leaning against the refrigerator.

"Yes, I already told you so! I think he unbalanced her, and she fell and hit the table."

"To your knowledge, is your sister suffering from a blood condition?"

"I don't know. She's a hypochondriac. She's always going for some sort of test and seeing some kind of new doctor, and I've asked her about her bruises—"

"The bruise on her head?"

"No, other bruises. She has lots of bruises. And I've asked her about them, and she tells me it's because of some obscure disease, but I'm a nurse, and I know better—those bruises are from Ron beating her."

"What was your 'altercation' about?"

"It was a family matter. About their son. About Jared."

"Have you had these altercations before?"

"Not really. Not like this. Say, isn't anyone going to ask Ron questions? And what about Jared?"

"They're questioning both of them separately, ma'am. Can you conclusively say you saw Mr. Ron Lassler hit Debbie Lassler?" His pencil was poised at the ready.

"I know he did."

"Date and location, please?"

"He does it in private. When nobody sees." Of all the images floating through her brain, she couldn't access that inconvertibly damning one. "Why the hell do you think she's lying there unconscious?" she asked, her voice loud, high, and fast, nothing like Ron's radio-friendly croon.

"Well, that is a very interesting question," said the officer. "Let's go back in the living room."

"I have to get to the hospital," Ron was saying. Jared sat with a third officer Erica hadn't noticed before, crumpled against a sofa pillow, sniffling, his palms pressed together like he was praying.

"Do you wish to press assault charges against Erica Richards?" the cop who'd been with Erica asked Ron.

Erica's mouth, dry and hot, felt disconnected from the rest of her body. She breathed quickly, sharp shallow intakes of air that did not fill her lungs. Her heart beat hard against her chest. Her right eyebrow pulsed.

"No, not currently," Ron said. "I need to see to my wife."

"Well, if no one remembers anything or wants to press charges, there's not much we can do. We do have a new domestic violence division, and we'll be reporting this incident to them. You all get to the hospital now. Have them take a look at your nose, Mr. Lassler. And, Mrs. Richards, we're going to need to question your husband. We'll be calling him."

———

Erica walked rapidly back to the house. Ethan answered the door. His voice was different than she'd ever heard it before: tight, controlled, cool. It frightened her.

"Where are the boys?" she asked.

"Watching TV. They were smart and went next door. Mrs. Kaiser gave them oatmeal cookies and gave me a lecture. I gave Sophia a bottle and changed her diaper. She's napping now." He pursed his lips together and stood there stiffly, even his body different than its normal loping, languid, confident self. From the background, Erica heard the singsong of *Fraggle Rock* and Jesse's and Jake's giggles.

"I have to get to the hospital," Erica said.

"What did the police say?" Ethan asked.

"Nothing much. They want to talk to you. I have to go and see how Debbie is."

"Want to tell me what's going on first?" Ethan asked, hands on hips.

"No, I will, I promise. I don't trust Ron."

She started Vince's engine before Ethan had time to object.

———

Back at the emergency room for the second time in a week, she found Debbie hustled away and Ron and Jared ensconced in plastic chairs. Ron was pressing a bunch of bloody tissues around his nose and staring blankly at an ad for home insurance. Jared was still sobbing softly, his bony shoulders trembling. Erica put her arms around him. He leaned into her. She wanted to ask him what he'd told the police.

"Get your hands off my kid!" Ron hissed. "By all rights, I should kick you out of here!"

Erica stayed put, leafing aimlessly through a six-month-old copy of *Golfing World*. She shivered in the frigid air-conditioning and sucked through a roll of lifesavers.

After about an hour, a doctor emerged, informing them that Debbie had, for all intents and purposes, suffered a stroke. A blood vessel had burst. There was massive bleeding in the brain. She was deeply unconscious, but she was young and relatively healthy, and if she was lucky, she could make a full recovery. They'd stabilized her vitals and were prepping her for emergency surgery. They were bringing all the powers of modern medicine in this world-class trauma hospital to bear.

Strokes like this in young women were unusual, the doctor noted. He suggested the possibility of an aneurysm. He questioned Ron about Debbie's medical history and medications. Ron replied that Debbie had always been fragile, noting her propensity for bruising, her frequent stomach ailments and sinus infections, the metal plate in her knee from a car accident, the pins in her elbow from the playground incident, her nervous exhaustion, and their recent "adolescent troubles" with Jared. He said he didn't know what medications Debbie had been taking and would check at home.

The doctor inquired about the bruise at Debbie's left temple. Apparently that was where the blood vessel had burst, in her left temple. Ron repeated his story about her hitting the edge of the coffee table when she fell, already unconscious, again referencing the mysterious blood disease.

"I've called for her records to check for preexisting conditions," said the doctor.

"And what happened to your nose, Mr. Lassler? There are some disturbing notes from the emergency response team."

"You can check the police report," said Ron.

"Ask at the main desk, and a doctor will take a look at it," said the doctor. "Meanwhile, my job is to save Debbie's life. If you'll excuse me, I'll get back to work." The doctor vanished behind the swinging wooden doors.

"You liar," Erica muttered. "You murderer. You know you hit her."

"You keep your mouth shut, you bitch," Ron said.

———

West Meadow, Long Island, was a place where God was rational and orderly, and evil was an aberration. God didn't come into the conversation much at all, actually. Parents in places like West Meadow placed their trust in the science of the body and of the mind, in medicine and in law. They directed their children into these professions. They believed in rational decisions and logical consequences. Erica had bought into this as much as the next person.

She knew Ethan, who grew up in Northern California with parents who did yoga and soaked in a wood-fired hot tub, believed even more strongly than she did in rational decisions and logical consequences. If circumstance A occurred, then that inevitably led to circumstance B. Circumstance B translated into a series of numbers and letters, which translated into electrical impulses, which then predicted the inevitability of circumstance C. His skill at applying these principles had earned him a fortune.

That night, lying on their water bed under the skylight, Erica told Ethan about her trip down to South Carolina, the horrors of the Pritima Center, and the way no one was going to save Jared if she didn't. She told him about Ashley's abortion. She related Jared's confessions about Ron and how they confirmed her worst suspicions. Ethan listened calmly, his chin resting on his elbow, his eyes, Erica convinced herself, sympathetic.

"This is all so damn stupid and crazy," was his only response.

She told him about getting high with Jared at Lauren's bar mitzvah and at various Sunday family dinners. She didn't tell him about the cocaine. Everybody deserved some secrets. Besides, she was going to quit anyway. She didn't like Anders or the park off Utopia Boulevard. It wasn't fun anymore. It wasn't worth it. Next time they met, she would tell him she didn't want any more T-shirts.

"This is the last thing I need right now," Ethan said. "With everything that's been going on."

"It's not all about you," Erica said.

"Do you think Debbie will recover?"

"She has to." Erica's heart was beating out of control again. She clenched and unclenched her fists, as if she could force the air around her into right angles, as if she could remake circumstances at her will.

Ethan sighed. "I need some sleep," he said.

———

The following morning, after Erica called the hospital and was assured that Debbie had come through surgery "as well as could be expected," Erica, Ethan, Jesse, Jake, and Sophia drove as planned to Dylan's Parents' Day. They watched Dylan win a tennis game and swim a mighty fast breaststroke, and sat on the bleachers in the mosquito-infested Pocono night listening to him nervously utter his five lines on stage. Erica wore a sundress and strappy sandals, and some mother from Westchester complimented her on her "marvelous clavicle." She retained her composure as she discussed with other parents the crises of camp: Were they serving artificially colored bug juice, as they appeared to be doing, or real fruit juice, as they'd advertised in the brochures? Should they install air-conditioning in the cabins? Was the tennis program too competitive? An isolated remnant of herself still held definitive opinions on all these issues.

Ethan and Erica took Dylan out for dinner, where they had planned to tell him his Aunt Debbie was very sick, but watching him chomp sloppily and happily into a bacon cheeseburger, a new field of freckles sprouting across his nose, they couldn't find the right moment to break the mood. They drove home Sunday, so Ethan could return to the Florida office.

⁓

Erica called the hospital and was transferred to the ICU, where the nurse at the desk told her again that Debbie was doing "as well as expected". They allowed her a fifteen-minute visit during which she watched Debbie sleep, her mouth slightly open, her body encumbered by a tangle of wires, monitors tracking her breath and heart rate.

"She's improving," Erica told Ethan, who was at his hotel in Florida.

At night, though, she slipped into a dream world where the rules of West Meadow did not apply.

There Debbie calls to Erica in a small voice, barely audible. Erica burrows deep under the starched white sheets of their shared hospital bed. "They can't hear what I'm saying," Debbie says. "They don't know what I want."

Even under the layers of the sheet, harsh light penetrates. Debbie is curled into a ball, the definition of her muscles melted away, her pale skin plumped up with water. Erica cannot find her face, cannot locate the mouth that whispers to her.

"What do you want, Debbie?" she asks. "What can I tell them?"

She can't interpret the sounds she hears. Debbie's syllables are microscopic; they come from a distant place. Erica believes what she hears Debbie say is "Speak for me," but she can't be sure if that is what she really hears or merely her own voice echoing back.

"What should I say?" she asks again. The tubes puncture Debbie's skin every which way: in her carotid artery with the nutrients; in her nose with the oxygen; out her bladder with a thin yellow line of urine. Her skin is mottled with bruises, a manifestation of all the collapsed blood vessels where the tubes can no longer go.

Erica wraps her arms around Debbie's tube-studded body. The air is tight, stinking of disinfectant. The catheter line wraps around Erica like a snake, entangling her with Debbie. She can't breathe and, in her asphyxiating panic, finally deciphers Debbie's words.

"Stay with me," Debbie is saying.

"No," Erica says firmly. "That's unfair. I won't. I can't." She twists the catheter line off her, untangling it knot by knot, letting it fall limp on the sheets, and without a glance back, she slips out from the bed and onto the slick linoleum of the hospital floor. She shoves the IV stand and the bed table covered with flowers and unread magazines aside and, nearly tripping over the television cord, runs out of the room and down the hall, goes down in the elevator, and runs past the reception desk and into the open air, thick with summer.

Erica wakes to the sun flooding through the skylight and Sophia crying in her crib. She wakes to another unreal day in the real world.

CHAPTER THIRTY-EIGHT

Over the next few days, Debbie slowly regained consciousness. She opened her eyes, she tracked objects, she took a few sips of liquid food, but she did not speak. Tests revealed facts borne out by her medical records and the medication bottles Ron brought in from home. It turned out that Debbie had been taking Coumadin, a blood thinner, because she was worried about blood clots arising from the pins in her shattered elbow. Apparently several months previously Debbie had complained to her doctor—one of her many doctors—of an ache in that elbow, and the doctor had mentioned the possibility of a blood clot. He never tested for a blood clot, but the mere mention of one was sufficient to inflame Debbie's anxieties, and evidently sufficient rationale for the doctor to prescribe the Coumadin. Debbie took aspirin for headaches, Tagamet for heartburn, and Valium to stay married to Ron. All these medications combined thinned her blood to the breaking point. All of these chemicals were ingested by a woman who, in her early twenties, warned Erica that smoking marijuana would lead to heroin addiction and who would have been horrified, had she known, that her predictions had come true, in a way, with a different drug.

Despite her myriad bad habits, Erica was sure that if Ron had succeeded in punching her, the most harm he would have inflicted was a black eye. Maybe a broken rib. Nothing she couldn't handle. But she'd dodged his fist, so he'd connected with his wife, who did not jump or dodge or fight back, who stood in his path like a ceramic bunny.

At least Erica had smashed Ron's nose in, given him the mildest percentage of the payback he'd deserved for years. But it was such a small and laughable triumph, one that did not meet her expectations for logical consequences or fairness. She hoped the blood on their white carpet left a permanent stain.

Debbie took most of her nutrition from a tube. Other tubes drained away the waste. The doctors suggested playing music to stimulate her brain. Ron, a stiff bandage covering the bridge of his nose, brought in his Englebert Humperdinck crap from WBEZ, where he no longer needed it because of their new adult contemporary format. Erica played Sting and Phil Collins, where her taste and Debbie's coincided. Jared played Michael Jackson, recalling one time he discovered Debbie dancing to "Thriller" in the kitchen. Debbie opened her eyes to all the music and occasionally contorted her lips into a shape that could be conceivably be characterized as a smile. The doctors tried experimental medications. Therapists exercised her limbs. Yet another tube drained out excess fluid from her brain.

Ron called the cruise company, who notified David and Suzanne as soon as they reached Bucharest. They flew home on the next available plane and drove immediately to the hospital. They blamed not Erica nor Ron nor Debbie's doctors for this horrible turn of events. From their perspective, what had happened to Debbie was a stroke, a random tragedy. It flew in the face of their belief in fairness. They complained bitterly of this new revelation of the unfairness of the universe.

The police called Ethan in Florida.

"What'd you tell them?" Erica asked, when he told her.

"That we had a family argument," Ethan said wearily. "That Ron has a bad temper. That I thought I saw him throw a punch, but that I wasn't sure exactly what happened, that all of a sudden Debbie was unconscious and bleeding on the floor."

"Did they ask you about Jared—about South Carolina?"

"Yeah, I told them you were in the Hamptons with friends. I'm getting kind of used to lying, you know."

Every time Erica allowed herself to stop and think another worry popped into her head. The police had already spoken to

Miss Peroxide, surely. How closely had Miss Peroxide looked at her, at Sophia? Would she suddenly remember some undeniable detail: the mole on Erica's left shoulder, say, or her emerald wedding ring? Might the police uncover the guard at the penitentiary, or the troll in the motel, or the overly friendly lady at the barbeque restaurant, or even the pheasant-hunting man in his pickup? Perhaps they would request the name and address of her imaginary hosts in the Hamptons. Justine had mentioned a time-share in Amagansett. She figured Justine wouldn't mind a little white lie, if it came to that, and she was right.

"Sure, you can use me as an alibi if you have to," Justine said. "I like the intrigue. "But what were you really doing? Wasn't that right before your sister's accident?"

"I don't really feel like talking about it," Erica said.

"No worries," replied Justine. "But between you and me, you shouldn't cheat on Ethan. You've got a good thing going with him. If my husband was as rich and cute as your guy I would never look elsewhere, believe me."

"I'm not—" Erica protested.

"It's okay." Justine cut her off. "We all need some fun."

<hr />

One day, two policemen showed up at her door. The more officious looking of the cops said that there had been accusations of drug use on their property. In a mild yet firm manner, he asked if they could look around.

"Do you have a search warrant?" Erica asked.

"No, ma'am," replied the cop in the same steady tone. "You're not required by law to let me in. But I would suggest that you do so."

Sophia pulled at Erica's leg. *Sesame Street* chirped on the TV. The microwave beeped. "What the hell," Erica thought. "Let whoever was behind this, Ron, or perhaps Nick, do their best." Let them find her diaper bag, or her plastic crayon holder. Let them look behind the toilet paper in the utility closet. If they found her coke where she'd hidden it, in an empty baking powder container behind the brownie mix, well, then, she supposed they deserved to arrest her.

They dumped toys and clothes on the floor, not bothering to clean up after themselves, but they didn't find a damn thing and even apologized gruffly as they left.

———

Summer camp, both day and sleepaway, came to an end. Jesse and Jake proudly showed off their Red Cross beginner swim cards. Dylan returned from the Poconos four inches taller and with a trunk of filthy, outgrown clothes.

She took the boys to visit Debbie. There was no use prolonging the inevitable. They'd ask questions, they'd look for her at Sunday dinner. Erica intended to visit while Ron was still deejaying his morning show, but the laundry dragged on, and the kids dawdled getting out of the house. When they walked in, Ron was already there, slumped in the one armchair, watching baseball. Debbie sat propped up against her bed pillows, wearing a Mets cap. Her eyes slithered from side to side. She smiled vacantly at them.

"She smiles like Kyle," Dylan whispered in Erica's ear. Kyle was a boy down the street with cerebral palsy. Erica herded the boys gently toward Debbie's bed. "Hello, Aunt Debbie," they all recited, dutifully polite. They fidgeted, clearly shocked and frightened by Debbie's puffed-up, medicated body, the spasmodic outbursts of her limbs, and her slurred mumblings.

"I won a tennis trophy at camp," Dylan said.

"Mmglh," muttered Debbie, like the sound was caught in her throat, more of a gag than a syllable.

Darryl Strawberry hit a home run with two runners on base, putting the Mets ahead, 5–3. "Whadya think, Deb?" Ron said, softly squeezing Debbie's arm. "Way to go, Darryl!"

"Mmglh." Debbie rolled her lips in on each other like the cement spreader on the twins' toy truck.

"Debbie never liked baseball," Erica said quietly. "I don't think she cares."

Ron sneered, his first acknowledgement of her presence. "Like you would know, Miss Rikki."

"I'm starting fifth grade," Dylan attempted bravely. "Next year I'm going to middle school." Tentatively he reached out, touching Debbie's wrist. Her fingers flapped, her thumb rising as if she wished to take Dylan's hand. Dylan smoothed her thumb over his, but simultaneously, Sophia overturned a vase of flowers, spilling water and dahlias onto the floor, and the twins discovered the rising and lowering mechanism at the foot of Debbie's bed. Debbie's legs jerked downward.

"Mmheeaee," she squealed.

"No!" Erica sharply pulled Jesse and Jake to her side. She reached in her diaper bag for a cloth to wipe up the water spill, but before she could do so Ron rose to his feet, gripping her tightly on the shoulder.

"Get your brats out of here before I bash their heads in," he said, squeezing harder. "And don't let me see you here again either. I told you not to come here. And don't let me see you talking to Jared. I've told him not to go near you." He pressed the nurse call button.

"Screw you," said Erica, pushing his snaky arms away, but nonetheless gathered her kids and left, colliding with the orderly and his cleaning cart. Shaking and nursing a bruise on her arm, she continued on to Roosevelt Field, where she bought $500 worth of children's jeans, corduroys, long-sleeved shirts, and sweaters.

She didn't tell Ethan about the incident when he returned home from work. He was staying in New York more frequently these days, meeting with lawyers, meeting with government officials, meeting with higher-ups at Grant Fishel. Everyone seemed to be telling on everyone else, as far as Erica could discern. He didn't talk about those meetings much. He didn't really talk much at all, just watched TV, went running, dispensed with the clove cigarettes and bought real tobacco ones, and when prompted, played with the kids.

He and the boys horsed around in the backyard castle after dinner and then came in and built more castles with Legos. As Erica was folding laundry in the basement, the phone rang, and Ethan answered. "Hey, Erica, it's someone named Anders for you," he called out from the kitchen.

Dylan turned on the Yankees game. "Want to watch with me, Dad?" he asked, but Ethan remained stubbornly by the refrigerator, nibbling on dill pickles out of the jar.

"Hi," Erica said softly into the phone.

"I hear you want to buy more T-shirts," Anders said.

"Yeah, my closet is empty," she said. "Tomorrow?"

"Who's Anders?" Ethan asked, as soon as she hung up.

"A father from Dylan's soccer league," Erica said. She feigned interest in the baseball game. Rickey Henderson hit into a double play, sealing the Yankees loss to the Twins.

"Henderson is having the suckiest season, don't you think?"

"I've never seen anyone named Anders at a game," Ethan said. He placed a Lego knight in position at the top of a turret.

"He's in the garment business. He imports T-shirts from India or something."

"Is that why you mentioned your closet?"

"Yeah. And there's practice tomorrow."

"Who's his kid?"

On television, a group of attractive young people drank beer on a boat. "I forget," Erica said.

"Do you have a teammate with a dad named Anders, Dyl?" Ethan built a bridge over the castle moat.

"I don't know." Dylan shrugged.

The twins crashed dump trucks into each other's knees.

"Bath time," Erica said.

———

On a morning as crisp and cool as if it had been ordered from an autumn catalog, school started. Erica walked all three boys to West Meadow Elementary, their new backpacks filled with pencils, crayons, and notebooks. At school practically everyone, including women she barely recognized, expressed their concern about Debbie and asked if there was anything they could do to help. They noted that Erica looked tired and worn, albeit enviably skinny. "Must be the stress diet," they sympathized. A few shared with her sad events from their own lives: a nineteen-year-old cousin run over by a truck, an aunt with melanoma. These tragedies, unlike her sister's, struck Erica as truly random acts of fate.

Every day after aerobics, Erica visited Debbie in the hospital. The timing of her visits allowed her to avoid Ron, who came in the early afternoon, and Jared, who came after school, and her parents, who usually came at dinnertime. She didn't deliberately try to avoid her parents, but their paths no longer coincided. Her mother never called. She never dropped over for coffee. She didn't sell real estate. Sunday dinner seemed on permanent hold.

The smell of the hospital nauseated Erica, that blend of disinfectant and recirculated fear. It amazed her that she'd ever wanted to work in such an environment. When she visited Debbie, she sat in a chair with wooden armrests, the seat upholstered with an itchy polyester weave, and blabbed inanely about her kids, about her exercise classes, even about the weather. Most days, tiring of one-way conversation, she watched baseball. A new cable channel re-broadcast games at any time of day. The apparently invincible Mets coasted toward victory, clinching the division title in mid-September. Meanwhile, the Yankees struggled, never catching up to the odious Red Sox. Debbie watched the images flicker across the screen with attention, but it did not seem to matter to her whether Dave Winfield hit a grand slam or Mookie Wilson struck out, or an aging actress sang the praises of Metamucil. She sucked on her lips and sometimes drooled. Occasionally her eyes blurred with tears.

One afternoon Erica made it to Babyland and bought Sophia a toddler bed. Having now achieved her goals of escaping both crib and playpen, Sophia set her attentions on escaping from her stroller. As Erica took her on long walks around the neighborhood, she pulled and bit at the nylon strap. But despite Sophia's earnest efforts, the locking clip remained intact.

Out of habit or obsession, or both, Erica found herself always walking past Nick's house. If he opened the door again, she told herself, she would say a distant and polite hello, maybe make a little innocuous conversation like she did, say, with Mrs. Kaiser next door. Every day as she approached his house, she practiced that conversation in her mind, but Nick never reappeared. Walking by one day she saw a For Sale sign out front. After that, she chose a different walking route and bought her iguana supplies at the PetMart in Roosevelt Field. She enrolled in an advanced step aerobics class, mastering routines requiring a complex series of steps, leaps, and arm motions. In class, this captured all of her attention, and walking back to the childcare room, she replayed the moves in her head.

Every two weeks she gave Anders a call and met up with him on Utopia Boulevard. She never got to know him any better. She kept telling herself she would cut down, she truly would, because it wasn't fun anymore, and her nose bled, and her heart beat too fast. But then two weeks would roll around again, and she got scared of feeling worse than she already did. She kept telling herself she no longer desired cheap happiness, that she no longer believed in that illusory sense of power and clarity. But in reality she sucked up any kind of happiness that might be on offer, and she desperately needed power and clarity, if only she could find it again. She played Jared's music constantly, and bought more of its like in the "alternative" section of Tower Records, next door to PetMart. She understood heavy metal now. Heavy metal wasn't about melody or dreaminess or romance or anything else she'd ever associated music with. Heavy metal wasn't really about music. You listened to it to drown out the chatter of your mind, to crush and obliterate.

Ethan gave testimony to the SEC with the intent of absolving himself of responsibility. The legal proceedings required his presence in New York, but Erica found she actually preferred the weeks he spent in Florida. She had pictured a trial, with judges and juries and witnesses, but all the proceedings actually took place behind closed doors, just Ethan and the lawyers talking. On those days, he came home late and said little, kissing the kids good night, eating dinner in front of the TV, and deflecting inquiries.

"Did they ask you about Stephan Langston?" she ventured.

"Oh yeah, Langston, Stanley, the whole crowd," he sneered.

"You'd rat on those guys? You worked with them every day. We went to parties together."

"What do you think this is, the Mafia?" Ethan fiddled with Dylan's Rubik's Cube. "Say, did Anders give you Dylan's soccer schedule yet?"

"Oh yeah, he did," replied Erica, flustered. She was still thinking about Shelley Stanley, her self-conscious couture and her nervous friendly chatter. Her balding, bellicose husband Stew with a propensity for belting out the University of Maryland fight song. Stephan Langston with his cracked horn-rim glasses, his fidgety fingers. She would not have sold out on these friends, these coworkers, these people no better than her. She would have let them be.

"Did you pick up my shirts at the cleaners?'" Ethan placed the Rubik's Cube, colors aligned, on top of the stack of records that still wobbled on the back of the TV.

In the beginning of October, the Nassau County Police finally called her in for an interview in a stale-smelling, institutional room in the Mineola courthouse. They began by asking her about her connection with Nick Stromboli; she told them they were old friends from their school days. They'd found her name in Nick's infamous phone book, but apparently Nick, in exchange for immunity, had given them names of cocaine suppliers from Queens to Texas. That explained his quick disappearance and satisfied the police. That wasn't why they were questioning her. There were bigger fish to fry in the Stromboli case. Instead, hers was one of those uncomfortable yet newly classified domestic violence cases. They didn't care about any drugs she might have bought, except as it pertained to Jared. Jared had admitted to the pot smoking, but the prior officers hadn't found any in her possession, and it wasn't as if she was his teacher or guardian, so all that earned her was a lecture, and then they moved off the subject of drugs.

The cops asked her what she knew about Jared's relationship with Ashley, about their sojourn in Philadelphia, about the Pritima Center and Jared's escape from there. In answer to all these questions, Erica supplied half-truths and mild lies. Erica told them that Jared was terrified of Ron, that Ron had hit him since he was a little child. She told them that he beat Debbie also, that Jared had confirmed it, that she'd seen the bruises. They asked for concrete evidence, but Erica could provide none. All these years, she'd never reported anything to the authorities. Jared didn't have any visible injuries, and as for Debbie, weren't those bruises the result of her medical condition? Now, if maybe she could call them when the abuse was actually occurring, they could do something. Although, the police admitted, it was too late for that.

But the police could find no concrete evidence of Erica's misdeeds either. They never produced witnesses from small Southern towns. They'd called Justine, and she'd given them the address of her time-share in Amagansett.

The officers shuffled their papers. One of them opened his knees unflatteringly and scratched the inside of his thigh. Erica looked out the smudged window; late-afternoon sun glinted off the cars in the parking lot. The days were getting shorter. By the time she got home, after picking up the twins from a playdate, Dylan from Hebrew, and Sophia from Lisa's, it would be dark.

"Have you already spoken with my brother-in-law, Ron Lassler?" she asked.

"Yes, ma'am," said Officer Scratchy, who appeared to be in charge.

"And Jared Lassler?"

"Yes, ma'am."

"What did they say?"

"We're not at liberty to tell you that, ma'am."

"You told me that domestic violence is a crime." Emboldened enough that her anger outweighed her fear, Erica sat up super straight and heard her voice rise high and tight.

"Yes, ma'am, it's a crime now," said Officer Scratchy. "But as you said, it's domestic. It takes place privately, and for any criminal prosecution, we need facts. We need witnesses. And we don't have any." The other policemen nodded in agreement.

They dismissed her with a handshake. Erica couldn't determine from the policemen's professional cool demeanor whether they believed a word she said or for that matter anything that Ron and Jared said, whether these official inquiries would land anywhere except a filing cabinet, whether it would ever matter. She doubted it. Vacancy enveloped her. All of this would come to nothing. Nothing as disastrous as she had feared, but nothing good—no more explosions but only a gray, sad fading away. She recalled her frenzied drive back and forth from South Carolina—the dark, empty mountain roads, the thick heat of the day, the speed, the fear, the absolute vivid intensity of it—with something bordering on nostalgia. Walking to the car, she passed the cops standing by a coffeepot, bantering about the upcoming Jets game.

———

At noon the next day she positioned herself by the cluster of trees at West Meadow High. Erica had not seen Jared in over a month, and the sight of him, sipping a milkshake, chatting with a petite girl in a tight orange T-shirt, jarred her. His Pritima Center buzz cut had totally grown out, and he'd gained some weight, but his jeans and shirt were stained and wrinkled.

"Not doing much laundry, huh?" was the first thing that popped out of her mouth.

"I just pick stuff up off the floor," Jared shrugged. "Mom always did the wash. What are you doing here at school?"

"I needed to talk to you somewhere where your father wouldn't find out."

They walked over by the football field. "Dad's sending me to military school," he said. "Next week. They've got the contracts signed and everything."

"Oh no!" Erica cried. "Can't you do anything about it?"

Jared shrugged. "No," he said flatly. "I can't."

"Have you seen Ashley, by the way? I haven't seen her since Ocean City." Out of the corner of her eye, Erica could still see the girl in the orange T-shirt staring at them.

"Her mom sent her away to school," Jared said. "Some boarding school in Vermont where they shear sheep and spin the yarn or something." Jared shifted his feet back and forth. He looked back at the girl.

Erica took a deep breath. "The police questioned me yesterday," she said. "Did they speak to you?"

"Yeah, of course," Jared said. "They asked me about you, and I told them you were my favorite aunt and my good friend and that you'd helped me out a lot with problems with my parents and stuff. That you weren't a dork like every other adult I seem to encounter. But I told them I ran away from the Pritima Center of my own accord. That I saw that agricultural extension lady leave, and when the garbage truck came in, I followed her out. Apparently they'd checked with the agriculture bureau down there, and they said they hadn't sent anyone, but I said, so what, maybe she was some crazy lady who snuck in to steal food or whatever—there's all sorts of strange people in South Carolina, believe me. Then I told them I hitched a ride to Ocean City where I met Ashley. That's what we'd planned to say—what Ashley suggested—if things didn't work out. I mean, don't worry about Ashley giving you up to the police. She's crazy about you."

Their plans. They'd planned ahead. They'd considered that things might not work out. At no point had such contingencies remotely crossed Erica's mind. Her breath felt sharp in her chest.

"I told them I hated the Pritima Center," Jared was saying, "And those religious nuts and the whole stupid South. I told them how they made me landscape, like, six hours a day, and it made my asthma go out of control."

"Did you tell them about your dad, how he hits you?" Erica asked. "And did you tell them how he hit your mom?"

"No," Jared said. "What's the point anymore?"

"There's still a point," Erica insisted. "The point is that it's very wrong. Domestic violence is an official crime now. Your dad shouldn't get away with it, and your mom can't defend herself anymore, not that she ever did. I told them everything I knew, but it's not going to mean a damn thing unless you corroborate what I said."

"I'm going away to military school," Jared said, slurping the dregs of his milkshake. "Next time I see Dad, I can bash his head in if I want to."

"What about your mother?"

"Like he can hurt her more than she's already hurt? Plus, I told you, he hit her only that once. If he hit her at all. Last time he was aiming at you." Jared threw the paper cup into a trash can across the path; it missed and rolled onto the grass.

"It's not fair," Erica said, her voice rising. "We can't just let it go after all this."

The lunch bell rang.

"I gotta go to Spanish," Jared said.

"Can I see you before you leave? Come by with a CD," Erica said.

"I better not," he said. "I feel like my father's watching me all the time, even when I know he's at work."

She reached her arms out toward Jared. He smelled like pastrami sandwich and hair gel. She felt the brush of downy beard against her forehead.

"Are you sure?" she asked.

"I saved your ass, Aunt Rikki," Jared said softly. "What more do you want from me?"

CHAPTER THIRTY-NINE

Erica and Ethan put their house on the market. The meetings with the lawyers had ended, but so had Ethan's welcome at Grant Fishel's Manhattan office. Erica tore through the rooms of their house, discarding broken, boring, and duplicate toys; pants with ugly stitching; goods she'd ordered from catalogs and never gotten around to unpacking. She no longer remembered why she had bought these items, and she supposed she should hold a garage sale or give them to charity, but that required too much effort. She threw them all in the trash. Sometimes, struck by a compulsion to replace what she was discarding, she drove to the supermarket. The rows of food looked colorful and beautiful, such an abundance there for the eating. She bought way too much: zucchinis, tomatoes, the last of the summer peaches, a giant watermelon, a ten-dollar jar of Spanish capers, a coconut cake from the in-store bakery. She found herself eating even though she wasn't hungry, just because the food looked so pretty and tasted good on her tongue. Such a reliable companion, food. Of course, excess consumption necessitated an extra call to Anders.

Out in the standard world, October proceeded as scheduled, bleaching the stickiness out of the air and granting West Meadow a brief moment of glory. Even the fumes from the expressway evaporated into the crisp air. The leaves turned scarlet. Erica sent out invitations to Sophia's first birthday party and bought her a doll with long yellow hair and a set of stuffed calico cows. Dylan's soccer schedule kicked into high gear. One Sunday in mid-October they escaped the parade of families inspecting their house and drove to a tournament fifty miles out in Riverhead. Dylan scored a winning goal. The sun sparkled off the trees. On the way home, they stopped at a farm stand and bought a freshly baked raspberry pie.

After dinner, Erica bleached raspberry stains out of the kitchen counter. More people were looking at the house Monday morning. Ethan stuck glasses in the dishwasher. "Anders wasn't at the tournament," he noted.

"Maybe his son quit soccer." Erica picked at her cuticles. They looked gross. She needed a manicure. "Carson," she added for good measure. "His son's name was Carson. He wasn't there either."

"That's weird, given that Anders was so involved with the scheduling and all," Ethan said.

Erica didn't respond, only scrubbed harder.

"I've got to help Dylan with some quadratic equations," Ethan said.

Sophia clattered pot lids across the floor. As Erica leaned over to pick them up, she felt Ethan's hair brush against her shoulder, and she lifted up her head, hoping for affection—a kiss?—but instead he whispered in her ear. "And another thing," he said. "You should eat better or sleep more or something. You look like crap."

———

Every day Debbie exhibited incremental improvements. The best the medical establishment had to offer had brought their skills to bear, and they'd succeeded: Debbie would live. She wiggled her fingers and toes and, with the diligent efforts of the physical therapist, sat up with the support of a wheelchair. Erica wheeled Debbie around the halls, taking her to the glassed-in walkway to view the fall leaves. She fed her applesauce from a spoon. Her guttural mouthings began to resemble comprehensible speech. Back in her room, Debbie ran out of steam and closed her eyes; she snored softly. Erica watched more baseball. The Yankees swept their last four-game series but still could not catch the Red Sox.

At aerobics, Lisa and Justine expressed concern over her sleep, her skin, her mental state.

"You need a manicure," said Justine. "And a massage. You have to take care of yourself."

"Maybe you should see somebody," suggested Lisa.

"I'm fine," said Erica. "Leave me alone."

Debbie's doctors transferred her to a rehabilitation facility. It smelled better there, like air freshener, and the walls were covered with generic prints of summer meadows and seascapes: Debbie's favorite art, in truth. The atmosphere of false cheer remained unchanged. Patients of varying capabilities struggled through the hallways with walkers or lolled in chairs, nodding like heroin addicts. All the aides were young, with lilting Caribbean accents. If Erica didn't know better, she'd think they'd been hired by Housemates.

After Debbie had been there about a week, one of them greeted Erica by name as she walked into the common room.

"Debbie's so lucky to have such a loving family, Rikki," she gushed. "I see how you visit every day, how you treat her. And that husband of hers—what a sweetheart! Come with me. Debbie's learned a new trick. She's playing Scrabble."

"Scrabble" involved helping Debbie correctly identify the letters and then form the words. Debbie's hair, combed by the aides, stuck out in wavy bristles so unlike her usual pixie cut, streaks of gray showing at the crown. She was wearing pink stretch pants and a matching scoop-neck shirt—easy to get on and off—that Erica knew the real Debbie wouldn't have worn to take out the garbage. Confined indoors, her skin was reddened and mottled, puffy with medication.

"Can you find me an *A*, Debbie?" Erica asked. Debbie studied the wooden letters with an intent but bland expression. After mistakenly picking a *T* and an *E*, she successfully located the *A*. They went through the same routine for an I and an M. Erica put the word "AIM" down on a double-word space.

They played until the board was almost filled, when Erica detected a presence hovering over her. She turned and saw the chatty aide, and then behind her, Ron, well ahead of schedule. She expected him to shoo her out, maybe even follow her into a hallway and press her against a wall, but he merely nodded curtly.

"How ya doin', sunshine!" he crowed.

Debbie blinked in the fluorescent light.

"You look beautiful, sweetie," Ron said.

"Hell-o Ron," Debbie slurred.

"Who's sitting next to you?" Ron prompted.

Debbie's brow wrinkled in concentration. "Rik-ki," she finally said, in a voice lacking both anger and forgiveness.

Ron evidently tolerated her presence now, but it had nothing to do with respect for her power, rather, the opposite. Erica was no longer dangerous. She was supposed to accept this situation for the rest of her life: Debbie's diminishment of self and this perpetuation of lies.

When she got home, she called Officer Scratchy, whose real name was Aaron McCloskey. Officer Scratchy was at a meeting. She left a message on his machine, but the rest of the week went by, and he never called back.

The following Monday, after aerobics, instead of going to the rehab facility, she drove over to Ron and Debbie's for the first time since that fateful August afternoon.

The front door was unlocked. She walked into the living room. Debbie's absence was palpable. The rust-colored blood stains were still there. A layer of dust covered the furniture. There were magazines scattered everywhere. She peeked into Jared's room. The sheets still lay crumpled from the last night he'd slept there, his bedspread fallen to the floor. His posters were still on the wall. He'd taken his record collection. She was about to peek under the bed to see if his dope stash was there, when she heard Ron walking down the hall.

"Hello?" he called out. He was wrapped in a towel, his nubs of thinning hair gleaming wetly. He smelled of shaving cream. His eyes narrowed when he saw her. "What are you doing here?" he growled. "Get out of my son's room."

"We have to talk," Erica said.

"What about?" His voice sounded soft and tired. "Haven't we talked enough?"

"We have to talk about Debbie." She followed Ron into the kitchen.

Ron stuck a strawberry Pop-Tart in the toaster oven. "Rikki," he said, "she's getting better every day. You saw her yesterday. She called you by name."

"She'll never be the same," Erica said. "You know that."

They stared each other down for a minute or so, then Ron took his Pop-Tart out of the oven. As he bit into it drops of steaming red liquid dripped onto his chin. His nose still looked pink and swollen. "I got laid off last week," he said. "There wasn't a market for my musical taste, they told me. And they want a younger voice for adult contemporary. More humor. More outrageousness."

"I'm sorry about that," Erica said.

"Want some coffee?" he asked, pulling out a jar of freeze-dried granules.

"No, thanks," Erica said. "Honestly, I'm sorry about your job, but we need to talk about August. You hit Debbie. That's why she tripped. That's why she fell. And you hit her lots of other times. Jared told me." Dizzy, she leaned against the counter.

"Get real," Ron said, putting down his unfinished Pop-Tart. His voice betrayed a trace of the old vehemence. "I didn't hurt Debbie. You heard the doctor. She had a stroke."

"You knew she was taking Coumadin. You knew she was taking blood thinner." Erica stood up. Leaning made her look weak, and that she could not permit.

"I did not!" Ron said.

"Don't lie to me," Erica hissed, closing in on Ron, as face to face as she had the other time, the time before. "I'm so sick of your lies. You knew she was taking Coumadin, and you hit her anyway. She had bruises all the time; she hid them under her clothes. She gave me all that bullshit about a blood disease, but I never believed her."

"She did have a blood disease. That's why her doctor prescribed the Coumadin."

Erica grabbed his wrist, digging into his tender skin, still damp from the shower. "The Coumadin caused the blood disease! It wasn't treating it!"

His staggering illogic left her reeling, without purchase. He was gaining his equilibrium back, she could tell. His shoulders stiffened. If he dared throw another punch at her, she would smack him in the temple. No wimpy nose punch this time. She would take him by surprise. She would knock him out.

"You're a murderer!" she snapped.

"Come again?" Ron asked. His eyes remained as impassive as ever, but his hands shook.

"You killed my sister! You think I don't know it? You can fool the doctors, and the social workers, and the police, and my whole damn family, but you can't fool me. I'm going to make you pay for this like you deserve!"

"Now, look here," Ron said, his voice cool and steady. "We've all been through a horrible tragedy. We need to be there for Debbie whether we like each other or not. Why don't we let the rest of this go?"

"Because it's a lie!"

"Speaking of lies," Ron said, "I know what Jared told the police. But he's a storyteller, that young man. His story could change."

"Jared told the truth," Erica said.

"Testimony can change," Ron said. "And you've got a lot to lose. Your rich little scheming hubby for one. Your four children for another. Maybe you'd better stop now. You always thought I was so stupid. You and your hubby both. You always looked down on me. You always made fun of me. You made fun of my musical taste. You made fun of my military service. You made fun of the fact I know how to screw in a lightbulb without calling a repairman. You think I don't know what you're about?"

Erica wanted the last word. She wanted at least that pitiful morsel of satisfaction, because she didn't trust in divine judgment, and that seemed the only other option left. But as she stood there, searching her brain for the knockout comment, she saw something new: Ron's eyes, swollen with tears.

"I love my wife," he said. "You think I don't love my wife? And I used to like you too, Rikki. You were so feisty. So sexy."

Those tears rendered her impotent in a way his threats never could.

"Your love," she finally choked out, "your love is not the kind of love I want."

———

That night, Erica watched the seventh game of the World Series. She'd been ignoring the series, a battle between two evils: Ron's horrible Mets and the despised Boston Red Sox. But she had to root for someone. For the first time in her lifetime as a Yankees fan she threw her loyalties to the Red Sox. She'd attended college in Boston, she told herself, only a mile from Fenway Park. Maybe this small shift in her alliances would serve as compromise, her bargain with the fates. In the ninth inning, with two outs and two strikes on the batter, the Red Sox held the lead. Erica allowed herself, prematurely, the pleasure of this small victory, and then Bill Buckner, at first base, let Mookie Wilson's baseball roll through his legs, and Ron's stupid Mets, his undeserving Mets, won the World Series.

CHAPTER **FORTY**

The sun continued shining relentlessly through an unusually warm November. Erica packed her family's life away in boxes. With each box, the house looked lonelier and sadder, deprived of its character. Before the real estate agents arrived with potential buyers in tow, Erica baked rolls of chocolate chip cookies and put Phil Collins on the stereo. Strangers paraded through her home, admiring the flowered accent tiles and marble vanity in the powder room.

For the first time in many years, Erica frequently skipped aerobics class. There didn't seem to be much point. No matter how much she kicked her legs or swung her arm weights, her legs still crinkled with cellulite and her upper arms hung thin and limp from their bones. No one complimented her anymore. Instead they treated her with a sincere, but nervous and distant, kindness. They all knew about Debbie and her stroke, and Jared's DDD troubles, and how Ethan, beset by scandal, had been forced out of town. Worse rumors circulated, Erica was convinced, when she wasn't around. Even loyal Lisa didn't expect her to look her best.

She did the coke in the basement. At first she restricted it to the cedar closet, but then she stopped bothering. It was not like Ethan was ever home anymore, and if the boys were off at school, or their multitudinous activities, or sleeping, who would be looking? Only Sophia, and Sophia, thank God, still napped.

The week of Thanksgiving the weather finally turned gray, raw, and wet. Even inside the house Erica shivered, wearing one of Ethan's baggy Irish sweaters all day long. Her nose ran. Her muscles ached. She put on the new Van Halen CD she'd bought at Tower Records. She remembered how Jared had loudly insisted that Eddie Van Halen was the best guitarist in history, that he put Eric Clapton to shame. Maybe. He certainly smashed and pulverized the strings. He made her eardrums tingle like she'd dunked her head into an icy lake. Whereas when Eric Clapton sang "Layla," his chords stretched out and thrummed and floated, taking her back to the day when she first heard the song on WNEW radio, taking her back to those mossy bricks of the Mackay estate, all those days when she couldn't get the melody out of her head. The woods were always impenetrably dark when she snuck out of her parents' house and walked through the trees, but when she lay down on the damp ground, her body suffused with heady anticipation, she watched the outlines of the limbs and leaves reveal themselves.

Van Halen only took her back as far as last spring on her parents' patio, her mother's pansies blooming in clay pots, the robin nibbling at the bird feeder, and Jared leaning intently forward, wearing his favorite black T-shirt with the skull on it. She'd felt remnants of that heady anticipation reawaken then, spread their tentacles and adapt to new air: a nascent, fragile conceit.

She should stop. Now. Today. She should file Anders's number away with her memorabilia, like a ticket stub from a concert, a trace of a vanished thrill.

Down the two flights of stairs and over the screech of Van Halen she heard Sophia's voice. In her high burble, she named objects in her room: "Birdie! Duckie! Bear! Blankie!" and then, her voice rising, a sense of urgency intruding, "Mama, Mama!" She rattled the rails of her baby gate.

This was the saving grace of Erica's life, the incessant demands of her children. They never allowed her more than a few minutes to brood. Marked and dirty she might be, but never purposeless.

The restaurant in Port Jefferson had leather-bound menus but smelled institutional, like Debbie's rehabilitation facility. Erica's mother had originally broached the idea of suspending Thanksgiving altogether, but her father, unhappy with that plan, made reservations at this inn that specialized in stuffy family dinners.

Ron was coming, ruining Erica's resolution never to see his face again. Jared was flying in, released from the military academy for the weekend. And Debbie was coming. For Debbie's first excursion outside institutional walls since her "attack," as her mother continued to refer to it, Ron was hiring a special handicapped van. They hadn't arrived yet. Ethan, Erica, and the kids settled in next to Mom and Dad at the long rectangular table.

They would fit in: all the other families eating there looked sad in some way. Across from them sat an ancient couple, the husband in a wheelchair, his wife assisting him in cutting up his food. An obese boy sat with his lumpy-looking parents and a sharp elderly woman in a Chanel suit. Next to them sat a Japanese family: a father in slacks and a sports jacket; a petite mother in red skirt and matching sweater; two silent little girls in flowered party dresses. They stared curiously at the cheese crust on their onion soup.

"I don't like onions," declared Jesse.

"Let me see if I can get you something else," said Erica. She raised her hand for the waiter.

Mom shook her head. "It's a fixed menu. I don't think they do substitutions, do they, David?" She looked at her husband for affirmation, but he merely shrugged.

"Where are Ron and Jared? They're late." Dad looked out at the circular graveled driveway, where a wind-whipped rain was driving the last shriveled leaves off a thick oak tree.

"They were meeting up with Debbie at Shady Oaks. They're all coming together in the van." Suzanne spooned onion soup into her mouth, wrinkling her nose in a gesture that reminded Erica of Debbie. The old Debbie. "Too salty," she complained.

"I hope the roads aren't too dangerous in this weather," David said, drumming his fingers on the table.

"We drove here perfectly safely," noted Ethan, leaning back in his chair. He and Dylan were passing a handheld electronic game back and forth.

"Iz everzeething satisfactory?" the waiter, evidently an immigrant from some Eastern European country, asked Erica.

"Can we get a replacement for this soup for my son? He doesn't like onions."

The twins crashed their Matchbox cars into the plastic turkey centerpiece.

The waiter nodded amiably. "I am sure. I will ask chef."

A large white van pulled up outside the bay window of the inn. Erica watched Ron and Jared step out to assist the driver as he slid open the door of the van and extended a ramp. Ron pushed Debbie's wheelchair down the incline. Debbie, dressed as if ready for skiing, sunk deep in her down hood and woolen scarf. Ron laid a blanket over her lap while Jared rushed ahead to open the inn's heavy wooden door. The wheelchair rocked from side to side as Ron steered over the gravel.

"I sure hope she doesn't catch cold. I sure hope this wasn't a mistake." Suzanne scratched the back of her neck. Both she and David stood up, making room for the wheelchair at the end of the table, pulling out chairs for Ron and Jared.

Jared remained standing, clearly uncomfortable with the forced intimacy of this family gathering. His hair was shaved into sidewalls just like his father's, and his whole body looked harder, stretched and taut.

"Hi," said Erica, hoping for a glimpse of connection, an undercurrent of shared mirth or pain.

"Hello, Aunt Rikki," responded Jared politely. "Whatcha doin', dude?" he asked Dylan, who was making occasional passes at his soup, reading *The Fellowship of the Ring* for the twentieth time, and playing the game whenever Ethan passed him the tablet.

"What happened to your hair?" asked Dylan.

"A buzz cut happened to my hair." Jared slid into his seat and took a bite of soup. "This stuff is nasty," he commented.

Erica sipped her soup, lukewarm and gluey. "You're not kidding," she agreed, wanting to exchange words with Jared, no matter how trivial or desultory. She stood up and walked over to Debbie. "Happy Thanksgiving," she said, kissing Debbie lightly on the cheek. Her skin felt papery and dry, like an aged grandmother's.

"Who's that, hon?" asked Ron.

"Rik-ki," answered Debbie, her hands shaking involuntarily.

"I wonder what happened to that waiter," Suzanne said. Her hands kept rising to her lips, like she wished she could smoke one of the cigarettes she'd given up twenty years previously. The twins engaged in a carrot-stick battle with the overweight boy at the opposite table. A carrot stick hit David in the cheek, but he pretended not to notice, sweeping the carrot into his napkin.

The earnest young waiter finally reappeared with bowls of chicken noodle soup. Jesse and Jake settled down, but Sophia, weary of gumming crackers, slid out of her high chair and circled the table. The little Japanese girls caught her attention. She pulled on their skirts and their family's orange tablecloth emblazoned with pumpkins. A water glass wobbled off the table and broke. The busboy rushed over to mop up the mess. Ethan looked up from his electronic game long enough to swoop Sophia into his lap. She punched the buttons of the game, laughing at how the colors on the screen changed at her command.

"We never should have eaten in a restaurant," said Suzanne, scratching the back of her head. "This was a mistake."

The main course arrived, flaccid turkey flanked by a mound of gooey stuffing, grainy mashed potatoes, canned green beans, and slimy canned yams with marshmallows. The old Debbie would never have served a meal like this. The old Debbie researched her holiday recipes diligently. She culled them carefully from *Woman's Day* or the food section in the newspaper, protected the recipe with plastic wrap, and prepared the dish as meticulously as a lab experiment, never varying so much as a quarter teaspoon from the recommended spicing. While everyone ate, she bustled around the table, clearing the dishes away before anyone had the opportunity to take seconds. Erica had never particularly cared for Debbie's holiday creations, but now that she would never eat them again, she missed them intensely.

Ron fed Debbie potatoes. Occasionally, responding to his murmured encouragements, she made her own ventures with the spoon, dribbling food on the napkin spread out over her lap.

"She's losing weight," fretted Suzanne, and indeed, under the medicated bloat, Erica could tell Debbie had lost her compact round definition. Her skin and muscles drooped on her bones like an unironed tablecloth.

Erica shoveled food into her own mouth. She felt a restlessness in her digestive tract, akin to nausea, and the mild sweet sameness of turkey, cranberry sauce, potatoes, and stuffing settled her stomach. When she looked up from her plate, she noted that Ethan had disappeared. Perhaps he'd gone outside for a cigarette. He was up to a pack a day now. He'd put Sophia back in her high chair, where she was contentedly smearing a marshmallow around the plastic tray. Dylan was still immersed in his book.

"Should you let him read at the table?" Suzanne asked.

"I don't mind," Erica shrugged. "It's for school," she lied. She wished she could sink into a book herself, or better yet, go back and sit in steamy Vince Volvo, spacing out to Van Halen. She could take Jared with her and rescue him from answering his grandparents' questions about military school. This dinner would be a whole lot easier to take if they were stoned; they'd gain essential psychological distance. Perhaps they might even find some elements borderline amusing.

"What classes are you taking, son?" asked Dad.

"The usual stuff," Jared mumbled. "English. Calculus. History. Chemistry. Mass murder."

Dad blanched. "Have you made any friends?" he asked.

"Not to speak of. This food here sucks as bad as the food there, by the way."

"I don't like it either," said Jake, rolling a Matchbox dump truck into the gravy boat, knocking it over into his grandmother's lap.

"Jake!" Mom barked. "You've stained my linen skirt."

"It's not Jake's fault!" Erica cried. "He's just bored."

"What do you care, Rikki?" Mom mopped up the gravy with her napkin. "You're leaving. You won't have to put up with us for much longer. Where's Ethan, anyway? Evidently he no longer cares to grace us with his presence."

Ethan's seat was still empty. "I don't know," Erica said. "Maybe he has a stomachache."

"Can't you make your children behave? Can't you have more respect for your sister? Every day she has to live like this." Mom's voice broke. Debbie slumped in her chair, her eyes closed. Jared sighed, leaning back wearily in his seat.

"My children are your grandchildren, you know. What do you expect them to do, stuck in this restaurant? This is a train wreck here"—Erica gestured around the table—"and you want us to stand here and rubberneck for the rest of our lives."

Mom scratched the back of her neck. "Train wreck? I don't know what you're talking about. Honestly, Rikki."

"Now, now." Dad placed his hand over Mom's. "This is a happy occasion."

"We'll never have Thanksgiving together again," Mom bawled.

"Sure we will," Erica started to say automatically, but then she stopped. Maybe next Thanksgiving they could visit Ethan's family and eat a calm barbequed turkey on their patio, on a warm afternoon scented with eucalyptus. Maybe they could deep-fry their turkey or whatever they did down South, all by themselves in their new home. Or they could skip the turkey entirely and eat barbequed shrimp on a Caribbean island. "You're right—we won't be back," Erica said. "In fact, we're leaving now. I'm going to find Ethan." She gathered all the toys flung over the table and on the floor. She picked up Sophia, grabbed the twins by the hands, slung the baby gear and entertainment bags over her arms, and, motioning to Dylan to follow, rose up from the table.

"You'll miss the pumpkin pie," Dad said.

"Too bad," said Erica as a Matchbox car fell out of the bag and rolled under Jared's chair. "Bye, Jared," she said. "Keep in touch."

"Whatever," Jared handed her the toy car.

She found Ethan at the bar, nursing a whiskey and watching college football. Ignoring the prominent "Absolutely No Minors" sign, she pushed her way up to the counter. "Let's go," she said.

"Say the word," Ethan replied. From the door of the restaurant, she watched him return to the table and say polite good-byes, kissing everyone on the cheek. Outside, darkness had fallen completely, and needles of sleet battered their faces. The fat boy was standing out there with his family, waiting for their valet-parked car. He and the twins resumed their acquaintance, running in and out of the slush-soaked bushes.

That Sunday, with sleet once again falling outside and apple-cinnamon potpourri simmering on the stove in their warm kitchen, a medical couple—a gastroenterologist and his wife, a pregnant dermatologist—made a cash offer on the house. It was $25,000 below their asking price, but Ethan and Erica accepted it.

CHAPTER **FORTY-ONE**

As soon as the doctors put down their contract deposit, Erica flew down to join Ethan for a whirlwind tour of Florida houses. Once again, she left the kids with Lisa. She owed Lisa a debt she could scarcely repay; she figured she'd buy her the Louis Vuitton bag she'd been lusting after.

Grant Fishel had changed its ways since the ebullient and expansive spring, housing Ethan and Erica in an anonymous Doubletree Inn by I-90 with no fluffy bathrobes and no orange-scented soap. They wandered through subdivisions with an agent provided by Grant Fishel's corporate relocations department, a woman named Rosalyn with streaked blond hair frozen into a flip and huge blue glass earrings shaped like dolphins. Rosalyn's nasal Jersey accent was softened and slowed by twenty years in South Florida.

She gabbed constantly, like Erica's mother used to, and Erica let the burble stream comfortingly through her ears. Yet as she ogled each tiled foyer, each Jenn-Air range or steam shower or ballroom-size closet, her disenchantment grew. These houses no longer exuded the luxurious magic of last spring, as if the twins were to return to Disney World and suddenly realize that Mickey Mouse was only an underpaid worker in a hot, smelly costume. Nor, she realized, was Florida far enough away from New York. Her great-aunts and great-uncles and assorted other elderly relatives lived there. Her parents would get over their huff soon enough and visit them; indeed, only a week after Thanksgiving, her mother had already invited them all over for latkes and menorah lighting. The Schrabner family vacationed every year in Fort Lauderdale. It was only a matter of time before she would she'd walk into her new supermarket and encounter someone who recognized her, who would call her Rikki. Her mind drifted back to the Smoky Mountains, beyond the reach of the highway, beyond the reach of the television and the telephone, where the one-lane roads dropped off steeply into darkness.

Ethan kept shaking his head, complaining that all the houses looked interchangeable, one stucco faux Mediterranean villa after another, with thick spiky grass in front and a kidney-shaped pool in the back. "Don't you have something, I don't know, more unique, more classy, than these suburban developments?" he asked. It was already early afternoon on Sunday, with Erica's flight back to New York scheduled for Monday morning. Time was running out.

"I don't know what else to show you, honey," said Rosalyn, shaking her head so that the glass dolphins rattled against the folds of her neck. She'd definitely had work done, Erica concluded. All the skin above her neck was stretched taut, her lips flat and thin under their cracked ruby lipstick.

"How about a house closer to the beach?" Ethan suggested. "With a larger yard and mature palm trees instead of these little skinny things." He waved dismissively at the scrawny specimens supported by wire, smelling of bark dust. Understandable disdain, Erica thought, considering he grew up among redwoods. "A view of the water would be nice."

Rosalyn rolled her eyes, even as her smile stayed put. Erica knew what was in Ethan's mind's eye: one of those houses along Route 1, the ones hidden far behind their gated entrances, the long driveways shaded by palms. Maybe he believed all the risk he'd taken for the benefit of Grant Fishel had earned him one of those. He was still an MIT geek at heart. He still didn't recognize his stumbling, half-innocent role in the scheme of things. Even Erica had figured out that those mansions belonged to the likes of Stephan Langston, or maybe Nick Stromboli's suppliers, once they all got out of prison.

As the sun set, Erica and Ethan settled on a compromise, a bungalow on the Intercoastal with a couple of waving pineapple palms and a boat dock, in a neighborhood south of Boca. It cost twice as much as their home in West Meadow, but with multiple bonuses sitting in savings, Ethan figured they could pull it off. He especially liked the idea of a boat, and Erica supposed the boys would also. Unlike the '30s-era homes down the block, this house was as brand-new as the ones in the subdivisions, constructed on the unwanted fringe of someone else's fabulously large lot. Erica did not want an old house, however elegant. This bungalow was as untouched as the tract homes with their Jenn-Airs and Jacuzzis. It still smelled of paint, and in the warmth of the early evening, the smell of fresh asphalt rose up from the driveway. She didn't want the worn stucco of the rambling mansion next door, streaked with moss. She didn't want any of the history those walls might contain.

"I'm sure this will be a lovely place to raise your beautiful family," Rosalyn said. They followed her back to the office to sign the papers.

CHAPTER FORTY-TWO

A moving service, paid for by Grant Fishel, packed up all but the most essential of their possessions and transported them to their new home. Erica and Ethan celebrated New Year's with a bottle of French champagne and caviar he'd gotten from a client, sitting in their empty living room in front of the fireplace. Without furniture, or piles of paper, or scattered toys, the house looked huge, larger, in fact, than the house they were moving to. Sammy remained in the family room. She'd taken him to the vet and obtained a special certificate of reptilian health; still, he'd need to fly in cargo. He was five feet long now. Periodically, he emitted a high-pitched squeal.

In the second week of January, with their closing date two days away, Ethan returned for what would be his last week in West Meadow. Lisa offered to take the kids Friday night, so Erica and Ethan could enjoy one last fling in Manhattan.

Erica dropped them off midafternoon. The weak light was already fading, a light snow beginning to fall, and she needed to drive into the city. Ethan had suggested she take the train—a few flakes of snow sufficed to send him into a transportation panic—but she preferred to drive and, truth be told, had an appointment with Anders en route. Her last. She'd need to figure out a new arrangement in Florida. If *Miami Vice* was to be believed, that wouldn't prove too difficult.

"Tell me the truth—aren't you going to desperately miss New York?" Lisa asked.

"I don't think so." Erica already desperately missed New York, but it was the New York of her past, or maybe only of her imagination. That was too complicated a truth to share with Lisa.

Lisa's face dropped, making Erica feel as if by rejecting New York, she was rejecting her personally.

"I'll miss you a lot, though," Erica assured her.

Lisa's round face, framed by wispy blond hair, brightened. "Well, at least I can visit you," she said. "It's not like you're falling off the face of the earth. It's not like that old boyfriend of yours in high school—what was his name?'

"Jeff."

"Yeah, Jeff. He went to that strange college in Oregon, right? Did you ever hear from him again?"

"No," Erica said. Jeff had sent her exactly one letter from Reed, which she'd ripped open excitedly, right in front of the Boston University student union mailboxes. All it did was describe some crazy party he'd attended where he rode a motorized couch. It made him think of her, he said; he thought she'd find it amusing. He'd signed the letter "Sincerely." The "sincerely" cut her to the bone. She did not write him back.

"Well, who cares—you're better off with Ethan," Lisa said, giving her a hug. "You guys go have a great time tonight. Okay?"

Erica drove home, changed into her leopard-print bustier dress and leather boots, and paced around the kitchen. She dreaded standing, overdressed, in that deserted and dark park off Utopia Boulevard, waiting for Anders to show up.

She poured herself another cup of coffee.

No one but Nick and Anders, and, she supposed, Stephan, knew about the coke. Even Jared thought she'd only tried it a few times. It amazed her how easy it was to hide something so big in plain view. No one was looking for it, because everyone she knew— from Ethan to her mother to Lisa to the ladies in aerobics class to the police—looked only for what they expected to see.

Her mind drifted to Sophia and how she often woke from sleep in a new location, opening up to that fresh moment with a wide-open toothless grin. That deep honesty, that wide-open vulnerable presence, everyone's birthright, slipped away while they weren't paying attention. Her own life stretched forward as far as she could see, a gray blur, each moment indistinguishable from the next.

She was as trapped in body and circumstance as Debbie.

She could no longer live that existence. She wouldn't allow it.

She would dip herself in a vat of acid; she would blast that line of moments open and rub them raw, and stare that pulsing river down.

She sipped her coffee, thinking of Anders shivering alone in the park, waiting for her. He wouldn't wait for long. He'd stalk off in disgust and then call another customer in his phone book. To him, she was nothing but an interchangeable commodity. She pulled out the last of her coke and dumped it on the kitchen counter, dividing it into lines, frantically, sloppily, wiping up the leftover grains like pastry scraps and shaping them again. She finished it all, the whole supersize bag of potato chips, right there in the kitchen, looking out at her hand-painted fruit tiles, the bowl of oranges, and the play castle with its crust of frost. Right there out in the open, where anyone could have seen her, if only they were looking. As she straightened up, she banged her knee against the edge of the counter. Blood streamed out of a ragged gash. She pulled down her ripped pantyhose and made herself stare at the red stream dribbling down her leg, willing herself not to give in to the dizziness and the shadows at the corners of her vision. She washed the cut with antiseptic, applied a Band-Aid, and changed into patterned leggings. Her knee stung as it moved against the nubby fabric.

She checked the clock, confirming that she'd missed her appointment with Anders. The snow drifted down as she drove into the city, melting before it hit the ground. The drops of whiteness shimmered in her headlights, and she pushed her way through the sparkling fog. Her leg throbbed. The rush of blood into the gash dissipated and then surged, in rhythm with her heart, in rhythm with the pulsing traffic. She drove over the Fifty-Ninth Street Bridge. This would be the last time she would traverse this tangle of concrete and lights and honking taxicabs, the last time she would park by a manhole spewing out steam.

She took Ethan to a club she'd wanted to go to for a long time. It was situated in a part of the New York City subway system that had long ago been closed off to use. To get there, you climbed down three steep flights of stairs to an old subway platform. The rails were blocked off at some point, obviously, but at the edge of the dance floor, all that you could see was their dark expanse, curving away as far as the eye could see. People were rumored to live down there, like moles. She imagined these creatures as pale and wet, their eyes clouded over from lack of light. She and Ethan leaned over the railing, their bellies hard against the metal. She wanted to scramble over it and explore the slimy depths of the tunnels, but instead they both drank watery margaritas, one after another. When she was ready, she took Ethan by the arm and steered him into the anonymous sway of dancers.

The music wasn't as clangorous and angry as Jared's heavy metal, but it shared the same incessant, hypnotic beat. To cleanse her head of everything else, she bobbed up and down on her heels. She twirled like a child. She raised her arms to the ceiling. She pressed her face into Ethan's chest. Aside from Ethan, she knew no one there, nobody, and nobody knew her. She was simply another sweaty body, crammed into a rayon leopard-print bustier dress with cutouts at the waist and a stinging cut hidden under her leggings. She drank more tequila until she landed somewhere at least approximating where she wished to be, where all the extraneous static evaporated, leaving nothing but her core. Her potent core. It still lay at the heart of her being, crystalline and invulnerable.

Ethan smelled so fine. His white work shirt, damp and unbuttoned. His arms, wrapped around the small of her back. His hips, pressed into hers. She'd lost him for so long. His absence, that impression in the mattress where his body used to be, that cool breeze under the blanket, had grown more real than his presence. But he was present now, in this moment, and so was she. She knew what she wanted. She'd assumed she wanted to be wasted, to be numb, to be lost, but no, this raw presence beat everything. She wanted Ethan, right there on this dance floor, in the midst of all these strangers, or maybe on the slick concrete of the tunnels, where it stank faintly of urine and years of accumulated grime. Anywhere but in their bed, on the plain mattress on the floor of their empty bedroom, on the one reserved set of flowered three-hundred-thread-count Egyptian cotton sheets. She raised herself on her toes and kissed him, on the neck, on the mouth.

"Who's Anders?" Ethan whispered throatily.

She looked into Ethan's eyes, wide and hazel and hurt, eyes that were searching for the wrong things. All the secrets she'd kept from him, and he was convinced of one she hadn't even contemplated.

"I don't know," Erica said. "I've never met him."

"Bullshit. C'mon, who is he?" Ethan gripped her tightly, pressing painfully against her ribs.

"He's a friend of Stephan Langston's," Erica said.

Ethan's grip relaxed slightly. "You doing some insider trading?" he asked, incredulous.

"You think I'm having an affair, don't you?"

He nodded.

"Well, you're wrong. I never wanted anyone but you. I don't want anyone but you. I love you. Don't you believe me?"

He nodded again. All around them, people pushed and shoved and twirled. Somebody stepped on her big toe. "Yeah," Ethan said. "If you say so. But who's Anders?"

A dark cloud enveloped her, vast and deep, the one that lingered close by all the time, waiting for her. The one she always clawed at and pushed down. The one she always thought she could beat. But she was done with lies and had nowhere to run. Let Ethan finally look inside her flawed crystal core. Let Ethan call her on her game. Let Ethan deal out her punishment.

Erica breathed in sharp and big. "He's a cocaine dealer," she said, awaiting the explosion.

"You're doing coke?"

"Yeah, I mean, no, not anymore. I quit. I mean, today; I mean, never again; I mean it truly. I decided today, in the kitchen, really, that that was the last time. . ." She rambled on, as if words alone could make her intent tangible, a solidity that she could cling to. She'd been looking down at the ground as she spoke, but now she looked up, back into Ethan's hazel eyes, awaiting the crushing blow. She could not evade what she could not erase. Let Ethan punch her where Ron had missed. Let Ethan crush her.

But instead, he cut her off, his arms running roughly down her back. "Erica, stop it. Don't tell me anymore."

"Are you serious?" She staggered, bumping into a dancer's

swaying hip and falling down onto her knees. She'd been holding her breath, and now she released it, gulping gallons of musty air, filling her lungs to bursting.

"Yes. Way too much information. I don't want to know."

"You mean that?" She reeled back on her heels. Someone stomped on her index finger. She gazed at the length of Ethan's blue jeans, his tanned hands reaching down for hers.

"Yes, didn't I make that clear? I got enough on my plate."

He pulled her up. His hands felt warm and moist, clutched around her waist where the cutouts were. He kissed her deeply.

"Let's go home," Erica said.

Outside, it was cold, the feeble snow already dissipating. The air smelled of diesel fumes and burnt toast. She breathed in that thick, unclean, familiar essence for the last time.

She drove home. The traffic was light, the roads clear.

A full moon appeared between two clouds, like a face in the window. Everyone was sleeping. Window shades were drawn, lights out, alarm systems activated. Their house was as dark as everyone else's, with all four kids sleeping at the Schrabners'. She parked in the driveway instead of the garage. She was wasted but so awake. She wished she could take Ethan to the Mackay estate, show him the bricks overgrown with moss, the cracked sink propped up against a tree, the concrete foundation eroded by weeds, but none of that existed anymore. The land was covered over with houses where people slept with their alarm systems activated.

Ethan had pushed the back of the passenger seat down and lay against the headrest, half asleep. He didn't even seem aware she'd stopped the car. She reached her hand under his shirt and stroked his chest, those tendrils of curls, that slight softness at the belly, so good, how could she have forgotten? She kissed his neck, his mouth. He turned his head and, barely opening his eyes, kissed her back. She untied the bustier portion of her dress. His hands reached out to stroke her breasts. She unzipped his slacks. He was in her power.

Vince Volvo, her unreliable but always dear friend, who would never travel these roads again, felt like the proper place to be. She couldn't return to high school and the stones and weeds of the Mackay estate. She couldn't return to college, to her first time with Ethan, on the loft bunk in his dorm room, with the door open. But she could be with her beautiful husband in her large automobile, no matter how she got there.

Everyone could see them, but she knew no one actually would, because no one would think to look, and besides, they were all asleep in their locked-up houses with their central heating and their televisions. But Ethan and Erica were awake, on a chilly, moonlit night with scudding clouds. They were still young, under forty, and they had the sense to know it. They were not stale. They were not static. They could make themselves new. She climbed on top of Ethan in the passenger seat.

Both of them, plastered to the moment, failed to notice she wasn't wearing her diaphragm. Erica didn't remember that it was exactly fourteen days since her last period, and that inside her an egg was primed and waiting. Squished together in the cramped confines of Vince Volvo, rubbing against the leather, elbows banging against the door handle, they fit together perfectly; they always had. Outside, it was cold; inside the car, they were warm. Outside, the world drowsed in a numbed sleep, but they were awake. Erica's arm slid against the gumminess of a melted lollipop. It smelled dense inside the car, like sugar and baby wipes and mud from Dylan's soccer shoes. Afterward, she drove the car into the garage—hilarious, driving in the nude—and they peeled themselves stickily from the seats and walked through their stripped-down kitchen, arm in arm and laughing.

EPILOGUE

JANUARY 1987

You seize upon a weak burst of midday sunshine and take Sophia for a walk around the neighborhood. You consider asking Lisa to join you, but she's chatting on the phone and, as you recall, had mentioned some undefined plans for later that afternoon. The scattering of snow that had fallen throughout the morning is now melting, sending spurts of muddy water up Sophia's stroller wheels, but the WNEW weatherman is predicting another storm that evening. You hope he is mistaken, because your plane flight to Fort Lauderdale leaves at 9:00 a.m., tomorrow and if it snows sufficiently, both getting to the airport and enduring the inevitable delays with four children promises to be hell.

Lisa, bless her, is driving you to the airport. You and the children, plus Sam the iguana, spent last night in her basement family room, camped out in sleeping bags. You've closed on your house, packing two weeks of essentials into five giant duffels. The new family, the two doctors plus their six-year-old son, four-year-old daughter, and live-in Jamaican nanny, are moving in this afternoon. You circle around your old block to avoid seeing their moving van. You don't want to think of strangers positioning their bed under your skylight. You don't want to think of them recarpeting the family room or steaming off Sophia's rainbow wallpaper.

Ethan keeps talking about how you'll inaugurate your new home with margaritas on the dock, but it's been raining unceasingly in Boca Raton, a residue of hurricane season. Every time you've visited Florida, it's been unfailingly sunny and hot, so it's never occurred to you that it often rains there, just like New York. You've been counting on Florida to clear up the cold that has settled on you, never reaching a drastic peak but leaving you drained and congested. Your throat is sore. You cough up a greenish glop of phlegm. Your head feels thick and heavy; you need a full pot of coffee and a six-pack of diet Cokes to jump-start your day. You've forgotten your scarf. Living in Florida, your mother will no longer be able to hassle you, at the age of 31, about not dressing warm enough for the weather, or forgetting your raincoat, or wearing shoes that do not match your pants. She will not have any idea what you are wearing at all. Your legs feel cold and achy flapping against the lining of your corduroys. The deep gash in your knee is only partially healed, and you keep ripping off the scab when you pick at it at night. You're gaining weight by the day even though you can barely eat; you choke down a slice of toast, and your belly strains against the waist of your pants. Your legs are still fast and long, your knees still knobby and scraped like a child's, but they will never power you as far away as you need to go.

You walk for a long time, crossing over the railroad tracks, past the low-income housing and the turn-of-the-century frame houses of Meadow Heights. You pass your parents' house, where no one is home. After you closed on the house, they took you out to dinner at a mediocre Italian restaurant and then left to visit old college friends of your father's in New Hampshire. For the first time in your memory, your father has forgotten to prune the rosebushes, and evidently to cancel the paper, as there is a big pileup of the Times by their front door. A young family with a toddler has moved into Nick's house. Nick is in jail for a plea-bargained six months. News of a drug bust in Brooklyn, perhaps courtesy of Nick's information, was splashed all over yesterday's paper. They were big fish, these drug dealers from Colombia that got sent away for twenty years. While you were a subatomic particle, as Ethan might put it. You never sold drugs to a single soul. All you ever did was buy them, like you might buy cookies at the supermarket. Like Debbie bought Coumadin at the drugstore. You were a subatomic particle, invisible to society's microscope, and now you are swimming off the glass slide away to subtropical seas. You peer in the door of the pet store at the tortoises and lizards and one lonely-looking furry white cat. You walk back to your parents' house and put their newspapers in the yellow plastic box your father normally reserves for this purpose. You walk back across the railroad tracks toward where, as you practice telling yourself, you used to live.

You pause at the West Meadow Elementary playground, which is empty due to the weather. The rubber baby swings are too wet for Sophia's tush, but you roll her stroller up onto the sodden bark chips anyway and, with your eyes, frame the scene like a photograph. The wooden play structure, with its towers and tubes and rope ladders. The tire swing. The rocking animals on springs, shaped like elephants and hippos. The low brick structure of the school behind them. In the near distance to the right side, the high school, the cluster of leafless trees, the gateway to the luxurious colonials of Mackay Estates. The thin line of sky, gray fighting with blue. The sharp air, tinged with moldy leaves and exhaust. This is the image you will conjure when your children ask you where they are from.

Dylan, Jesse, and Jake will carry their own memories, of course. For a while their image of West Meadow will be as vivid to them as it is to you. But they are children, resilient and adaptable, and without reinforcement, these images will recede, and others, more current and pertinent, will rise to the forefront. Their voices will soften and slow. Their skin will turn a permanent shade of tan. Their life in West Meadow will become a faded remnant of early childhood, odd elements occasionally recalled in the context of something else, background to a dream. As for Sophia, she will remember nothing of this. You wish for all of them what you will never have for yourself, what you know to be impossible for anyone: blank pages to write their histories on.

Airplanes and moving vans cannot take you far enough away. That place—beyond roads, beyond phones, lost in fog— exists, but the path there, you now realize, is forever closed to you. It's closed for your husband, as well. Ethan still works for Grant Fishel, doing, as far as you can determine, essentially the same things as he's done all along. Maybe the actions that have been determined by the courts and by public opinion to be acceptable will no longer be acceptable a year from now. Maybe one of his disgruntled, betrayed superiors will rearrange his loy- alties. Maybe the underpinnings of Grant Fishel's whole abstract empire will collapse. You understand the potential for collapse now. It is stashed in your bones; it stares back at you with your own eyes.

In a few weeks, as you arrange your possessions in your new home, while you enroll the boys in their new schools and dangle your legs off the dock, while you sniff the yellow wild sage that blooms in your yard all winter, Debbie will come home from the rehab center to her new ranch house in Albertson. Ron, who now manages a Tower Records in Hauppage, will rent his own customized van and wheel her up the entry ramp built by a contractor buddy of his, but everyone's expectation is that slowly, painstakingly, she will regain her ability to walk. She might always require a cane or maybe one of those motorized scooters. With the help of extensive therapy, she will also regain her speech, her doctors believe. Progress will be slow, though, measured and self-conscious: her rapid-fire patter is a thing of the past. Never again will she gab about Phil Donahue while frosting some boring lady's hair.

You've relinquished your part in this. You aren't very good at what's required: the tediousness, the inane conversation, the refusal to acknowledge the avoidable catastrophe that put her in this situation. All your life Debbie told you how impulsive and unreliable you were, how all you did was get her into trouble. She never wanted your kind of love, she never wanted the kind of help you offered, and now it is too late.

As you look around this playground you have known your whole life, you still see Debbie swinging next to you on that old metal swing wobbling in its concrete base. Somewhere below the fresh asphalt, the blood from her elbow fracture still stains the ground. You prefer to think of her in her cast, cluttered with signatures and drawings, playing jump rope with her friends. Even in the cast, you have to admit, she was pretty adept at jump rope.

Jared for a time felt as much your child as the ones born from your body, but of course that was never true. You always want too much. You hope, if he remembers nothing else, he remembers how the gate opened up at the Pritima Center like you'd willed the garbage truck to enter. You hope he will see other gates in his life, the ones that stand there in plain sight, and understands he can walk through them like he has every right to do, by looking straight ahead and putting one foot in front of the other.

The new baby growing in you remains your secret for now. Already, you think you see a little bulge peeking out of the waistband of your corduroys. Five children, how absolutely insane. No one you know has five children, but no one you knew had four, for that matter. Your child is bound to you in hunger, and she will suck food and air from your body and take from you anything she requires to survive. Her heart already beats. The heart is the first organ that fully forms. She will grow inexorably, blood pulsing between your two consciousnesses, arms forming, legs, head, fingers, pushing out against your belly, creating bumps like marbles in your skin as she kicks, reaching down toward the light, making herself known. You don't need any cocaine. You don't need any chemical high of any kind. Like you told Justine, a couple of lifetimes ago, childbirth is the best rush ever.

You need to allow one day to follow another, permeated

by the white noise of the ordinary. As many times as you have tried and failed to penetrate the fog surrounding the afternoon of Debbie's collapse, one image remains inviolable: you, at the end, still standing. Whether you deserve that gift is perhaps irrelevant. This is the gift you've been granted, and you will run with it.

A cocker spaniel bounds past Sophia's stroller, followed by a woman in a fur coat holding tight to her extended leash. "Doggie!" Sophia exclaims. Then that spaniel is followed by another, then another. Soon the playground is awash with cocker spaniels, sniffing each other's butts, yipping, peeing against the play structure, kicking up wood chips and mud. You have never seen so many of the same kind of dog in the same place. Then Lisa strolls up the hill with Penny, and the realization dawns on you: this was her plan for the afternoon; this must be the monthly gathering of the cocker spaniel club she's talked so much about. "Doggie, doggie!" exclaims Sophia as each spaniel appears, until her system short-circuits, and she can only stare in stunned wonderment. She wants every one of those doggies, all of them at once, wants to run her chubby hands through their damp spiky fur, wants the press of their wet noses on her cheek, the kiss of their smooth pink tongues. She wants it now, no, before now. She wants it as badly as anything she has ever wanted in her fourteen months of life. She works the nylon strap of her stroller, manipulating it through the plastic loops and past the restraining teeth. She flexes her fingers and, gripping with all her might, pulls up the snap. The strap falls loose. She is free! She slithers down under her seat, onto the footrest, onto the slush-drenched bark dust. She staggers to her feet, and she is off.

You follow your daughter into the windy winter afternoon.

ACKNOWLEDGMENTS

I want to thank the members of my writers critique group who cared tenderly for this manuscript in its infancy and childhood: Lisa Alber, Michael Bigham, Dawn Cadwell, and Jeannie Burt. Thank you to my daughters Gabrielle and Jessica and my cousin Kathleen Fitzgerald for your careful and honest feedback. Thank you to Genevieve Gagne-Hawes at Writers House for guiding me through several rewrites. Thank you to my son Lukas for nagging me to "get an agent". Thank you to my neighbor and friend Kim Bissell for your advice and support. Thank you to my wonderful publishing team of Mary Bisbee-Beek, Ann Weinstock, and Kristen Weber. A multitude of thanks to my husband Zak. I waited a long time to show this book to you but once I did you became my greatest backer.

And thank you always to my continually expanding family: my husband Zak (again); my children Gabrielle, Jessica, Alex, and Lukas; my son-in-laws Tom and Matt; and my grandchildren Halle, River, Lillianna, and Leda. You provide the chaos that is life and the context for everything I do.

CREDITS

BOOK CLUB
DISCUSSION GUIDE

1. How does the book's 1980s setting inform the characters and plot? Do you think this story could take place today?

2. How does the suburban setting inform the characters and plot? Which aspects of this story are unique to upper middle class suburbs and which are more universal in nature?

3. Are you more sympathetic to Erica or to Debbie, or to both women equally? What do you view as their strengths and weaknesses?

4. Do you think Debbie bears any culpability for what happens to her or do you see her simply as a victim?

5. How do you think Erica gets away with having so many secrets—from her husband, from her family, from her friends?

6. Do you think Jared's behavior justifies the degree of his parent's intervention?

7. What is your opinion of Ron? Whether he actually beats his wife or son is left unclear. What is your gut feeling on this issue?

8. How do you see Erica as a mother?

9. How do you see Ethan as a husband? Do you think he views Erica as a full person?

10. Do you think Erica's attitudes and actions at home and Ethan's attitudes and actions on Wall Street parallel each other in any way? How are their characters alike and different? What holds their marriage together?

11. What do you think motivates Erica to use drugs? Why cocaine in particular? What holes in her life is she filling? Do the holes come from without or within or both?

12. Why does Jared have such a hold on Erica's heart?

13. Where does childhood end and adulthood begin? Are there risks created by not drawing a clear line between the two? Why do you think Erica is so drawn to adolescents and adolescence? Do you agree with Debbie that you cannot be a friend to your child (or nephew)?

14. Erica endures a number of escapes and near misses that could have destroyed her life. But at the end she is "still standing". Do you think this is fair? Do you think she deserves a comeuppance?

15. Why do you think Ethan essentially shrugs off Erica's confession, telling her that he "has enough on his plate"?

16. Do you think, by the end of the book, that Erica has been changed in any way by her experiences? Has Ethan?

17. What do you think the future holds for Erica and why? Will she stay off drugs? Live her life differently? Reconcile with her family?

18. *Wrong Highway* touches on some charged issues: drug addiction, abortion, Wall Street malfeasance, to name a few. Did you come to any of these topics with preconceived notions that affected your perception of the book?